Galla Placidia

Empress of Rome
in a Time of Turmoil
(389-450 A.D.)

SONIA SORRELL

UNIVERSITY PRESS OF THE SOUTH

Published in the United States by:
    University Press of the South, Inc.
    5500 Prytania Street, PMB 421
    New Orleans, LA 70115 USA

E-mail: unprsouth@aol.com   Fax:(504)866-2750   Phone:(504)866-2791
Visit our award-winning web page:
                http://www.unprsouth.com
Visit our partner's web page:
                http://ww.punmonde.com
Acid-free paper.

Sonia Sorrell.
Galla Placidia. Empress of Rome in a Time of Turmoil, 389-450 A.D.
First Edition.

Fiction Series, 12.   Italian Studies, 2.
vi + 413 p.
Includes Preface.

    1. Roman Empire. 2. Classical Studies. 3. Rome. 4. Galla Placidia. 5. Women's Studies. 6. Christianity. 7. Emperor Theodosius I. 8. Goths. 9. Imperial Patronage. 10. Ravenna.

ISBN: 1-931948-38-0.
Library of Congress Catalog Card Number: 2004105453.

DEDICATION

This book is dedicated to
John R. Elliott
my husband and my best friend

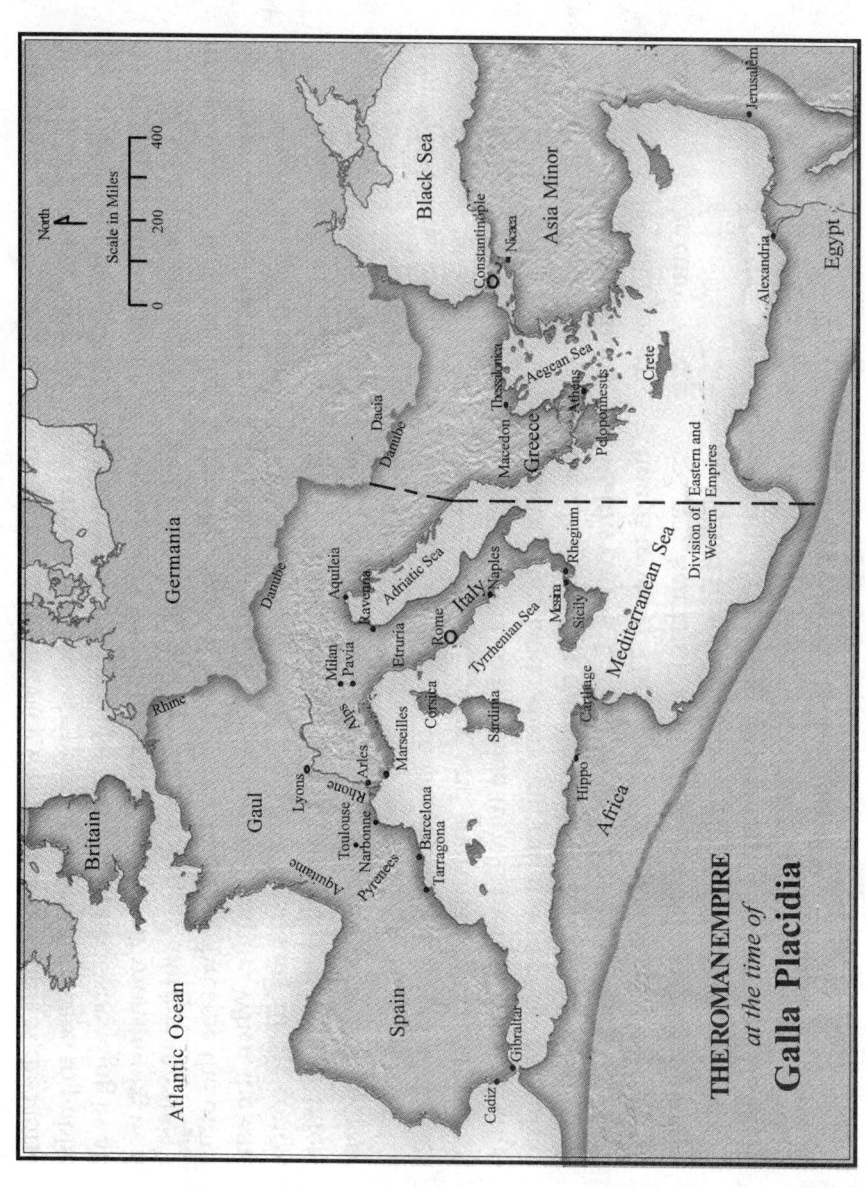

North

Scale in Miles

0   200   400

Atlantic Ocean

Britain

Germania

Gaul

Rhine

Danube

Aquitaine

Toulouse

Narbonne

Pyrenees

Lyons

Arles

Rhone

Alps

Marseilles

Milan

Pavia

Ravenna

Aquileia

Danube

Dacia

Danube

Black Sea

Constantinople

Nicaea

Asia Minor

Thessalonica

Aegean Sea

Athens

Macedon

Greece

Peloponnesus

Crete

Alexandria

Egypt

Jerusalem

Division of Eastern and
Western Empires

Spain

Barcelona

Tarragona

Gibraltar

Cadiz

Corsica

Sardinia

Etruria

Rome

Italy

Naples

Tyrrhenian Sea

Messina

Sicily

Rhegium

Adriatic Sea

Mediterranean Sea

Carthage

Hippo

Africa

THE ROMAN EMPIRE
at the time of
Galla Placidia

PREFACE

This is the story of Galla Placidia, a woman born at the major turning point of history, when the ancient pagan past was overtaken by the young religion of Christianity. Daughter, sister, wife, and mother of Emperors, Galla Placidia was instrumental in leading Rome through the turbulent transition from a pagan to a Christian state. This story is based on true historical events of the first half of the fifth century AD. The principal Roman and Germanic characters in this story actually lived. No gratuitous violence was added—the events of the period were sufficiently violent and tumultuous to satisfy any novelist's desires. When necessary, any lacunae in the information about the life and times of Galla Placidia have been filled with incidental fictitious characters, events, and locations. It was not my goal to recount recent academic research on the life of Galla Placidia; other scholars have already done that admirably. My goal was to use known and accepted facts and information about the life and times of Galla Placidia to create a vivid, exciting, and living portrait of one of the most fascinating and powerful women in history.

Galla Placidia was born the daughter of Theodosius I, the emperor who made Christianity the official religion of the Roman Empire. Upon the death of Theodosius, Galla's two half brothers, Honorius and Arcadius, ruled the Empire. Galla's privileged imperial youth was abruptly ended in 410 when the Goths sacked Rome and abducted Galla, holding her for a ransom of land and grain. Galla's brothers refused to pay the ransom and Galla was forced to accompany the Goths as they sacked and plundered their way through Italy and eventually into France and Spain. After several years of fruitless negotiations with Galla's brothers, the Gothic chieftain Athaulf married Galla in an act of defiance against Rome. Galla's marriage was blessed with the birth of a son, but her happiness was short-lived. First her infant son died and then her husband was assassinated. Only then, five years after her abduction, did Galla's brothers give in and pay the ransom. Galla Placidia was restored, alone, to Rome. The Rome that Galla found upon her return had changed as dramatically as Galla herself had changed.

Galla's restoration to Rome was not the end of her adventures. Now older and wiser, Galla set about to continue her father's dream of creating a truly Christian Roman state. Galla married Constantius, who later became emperor of Rome. When Constantius died a few years into his reign, Galla ruled as regent for their young son, effectively becoming Augusta Galla Placidia, the most powerful individual in Rome. During those years, Galla strengthened the Christian religion with her imperial patronage and by building numerous churches. One of the most beautiful structures that Galla commissioned was her own mausoleum, the Mausoleum of Galla Placidia in Ravenna, but Galla was never entombed there. Even in her death, Galla's story goes beyond the ordinary. Galla was in Rome, not Ravenna, when she died--her body was laid to rest alongside the Great Fisherman himself in the catacombs beneath St. Peter's Basilica.

ACKNOWLEDGEMENTS

All my life I have opened books to find brief dedications such as, "To Mary." As a wife, I recognize that the Marys of the world are the ones who see that life moves forward while a book is being created, shouldering not only their share of life's burdens, but the author's share as well. In this day of two-career families, it's as often a Tom as a Mary who gives selflessly while an author disappears into a room to write for hours on end. Such is the case with the book you are now holding. This book is not the creation of one person, but two.

I first read about Galla Placidia many years ago and over the intervening years I have lectured to my students about her adventures and her contributions; I have even encouraged my students to write her story. It was my husband, John R. Elliott, who suggested that I write the story myself. He set up a room where I could write; he took over the hundreds of daily chores; he helped locate the source materials; he traveled with me on numerous occasions from Lisbon to Istanbul visiting related sites and libraries; and he typed the manuscript, edited the text, pointed out inconsistencies, and suggested plot development. No, he didn't write the words contained in this book, but those words could not and would not have been written without him. It is time for those who truly do make a book possible to get credit where credit is truly due. This book is *by* Sonia Sorrell *with* John R. Elliott, without whom this book would have remained only a dream.

I am indebted to Nissa A. Clark, my editor, for her keen attention to detail and her excellent suggestions. I would also like to express my gratitude to Lisa Hanslip, Emilie Fitzhugh Sizemore, and Dana Collier Zurzolo for their support and encouragement. In addition, I am grateful to Jose, Lola, Teofilo and Sonia Solano for their patience and help while I completed this book. Ultimately, I want to thank Birgitta Lindros Wohl for introducing me to the study of ancient Rome. Galla Placidia would be grateful to each and every one of you for helping to tell her story.

GALLA PLACIDIA - GENEALOGY

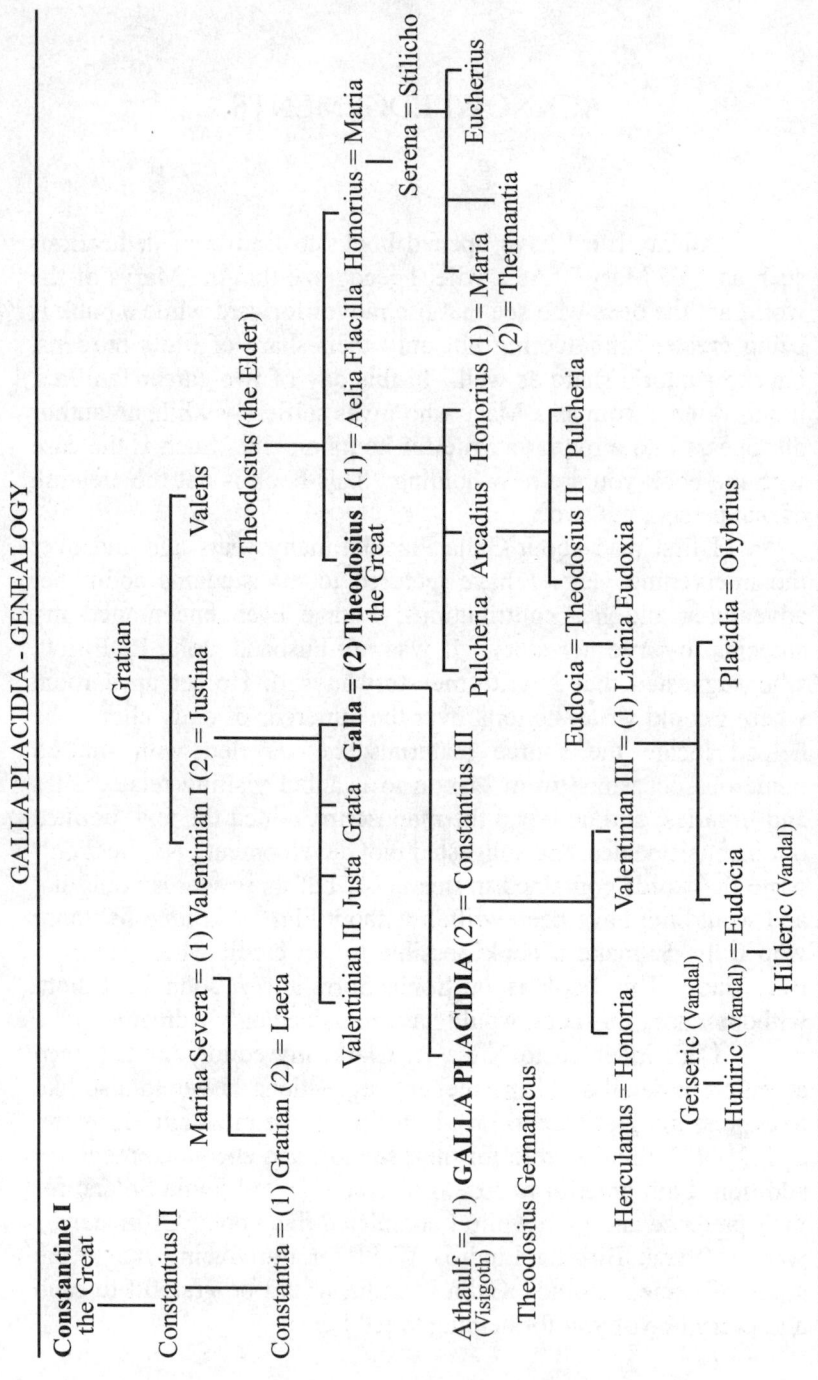

PROLOGUE
415 A.D.

For the third time that morning, Galla had to stop to fix her sandal. She knelt down on the dirt road, unwound the broken strap from her dust-stained ankle and bit off the ragged end of the leather cord. Gravel pierced her knee. She growled deeply.

"How much farther can it be?" Galla wondered impatiently. "I've traveled this road a hundred times and it never seemed so long before."

She knew she was on the right road. So much had changed since she was last here, that she made certain to take the coast road the entire way. As long as the rugged coastline was on her right, she knew she could not miss her destination.

"But how much farther?" she wondered anxiously. She threaded the worn leather cord through the hole in the sole of her sandal. She tied it tightly, giving it an extra tug to make certain it would hold. She sighed wearily, dragged herself back up upon her feet and picked the sharp gravel out of her knee. Her amber eyes stung with tears but did not overflow.

The mule snorted angrily and tossed its head to gain attention.

"Poor mule," she thought. "You're tired, too. You must think me mad to keep driving you on this way."

The mule stared at her dumbly.

"Come on mule, it can't be much farther now. And when we arrive at the farm you'll have fresh oats--all you want--and a good, long rest."

She, too, longed for a good meal and a long rest. She had traveled for eight weeks and her last meal was midday yesterday. Her head was light with hunger and exhaustion. But she couldn't give up now, not when her goal was so close. She poked a stray strand of her auburn hair back into the knot atop her head.

She lifted the reins of the harness over the mule's shaggy head and started off again down the dusty, pot-holed road. She had only gone but a few steps when she felt the leather sandal strap break and snap against her skin. She swore out loud, ripped the sandal from her foot and threw it forcefully over the cliff and into the sea below. As soon as it left her hand, she regretted her impulsive gesture.

She stomped her naked foot into the dust and she felt tears well up again in her eyes.

"No, I won't cry. I won't give in. I must get home. I must!" Her throat ached and she tried to swallow down the lump that was rising up inside it.

She hated that feeling. She had known it before. It was a girlish, helpless feeling that always came when things seemed at their worst. She knew she had to get it under control or it would control her.

"Stop it!" she hissed out loud. "Stop it. Such feelings are weak and ignoble. You are not weak and you are not ignoble. You are Galla Placidia, of noble Roman birth, and you are going to control these childish emotions!"

She lifted her head and blinked back the tears with a long, deep breath. She took a second, deeper breath and pulled her shoulders back until she felt the muscles stretch across her chest. She took a third, perfunctory breath and the helpless feeling began to pass. She was in control again. It was time to move on.

Galla and the aging mule lurched forward and began to proceed along the road once again. The mule lifted each foot with effort and slammed it down again, dust rising with each step. Galla's usual long stride was now reduced to a slight limp, her steps alternating between a sandal and a naked foot.

It was not yet midday, but the sun was already high in the sky and its rays were hot and strong. The lambskin sheath that had afforded Galla such warmth and comfort up north now pricked and chafed her skin. She lifted her arms slightly to keep them from rubbing against the coarse fur. She thought briefly of the lovely silk togas she had worn as a girl. They were as light and cool as a spring breeze and had felt wonderful against her body underneath. But that was long ago--another life really. So much had happened since then, it was as if she were thinking not of herself, but of another young girl.

A huge wooden cart rumbled past her on the road and the noise brought her back to reality. A rough peasant cursed at her for not moving out of the way more quickly and he spat upon the ground in front of her.

She hadn't seen another person on the road all day and, although his crudeness made her wince, she gathered the nerve to speak to him.

"You!" she shouted. "You there! Could you tell me how far it is to the villa of Theodosius Flavius?" How strange it was to utter those words--Theodosius Flavius--her father's name. And how strange also, to be forming her tongue into Latin again. How long had it been? Could it really be five years? She wasn't really sure. The peasant on the cart continued on his way.

"You!" she demanded. "You there! I'm talking to you! I am Galla Placidia, daughter of the Emperor Theodosius, and I demand that you stop and address me properly."

The ruddy-faced peasant glanced over his shoulder and spat once again. He pulled back his lips into a black-toothed grin.

"And I'm the Queen of Egypt," he whined, mocking her female voice. He laughed hoarsely and slapped the harness straps on his old horse causing the cart to proceed forward faster. The cart rumbled away, disappearing over the crest of a hill, the old man's laughter fading with the dust.

Galla stood dumbstruck, her jaw dropped in amazement. How dare he! How dare he! When she reached home, she'd tell the guard to search him out and drag him before her for an apology. Queen of Egypt indeed! Whatever indignities she had suffered during the last five years, she was in *Rome* now--*her* Rome--and she was going to resume her rightful position as daughter of Theodosius the Great and sister of Arcadius Flavius and Honorius Flavius, rulers of the Eastern and Western Empire.

She pulled herself up to her full five-feet-seven inches and lifted her proud Flavian chin. She ran her hand over her face. Had she changed so much? Her cheekbones were still high and well defined; her nose still straight and chiseled; her mouth still full and perfectly formed.

She drew her hand from her face and looked at it abstractly. This was not the hand of the highest born woman in Rome. This was a hand brown from the sun and calloused from labor. She looked down at her thin, gaunt figure, shapeless under the heavy gray sheepskin. No, this was not the figure of the young Roman noblewoman who walked this coastal road all those years before. She looked at her feet--one wrapped in a crude barbarian sandal and one dirty, brown and naked. She smiled sardonically.

No wonder the old man had mocked her. Where a young, beautiful and voluptuous aristocrat had once stood, now stood a thin and weathered peasant. Where once had stood an elegantly perfumed patrician, now stood a beggar reeking of bear grease and sweat.

"Oh Father, oh Father, how glad I am that you are not here to see what has become of your Little Acorn. You were so proud of me. Even with your two sons, you loved me best. I remember how the noblemen used to laugh at you when you bragged on and on about your Little Acorn. You said I was worth a dozen sons. And now look at me, thin and weathered as an old piece of jerky. Peasants laugh at me as if I were a street urchin. Oh Father . . . "

The sound of galloping hoofs wakened Galla from her musings. A young man was racing along the road on a fine white Arabian. Galla sheepishly held up her palm to him and waved for him to stop. The young man pulled back the reins and drew his horse to a walk.

"Tell me, please sir," she looked up entreatingly, "I'm looking for a villa, it's just north of the city of Rome, somewhere along this road. It's the estate of Theodosius Flavius. Can you tell me how much farther it is?"

The man looked down upon the frail figure of the young woman. "It's just over this rise--but you needn't go begging there-- they are Roman nobility and have no love for Gothic riffraff like you. They'd rather give you a good beating than a crust of bread. Move along now, you'll not find a welcome here."

Weariness, hunger and frustration caught up with her and Galla let out a long mournful wail. The young man reached into the pouch hanging at his waist and drew out a small coin. "There," he said, tossing the coin in her direction. "You may be a Goth, but you are a woman and I can't let you go hungry. Just see that you're off this Flavian land by sundown." He kicked his heels into the mare and galloped off.

His words echoed in her ears. "Flavian land . . . Flavian land . . ." She was here--she was home. Flavian land . . . *her* land.

She dropped the reins of the mule and ran up the rise in the road ahead of her. She looked unbelievingly across the wide valley --this couldn't be her home--where were the gardens, the fountains, the exquisite villa shining in the sun atop the far hill? He was wrong, that haughty young man. This was not the grand estate of the first family of the Empire. Her eyes scanned the landscape, searching for a familiar sign, some indication that she had, indeed, reached her beloved home. Nothing, nothing was familiar.

Just as she was about to turn back to return to her mule, something caught Galla's eye. She squinted her large amber eyes to see more clearly in the bright noonday sun. Could it be? Could it really be? There, in the V of the valley, was a large fallen oak tree, nearly overgrown with grass and wild vines. Galla's eyes followed the curve of the twisted old tree. Galla smiled mournfully. It was the old oak tree she had known so well from her carefree days as an impetuous child.

A dull pain tugged at her heart. Yes, she was home. But it was not the home she had pictured so often in her mind during her years in the north. That home of her youth was grand and opulent. That home was the home of her father the Emperor and his father before him. That home shone in the brilliant Italian sun like the palace of Jupiter himself. Now, in its place, was only rubble. What had been elegant gardens and beautiful pools and fountains, was now only tangled and twisted vines and weeds.

Galla's heart sank and she felt drained and old. She left the road and walked slowly down into the valley in which she had spent her youth, child of the most powerful man on earth. Those were blissful, magical years, made all the more so by a child's utter ignorance of fate and fortune.

Galla reached the old toppled oak and ran her hand along its rough bark. Memories came rushing back and made her head swim. "There!" she thought, "There! That slash in the old oak's trunk! That is where young Eucherius failed to maneuver his chariot properly during his jump. Poor Eucherius, Fortus and I were so hard on him . . ."

Fortus . . . Fortus . . . The sound of his name in her head opened a dam of emotions that had been closed up for too long. Out flooded all the feelings that she had held pent-up within her for so many years. Fortus . . . Fortus . . .

Suddenly dizzy and weak, Galla grabbed a branch of the old oak to steady herself. She stepped up on a rock and drew herself up onto the fallen oak and sat down, her thoughts swimming in her head, her heart pounding until it throbbed in her ears.

"Oh Fortus, where did it all go? The world was *ours*--we were so happy! How could God have allowed this terrible fate to befall us?" She looked down at her right hand at the tiny bronze ring on her little finger. "Fortus gave me that ring seven years ago. Could it really be only seven years? It seems as if a lifetime ago!"

She twisted the tiny ring back into its proper position, placing the small oval surface on the top of her finger. There, in small neat letters, was the chi-rho cross, symbol of her faith. She felt ashamed of herself. "God did not cause this terrible calamity," she thought. "Fortus would be ashamed of me for thinking so." Other than her father, she had never known another man with such blind, adoring faith as Fortus.

Staring at the delicate ring, she tried to imagine Fortus' features--a face she had not laid eyes upon since that terrible night five years earlier. She struggled to reconstruct his face in her mind's eye. Beautiful teeth . . . she remembered beautiful white teeth and an easy smile. Soft brown curls--yes--and gentle blue eyes . . . eyes the color of the Mediterranean. She remembered his strong hands and how small her hand had felt in his. And then there was his voice--deep and clear and even. She remembered his laughter and how, when Fortus raised his head and laughed, she laughed, too. "How we all loved him," she thought, "and I more than anyone."

Galla looked out over the valley--her mind racing back in time . . . gone were the ruins of the present and in their place was the magnificence of the past. There, up on the crest of the hill, stood her father's palace--the most beautiful palace since Hadrian's villa at Tivoli. It shone bright white in the sun like a glorious crown atop the terraced hillside. Water splashed gaily as it cascaded down the stepped waterfalls into the pools below. Color --everywhere was color--flowering trees and roses. Birds sang sweetly and the sound of youthful laughter filled the air.

She was no longer the thin and worn Galla, she was once again the Galla of her youth . . . brimming with energy and life.

PART I

CHAPTER I
408 A.D

"Catch me, Fortus! I bet you can't!" Galla laughed and dug her heels into her horse's side. The horse sailed down the hillside, its black mane flowing against Galla's body. Galla shrieked with glee as she maneuvered her horse over the stream and around the big oak tree. She loved the feeling of the wind in her long thick tresses--she loved the thrill of speed and danger. She dug her heels in farther and pushed her horse harder. She was yards ahead of Fortus, but he was catching up quickly. "No one rides as well as Fortus," she thought, "except me."

She drew up her horse and stopped atop a small hill and looked back at Fortus racing towards her. It was as if horse and rider was one animal--all muscle and strength and desire. Instead of his Imperial guard uniform, Fortus was wearing only a kilt and his broad chest shone deep bronze in the sun. A familiar tug pulled at Galla's heart as she looked at this young man--part human, part god.

Fortus flew up the hill and stopped abruptly just inches from where Galla sat upon her horse.

"Why did you stop?" Fortus demanded. "I was catching up with you! If you'd continued, I could have caught you."

"No you couldn't," laughed Galla. "I only get caught when I want to get caught, like now," she murmured softly and slid off her horse.

Fortus looked down at her and smiled. He dismounted with an air of studied casualness. What mischief was this beauty up to now? He could never tell with Galla quite what she was thinking. She wasn't like the other girls who were so transparent in their seductions. Galla was different. She'd always been different, ever since they met thirteen years before when they were only five. Oh, what a sight she was then--all knobby knees and long fawn-like legs.

Fortus remembered the first time he ever saw Galla. His father had come down from Milan to meet with the Emperor and Fortus had accompanied his father. When the guard ushered them into the audience hall, there was the Emperor himself, down on his hands and knees, with Galla riding astride his back, flailing her legs and ordering him to gallop.

The Emperor did not rise when Fortus and his father entered the room. Galla spied the visitors and tugged the Emperor's ear in their direction. The Emperor turned his head and proceeded towards them on all fours, neighing loudly as Galla patted his head, offering him honey cakes and commending him as the best horse since Alexander's Bucephalus.

When the horse and rider had reached the visitors, the little girl dismounted regally and introduced herself as "Galla Placidia, daughter of Theodosius, the great Emperor of Rome and the greatest steed ever to race in the Circus Maximus." With that, the Emperor collapsed in laughter upon the floor and Galla fell on top of him, laughing so hard she nearly choked.

Fortus loved her immediately. She wasn't like any other girl he'd ever known--or any *boy* for that matter. There wasn't anything ordinary about her--she was smarter, quicker, prettier, taller and more wonderful than any other child he'd ever met. She was also meaner, ruder, more spiteful and more ornery than any other child, too. And Fortus adored her.

As they stood now atop the hill overlooking the lush fertile valley of her family estate, Fortus still saw the headstrong, willful child in the beautiful young woman before him. The years had no effect on her strong personality--it was still as sharp and keen as always--only the outward aspects of her person had changed. No longer were her knees knobby or her legs like a clumsy fawn. Before him stood a magnificent creature, tall and beautifully formed. Only the mischievous twinkle in her lovely amber eyes belied her air of sophisticated composure.

Galla stepped towards Fortus and looked up seductively into his eyes. She placed her cool hand against his bare chest.

"Fortus," she purred, "if I wanted something very badly, would you give it to me?" She drew her hand across his chest and wound a forefinger into the hair tugging gently.

Fortus' heart pounded. "Yes, Galla, I would give it to you if it were in my power to give."

"What if it were something forbidden, something the daughter of an Emperor should not ask for," she said haltingly, placing one hand on Fortus' shoulder and the other hand low on his trim waist.

Fortus' breath came quickly--he struggled to be calm and casual.

"As I said, Little Acorn, I would give you whatever it is in my power to give."

Galla smiled sweetly and stepped closer, her breasts just touching his chest.

"Even if it were something very bad--something beneath the position of the Emperor's daughter?" Galla cooed softly. She placed her lips so close to Fortus' mouth that he could feel her warm breath mingle with his own.

Fortus felt every muscle in his body tense, the blood rushed from his head . . . "Anything, Galla, anything. What is it you desire? Perchance I too desire it, my Little Acorn."

"And you promise me you'll say yes, Fortus, if I ask?" Galla whispered, pushing her full body against his.

"Yes, Galla, yes," Fortus stammered.

"Then I want a rematch of that race!" Galla stated firmly, pushing him away. "And I'll prove to you that you couldn't catch me--you never could and you never will!" She laughed defiantly, aware of the feelings she was able to arouse in Fortus and the anger that was taking hold of him.

Fortus turned and took a few powerful strides away from her, straining to regain his composure. "She did it again!" he thought. "I'm such a fool. She always fools me, manipulates me, and I play right into her hands. Oh, but what beautiful hands they are." He turned back towards Galla and smiled sheepishly.

"As I said Galla, I will give you anything that it is in my power to give--and if it's a race you want--I'll give you the best darn race you've ever run. Mount up!"

Galla laughed and tossed her hair playfully. "I love you Fortus, honestly I do!" she said to him over her shoulder as she swung herself effortlessly up onto her horse.

Fortus, too, mounted his horse. He looked over at Galla. He knew he wouldn't win the race, even if he could, a fact about which he was not quite certain. He would see to it that she won the race, not because she was the Emperor's daughter, but because she was Galla, and Galla always won.

CHAPTER II

Galla pushed open the kitchen door and strode in, her eyes shining brightly with excitement. Eli was stooped over the fire, adding some charcoal. Eli slowly straightened up her aging frame and flashed a look of angry disapproval at Galla.

"Where have you been, you naughty girl?" Eli demanded. "Your uncle has been in three times checking to see if you've arrived home from your wanderings. He's absolutely furious. The guests are already on their dining couches and have finished the first course. Look here--the squabs are ready and about to be served." She pointed to a huge silver tray full of broiled squabs.

Galla smiled meekly and the flush of victory drained from her face. "I'm sorry Eli, I lost track of the time, we were having such fun. It really was an extraordinary day." Galla leaned over and kissed her nurse's graying head.

"Extraordinary," Eli sighed. "You're extraordinary, running all over the countryside at all hours of the day and night, just like a wild animal, with no thought for your family or your reputation. Now get in to your quarters and get bathed. I've laid out your beautiful new Egyptian sheath. And hurry! If your uncle Julius has to come in one more time, I'm afraid of what he'll do!"

Galla sneaked a leg of one of the squabs that Eli was carefully arranging on the serving tray, turned on her heel and strode off towards her rooms in the east wing of the vast palace. Her heavy riding sandals rang on the marble floors as she walked along the long corridors.

Arriving at her room, Galla undressed quickly and slipped into the bath that was awaiting her. It felt cool and soothing against her sunburned skin. She would have preferred to remain soaking in her bath than to face an evening of dull conversation with her relatives and their guests. But Eli's warning echoed in her ears and Galla stepped from her bath and was toweled dry by her servant girl.

"Will my Lady be wanting her silver sandals or the gold?" Anta inquired anxiously. Eli had obviously ordered Anta to dress

Galla quickly and now poor Anta hovered between Eli's anger and her mistress Galla's displeasure.

Galla saw the young girl's fear and said, "The silver will be fine, Anta," amused at the fear that the aging Eli could instill in the entire household when she was worked up.

Galla thought of Eli and how Eli had been not too much older than Galla was now when Galla's mother had died and Galla's care was left in Eli's capable hands. Galla was only six at the time and now the memory of her mother was clouded by time. Galla's childhood memories centered around the loving security of her good nurse and the deep affection of her father. But those years were cut short when Galla's father died not long after her mother. Her later childhood was a series of distasteful recollections of long journeys between government centers, heated custody debates, and painful family battling.

Galla was brought back from her musings by Anta's voice, "There, my Lady, you are ready."

Galla picked up the polished bronze mirror and gazed at her reflection. Where only twenty minutes before had been a dirty tomboy, now stood a respectable Roman aristocrat. Galla smiled at the deception. She glanced gratefully at Anta. How fortunate Galla was to have such a skilled Greek servant. No one in the dining hall would guess that underneath Galla's polished exterior was the ardent horsewoman who defeated one of Rome's most accomplished soldiers only an hour before.

When Galla entered the grand dining hall, all that remained of Eli's lovely stuffed squabs were bones scattered randomly on the floor. Servants scrambled to pick up the debris before the third course was served.

Galla's uncle Julius looked up and frowned severely at Galla as she paused by the tall bronze doors. His angry expression softened as he scanned her elegant appearance. The close-fitting white Egyptian sheath clung tightly to her beautiful figure and was belted at the waist by a broad band bearing the Imperial insignia. The white pleats of her gown fell to her slim ankles and revealed delicate jewel-studded silver sandals. The stylish dress was sleeveless, and Galla's lovely long bronzed arms were wrapped in silver coils resembling snakes. Her abundant auburn tresses were piled high atop her head and were bound with silver ribbons. Long silver earrings framed her oval face, tinted pink from her day's outing, from which Galla's lovely amber eyes shone brightly. When Galla saw her uncle's look of reproach soften into an approving appraisal, Galla flashed her most brilliant smile and he returned it, beaming proudly.

"How beautiful she is," he thought to himself, "and how regal and commanding. If only her two brothers had one quarter of her intelligence and energy, I could go to my grave knowing I had fulfilled my sacred duty to their father and left the empire in good hands. But just look at those two," Julius glowered at the two brothers reclining on their dining couches, guzzling wine and laughing hoarsely with their friends. "The two together couldn't rule this *house*, let alone an Empire. Yet rule they do, as *Emperors* of the entire Roman state, ruling it right into oblivion with over taxation and indifference. If only Galla had been a boy, if only the reins of government could have been placed into her hands, if only . . . " Julius looked back to Galla who had followed his glance and she now smiled back at him sympathetically.

Galla moved slowly in his direction, nodding good evening to the guests as she caught their eyes. She looked in the direction of her two brothers, acutely aware, as she always had been, that they were not her full-brothers, only her half-brothers, sons by her father Theodosius' first marriage to Aelia Flacilla, an arranged marriage of state. Later, after Aelia's death, when on one of his many travels from Rome to Constantinople, Theodosius had met and fallen in love with a beautiful Thessalonikan girl named Galla who was to become Galla Placidia's mother. This was not a marriage of state, but a marriage of deep affection. Only one obstacle had stood in the way--her family's adherence to the Arian sect of Christianity. Eager to marry into the Imperial family, the prospective bride's family gave up their Arian ties and became followers of Athanasius, who preached the indivisibility of God the Father, the Holy Spirit and Jesus Christ. Upon the family's rejection of what Theodosius considered their Arian heresy, the marriage ceremony was held. It was a marriage of true love, and out of their union, Galla Placidia was born.

Galla's brothers did not look up to acknowledge Galla's nod as she glided across the floor. Arcadius and Honorius were engaged in lewdly appraising the physique of a young Celtic slave boy. The proud young slave stood rigid as the two men lifted his tunic and exchanged comments on his various attributes. Galla flushed with anger, yet she knew this would only serve to amuse and encourage her two brothers who were already inebriated at this early stage of the banquet. Galla stifled her anger, set her mouth in a smile, and continued across the vast hall.

Galla reached her uncle's dining couch and perched lightly upon the corner. Julius held up his cheek and Galla kissed it warmly. Other than Eli, her uncle was the only remaining member of her household whom Galla truly loved. Although Julius could never replace her father Theodosius in her heart, Julius had taken Theodosius' request to serve as guardian to Galla quite seriously and they sincerely loved one another. Julius was not, in fact, an uncle by blood, but Theodosius had loved him dearly and called him brother, so Galla grew up calling Julius "Uncle" and she loved him as if he were, indeed, her true uncle.

Julius offered her the last remaining squab on the small serving table next to his dining couch. Galla reached out and picked up a bunch of red grapes instead and popped one into her mouth.

"And what have you been doing with yourself all day my fine niece?" Julius said loudly enough for all the guests to hear. "You haven't been within the palace walls all day. Perhaps you went into Rome to the library or to consult with the Holy Fathers at St. Peter's Basilica."

Galla leaned back and appraised her uncle. Library? Holy Fathers? What was he talking about? He himself had seen her off early this morning, when she and Fortus had ridden out of the courtyard and off across the countryside to the north. Rome was to the south. Had the wine already reached his head as it had her brothers'? "That certainly must be some vintage," she thought to herself as she took a sip from the gold cup on the table.

"Tell me about your day," Julius continued, "perhaps you spent it translating Greek, or in more womanly pursuits, like weaving," Julius tossed a look over Galla's shoulder to the dining couch in the corner.

Galla followed his glance. "Oh no!" she muttered out loud. Julius squeezed her hand to silence her. *That* was the reason Julius was lauding her "womanly" virtues . . . Eucherius was present at the banquet. In her attention to her brothers and to Julius upon her entrance, she had not glanced to the other side of the hall. If she had, she could not have missed that overbearing lump. If she had known Eucherius would be there, she would have spent the night in the countryside. But too late now, she was there and Julius' boasting had drawn Eucherius' attention to her.

Looking up from his plate, which he held just inches from his face, Eucherius licked his fingers and smiled a greasy grin at her. Galla's stomach turned. She formed her lips into a polite smile and nodded. His grin widened, revealing bits of the dinner he had just been devouring. Galla quickly looked down at her wine cup and busied herself rearranging the little serving table.

"Pigs' feet," she thought, "that's it, pigs' feet. That's what he reminds me of, cold, pickled pigs' feet, all white and bloated and tasteless." Somehow she could not restrain herself from looking up again--like after a terrible accident in the Circus Maximus when she didn't want to look but somehow couldn't stop herself. Galla looked up at Eucherius again. He was talking to his mother Serena who was reclining on the dining couch next to his. Chunks of food fell from his mouth as he spoke animatedly about Galla, gesturing a plump, white, oily finger in Galla's direction.

Serena, listening half-heartedly to her son's babbling, turned her cold green eyes on Galla and curled her painted red lips into an affected smile. Her white face and her black hair gave her a corpse-like appearance. Serena was one in a long line of conniving Roman matrons who dominated their children's lives in the best interest of their own social statuses. She and her husband Stilicho had been granted the guardianship of Galla's two brothers, Arcadius and Honorius, upon Theodosius' death. Relatives by both blood and marriage, Serena and her husband Stilicho sought every opportunity to promote a marriage between their son Eucherius and the noble Galla Placidia to thereby solidify their position and power in Rome.

Galla looked back down and pretended to occupy herself with the third course of roasted venison in onion sauce. She could still feel Serena's piercing stare. "You call yourself 'Cousin' and yet you want me to marry your son," Galla thought to herself. "If my father were here today, he'd ban you all. He never would have allowed you to rule and dictate our lives this way. Those fools Honorius and Arcadius, if only they had a brain and a backbone between them, they'd stand up and throw you all out." Galla glanced over at her two brothers who were now engaged in forcing the slave boy to eat spiced sea urchins. The boy's face ran with tears of anger and frustration, causing the brothers to howl with laughter.

Galla turned her attention back to Julius, her only refuge in this array of sordid humanity. "Uncle," she said, "Fortus and I devised the most wonderful race track today--out in the wide valley just north of here." Julius threw her a disapproving but bemused look. Galla continued on, "We created a track, well, *kind* of a track, around the outside of the valley and the finish line is just past the big fallen oak tree in the middle of the valley. We had the men build a ramp and in order to reach the finish line, you must ride your horse up the ramp, jump the old fallen oak and ride up the hill. It's wildly fun," she exclaimed, "and Fortus is splendid at it. Will you join us tomorrow? You do know the old oak, don't you?"

Julius smiled sadly. Yes, he knew the "old" oak as she called it. In his youth, her father and he also used it for their races, only in those days the oak was young and strong and it stood tall in the center of the valley. It was Theodosius' favorite place to go to get away from the demands of the Empire. As assistant to the Emperor, Julius often had to seek out Theodosius, and he usually found him in the valley seated under his beloved oak tree. Its branches were privy to more affairs of state, and heart, than were most men in Theodosius' life. Julius was a rare exception, a man whom Theodosius truly loved and respected. The two would sit for hours under the big oak and talk of life, of love, of empire, and of God. Theodosius often compared the oak to the Empire itself-- the oak's strong trunk represented the strong centralized government of Rome reaching out its benefits to all the provinces which he imagined as the branches, with both trunk and branches drawing strength and sustenance from their deep roots in the solid ground of the Christian faith.

Theodosius had even confided to Julius that it was on the soft grass, in the early spring, beneath the big oak, that Galla had been conceived. That is why he always referred to her as his Little Acorn. If only he could see his Little Acorn today--what a magnificent oak she was now. Theodosius could have asked for nothing more even if she had been a son. And what a cruel twist of fate, for Galla and for the Empire, that she had not been born a son.

Yes, Julius knew the oak tree. He had watched from the palace veranda, the night that Theodosius died, as a violent thunderstorm unleashed its fury across the broad north valley. In a blazing flash, lightning fell the huge oak tree, causing it to crash so hard against the earth that Julius felt the tremor far up the hill on the veranda. Julius saw his future fall with it. As much as Theodosius had loved Julius, he was aware of Julius' advancing years. In his will, Theodosius had appointed Stilicho the legal guardian of the Emperor's two sons, Honorius and Arcadius, which included the honor and responsibility of raising and educating the two boys. To Julius, his trusted but aging companion, Theodosius bequeathed a substantial income and, something much greater and more precious, the co-guardianship of his Little Acorn, the thing that, next to his Christian faith, Theodosius held most dear in all the world.

"Uncle! Uncle! Are you listening?" Galla gently shook the old man's shoulder, thinking he had lost his train of thought. "I asked if you knew that big old oak tree--the one that fell down all those years ago?"

"Yes," Julius smiled softly at Galla, "I know the old oak tree."

"Well, that's the tree we have to jump. It's very big you know. I did it and so did Fortus, but none of the others could. Even some of the *Praetorian* Guard tried, but they failed."

"I bet *I* could jump it," a loud shrill voice whined from behind her. Galla looked up to see Eucherius peering down at her, alternately chewing on a rib bone and sucking sauce off his fat fingers.

"What?" Galla said flatly.

"I bet *I* could jump it," Eucherius whined boastfully.

"Oh, Eucherius, I'm certain you're a marvelous horseman," Galla lied, "but you don't know the tree I'm talking about. It's a special tree, a . . .a . . . very big tree, a . . . a . . . very difficult maneuver . . ."

"*I* can do it," Eucherius interrupted, his large tongue reaching out to lick the sauce dripping off his protruding lips. "I can do anything, Mother said so. She said, 'Eucherius, you can do anything if you set your mind to it.' So I can do this. *I* can jump that silly old tree."

Into Galla's mind flashed a picture of a hippopotamus leaping over the old fallen oak and getting stuck halfway over--front legs on one side, back legs on the other--teetering back and forth and bellowing for help. She laughed impulsively at the image.

"You're laughing at me, Galla! Don't you *dare* laugh at me! I'll tell my mother I don't want to marry you and *then* where would you be? An old maid--*that's* what you'd be. Everyone knows you have no real prospects--you're not in line for the crown and your brothers are only offering a pittance of a dowry. *They* hope you end up an old maid in a convent and if it weren't for *me*, you just might. So you'd better be nice to me if you know what's good for you!" As his anger increased, his face grew redder and his fish-like eyes bulged farther and farther out from his head, all the time he was waving a ragged rib bone in her face.

Galla was frozen with anger, which Eucherius interpreted as fear, so he railed on and on at her. Julius didn't dare silence this young stuffed pork chop, son of the powerful Stilicho.

A few minutes before, Galla had tried to discourage this puffy young windbag's boasting because, in some inexplicable way, she actually pitied him, he was so weak and pompous and unlikable. But now, with this outrage, she made an abrupt tactical change.

"All right, all right, Eucherius, I was just looking out for your welfare. We all think so much of you here, we wouldn't want anything to happen to you, *I* least of all, since my future appears to be so totally in your hands. If you think you can do it, I would be very proud to show the entire guard the exceptional prowess of my cousin and future fiancé." Still seated, she bent deeply at the waist in a mock bow.

Eucherius straightened up and smacked his fat lips. "You're going to be a difficult wife, Galla Placidia, and I'm going to have to rule you with a heavy hand, I can see that even now. Oh, what a burden my ancestors have placed upon me," he sighed. "What time shall we meet tomorrow for the race?"

Drawing on all her strength to control her fury, Galla stated calmly, "At twelve noon--the sun is at its highest and will not be to anyone's disadvantage. We'll meet at the palace end of the big valley. Is that agreeable to you, *Cousin*?"

"Well, all right, I guess so." Eucherius looked down at the rib he had been flailing during his tirade and he saw it no longer held any meat to speak of. He threw it on the floor next to Galla's lovely silver-sandaled foot. "See you tomorrow," he muttered. "And you'd better be there!" he added as he waddled off to his dining couch stopping briefly at a serving table to pick up a handful of chicken wings.

Galla took a deep breath to regain her composure. The hippopotamus still teetered in her imagination and the picture served to regain her good humor.

"Galla," her uncle interrupted her imaginings, "do you really think this is such a good idea?" he queried.

"But Uncle, you heard him! I can't let him get away with that! That big tub of lard! Rule me with a heavy hand, ha! I'd rather hit him with a heavy club!" she whispered harshly.

"Galla, Galla! Stop it, stop it. Think of what you're doing. *That*, tub of lard that he might be, is your hope of a secure life. Your future is not assured by any means. Your father's fortune went by law to your two brothers. You are at their mercy. You must think to the future. Even though the chance is remote, there is the possibility that *your* son and not theirs' might one day rule the Empire."

Galla rolled her eyes. Julius looked at her reprovingly and continued, "Yes, there *is* that chance, depending upon whom you marry and how long your brothers live. By offering a meager dowry, your brothers are assuring that you will have no suitors of high birth. The way they have it planned, Eucherius may well be the only alternative to the convent--and we both know you'd make a terrible nun--'obedience' is not in your vocabulary."

Galla smiled meekly. Her uncle continued, "Whatever else in which Eucherius may be lacking, he is not lacking in political ties nor in financial security. You may not be the happiest Roman wife, but you will not be the poorest nor will you be the least powerful."

Galla looked over at her uncle with a pitiful expression. "I'm sorry, my dear," he said softly. "We are not ordinary persons with ordinary lives. We owe our lives to Rome. It is our *pietas*, our duty, and we must obey."

CHAPTER III

Galla awoke before dawn. She sat up and slipped silently out of bed, careful not to awaken Anta who was sleeping soundly on the floor at the foot of Galla's bed. Galla went into her dressing room and washed her face with cold water from the marble basin. She brushed her long hair quickly and then tied it into a neat knot atop her head. She would have time for the rest of her toilette later, now she was eager to go to the stable and prepare her horse for the day's events.

Galla pulled on a short tunic, then she tied a pair of sandals together and threw them over her shoulder. She didn't want to awaken the entire house with the sound of her sandals against the polished marble floors. Galla gently pushed open the tall bronze doors. The guard outside was snoring softly as Galla tiptoed silently past him as she headed for the kitchen.

Eli was already awake and hard at work baking bread for the day. She was leaning into the oven pulling out two freshly baked loaves. She jumped with surprise when she looked up and saw Galla.

"You scared me!" Eli reproached. "What are you doing up at this hour? You should be getting your beauty sleep, not rummaging around like some gypsy beggar!"

Galla smiled sheepishly and picked up one of the freshly baked loaves of bread. It smelled warm and delicious and it reminded her of when she was a little girl and Eli would let her "help" in the kitchen. Galla tore the loaf in two, poked one half under her belt and bit into the other half.

"Oh, go off with you then," Eli moaned. "I know there's nothing I can say to stop you. Where you got these wild ways, I'll never know. Get out of here now, just be sure to be back for breakfast. Today is Eucherius' birthday and he requested a special meal; he's been ordering it for weeks. You'll be expected to be there. Now, don't go looking at me like that, he's not *my* cousin."

Galla, who had been visibly expressing her displeasure, screwed-up her face even tighter until Eli had to laugh. Galla loved to see Eli laugh; it was so much like the old days.

Galla stepped over to her old nurse and hugged her tightly. Tears rose in Eli's eyes and to hide them she turned away saying, "Now get along, I've got a lot to do--after all, making breakfast for Eucherius is a greater task than making breakfast for an entire Legion." Galla laughed loudly and went out of the warm, sweet-smelling kitchen, into the cool dampness of the early dawn.

As Galla approached the stables, two guards saluted her smartly. "Does Your Highness require her horse?"

"No, not now," Galla replied without looking at the guards as she strode past them into the stable.

Galla loved the stable. She loved the darkness, the smell of new hay and horses, and the sound of the horses' soft snorting. She walked over to the stall where her stallion Odysseus was eagerly extending his head awaiting her gentle caress, his soft brown eyes alert with intelligence.

"Good morning, Odysseus." Galla patted him on the neck as she slid under the chain and into his stall. The stall was warm and quiet. Galla ran her hand over the horse's fine black back.

"What a magnificent creature," Galla thought, as Odysseus nudged her gently and poked his nose into her hand. "Yes, yes, I brought you something. Here," she said. "If Eli knew what I was doing with her freshly baked bread . . ." Galla smiled at the thought and felt slightly guilty. Odysseus took the bread greedily and began munching rhythmically.

"Did you have a good night Odysseus? I hope you slept well. Remember the game we played yesterday? You enjoyed it, didn't you? So did I. Well, we're going to play it again today, only *this* time, it will be even more important that we win." Odysseus looked Galla directly in the eyes. "You understand, don't you boy? Good. Well, you have a restful morning and I'll see you later."

"Guards!" Galla said loudly as she slipped out of the stall. The two guards ran towards her. Galla ordered fresh oats and plenty of water for her horse and asked that he be curried and then walked around in the paddock. "I'll be back a little before noon," she said, and she walked out of the dark, quiet stable into the daylight.

She had halfway expected to see Fortus there. He often went to check on the horses early in the morning. She looked around but Fortus was nowhere in sight. She wanted to tell Fortus about the events of the previous night, to give him *her* side of the story and to explain why she *had* to accept Eucherius' challenge. Fortus wouldn't be happy with her. She had placed him in a very difficult, even a very dangerous, position. Fortus now had to race against Eucherius, one of the most prominent and powerful young men in Rome, even if he *was* a big tub of lard.

"Oh," she moaned to herself, "that makes it even worse, doesn't it? Fortus, the strongest of the royal guard, racing against a big tub of lard. What will people say of Fortus? They'll think he's lost his mind."

Galla looked around worriedly. "If only I could get to him, to explain . . ." Galla's thoughts were interrupted by trumpet blasts announcing the occasion of a royal festivity. "Oh no! Eucherius' birthday! And I'm late already!" Galla raced off to the palace to wash and to dress for the birthday breakfast.

The breakfast was served in the peristyle garden that overlooked the sea. The morning was bright and clear and the birds sang in the trees. It was as if all nature were ignorant of Galla's concerns as she walked into the garden.

The guests had already arrived and were standing around several tables laden with delicacies. Servants strolled about refilling partially empty goblets and removing discarded plates. Galla was always amazed that guests who had eaten to the point of illness only hours before, could awake early and eat and drink as if they had been starving for days.

Eucherius had ordered the couches from the dining hall to be moved out into the garden. He was sprawled languidly across a high stack of silk cushions atop a carved marble couch, proclaiming officiously that fresh air increased his appetite. Everyone laughed loudly and commented how glad they were to see him in such good spirits and with such a healthy appetite.

Galla skirted the main group of diners and sought refuge in the little tholos at the end of the peristyle garden. It was a small round space, screened off from the rest of the garden by a row of columns. She sat down on a marble bench and a young servant boy handed her a cup of wine and a plate of sliced cold chicken with artichoke hearts.

Galla looked up to thank the boy and she realized that it was the young Celtic slave boy whom her brothers had spent the previous night taunting and humiliating. Galla said softly, "I'm sorry. I mean I apologize, for my brothers, that is," she felt awkward addressing a slave in so familiar a manner, yet she continued, "I apologize for Honorius and Arcadius; they, they were wrong." The boy smiled politely at her and lifted his shoulders to signal incomprehension.

Just then a voice boomed out, "Did we hear our names?" Arcadius and Honorius rounded the corner and entered the tiny tholos. "And what were you saying about us to this luscious young boy, my beautiful sister?" Honorius inquired cheerfully.

Galla could tell from their expressions that they hadn't heard the words of apology that she had uttered. "I was just telling this slave to go and ask my two charming brothers to join me here that we might breakfast together and enjoy one another's company," Galla lied.

"Oh, no use talking to that boy," Honorius laughed. "He doesn't speak a word of Latin, and if I have *my* way, he won't *learn* one, either. A good slave is an ignorant slave." Honorius pointed at the cup and plate Galla was holding and signaled the slave to fetch two more. The boy scurried off, grateful to be out of the brothers' company, if only for a few minutes.

Honorius and Arcadius drew up two benches and sat across from Galla. "And why aren't you with the rest of the guests, Galla?" Honorius drawled as he gave Galla a sidelong glance. "It's your duty to be charming and to entertain our friends. I must say you've been standoffish lately and I for one don't like it. What do you say, Arcadius?"

Arcadius looked up at Galla and then at Honorius. "I don't know what to think, Honorius. I never did understand women. Frankly, I don't know if there *is* much to understand really."

"You're probably right there, Arcadius," Honorius responded jovially and looked back at his sister. Galla laughed too. She knew to do otherwise was to continue and increase the insults against her and her gender.

"Yes," Galla said, "you mustn't worry about me and what I'm thinking. None of it is of any importance, not to you two anyway, the co-emperors of *Rome*. You have so many other concerns, don't let me be one of them."

"Well-spoken, little sister!" Honorius reached out and patted the top of Galla's head. "You're a good Roman woman, quiet and knows her place. See that you keep it that way, eh?" Galla stiffened slightly.

Arcadius could see a pending feud and, eager to maintain decorum in front of their guests, he changed the topic of conversation. "What a splendid, perfectly splendid day to celebrate Eucherius' birth. And it *is* an occasion to celebrate, isn't it siblings? After all, one day he'll be Galla's husband and our brother-in-law, won't he?" Galla shuddered slightly but her brothers didn't notice.

"Yes, *one* day, Arcadius, but no rush," Honorius retorted. "That's in the future."

"I don't know," Arcadius countered. "Galla isn't *young* you know, she's eighteen. Most the girls her age are already married and mothers."

"Quiet, Arcadius, you don't know what you're saying. That Gaelic wine has reached your brain and the sun hasn't reached midday. Galla will marry when I say so and I say she will wait. There's plenty of time for that later."

"Why when *you* say, Honorius?" Arcadius said thickly, the wine numbing his speech. "Because you want *your* son to be Emperor? Well you don't have a son, but I do. *My* son will rule Rome one day. *If* you have a son, he will be second in line." Then, changing his tune, Arcadius added amicably, "And both of us will have *many* sons, so what difference does it make if this wretched creature gets married and has a few bastards? Her children will never rule Rome! And Stilicho can just forget about ruling Rome through his son Eucherius."

"Shut up, Arcadius, you fool!" Honorius whispered hoarsely. "That's enough!"

"Yes, I agree, dear Brother," Galla interrupted, "that *is* enough. Neither one of you need worry about marrying me off now or later. I'm in no hurry to marry now and perhaps not ever," Galla said calmly.

"Well-spoken again, my little sister. You make me proud to have such a noble Roman woman in my household!" Honorius pounded his palm against her back. "Now, where is that worthless Celt? I want more wine. Where *is* he? Arcadius leaves for Constantinople this afternoon and we must toast his departure!"

Galla stood up, placed her cup and plate on a small table and said, "I'll fetch your breakfast myself, dear brothers," and she walked out of the tholos with both brothers praising her in loud, drunken voices. Galla spied the young Celt heading for the tholos with trays laden with food and drink. "Honorius and Arcadius will never miss me," she thought, "not in the condition they're in," and she slipped out of the garden and headed for her chambers.

"Constantinople," Galla thought as she entered the palace, "seat of the Eastern Empire. How I remember those long, arduous journeys between Rome and the Eastern capital. Father used to make the trip regularly and he often took me and the household. I hated the difficult conditions, but I loved being with Father. *He* knew how to rule an empire, strict ties between East and West. Those fools Honorius and Arcadius only meet to drive the two capitals farther and farther apart."

Galla was glad that Arcadius was leaving. His visits were always occasions for family quarrels and political factioning. It would be good to have him out of the villa again. Dealing with Honorius alone was enough. Galla hoped that Honorius, too, would soon return to his palace at Ravenna, and then she could have the villa to herself again and be free of her two quarrelsome brothers.

"I envy my brothers' ability to act independently," she thought. "They can come and go as they please. If *I* wanted to travel to Constantinople or Ravenna, or anywhere, for that matter, it would be forbidden. No, I have to stay here at the villa, with my brothers and Stilicho and Serena watching my every move. I'll probably never go anywhere again," Galla thought glumly as she turned the corner and headed down the marble corridor to her rooms.

Galla arrived at her chambers to find Anta waiting anxiously for her by the door. Anta held out a small scroll. "This came for you, my Lady. The messenger said it was urgent."

Galla took the scroll and examined the seal. It was a tiny chi-rho cross, neatly impressed into dark blue sealing wax. It was from Fortus. Galla's heart missed a beat. "Oh, no, he *knows*," she thought as she quickly opened the scroll and read,

> To Her Royal Majesty,
> Galla Placidia Flavius--
> Greetings from your faithful servant,
> Fortus Agrippa Lepidus.

"Uh, oh," Galla thought, "he really *is* mad. He only uses such formality when he wants to irritate me." She continued reading,

> If it pleases Her Highness, I would like to request the honor of her company for a brief meeting at her earliest convenience. I will await her pleasure at the top of the north valley.
> With highest respect,
> I am her faithful servant,
> F. A. Lepidus.

Galla moaned and threw herself down onto a chair. Anta began unlacing her sandals. Galla could tell from Anta's quick movements and anxious glances that even this little slave girl had heard about the pending race. "Word travels quickly," Galla thought.

Galla's birthrights were many, but privacy wasn't one of them. By now everyone in the palace knew about the race. Galla reproached herself for making such a foolish challenge to Eucherius. She replayed the events of the previous evening in her mind--Eucherius' whining, his haughty arrogance, the half-eaten rib bone . . . as she relived the events, her anger rose-up again.

"I don't care who knows it," Galla thought defiantly, "That tub of lard deserves it. What right has he to treat me as if I were a slave girl? *I'll* show him. I don't care what Fortus says."

Galla's anger increased and she resolved to be firm with Fortus. She knew Fortus would try to talk her out of this race. He'd ask her to apologize to Eucherius and to forgive him. Sometimes Galla just couldn't understand Fortus. There he was, the most honored soldier in his regiment, with hundreds of awards for his bravery and strength, and yet sometimes he seemed like such a coward, with all his talk of Christian apologies and understanding and forgiveness.

Sometimes Galla wondered if Fortus used his Christianity to mask his fear, like the time the huge drunken Macedonian drove his chariot straight at Fortus as he was crossing the Via Appia. Fortus had to jump out of the way into the mud and the big foreigner only laughed at him. Galla was present and she was livid with anger. She had thrown her hunting knife to Fortus, expecting him to use it on the offender. Instead of using the knife on the big drunk, Fortus used it to scrape the mud off his tunic, all the while ignoring the man's insulting laughter. Several Romans had stopped to watch Fortus, the grand Imperial soldier, show the Macedonian lout a lesson, but when Fortus began calmly to clean himself, the Romans wandered off, muttering disparaging remarks about cowardice and fear.

Galla was embarrassed and ashamed. She demanded to know why Fortus had allowed the man to make a fool of him.

"It was he who was the fool, Galla, and I would have been a fool, too, if I had reduced myself to his level," Fortus had replied.

"But your dignity, your pride," Galla had stammered.

"Here is my dignity and my pride," Fortus responded as he held up the tiny cross he wore on a leather strap around his neck, "It's all the dignity and all the pride I'll ever need."

Galla hadn't understood him then, nor did she understand him now. Christianity with all its loving and forgiveness was fine in its place, but not at the expense of one's dignity. Dignity, pride and position had to come first. They were what made Rome great. Where would Rome be now if it had always turned the other cheek?

"No," Galla thought, "Fortus just doesn't understand. It's not his fault. He's not of noble birth, that's all. One really has to be of noble birth to understand how important it is to maintain one's dignity."

Galla finished dressing and headed for the stable. The grooms had prepared Odysseus and he stood shining in the sunlight, his muscles quivering with pent-up energy. Galla mounted her horse and felt the surge of excitement she always felt when seated on this magnificent animal. No one could beat her today; she felt it in her bones. She galloped off to the north valley.

Fortus was waiting for her. He watched her as she galloped towards him. When she drew up her horse alongside his, he dismounted and gestured for her to do the same. Galla slid off her horse and walked over to where Fortus was standing.

"Well, that was quite a formal invitation you sent me, Fortus, " Galla said in her most officious tone. "Well, I'm here, what do you want?"

Fortus cocked his head and looked at her, torn between anger and admiration. Part of him wanted to slap her soundly for her foolish headstrong ways, yet another part of him admired her steadfast resolve, so rare in one of her gender.

"Galla," Fortus began gently, "about this race . . ."

"It's already arranged," Galla interrupted, "and besides, you weren't there and you don't understand what happened."

Fortus looked up, took a breath and began again, "I understand that you have placed me in a very awkward position. If I lose, I am disgraced and run out of the Imperial guard. If I win, I'll probably be sent to the most remote post in the Empire, or, even worse, Eucherius could have me executed."

"Oh Fortus, you're always so dramatic. It's only that tub of lard Eucherius."

"It's not Eucherius who concerns me, although I think you do not fully realize that that "tub of lard" as you call him, is one of the most powerful tubs of lard in the Empire. The one who concerns me is his father, Stilicho, *your* cousin Serena's husband and *my* commanding officer."

"What does Stilicho have to do with this--it's just a silly race," Galla countered.

"There's no such thing as a 'silly race,' or a 'silly' anything, when it comes to matters of state," Fortus said firmly. He looked hard into Galla's eyes. "Could you really not know what's happening?"

"What do you mean? *What's* happening?" Galla said, her curiosity tempered by defense.

"Galla, my darling, your cousin Serena and her husband Stilicho are determined that you marry their little tub of lard so that they can rule through you and your son."

"Oh, *I* know all that. What does that have to do with this race? I'm not going to *marry* Eucherius today, I'm just going to put him in his place."

"That's *just* the point, Galla. Your brothers would love to see you put Eucherius in his place and disgrace him and his father. It would give them one more reason to put you in a convent, or to lock you up in an asylum for being mad. Your brothers will go to any length to see that you don't marry--not Eucherius, not *anyone*," Fortus added painfully. "If you were to marry and to have a son, it would jeopardize their sons' right to rule, and your brothers are busy enough trying to secure the throne for their heirs, without worrying about one of yours."

"Oh Fortus, really, what's all this talk of marriage and of heirs? I have no intention of marrying anyone, not now and probably not ever."

Fortus looked down and Galla could tell he was hurt.

"Oh Fortus, if I were to marry *anyone*, it would be you," she teased.

"No, Galla, you know as well as I do, that would be impossible. The daughter of Theodosius the Great cannot marry a common soldier who depends on the kindness of her brothers for his next meal and a roof over his head."

His tone was serious and he looked at her sadly with his clear blue eyes. Galla suddenly realized that he was earnest and that he was actually discussing marriage with her. Something stirred within her. She had grown up with Fortus. She loved him dearly, as a friend, as a comrade, but all of a sudden she felt something new, something she had never felt before.

Galla turned and took a few steps away. The sun was at its full height and the sound of horses approaching could be heard in the distance.

"They're coming," Fortus said as he stepped in front of Galla and took her hand. "I love you Galla, I want you to know that. What I do today, I do out of my love for you."

"What do you mean? What are you going to do? Tell me. You must tell me."

Just then Eucherius' voice could be heard high above the voices of the others and the sound of horses' hoofs.

"Yoo hoo, Galla, where are you? We're here!" Eucherius' voice rang out in a shrill singsong.

"He sounds *drunk*," Fortus said in disbelief as he dropped Galla's hand. "How can he be drunk and its barely noon?"

"Oh, its his birthday, and there was this breakfast party . . ." Galla said meekly.

"His birthday? A breakfast party? He can't race like that, he'll kill himself!"

"With any luck," Galla offered, trying to lighten Fortus' mood.

Just then, a huge chariot carrying Eucherius appeared at the top of the hill. Eucherius had about twenty horsemen with him and they were all laughing and shouting raucously.

Galla and Fortus looked at Eucherius in amazement. They had expected him to arrive on one of the Imperial stable's finest horses. Instead, here he was dressed in a long, flowing gold toga, driving a silver war chariot, complete with treacherous spiked wheels.

The chariot thundered over the hill and towards the grassy area where Galla and Fortus stood dumbfounded.

"What does he think he's doing?" Galla queried. "Is he crazy? This is a *horse* race. This track isn't meant for a chariot. Can he really be that dumb?"

"No, Eucherius is neither crazy nor dumb. I'm not sure *what* he's up to, but you can be sure it's not good." Fortus took a step forward and shaded his eyes to get a better look at Eucherius and the chariot shining in the bright noonday sun.

Eucherius drove his chariot straight towards Galla and Fortus, forcing them to hurry out of the path of danger. The chariot rumbled past them, followed by Eucherius' boisterous entourage. Eucherius drew up the reins of the two horses pulling the chariot and stopped a few feet beyond where Galla and Fortus had dashed for safety. The other horsemen also reined in their horses and Galla and Fortus found themselves surrounded by overly heated horses and overly drunken men.

"*There* you are, Galla," Eucherius whined. "Who's that you've got with you?" Eucherius leaned close to get a better look. "Oh, nobody, just that soldier, whatever his name is. Galla, you really should be more careful with whom you talk . . . racing against someone is one thing, *socializing* is quite another. All right, well, we're here, where's this silly race track you're so proud of?"

"Silly," Galla thought of Fortus' words, "There's no such thing as a 'silly' anything when it comes to matters of state."

Looking now at Eucherius, standing aloof and confident in his armor and shining war chariot, Fortus' words took on new meaning. When Eucherius was reclining on a dining couch with a turkey leg in his hand, he looked comical and ineffectual. But dressed in an Imperial gold toga and polished bronze cuirass, driving a massive war chariot, and accompanied by twenty muscular Imperial guards, even a tub of lard can be a formidable opponent. Galla swallowed hard, trying to control the lump of apprehension rising in her throat.

"Well, cat got your tongue Galla? I said, where is this track that's supposed to be so difficult?" Eucherius demanded.

"Eucherius, the track I was talking about is a race track for *horses*, not for *chariots*. It's difficult enough to maneuver a *horse* over the course . . ."

"That's just the point," Eucherius interrupted. "That's why I brought a chariot. You said that soldier-friend of yours could do it. You said even *you* could do it, and you're only a *girl*. So if a mere soldier and a girl can run the course on a horse, then *anybody* can run it on a horse. *That's* why I brought the chariot. Has *anyone* run the course with a chariot and *two* horses?" Eucherius asked, smiling smugly.

"Well, no . . ." Galla stammered, "but . . ."

"There then, it's as I said. *That's* why I brought the chariot, to show you how a skilled charioteer can beat a common soldier and a mere girl. Now, where's that track? Where do we begin?"

Eucherius' gloating and superior attitude were all Galla needed to forget Fortus' words of warning.

"All right," Galla began, trying to hide her rising irritation, "we start here at the top of this hill. We ride one lap around the rim of this valley and then we ride down into the valley and across that stream." Galla pointed to a stream that traversed the near side of the wide valley in front of them. "Then comes the fun part . . . we ride straight towards that big fallen oak tree, ride up that ramp, and jump over the tree. *If*," Galla quickly corrected herself, "*when* you land on the other side, you ride up the far hill. The one who gets to the top of the far hill first, wins. It's very simple, really," Galla smiled as she watched Eucherius' face as he studied the huge old oak tree.

Eucherius looked down at Galla quizzically. "*That* oak tree?"

"Yes, *that* oak tree," Galla replied.

"The big fallen oak tree in the center?" Eucherius asked slowly.

"Yes, the big fallen oak tree in the *center*," Galla said in her most casual voice.

"And you say you and this soldier-boy have done it before?" Eucherius said as he looked directly at Galla.

"Yes, that 'soldier-boy' and I did it several times yesterday. Just ask anyone who was here. It's really a *lot* easier than it looks. *Anyone* can do it . . . soldier-boys, even girls. Now that I see it again, I'm really ashamed of myself for making such a big deal of it last night."

Galla glanced quickly in Fortus' direction and saw him staring at the ground, the muscles in his temples revealing his tension.

Galla felt a pang of remorse and said to Eucherius, "I'm sure it's much too easy for you, let's just forget it, all right?"

Fortus looked up at her, his eyes revealing his approval.

Eucherius blurted out, "You're not going to get off *that* easily, Galla. I don't believe either one of you jumped that big tree. I want you to *prove* it, *prove* you jumped a horse over that big tree. You and that boy run the course. If you make it, and I say *if*, then I'll do it with two horses and a chariot and then I'll be best. I *will* be best, then, won't I men?"

The drunken guards in Eucherius' entourage all nodded and jeered in agreement.

Galla looked at Fortus who was busy assessing the situation. Fortus slowly nodded his consent and Galla said, "All right, Eucherius, we'll go first. *If* we make it, then you'll race the course. *If* you make it, we'll all agree you're the superior horseman."

Galla thought to herself, "He'll *never* make it, not with that big clumsy war chariot, so *we'll* never have to say he's a superior horseman." She felt her confidence return as she mounted her horse and she and Fortus rode up the hill to the starting point. When they reached the top of the hill, they stopped to await the starting signal.

Just then Stilicho and Serena appeared at the crest of the hill. They were riding in a litter being carried by four bronze Numidian slaves. Stilicho's blonde hair and broad Germanic features contrasted sharply with Serena's pale chiseled features and coal black hair.

The slaves carried the litter to a clearing in a grove of trees. They then set out two dining couches and two small serving tables. Stilicho and Serena regally exited the litter and carefully seated themselves on the couches. The well-formed African slaves hurriedly brought out gold goblets and poured wine for the two.

Stilicho proudly surveyed his son and the shining chariot beneath him. Stilicho's wide mouth stretched into a grin and he waved slowly to Eucherius and his comrades. Serena sat stiffly, staring coolly directly at Galla. Galla thought how like an ice sculpture Serena looked, tall and cold and motionless.

Galla turned to Fortus, "Well, this *is* an occasion, isn't it? You were right, Fortus."

"I didn't want to be right," Fortus replied, "but those two are so transparent it's easy to see right through them. Well, at least we won't be defeating their son directly. And, who knows, perhaps that big tub of lard *can* make it over that jump." Fortus smiled his warm smile at Galla.

Galla's heart quickened to see that look in Fortus' eyes. "How breathtakingly handsome he is," she thought. "Why haven't I noticed that before?"

"Fortus," Galla began, "about the conversation we had earlier, about marriage, about *us*, I mean . . ." Just then the horns blew to announce the approaching start of the race. Two mounted guards rode up carrying flags to mark the starting line. They positioned themselves on either side of Galla and Fortus.

"We'll talk about it later, Galla," Fortus responded. "Meet me at the tree at dusk. And now good luck, Galla, race well."

The starting horn blasted and the race began. The two horses were excellently matched, as were their two riders. As the crowd cheered loudly, Galla and Fortus maneuvered their horses around the rim of the valley and then down onto the valley floor and across the shallow stream. Fortus led the way until his horse slipped on the mossy rocks in the streambed.

Galla and Odysseus flew past him as his horse regained its footing. It was a long straight run across the valley floor to the makeshift ramp leading to the fallen oak tree. It was as if Odysseus never touched the ground as he flew across the flat basin of the valley. Then up, up the steep wooden ramp and suddenly both he and rider were airborne, sailing freely across the tree and landing soundly on the ground on the other side and galloping off.

Galla heard the sound of Fortus' horse galloping up the ramp and then silence as he, too, sailed through the air and over the tree, landing in the same spot that Odysseus had just vacated. It was neck and neck up the far side of the valley, the two horses striding in unison so close, that the riders could have reached out and touched one another. Up, up the hill to the finish line and the cheers of the waiting crowd. The two horses crossed the line at exactly the same moment as the finish line guards called in unison "Tie!"

Galla and Fortus allowed their mounts to race past the finish line and over the brink of the hill, spending the last of their momentum. The sound of speeding air rushed in Galla's ears and she felt exhilarated. She drew up her horse and smiled broadly at Fortus. He, too, was experiencing the thrill of a race well run and his eyes shone with pleasure.

"Well done, Galla, well done," Fortus shouted. It was only then that Galla realized that they had tied and that *she* had not won the race. The day before she would have counted this a failure and demanded a rematch. But somehow today was different. Today she was happy to end the race tied evenly with Fortus.

"And you, Fortus, well done, too. An excellent race--an excellent opponent," Galla beamed proudly at Fortus. Their eyes met. It was as if an invisible thread ran between them, connecting them, even though they were several yards apart.

A loud commotion on the far hill finally drew their eyes away from one another. It was Eucherius and his men preparing for the start of Eucherius' solo run in the chariot.

"Hail! Hail! The victor Eucherius!" the men shouted in a drunken chorus. Eucherius drove his chariot to the starting line, weaving slightly along the way. He waved to his cohorts as if he were a victorious general celebrating a great triumph in the streets of Rome. The more he waved, the more the men cheered.

The huge silver chariot and its driver reached the starting point and the two starting guards took their places. Galla and Fortus, drawn out of their reverie, watched as Eucherius waved to Stilicho and Serena.

Galla looked at Fortus. He was still mounted on his horse and his hands were gripping the reins tightly. "Galla," he said without looking at her, "pray with me. Pray that Eucherius doesn't kill himself. Ask God to forgive us." Fortus bowed his head and Galla did likewise.

With a sudden blast of the starting horn, the race began. The huge chariot lumbered around the rim of the valley, lurching from side to side. When the circuit was completed, Eucherius drove down into the valley, his two horses racing hard to keep ahead of the heavy chariot that was building momentum behind them. Eucherius leaned forward and whipped his horses brutally. Shouts and cheers of encouragement rang out across the valley. Galla and Fortus watched silently from the far hill. They saw Eucherius lurch forward and nearly fall out of the chariot as one of the big wheels struck a rock. Stilicho leapt to his feet and Serena cried out in fear for her son.

Eucherius drove the horses onward, beating them unmercifully with his whip. He forded the stream, the wheels rumbling across the hard rocks on the river's bed. Next was the long straightaway on the valley floor. Eucherius loosened the reins and whipped the horses again, urging them to gain the speed it would take to climb the ramp and clear the big oak. Onward, faster and faster, the horses ran. Then up the ramp they charged at full speed, drawing the chariot and Eucherius behind them.

"Good, that's it," Galla thought, "let the horses have their heads, let them run the race, they can do it, good . . ."

Just as the chariot headed up the ramp it leaned back at a strong angle. Eucherius began to slip backwards. Rather than grabbing the chariot to brace himself, he pulled in on the reins, drawing in the horses' heads abruptly. The horses slowed but it was too late, they had reached the end of the ramp and there was nowhere to go but over the huge oak.

Fortus saw the disaster coming and he lowered his head. Galla stared, transfixed, as the two horses somersaulted over the old oak tree and as Eucherius and the huge wooden chariot landed on top of them.

Galla's hand flew to her mouth to stifle a scream as she strained to see. Serena's shrill cry could be heard above the shouts of the men. Everywhere was movement and confusion. Only Eucherius and his horses were still and silent. The crowd rushed towards the chariot; Stilicho shouted orders and called for his litter.

When the men reached the chariot, Galla heard Stilicho cry out to Serena, "He's alive! Just barely, but he's alive. Send for Ptolomy and the other physicians." The men carefully lifted Eucherius out of the chariot and onto the litter.

In minutes the litter was carried away and the valley was empty. Eucherius' two horses lay motionless under the broken war chariot. Galla and Fortus remained silent. The events of the last hour replayed in Galla's mind. It didn't seem real. "If only Eucherius had grabbed the chariot and not the reins, if only . . ." she thought dully.

Fortus' voice broke through her hazy thoughts. "You'd better go back to the palace and see how he is. Act concerned. Take care of him. Stilicho and Serena will blame you, so you must do everything you can to make amends. You *must*, Galla."

"Yes, Fortus, I know I must. All right, I'll go. What about this evening? Can we still meet this evening?"

"See how it goes. If he improves, yes. If he doesn't, well I don't know if we'll ever see one another again." Fortus took her hand and kissed it softly. "Now go, *quickly*."

Galla galloped off leaving Fortus alone in the wide valley. He sat on his horse surveying the place where he had spent so many years in youthful innocence. Now it all looked so different.

Suddenly in the distance he thought he heard a noise; he listened more intently. Yes, it was a noise, a muffled wheezing sound. Fortus rode towards the sound. As he approached the big oak, he realized the sound was coming from one of Eucherius' horses. It was still alive.

Fortus dismounted and surveyed the scene of the horrible accident. A long gash in the tree marked the spot where the chariot wheel had failed to clear. The one horse was obviously dead, its head was bent back and its neck was broken. The other horse was breathing laboriously. Fortus examined its injuries . . . two broken legs and blood oozing from its nose. Tears rose in Fortus' eyes. He dearly loved horses . . . they were so loving and faithful, they'd give their hearts for you, just as these ones had today. Fortus knew he couldn't let it suffer any longer. He knelt down and stroked its muzzle. Its big brown eyes looked up, pleading for help. "Yes, boy, yes, you're going to be all right. You're going to a better world than this one." Fortus drew his sword, took a deep breath, and plunged it deep into the horse's neck. Fortus stood up and wiped the sword against the oak tree. He remounted his horse and rode slowly out of the valley.

Galla arrived back at the palace, turned her horse over to the stable guards and headed straight for Eucherius' quarters without stopping to change her riding clothes. Two guards were stationed in front of the tall bronze doors. As Galla approached the doors, the guards widened their defensive stances and crossed their lances over the entrance.

"I'm here to see Eucherius. Tell him Galla Placidia requests to be admitted."

"We have orders that no one be admitted, Your Highness, not even you."

"Who gave those orders?" Galla demanded.

"Serena, Your Majesty," one of the guards said, his tone revealing his apology.

"Well, can you at least tell me how my cousin is? I'm very worried about him. Will he live?"

"We don't know, Your Majesty. No one has told us anything except that we are to admit no one. Stilicho, Serena, and the Imperial physicians are with him now."

The other guard cleared his throat, indicating that the guard who was speaking was perhaps disclosing more than he should. The man fell silent.

Galla knew the difficult position the guards were in and she didn't press them for any more information. She thanked them, turned, and walked slowly towards her wing of the sprawling villa. She couldn't decide if she was angry with Serena for issuing the restraining orders or grateful. Part of Galla wanted to fulfill Fortus' request that she nurse and care for Eucherius; the other part was glad that she didn't have to face him.

When Galla reached her apartments, she found them empty. "Anta must be on an errand or at her midday meal," Galla thought, pleased to be completely alone. She sat down at her dressing table, which overlooked the rolling hills of the countryside to the east. How beautiful and calm the world seemed. It was hard to believe all that had happened that morning . . . the race . . . the accident . . . Fortus . . .

Fortus . . . the thought of Fortus made Galla's pulse quicken. Only yesterday he was a friend, a comrade and now today, how differently Galla felt. She longed to see Fortus, to tell him how she felt, to ask him how long he had felt this way about her.

"Please, God," she prayed. "Make Eucherius live. Forgive me for my thoughtless, headstrong ways. Help me to be better, to think before I act."

A soft knocking on the door interrupted Galla's prayer. "Come in!" she commanded impatiently.

The door opened and Eli's stocky frame scurried into the room. Her face was taut with concern.

"Galla, dear, I'm glad I found you. They don't want me to tell you, but Eucherius is fine. Just a small blow to his head and a big blow to his pride. I just *happened* to be passing by his door," Eli looked down, avoiding Galla's eyes, "and I heard Eucherius say he wants you to suffer and to feel bad for what you did. He wants to keep you in suspense. Then, when you finally learn that he's all right, you'll be grateful and indebted to him." Eli looked up again to see if Galla approved of her eavesdropping.

"Thank you, Eli. You are a dear. Keep me in suspense, eh? That family never stops plotting and conniving, do they? Oh, Eli, what would I do without you?" Galla smiled and stroked the old nurse's hair.

Eli beamed proudly. "I'd better get back to the kitchen before anyone finds I'm gone. If I hear anything else, I'll let you know." Eli started to walk out of the room.

"Eli," Galla said, "how does one know when one is in love?"

Eli stopped abruptly and turned back to look at Galla. "In love? With *Eucherius*?" Eli said with such a look of shock that Galla had to laugh.

"No, *no*, not with Eucherius, perish the thought! With just *anyone*, anyone in general. How do you know if you're in love?"

Eli took a few steps back towards Galla and said, "Well, it's been many years, but I was in love once. I was just about your age. Oh, he was a lovely lad, a stable boy, very tall and handsome. I remember I felt very good--but kind of sick--all at the same time. It's like getting an invitation to a special party, and when you get there you are very nervous, but still you have a wonderful time. Oh, I don't know, don't ask me, it was so long ago."

"What happened to him?" Galla asked.

"Him?" Eli asked blankly.

"To the handsome stable boy?"

"Oh, I don't know. It was the year your dear father, God rest his soul, took the entire household to Constantinople. When we returned to Rome, the boy was gone. I asked and asked after him, but nobody even *remembered* him. Kind of funny, isn't it? The love of my life and no one remembered him."

Eli picked up the corner of her apron and dabbed her eyes. "Well, I better get back to the kitchen. Now, don't you worry your pretty head about falling in love. When it happens, you'll know it. And *you* won't forget him either, not ever." Eli turned and shuffled out of the room.

Galla got up from her dressing table, went to her bed and lay down. She suddenly felt very tired. The paucity of sleep the night before plus the events of the day caught up with her. She closed her eyes and slept until Anta awakened her for dinner.

Galla awoke with a start, fearing she had missed her appointment with Fortus. She was relieved when she saw that it was only late afternoon and that several hours remained until dusk.

Anta announced that Julius had asked Galla to dine with him in his private apartments and that Eucherius and his family would not be joining them. Relieved that she did not have to face Eucherius or his family, Galla began to order the clothes she wanted to wear that evening—her best black silk dress, the jeweled sandals, the cashmere shawl . . .

Anta looked at her quizzically. The little slave knew that these were Galla's most treasured articles. "All this for a simple dinner with her uncle?" the girl wondered to herself as Galla requested a massage with the scented oils from Parthia.

After her massage, Galla soaked in a tub of hot water sprinkled with Egyptian lotus blossom perfume. She had Anta do and redo her hair three times before it suited her. Then she dressed and put on her finest gold jewelry. At last Galla was ready and she hurried off to dine with her uncle.

Julius was waiting for her in his apartments. The serving tables had been set and the servants stood at attention. When Galla entered the room, he dismissed the servants and carefully closed the doors behind them. He didn't notice Galla's special attire or her impeccable coiffure. His thoughts were on other matters.

"Please be seated, Galla. I'm glad you could come. We don't get to spend much time alone together anymore, do we?" Julius busied himself pouring wine from the silver pitcher.

His apartments were conservatively and tastefully decorated, a reflection of his world travels and masculine life style. On one wall were half a dozen zebra skins, mementos of his African campaign. On the far wall was a beautifully carved interlace pattern on a huge Celtic shield, a reminder of his campaign to pacify the discontent in Britain. In a corner stood an exquisite Egyptian obelisk, purchased on a trading expedition to the Red Sea. Among the numerous souvenirs of military campaigns and trading expeditions were maps of all the provinces of the Empire. Galla filled with pride when she looked upon these symbols of greatness--the greatness of her beloved guardian -- the greatness of her beloved Rome.

Julius handed her a gold goblet filled with deep red wine. He looked especially handsome this evening in his deep blue tunic. His silver hair shone in the late day's sunlight and his clear blue eyes looked directly at Galla.

"Here," he said. "Drink this. From what I hear, you need it, after the day you've had." He sat down on a leather camp chair across from Galla's more luxurious padded armchair. "Well, I've heard *their* side, now let's hear *your* side."

"Good old Uncle Julius," Galla thought, "always the practical, direct, no monkey-business Roman. *Virtus, simplicitas, gravitas*--manliness, directness and seriousness--all the Roman virtues wrapped into the thin, elegant frame of one man. Sitting across from this bastion of Roman *pietas*, Galla felt very young and very foolish. She took a long drink of the aromatic red wine and then proceeded to tell Julius all about the events of the day, all except the part about Fortus and her newly discovered feelings for him.

When she was finished, her uncle sighed deeply. He got up, prepared two plates of cold chicken and dates, handed one to Galla, and returned with his plate to his army camp chair. He ran his hand over his chin and sat for many minutes in silent contemplation, not eating, just thinking.

Galla hadn't had a thing to eat since breakfast and she was ravenous. She promptly downed the meager portions her uncle had served her, he always ate so sparingly, and she got up to help herself to some vegetable stew and fruit tarts. She looked at her uncle.

Julius said, "Go ahead, eat. You're young, you need your strength," and he refilled their goblets.

When they were seated again, Julius looked straight at Galla and said, "I've been debating how much to tell you, how much you need to know . . . I've always tried to keep problems away from you, to let you enjoy your childhood and youth while you could. On one hand, I say to myself, 'She's a woman, how much does she really need to know about matters of state?' and on the other hand, I say to myself, 'She's the daughter of Theodosius the Great and, as such, she *is* the state--anything that concerns the state, concerns her.'"

Julius paused and then began again. "Galla, there are many things I have kept from you, things that I thought might distress you. But now I feel that you must know."

Galla felt sorry for the old man struggling so hard to protect her. "If it's about Serena and Stilicho trying to marry me off to Eucherius, and my brothers trying to send me to a convent, I already know all that, so don't distress yourself, my dearest uncle," Galla said sympathetically.

Julius smiled slightly in appreciation of her solicitude. "I wish it were that simple, Galla. Yes, that is part of it, but there's more, so much more, that's threatening your future and even the future of Rome itself." He put down his cup and leaned forward towards Galla, one elbow on each knee and his hands clasped tightly together.

"Galla, remember when I tutored you in history, we studied all about the Goths, those ferocious marauding Germanic tribes north of the Danube?"

"Yes, I remember very well, and Stilicho taught me the Germanic language Gothic that year, to complement my studies of the Goths. What about them?"

"Well, for sometime now, the Goths have been quite restless. We've tried and tried to pacify them. We've even offered political appointments and financial help, but to no avail. They are steadily pushing south, crossing our northern frontiers and attacking our outposts."

"Can't we do something, perhaps send a new garrison to defend the northern border?" Galla asked, beginning to wonder why her uncle was discussing these remote barbarians and what possible effect they could have on her.

"We've already sent all the men we can spare. If we send anymore, it would leave Italy, and even the city of Rome itself, defenseless. We're spread too thin already. This isn't anything new, the northern tribes have been gnawing away like rats at our borders for generations and we've always managed to push them back. But, little by little, the hole they chewed widened and now it's too wide, they're crossing the frontiers in hoards. To compound the problem, they have a new leader, and a damn fierce one, I'm told. His name is Alaric and he's managed to organize a formidable army." Julius paused and took a sip of wine. Galla sat silently, her interest piqued.

"Alaric is, at this moment, outside Pavia, one of our Roman garrisons. He is threatening to attack."

"But Stilicho is Master of the Soldiery, can't *he* do something? Can't *he* send some troops from somewhere else to defend Pavia and to stop this Alaric?"

"Ah, you've hit upon the *real* problem, and that's what I've been debating whether or not to tell you. I've decided that you have a right to know, just in case."

"Just in case what?" Galla asked slowly.

"Just in case, that's all," Julius said, lowering his already subdued speaking volume. He continued, "As you know, Stilicho is Germanic by birth and a Roman by citizenship. I believe he's somewhat *torn*, shall we say, between his allegiances. He hasn't quite decided whether to support his birth country or his adoptive country."

"Do you mean you think he'd back the Goths and this Alaric?" Galla said in shocked disbelief.

"I don't know. And that's what worries me. You can trust an ally, you can even trust an enemy, but never trust a man who sits on the fence and doesn't jump one way or the other. The ancient Greeks knew that. Do you remember what they did with anyone who didn't commit to one side or the other during a war?"

"Yes," Galla replied, "they executed him, publicly, as an object lesson to others."

"That's right," Julius said, pleased that his tutelage had fallen on such fertile ground as Galla's brilliant mind. "Stilicho has proposed a 'compromise' as he calls it. He wants to admit as many Germanic men as possible into the Roman army and to offer them Roman citizenship in return for their support against further invasions by the Germanic tribes like the Goths. The Roman soldiers want no part of it and they are rebelling against Stilicho's policies. They see Stilicho as a traitor against Rome, a *Germanic* traitor. They say Stilicho could have had Alaric assassinated several times, but he didn't."

"What do *you* think, Julius? Do *you* think Stilicho is a traitor?"

"I don't know for sure. He's done nothing either way to prove himself loyal to Rome or a traitor to Rome. I *do* know that he's lost the trust of the people. As fast as he's gaining Germanic support with his policies, he's losing Roman support. It's a very dangerous situation, made even more dangerous as long as he resides here within the palace walls."

Galla sat stunned. She blinked her wide eyes, trying to absorb all she had just heard. It seemed unbelievable that Stilicho, who held the highest post in the Imperial army, could be undermining Rome with the power entrusted to him by her father. And Serena. Serena was *Roman*, the daughter of her father's sister. Could Serena know all this? Was she part of it?

Julius stood up. "You've had a long day, Galla. You'd better go get some rest. Try not to think about all this tonight. We'll talk about it again if I hear of any new developments. And, by all means, keep what I've told you in strict confidence. Don't tell anyone, and I mean *anyone*--not Anta, not Eli, and not Fortus."

Galla looked out the window quickly. It was nearly dusk.

"Promise me, Galla, not a word to anyone. It could mean our lives."

"I promise, Uncle Julius, not a word to anyone." Galla stood up and kissed Julius on the cheek. "Thank you, thank you for sharing this with me. Let me know what happens."

"Good night, Galla, sweet dreams."

"Good night, Uncle Julius, rest well. God bless you."

"And you too, Little Acorn."

Galla left Julius' apartments, but instead of turning right towards her own rooms, she turned left towards the service door. She could hear Eli and the others in the kitchen as she tiptoed past the pantry door and out into the early evening.

The night air was warm. It was nearly summer and the air felt soft and balmy. Galla walked the well-worn path that led north to the wide valley. The birds were singing their last notes of the day and the crickets were tuning up for the night. Galla's pace quickened in anticipation of her meeting with Fortus. She thought about how good it would be to see him, to tell him how she felt, to hold him, and, perhaps, to kiss him.

Her fast walk became a run and soon she was at the valley's edge. Down in the basin of the valley she saw that a small campfire had been lit beside the old oak tree. "It is Fortus," she thought, excitement surging within her. "He's waiting for me." And she ran down into the valley and to the oak tree.

As she approached the tree, the outline of a figure became silhouetted against the opalescent sky. Galla slowed her steps. She looked more carefully at the figure by the tree. It was too short, too thin to be Fortus. The figure turned and the fire caught the features. It wasn't Fortus--it was his servant, a young Thracian boy named Alcibiades.

Galla approached the boy. "What are you doing here? Where is your master?" Galla asked, apprehension rising within her.

The boy took a step closer. Galla could see that his eyes were red as if he had been crying.

"My master cannot come, Your Highness. He sends you these." Alcibiades held out a tiny scroll and a small silken drawstring purse. Galla took them and noticed her hands were beginning to tremble. She moved closer to the fire and unrolled the scroll.

Galla, my darling,

It is with heavy heart that I write this letter. I cannot meet you this evening or any evening. Stilicho has removed me from my post as palace guard and has sent me to defend the walls of the city of Rome. I care not that he has taken the exalted position of palace guard from me and placed me in the barracks with the infantrymen defending the walls. I do care that he has removed me from your most cherished presence. I long to be with you, to hold you, to show you my deep love for you. Perhaps this turn of fate is for the best, since I know that we can never be together completely as man and wife.

Galla stopped reading for a moment to blink back the tears rising quickly in her eyes. She continued reading,

I will pray for you everyday. May God bless and keep you. Pray for me.
> Your devoted Fortus.

Galla steadied herself against the old tree. Tears of anger, frustration, and sorrow ran down her face. The boy saw her tears and he, too, began to cry.

Galla composed herself long enough to say, "Thank you, Alcibiades, for bringing me this letter. You had better go back now before anyone misses you. You have served us well."

The boy tried to smile, but his sobs revealed his despair. He ran up, knelt down before Galla and kissed the hem of her dress. Galla leaned over and helped the frail boy up. How like Fortus to take the most helpless and sensitive of the staff and make him his personal assistant. Galla placed her hands on the boy's shoulders and looked at him seriously.

"Watch over your master, Alcibiades. Keep your ears and eyes open. Sometimes the tiniest fly on the wall has the best view. He needs you. When you can, bring me news of him. Now go and be careful." She pulled the lad towards her and gave him a quick hug. Then she pushed him away and he ran off, disappearing into the darkness.

The fire crackled and began to die down. Galla pulled herself up on the old oak and sat nestled between two branches. She placed the tiny blue silk drawstring bag in her lap and began to pull it open. She was calmer now. Her hands were steady again. She opened the little bag and turned it upside down. A small bronze ring landed in her lap. She picked it up and examined it by the firelight. It was finely carved and very delicate. The back was a narrow plain band. The front was a small neat oval. In the center of the polished oval was carved a minuscule chi-rho cross. Galla held the ring against her heart and looked up at the stars, which were beginning to shine in the night sky. "I won't forget you Fortus, not ever."

She looked back down, took the bronze ring in her left hand and slipped the tiny circle onto the little finger of her right hand, carefully centering the oval atop her finger. An odd feeling of peace came over her, and in some way she felt closer to Fortus than she had ever felt before. Galla sat on the old oak until the campfire shed its last rays, then she climbed down and walked slowly back to the palace.

CHAPTER IV

It rained most of the following week. Not a hard rain, but a soft continuous rain that marked the end of spring and the beginning of summer. Galla spent the majority of her time in her rooms reading. Julius' talk had renewed her interest in the unsettled barbarous tribes to the north. She pored over long neglected texts from her days as a student. She had been more fortunate than most young Roman girls. She had been allowed an education, limited, to be sure, but still she had a good foundation in the basics--reading, writing, history, mathematics, astronomy, the arts, and even some foreign languages, Greek and Gothic among them.

Julius had supervised most of her learning and when his knowledge failed, which was seldom, he brought in others to instruct the young Galla. It was from Julius that Galla gained her immense love of texts and she collected them prodigiously. She had set aside one of the rooms in her quarters as a library. Here she carefully placed her treasured texts, scrolls mostly, but books were becoming more and more available. Whenever possible, Julius would bring her a book when he returned from his many travels.

It was late afternoon and Galla was seated at her dressing table reading. Her window faced east and the light was beginning to dim. She was contemplating lighting an oil lamp when she heard a knock on the door.

"Come in," Galla said absently.

The door opened and a young slave girl entered the room timidly.

"Yes, what is it?" Galla inquired without looking up. There was no reply.

"What is it? Who's there?" she said with some irritation as she turned to see who had disturbed her concentration and was now mute. She saw the tiny slave, who couldn't have been more than six, standing at the door, still holding the big bronze handle. Galla's tone softened.

"Come in, my dear, what is your errand?"

The tiny girl rolled up her big brown eyes to look at Galla.

Growing somewhat impatient, Galla said, "Come on, come on, I don't have all day, if you have a message, give it to me."

The little girl scurried across the floor, handed Galla a scroll, and then raced out of the room, failing to close the doors behind her.

"Guards, shut the door!" Galla commanded. There was no response. "How odd," Galla thought, "where are they?" She got up, crossed the room and closed the doors herself.

Galla sat back down at her table and opened the scroll. It was from her brother Honorius. He wanted her to join the family for dinner.

"Oh bother," thought Galla. "It's been so pleasant the last few days, being alone and taking meals in my room. I wish that Serena and the others were *always* mad at me and always kept me out of their presence. Well, they must be cooling off. Perhaps they will share the wonderful 'news' of Eucherius' 'recovery.'" Galla threw the scroll into the small basket on the floor beside her table. She went into her dressing room to change for dinner.

When Galla arrived at the dining hall, she found the family assembled on a small circle of dining couches in one corner of the vast hall. Everyone was present--Julius, Honorius, Stilicho, Serena, and, much to Galla's discomfort, Eucherius.

"Good evening, Galla," Honorius said stiffly. "Thank you for joining us on such short notice."

Galla noticed that her brother actually sounded sober for a change. "How novel," she thought, "he must be up to something." Galla reclined on the only empty couch and a slave poured a glass of wine for her.

"Any news from Arcadius?" Galla asked politely, not really interested in the response. "He must be in Constantinople by now, if the weather didn't slow his journey."

"How interesting that you should ask. Yes, there *is* news of Arcadius," Honorius said with uncommon seriousness. "That's part of the reason I wanted you here tonight, to tell you that Arcadius has been taken ill, rather seriously, I'm afraid. He's at his palace in Constantinople."

"Oh? What's the problem?" Galla asked, revealing a concern that surprised even her.

"The doctors don't know. He has a high fever and can't keep anything down, even the medications," Honorius replied.

The loud sound of metal against metal drew Galla's attention. She had purposefully avoided eye contact with Eucherius when she entered the room and now she could hear him clanging things about on his serving table, like a small child trying to get a grown-up's attention. Galla ignored him.

"Perhaps it's the rain," Galla offered. "It's been unseasonably cool and damp even in the East, I hear. That often settles in one's bones, particularly in someone of *his* age." Her brother Arcadius was only a dozen or so years older than Galla, but she had not forgotten the reference *he* had made to *her* age that day in the tholos at Eucherius' birthday breakfast. "When the sun comes out again, he'll be much better."

"If he *lives* to see the sun again," Honorius sighed, not bothering to hide his true indifference in the matter.

Eucherius, who had been slamming around the metal objects on his serving tray to draw attention, could finally control his anger no longer.

"Arcadius, Arcadius! That's all I hear! Has anyone asked about *me*? What about how *I'm* feeling? *I'm* the one who almost *died* a week ago," Eucherius shouted in his high, nasal voice. "And you, Galla Placidia, you of all people! You should be asking about my health and begging my forgiveness!"

Galla knew that all eyes were on her and Fortus' words rang in her head. "Oh Eucherius, you looked *so* good when I saw you here this evening, I just assumed you were restored to perfect health!" She smiled, pleased at the resourcefulness of her own mind. "I came to see you immediately after your accident, but the guards wouldn't admit me. I've asked after you everyday. I am concerned, really," Galla paused, fearing that if she said anything more, she'd reveal her true feelings.

"Well, I'm not all right, Galla. That was a terrible accident. I ache all over and I've completely lost my appetite," he said as he threw the bones of a second chicken onto his plate. "If I didn't know better, I'd say you and that soldier boy were trying to kill me!"

Galla simply could not resist, "What makes you think we weren't?" she teased.

"Because you two wouldn't have enough nerve! Well, whatever you two were trying, you should be sorry."

Galla sighed and thought of Fortus. It had been more than a week since she had seen him and she missed him dearly. "I *am* sorry, Eucherius," Galla said slowly, "more than you'll ever know. I don't think I'll *ever* forgive myself for mentioning that stupid race. But what is done is done. We can't relive the past. I want you to know that I am very sorry and that I was very foolish."

Eucherius stopped gnawing on a pork chop and looked over at Galla. "Well, I think you actually mean that, Galla. I've never heard you sound that sincere. There may be hope for you yet. I accept your apology. You know, I feel better already. I think my appetite is returning. Slave! Slave! Bring me another chicken! And, oh yes, one of those big pastries with the cream filling, yes that one. Good." Eucherius began tearing apart the broiled chicken, forgetting all about Galla and the others.

There was a long silence while everyone was consuming the third course of turtledoves cooked in Iberian wine sauce.

"Honorius," Galla began, "I noticed that the slave you sent was barely six years old. Isn't she a bit young to be sent on errands?"

Honorius acted as if he hadn't heard his sister's question.

"Honorius," Galla raised her voice slightly, "why is such a little girl running the errands that the pages should be doing? And, something else rather odd, when I called for the guards to my apartments, they weren't there. What do you know about that?"

Galla saw Honorius and Stilicho give one another a quick, concerned glance.

Honorius finished the turtledove he was eating and he wiped his hands on a towel. "We've had to make some changes. We didn't really need all those slaves underfoot, so we've sent several of them where they can be of more use."

"More use?" Galla asked.

"Yes, more use. Now eat your dinner. The slaves are no concern of yours. If I had known you were going to be so inquisitive, I wouldn't have invited you here tonight. Galla, you must really learn to leave the running of this household to me. After all, I am the Emperor, a fact which you do not seem to acknowledge very often."

Galla quietly sipped her wine and wondered what Honorius and Stilicho were up to; they both seemed so tense and serious.

Just then, a guard burst through the doors to the dining hall, "The messenger from Constantinople has arrived, Your Majesty. He's waiting in the entrance hall as you requested." The guard saluted stiffly.

Honorius leapt to his feet. Galla started to rise but he stopped her. "No, you stay here, Galla. Don't interrupt your dinner. It's probably nothing," Honorius said and walked quickly out of the dining hall.

It was over an hour before Honorius returned. Dinner was finished and Stilicho and Eucherius were playing dice. Julius was reading a book and Serena was plucking the strings of a small harp, trying to work out the tune of a new song. Galla was just about to excuse herself and to return to her rooms when Honorius entered the hall. His face was pale and somber.

"My family," he said solemnly, "I have bad news, very bad news. Arcadius is dead."

There was silence. Each person in the room was shocked by the news and each one was busy deciding how this death would affect himself or herself personally. Honorius crossed the floor and picked up his wine goblet. He drank down its contents without stopping for a breath. He was visibly shaken.

"How strange," thought Galla when she saw Honorius' reaction to the news. "I didn't think Honorius even *liked* Arcadius, they were always arguing so."

Honorius put down the goblet and said, "Bishop Theophilus is waiting for us in the chapel."

Honorius walked out of the room and the others followed.

Galla seldom went to the palace chapel. It was built over two hundred years earlier when Christianity was still a forbidden religion in Rome. In order to afford security for the worshippers, the chapel was built under the villa foundations, cut deep into the tufa rock bed. It was always cold and damp down there and the heavy smell of stagnant water, rotting moss, and decomposing corpses always nauseated Galla. When she was little she had asked her father why he didn't build a new, magnificent chapel above ground, one that was worthy of the most Christian of Emperors. Her father had replied that the old subterranean chapel made him feel close to his ancestors, the early Christians who suffered and were martyred for their belief in Jesus Christ.

The family members made their way down the narrow, winding steps into the underground catacomb tunnel leading to the chapel. The slaves had prepared the way and had placed lighted oil lamps in the tiny recesses cut at regular intervals along the rock walls. The familiar putrid smell stung Galla's nose and she longed to run out of this dismal tomb.

They finally reached the chapel. It was a square room with a domed ceiling, all cut out of the living rock. The rock had been plastered over and painted with frescoes of stories of the life of Christ. But time and dampness had taken their toll and the ancient paintings were stained and peeling.

Honorius took his place next to the Bishop at the altar. The Bishop began to chant and every so often the family would respond in song. The service dragged on and on. Galla felt the cold chill penetrate her bones. She was wearing only a thin silk dinner dress and sandals. Her feet were numb and her hands were stiff with the cold.

Finally, the service was over and the family filed out of the chapel, down the long narrow corridor of the catacomb, and up the winding stone steps into the welcome warmth and sweet-smelling air of the palace. The family members bade one another a good evening and they headed off for their respective quarters.

When Galla returned to her room, she took off her clothes, which had absorbed the foul odor of the subterranean chamber. She rinsed herself in the basin of water on her bed stand. She put on a fresh white linen nightgown and climbed into bed, pulling up the blankets for warmth.

"I loved my father dearly," she thought, "and I agreed with almost everything he ever did or said. But I can't agree with him about that chapel. I *know* that's where our ancestors worshipped in secret, but by *force*, not by *choice*. I don't feel worship should be like that . . . clandestine, cold, and uncomfortable. I believe worship should be joyous and in the bright light of day, full of warmth and love. No, Father, I can't agree with you on this point. If I ever have the means, I'll build places of worship that will be full of warmth and life." Galla's thoughts blurred and exhaustion overcame her. She fell asleep and dreamed of building beautiful places of worship, full of joy, color, and radiance.

It was nearly midday when Galla finally awoke. Anta had removed the untouched breakfast tray and was placing the fresh luncheon tray on Galla's bed table.

"Goodness," Galla thought, "have I really slept this late?" It was unusual for Galla to sleep late; she was normally one of the earliest risers in the palace, with the exception of Julius, who was invariably out of bed before sunrise.

Galla realized that the news of her brother's death had affected her more than she thought. Although there was no love lost between them, Arcadius was her father's son and therefore was a part of him. Her small family had grown smaller still and the outside world looked bigger by comparison.

And the Empire--who would replace Arcadius in Constantinople and rule the East? Honorius couldn't rule the East, not when the West was in such dire threat of Germanic invasions from the north. Arcadius' son was only a child; it would be years before he'd reach his majority. What would become of the Eastern Empire until then? Would there even *be* an Empire then?

Galla surprised herself with her wondering. She had always taken for granted that the Empire would last forever. Now, here she was, for the very first time, questioning whether the Empire would be intact in the very near future. "After all . . . other great Empires have come and gone," Galla thought, "look at Egypt, and Persia, and even Alexander's great empire, why not Rome?"

Galla shook her head to cast out this disturbing thought. "Impossible, absolutely impossible. Rome has been here for over 900 years . . . it certainly isn't going to end during *my* lifetime. Even with all our faults and problems, we're still the greatest and most powerful Empire in history. Empires like ours don't end overnight."

With that reassuring thought, Galla got out of bed. She walked over to the window and looked out. It was a cool, gray day, but it wasn't raining. She decided that she'd been indoors too long and that a long walk would do her good. She washed quickly and dressed in a light woolen dress and cape. Anta stopped her on the way out the door and gestured to the untouched luncheon tray. Galla picked up a few figs and placed them in her pocket. The memory of the stench of the catacombs still lurked in her mind. "I'll eat later," she told Anta as she walked out of her apartments.

The villa was empty and silent and Galla saw no one as she strode along the marble corridors. The courtyard, too, was vacant. Galla continued on to the well-worn path to the north valley.

The long rain had encouraged the trees into full bloom. Their fragrant flowers helped to rid Galla's memory of the foul odors of the previous night's visit to the chapel. The overcast sky cast a pale gray light over the lush green countryside. Here and there, puddles reflected the clouds overhead. The earth was soft under Galla's leather boots.

Galla reached the rim of the valley and surveyed the remarkable changes the deep rain had made. Where only tiny buds had been, now were leaves and greenery. Wildflowers and thick grasses competed for space, creating a shaggy, green carpet on the valley floor. Only the old oak remained leafless and barren.

As she approached the old oak, Galla noticed that Julius had arrived ahead of her. He was seated on a heavy blanket by the base of the tree; only his silver hair belied his camouflage of green and brown woolen shawls.

"Uncle Julius! Hello! What brings you here?" Galla inquired, pleased to see the old man.

"Galla. You came. I was hoping you would," Julius said as he struggled to his feet.

"Sit down. Sit down, Uncle. Don't get up for me. It's just your Little Acorn. Sit down. Spread out that blanket a little farther and I'll sit down with you. I haven't walked in several days and I believe I'm already out of shape," she said between breaths, half out of truth and half out of empathy for the old man's age and labored breathing.

Julius spread out the blanket and Galla seated herself next to him just like when she was a little girl and Julius was about to read a story to her. Julius lifted a blanket and wrapped it and his arm around her. With his other hand, he offered Galla a mug of hot cider. Galla took it appreciatively, the smell of apples and spices pleasing her senses.

"You come well-prepared, Uncle. Were you expecting me?"

Julius responded, "Not expecting, just hoping."

Galla sipped the warm cider. She looked up at Julius. "What are you doing out here, Uncle?"

"I just wanted to get away from the palace, that's all, just get away and think. This old oak always was a good place to think." Julius patted the tree affectionately, his smile fading as quickly as it had come.

"Galla, I want to say how sorry I am about Arcadius. I know you two weren't close, but he *was* your brother and you are probably feeling his loss."

"Yes, I guess I am. I didn't think I would, but I am. It's as if, little by little, my childhood is fading away. First Mother, then Father, and now my brother. It seems so incredible that Arcadius is gone. Only days ago he was here and seemed in the best of health.

"Yes," Julius said slowly, "it does seem incredible."

"Has Honorius learned what caused Arcadius' illness?"

"It appears it was something he ate," Julius paused. "I don't want to upset you, Galla, but I find the whole situation very suspicious. There are too many people who will benefit from Arcadius' death. One must really wonder if Arcadius died of natural causes or if it was intentional."

Galla stared at Julius in dumb amazement. "What does Honorius say? Does he suspect anything?"

"Honorius is too busy to look into the matter. He's too busy speaking in the Senate. He has asked them to depose Arcadius' young son and regent and to place Honorius on the throne at Constantinople."

Galla sat silently, that sickening feeling of angst rising within her that she knew so well from a childhood spent in a palace full of intrigue and plotting.

Julius continued, "And then, Stilicho, too, would benefit, by his appointment as Master of the Soldiery of both the East *and* the West. What a convenient position from which to promote his Germanic cause." Julius continued speaking, almost as if to himself, "And then there are the Germanic tribes who would benefit . . . the death of the Eastern Emperor might be the end of a united Rome and the end of the resistance a united Rome can offer against their repeated forays across our borders. No, Galla, there are just too many people who would benefit by Arcadius' death not to question the cause of his death," Julius sighed. "And it's the fact that Honorius doesn't question the cause that interests me."

Galla felt a cold chill run down her spine and she shivered. "I'm sorry, Galla," Julius apologized, "I shouldn't have spoken so bluntly."

"No Uncle, I'm just cold, that's all. I'm glad you spoke bluntly. I find Honorius' actions interesting, too. I've always known he was ruthless and cruel, I guess I just never knew to what degree. I think I'm beginning to understand, too, why you and Fortus have been so concerned about me and my behavior. Do you think Honorius thinks of me as a threat to his power?"

Julius looked up quickly, surprised that Galla could put the whole picture together so quickly.

"No, not as a threat," Julius responded, carefully selecting his words, "not as long as you stay in the background. As long as you don't challenge him, and as long as you remain unmarried and childless, he has no reason to fear you. As a matter of fact, right now you're a benefit to him."

Galla knit her brows, trying to grasp Julius' meaning.

"Right now, you're his carrot in front of the horse. Stilicho is the horse, and you're the carrot Honorius is dangling in front of Stilicho. As long as Stilicho thinks there's a chance that you'll marry his son, then there's a chance that Stilicho might remain loyal to Rome. Stilicho has a brilliant mind and he didn't get to where he is by thinking small. He has set his sights on the Eastern throne and he's making plans to have it widened so it will fit his son's fat rump," Julius added bitterly.

"Eucherius--on the throne at Constantinople? Why Uncle, it would be a disaster!" Galla gasped, revealing her dismay.

"I agree. And so does Honorius, but for other reasons. You and I don't want Eucherius on the Eastern throne because we know that Eucherius is neither mentally nor physically able to rule the East. Honorius doesn't want Eucherius to rule the East for another reason, because Honorius wants it for himself."

"Honorius can't rule the *West* properly, let alone the East *and* the West!"

"You know that and I know that. Stilicho knows it, too. Practically everyone in the Empire knows it except Honorius himself. That's the problem with tiny minds, they can't see their own shortcomings."

"Julius, if Honorius *does* manage somehow to assume power at Constantinople, then I cease to function as a carrot. What reason would Stilicho have then to marry me to his son?"

"Ah, Galla," Julius smiled and hugged her tightly, "you're so like your father, always one step ahead. Yes, Stilicho wants the East; he also wants the West and the North, if the truth were known. But what he may want more than anything is a place in history--the history of Rome."

Galla looked at her uncle, her wide eyes revealing her incomprehension.

"*History*, Galla, isn't that what it's really about? Why do men do such foolish and outrageous things as attack neighbors and create great empires? Oh, greed, to be sure, but that's temporary. I think the real reason is *history*. We want to leave our mark on this earth before we go to join our Maker. We want future generations to know we were here. Each one of us wants to leave something of ourselves so that our memory is kept alive. Each one of us leaves our mark differently--some write beautiful literature, some create magnificent artworks, some create great empires. Most of us leave our mark by creating future generations. Children are our way of leaving something of ourselves and keeping our memory alive. I believe that's how Stilicho plans to leave his mark, through his children and their connection to the Imperial family of Rome. He became part of the Imperial family when he married Serena, but that's a tie by marriage only. It's through his children and his children's children that Stilicho is joined to the Imperial family by blood. That's why he married his daughter Maria to Honorius when they were only in their teens, he hoped to continue his bloodline in the Imperial family. Poor little Maria died soon after the wedding before she could give Stilicho a grandchild. Then Stilicho concocted the plan to marry his son Eucherius to you--a second chance to gain immortality through the Imperial family tree. But it looks like Arcadius' untimely death and Honorius' aspirations to the Eastern throne have ended that dream, at least temporarily. But Stilicho has one more trick up his sleeve along those lines--his youngest daughter Thermantia."

"You mean the little girl who was given to the service of the convent of St. Mary? She's a nun with the Holy Sisters, what plan could Stilicho have for her?"

"I've heard a rumor that Stilicho and Serena are planning to take her out of 'retirement' as they call it, and to put her back on the front lines, so to speak. Forgive me, Galla, if I speak indelicately, but these are indelicate times."

"Go ahead Uncle. I want to hear their plan."

"Stilicho is a student of Homer. Homer said that no man avoids misfortune if he stands firmly on both feet. What he meant was that a man has to be ready to change his stance on things . . . he must be prepared to jump if he needs to. It appears that Stilicho is ready to jump if his plans for Eucherius and you and the Eastern throne don't materialize. He has offered his daughter Thermantia to Honorius in marriage."

Galla sat upright. "What? Thermantia can't marry Honorius! She's a nun! She's spent her entire life in a convent! She knows nothing of the real world or of men--or of Honorius and his perverted ways. Oh Uncle! It would be cruel, the poor little child, how could Stilicho do this to his own daughter?"

"Stilicho doesn't look at it that way. He feels he's giving his daughter the opportunity to become an Empress, not only of the Western Empire, but, if Honorius can convince the Senate, of the East as well, perhaps the greatest honor any woman has ever had.

Few women have ever had the honor of being Empresses of a state that vast or that important."

"Oh but the price she'll have to pay for that honor is *her* honor. Uncle, you know as well as I the life Honorius has led, prostitutes and concubines, girls and boys. I've heard the stories of the parties. Honorius dresses himself in the trappings of a Christian emperor, but he undresses himself like the basest of the pagan heathens."

Julius lifted his eyebrows, surprised to learn that Galla was aware of Honorius' debaucheries.

"To sacrifice a nun to Honorius," Galla continued, but Julius interrupted, "Or to sacrifice you to Eucherius. Which one do you prefer?"

Galla let out a long exasperated sigh. She felt as if she'd just been dealt a strong blow to her stomach. How infuriating! How frustrating! These men were trading women's lives as if they were trading horses at a bazaar. How unfair! How unjust!

"I'm sorry Galla. I've spoken frankly and now I've upset you. You were bound to hear about Thermantia soon and I wanted to prepare you, but I see I didn't do it very diplomatically."

"Oh, it's not *you*, Uncle Julius, it's *them*. Treating women like things instead of people, marrying us off to the highest bidder, as if we had no feelings, no minds of our own. It's just not right, that's all!"

"No, Galla, it's not right, but then very little is right in our world. Our duty is not to ourselves, my dear, our duty is to Rome. Somehow, some way, we must hold this rusty old Empire together. Millions of people depend on Rome--for employment, for trade, for currency, for grain . . . the list goes on and on. If Rome should ever cease to supply those millions with the necessities of life, I shudder to think what would happen."

"But Uncle, you speak of 'Rome' as if it were a thing, an entity, when all it really consists of is Honorius and a few wealthy old men in the Senate," Galla looked up, hoping her reference to the elderly members of the Senate had not offended Julius since he was one of those members. Galla added quickly, "After all, Rome doesn't exist on its own--*we're* Rome."

Julius hugged Galla tightly. "Yes, Galla, *we're* Rome. It's up to us to see that Rome lives on. We must continue the Roman task our ancestors began--to bring peace and law and government to all peoples. And it's up to us to keep the *idea* of Rome alive. As long as the people *believe* that Rome is strong and invincible, then the *idea* of Rome will continue."

Galla let out a long, deep sigh. "I know, Uncle. I guess I've always known it. 'Rome comes first.' Those are the first words I remember hearing as a little girl. Whenever I objected to those long state dinners, or to our uncomfortable journeys to Constantinople, or to whatever seemed unpleasant or unnecessary, those were the words I heard, 'Rome comes first.' I hated those words when I was young, and I'm not sure I like them any better now. I know that millions of persons across the Empire depend on Rome for their well being, but what about *my* well being? It would be different if I could actually *do* something for Rome . . . if I could pass legislation, or vote in the Senate, or even hope one day to be Emperor and to straighten out some of this mess. But, no, I'm a woman. All I can do is sit idly by and let others decide my future. My biggest contribution to Rome so far has been to serve as an Imperial carrot to be held out in front of Stilicho's greedy nose."

Julius laughed softly and kissed Galla's forehead. "Ah, but what a *lovely* carrot you are . . . and a very important carrot, I might add."

"Yes, Uncle Julius, but keep in mind that horses *eat* carrots. Let's just hope Honorius keeps that in mind, too," Galla smiled weakly. Her head had begun to throb and the cold air was beginning to creep through the woolen blankets. "I think I'll go back to the palace now, Julius. I'm feeling very tired. Are you going back now, too?"

"No, not now. I think I'll stay here a little while longer. You go ahead my dear."

Galla got up and shook her arms and legs, which were stiff from sitting on the cold damp ground.

"Uncle," she said, hesitantly, "have you heard any news of Fortus? You do know that Stilicho has sent him to defend the walls of Rome, don't you?"

"Yes, Galla, I'm sorry. I know you and Fortus are good friends. I think Stilicho knows it, too. Only a blind man would allow someone with Fortus' attributes to get that close to his carrot." Julius winked.

"Is Fortus all right?"

"Yes, he's fine. The commander at Rome reports that Fortus is doing a marvelous job directing the repairs on the defense walls. And the way things look, we may need those walls one day. Now, you run along, go get some rest. I have some more thinking to do. God bless you Galla."

"God bless you, too, Uncle Julius," Galla said as she bent over and kissed the old man's head, "I love you." Galla wrapped the blankets over Julius' shoulders and she left him, deep in thought, seated under the old oak tree.

CHAPTER V

Galla arrived back at her rooms to find that a large scroll had been delivered during her absence. Galla picked up the heavy vellum scroll and saw the familiar large Imperial eagle impressed into brilliant purple sealing wax. It was from Serena. Only Serena would be so obvious in her allusions to her Imperial status, tenuous as they might be. Galla unwound the scroll and read Serena's florid handwriting.

> My dearest Cousin,
> I beg that you will do me the honor of accompanying me to Rome this afternoon. My darling daughter Thermantia has asked to pay a visit to the palace, and I, her most devoted mother, am going to fetch her myself. I would very much enjoy the pleasure of your company on my journey. I will await your reply.
> Your loving cousin,
> Serena

Galla threw down the scroll and scoffed, "Your loving cousin, ha!" Galla was glad that Julius had told her about Stilicho's and Serena's plans to marry Thermantia to Honorius. "They don't waste any time, do they?" Galla thought. "They're just like vultures. Arcadius is hardly in his tomb and they are already trying to fill his throne." The thought sickened her.

Galla tried to remember Thermantia. The last time Galla had seen her was when they were at the wedding between Thermantia's sister Maria and Galla's brother Honorius. Galla and Thermantia were both very young and very excited about the wedding. The two girls had been allowed to carry baskets of flower petals, which they scattered along the path of the bride and groom. The little girls felt that the marriage between their siblings had made them "sisters" and it was the closest Galla had ever felt to having a real sister. Galla had been devastated when, on the day following the wedding, Thermantia had been sent to the convent of

St. Mary's in Rome. Galla was infuriated that no one had allowed her to bid farewell to her best friend and she ran to Serena to demand an explanation. Serena had explained coldly that she had two daughters and that the day before she had given one daughter to the glory of Rome and that day she was giving the other daughter to the glory of God. Galla never heard from Thermantia again.

"Poor little Thermantia," Galla thought sadly, "uprooted from the palace home of her childhood, and now uprooted from the convent home she has come to know. I wonder if she has any idea what her parents have in mind for her. She'll be so ignorant, so unprepared," a wave of pity washed over Galla. "As much as I don't like being a party to this evil plot, perhaps if I go along to meet her, I can help ease the transition for her. After all those years in the sheltered security of the convent, it will be very difficult for her to adjust to palace life again--especially palace life as it is these days."

Galla wrote a quick note to Serena stating that she would be happy to travel to Rome to fetch Thermantia and suggested that they meet at the palace entrance shortly after the midday meal. It was not a long journey to Rome; Galla could ride Odysseus there in less than an hour. Serena, however, didn't care for horseback riding, she preferred to be carried in a litter, and so Galla resigned herself to a tedious four-hour journey.

Galla ate her midday meal alone in her apartments and then Anta helped her dress in warm clothes for the ride to Rome. Galla arrived at the palace entrance to find Serena's litter, her four Nubian slaves, and two Imperial palace guards prepared for the journey. Only Serena was not present.

"How like Serena," Galla thought. "She loves to keep everyone waiting--it makes her feel so important. Well, she'd better hurry. We're getting a late start as it is. If she's any later, we'll have to stay in Rome tonight and return to the palace in the morning." Even with the four muscular African slaves and two of the armed Imperial guards to accompany them, the highway to Rome was not a safe place to be at night. Unemployment was high in Rome and the police force was spread too thin to afford protection outside the walls of the city.

Galla waited nearly an hour for Serena to arrive and was just re-entering the palace when Serena appeared at the door with three maidservants flitting about her tending to last minute adjustments to hair and garments.

"Oh, you're here, Galla darling, good. I'm ready. Let's go. If we don't hurry, we'll have to spend the night in Rome, you know, and we don't want to do that, now, do we?" Serena trailed off in a cloud of flowing scarves and heavy perfume. "Come along, dear, come along. Let's not keep everyone waiting." Serena stepped regally onto the litter and seated herself in the center of the cushioned seat that faced forward, leaving Galla no place to sit except the tiny wood bench that faced the back of the litter. Galla mounted the litter and sat down facing Serena.

Serena's maidservants placed bundles of hot food from the kitchen on the floor of the litter and then placed two bottles of wine on the seat next to Serena. Serena said, "It's always good to be prepared, one never knows what one will find along the road to Rome, you know." The maid poured a large goblet of red wine for Serena. "Would you care for one, dear?" Serena asked half-heartedly.

"No, thank you, Serena, perhaps later," Galla replied.

The four large African slaves picked up the massive litter, carefully balancing the weight among them, and began the trek south to Rome. Galla thought about how much she disliked riding in litters, it was so slow and cumbersome. And it seemed so wasteful to have four slaves occupied doing the same work that two horses could do. As Galla's thoughts drifted off to matters of efficiency and the economical use of slave labor, Serena rattled on and on about recent social events in Rome, lamenting that Stilicho's duties kept them at the Imperial country palace and not in the festive social circuit of the city.

Serena maintained a house in Rome, and she and Stilicho often visited there when Honorius did not require his services at the palace outside Rome. Now she was talking on and on about her recent redecorating projects--the enclosure of a new peristyle garden and the addition of a domed dining hall in the ancient tradition of Nero. She gave glowing reports of the new wall paintings and the new pool sculptures that she was having installed at her city palace.

Galla listened more intently as the list of repairs and additions went on and on. Serena recounted her recent purchases of bronze sculptures, gold candelabras, marble dining couches, and imported linen draperies from Egypt. Galla began to wonder where Serena was getting the money for all these purchases. Surely Honorius wasn't giving Serena all the funds needed to refurbish her Palatine villa, he had just reduced the number of his own palace servants in order to reduce spending. And Stilicho's post of Master of the Soldiery was a military appointment and did not command vast sums of money unless he was on a military expedition, in which case he could plunder local resources and benefit generously, which was not the circumstance at the present.

Galla was still wondering and Serena was still talking when they reached the north gates of the city of Rome. The Imperial litter needed no other identification; the guards at the fortified wall opened the gates, came to attention, and saluted the two women as they passed through the gates.

Galla was always struck by the transition from the countryside to the city within the walls. One minute there was the peaceful tranquility of the quiet farms and vineyards, the next minute there was the cacophony of rumbling carts, braying animals, street merchants screaming their wares, and the sounds of over one million residents who were noisily going about their daily lives.

"Galla, darling," Serena's high voice interrupted Galla's musings, "it really was such a long journey, I'm suddenly much too tired to deal with Thermantia and all that tonight. We'll spend the night at my villa and go to the convent in the morning. Guards! To the Palatine villa!" Serena commanded in a loud voice, not waiting for Galla's response to the sudden change of plans.

They arrived at Serena's villa to find it fully lighted and the servants waiting at the door. Galla realized then that the change of plans was not as "sudden" as Serena had led her to believe. Galla wasn't sure what these events meant, but at the moment the sight of the brightly lit villa and the smell of roasting boar was a welcome relief from the hard seat of the litter.

Galla followed Serena off the litter and up the stairs to the villa. Inside, it was all that Serena had described and more. The entrance hall was painted in the latest fashion of architectural vistas and vast landscapes. On the ceiling, painted birds fluttered and soared. On the floor, mosaic lions strolled amidst tiled palm trees. The room was lit with hundreds of gold oil lamps suspended from the ceiling by chains. Servants lined both sides of the entrance hall and they bowed stiffly as Serena and Galla passed by.

The huge atrium was likewise decorated in the most lavish of stylish, and expensive, tastes. Galla was to find the entire villa remodeled and redecorated with materials imported from as far away as the Indus River.

"How different from my father's villas," Galla thought with disgust. "This is how the ancient *pagan* Emperors lived--Emperors like Nero and Caligula. My father lived more conservatively, more like the later Christian Emperors. He would not have approved of this. Still, it *is* lovely, like a splendid paradise within the walls of Rome."

"Galla, darling," Serena interrupted Galla's thoughts, "my maid Lastia will show you to your room. I think you'll find everything you'll need there. I'm sure you'd like to rest. Shall we dine, say, in two hours?" Without waiting for a reply, Serena disappeared behind two tall bronze doors inset with panels of intricately inlaid lapis lazuli and silver.

Galla found her room in keeping with the rest of the luxurious villa. Serena had the room well prepared for her female guests. In the dressing room, the closets were filled with expensive gowns and jewel-studded sandals. In her bath, Galla found the shelves laden with glass vials of scented oils and exotic perfumes. Galla walked into the bedchamber and sat down upon the beautifully carved African mahogany bed, which was piled high with silk-covered pillows. She asked the maidservant Lastia to wake her in one hour and drifted off to sleep on a cloud of soft eider down.

When Galla awakened, she bathed and dressed for dinner. She could not have been more pleased with her appearance. She had traded her heavy woolen traveling clothes for a saffron-colored silk chemise, drawn in at the waist by a gold embroidered belt.

Lastia had arranged her hair in the current fashion of a single thick braid entwined with gold ribbons. On her feet she wore gold sandals with yellow topaz decorations. As Galla left her apartments, she secretly wished that there would be some dinner guests who could admire her fashionable attire, which was such a change from her usual country dress.

When Galla entered the dining hall, she found that her wish had materialized. The hall was filled with guests . . . at least one hundred of Rome's most wealthy and prominent citizens were in attendance. Again, Galla had the feeling that Serena's sudden change of plans was really arranged well in advance.

Galla paused at the door, waiting to be shown to her dining couch. An elegant young man approached her and bowed deeply.

"If I may have the honor," he said as he smiled and held out his arm. Galla placed her hand lightly on his wrist. As they walked the length of the dining hall, Galla felt as if all eyes were on her. She recognized several of the guests--prominent senators and generals among them.

Galla and her escort reached the far end of the hall where three empty couches remained. The young man led Galla to one couch and he sat down on the couch next to hers. He poured wine into the goblet on her serving table. Galla looked around the room searching for Serena but she was nowhere to be found. Galla surmised that Serena was late as usual and that she would make a grand entrance when all the guests had arrived and could serve as an appreciative audience.

The young man next to Galla had not spoken since the few words at the door. Now he sat, staring intently at Galla, obviously pleased with what he saw. In spite of feeling somewhat ill at ease at his overt attentions, Galla politely introduced herself.

"I am Galla Placidia, the sister of the Emperor Honorius."

"Oh, I know who you are. Everyone knows of the beautiful Galla Placidia. We've even met before, at a party at your villa. It was long ago, but I haven't forgotten. No man could forget you." He leaned forward and reached out to take Galla's hand.

Galla drew her hand back out of reach of the forward young man.

"Please forgive me then, sir, if I do not recall *your* name."

"I am Marcus, son of Senator Marcus Cornelius--that's my father over there." The young man nodded in the direction of an elderly man who was engaged in an animated conversation with a pretty young girl one-third his age.

"Ah, yes, Marcus Cornelius. I've heard of your noble family." Galla smiled sweetly, concealing that what she had heard about his noble family was that they were as poor as dormice and that they practically starved when there were no banquets to attend. Galla knew of many such families in Rome. They could trace their lineage back to the first patricians of the early Republic, but they had lost their wealth by one means or another and now they lived on their titles and the invitations those titles brought. These were Romans who would rather live as perennial house guests than to work for an honest day's wages.

Galla surveyed the young man next to her. His skin was pale and smooth, no doubt from spending days indoors at the baths. He was quite handsome, almost too handsome, as if he had spent too many hours fussing over his wavy blond hair and his fastidious attire. Marcus saw Galla's appraising look and mistook it for flirtation. He smiled broadly and reached again for Galla's hand, which she withdrew still farther, feigning a need to smooth her gown.

Just then the doors to the dining hall opened and two trumpeters announced the arrival of Serena. The guests all stood up and applauded as Serena walked regally across the vast hall. Galla had seldom seen anything like the reception Serena received. Such attention and reverence were traditionally reserved for the Emperor alone. The fanfare continued as Serena slowly walked the length of the room. She was dressed in an elegant flowing black dress that matched her coal black hair and accentuated the creamy white skin of which she was so proud.

Galla thought that, for a woman of her age, Serena was still quite striking. Galla watched the guests as they welcomed their hostess. Serena was obviously quite popular, or perhaps it was her lavish banquets that the guests were really applauding.

Serena reached the far end of the hall and nodded regally in Galla's direction. At her approach, the young Marcus sprang to his feet and bowed deeply at the waist. Serena waited for him to straighten up and then she stepped forward and kissed him on the lips. It was not a short kiss of greeting that one would give a dinner guest, and a much *younger* dinner guest at that, but a long, passionate kiss that modest women would have reserved for more private quarters. The crowd howled their approval.

After an embarrassingly long time, Serena and her young friend separated. Serena glanced in Galla's direction and was much amused by Galla's shocked amazement. Serena laughed loudly. "Well, my darling Marcus, have you met my little cousin from the country?"

"Yes, indeed I have," Marcus said excitedly. "You didn't tell me she was so lovely, Serena."

Serena, obviously displeased with Marcus' enthusiastic reply, replied coldly, "She's betrothed to my son, you know, or at least she will be soon. Come Marcus, pour a cup of wine for me, won't you darling? It always tastes better when *you* pour it for me." Serena took Marcus' arm and carefully seated him facing her and away from Galla.

Galla had much to think about as the banquet wore on and on. Galla was well-trained to sample only a few bites of each course as it was served, thereby to be able to participate politely in a long banquet of many courses and not to appear rude by refusing to taste every dish. Tonight, however, after the tenth course, Galla had to refuse any more. She had been to many banquets hosted by some of the wealthiest persons in the empire, but never had she witnessed anything like this. The exotic and expensive dishes included flamingo boiled with dates, boiled ostrich with sweet sauce, sows' udders stuffed with salted sea urchins and patina of brains cooked with milk and eggs. Entertainment was provided to accompany each course--there were lush belly dancers from Parthia, lithe acrobats from Egypt, and muscular wrestlers from Gaul.

After three hours of eating, drinking, loud music and energetic entertainment, Galla had had enough. She left her dining couch and went to say good night to Serena who was now sharing a single dining couch with the young Marcus. Galla thanked Serena for the memorable dinner and then asked to be excused, politely adding that the long ride into Rome must have tired her more than usual. Serena quite gladly waved the younger woman off and quickly returned all her attention to the handsome young man lying next to her on the couch.

Galla left the noisy dining hall and walked down the empty corridor to her quarters, grateful to be away from the deafening sounds and overpowering smells. As she approached the doors to her apartments, a guard abruptly stepped out of the shadow of a column and stood in her path. Galla, startled, jumped back and started to cry out.

"No!" the guard whispered, "Do not call for help. It's Pontus, your servant from the palace, my Lady."

Galla examined his face and regained her composure. "Pontus, what are you doing here? Why are you no longer at the palace?"

"Forgive me, my Lady, I don't have time to discuss that now, someone might see me. I only came to bring you this." He drew a tiny scroll from under his cloak and placed it in Galla's hand. Galla looked down and saw a tiny chi-rho pressed into the familiar blue sealing wax. It was from Fortus. Galla looked up to thank Pontus, but he was already hurrying quietly down the hall.

Galla entered her room and closed the heavy door behind her. She sat down on the bed and unsteadily unrolled the tiny scroll.

> Galla, my Love,
> Pontus saw your litter as you entered the gates of the city today and he rushed to tell me the wonderful news that you are here in Rome. If the situation allows, I would very much like to see you. I will wait by the open end of the new peristyle garden that is still under construction. Do not take any chances, if either one of us were to be caught, the consequences would be dire. If you cannot meet me, then I send my love.
> Your devoted Fortus.

Galla's heart raced--Fortus, here, so close! She raced to the little dressing table and began to unwind the stylish braid and gold ribbons. She brushed out her hair and she washed her face so she'd look like herself again, not like one of the artificial young Roman women she had seen at the banquet that evening.

As Galla was deciding what to wear for her reunion with Fortus, the maid Lastia noisily entered the room.

"Oh no! She'll ruin everything!" Galla thought desperately. She continued looking through the closet, busily trying to think of a way to get rid of Lastia.

The maid walked over to the bed and started to fold down the blankets. She stumbled and caught herself with the bedpost. She staggered to her feet and uttered a profanity.

"She's drunk!" Galla thought jubilantly, "She's drunk! I bet there's a party in the kitchen to match the party in the dining hall. What luck!"

"Lastia," Galla said, trying to sound calm.

"Yesh?" Lastia slurred.

"I'm really very tired. I think I'll just go directly to bed. I won't need your services this evening. You may go now."

"Yesh, m'laydee." Lastia drawled, then wove her way unsteadily to the door.

"Oh, Lastia, please wake me in the morning when Serena arises, I don't want to keep her waiting."

"Oh, Shereena's gone. Gone withim. Shee won't be back tonight. Never is when she goes withim."

"Very well, Lastia, thank you. Have a good evening."

"Thank you, m'laydee, you're niche, reeley niche," and Lastia stumbled out the door, slamming it carelessly behind her.

Galla stood in utter disbelief. She could not believe her good fortune. In a few minutes she would be with Fortus. She hurriedly undressed and put on a simple light blue sheath and wrapped a loosely woven blue shawl over her shoulders. Fortus liked blue and she wanted very much to please him. She laced a pair of dark blue sandals around her narrow feet. She looked in the mirror and was happy with what she saw. The fatigue and heaviness that plagued her at the banquet were now entirely gone and she felt radiant and full of energy.

She drew the shawl over her head and quietly opened the door to her apartments. In the distance, she could hear laughter and music still coming from the dining hall. Galla tiptoed silently along the corridors until she finally reached the new peristyle garden. She stopped and surveyed the garden to see if anyone was there. Then she walked quickly along the walkway towards the unfinished end of the enclosure.

It was very dark and clouds covered the moon. Galla picked her way through the construction rubble, trying not to make any sound that would draw attention. Just then, the clouds parted and moonlight bathed the garden. Galla was startled to see a man standing just yards in front of her. It was the guard Pontus. He held out his hand and Galla took it. He led her through the maze of construction materials and helped her to scale the temporary wooden fence at the end of the garden. He jumped down the other side of the fence and then, taking Galla's narrow waist in his hands, he lowered her down off the fence and onto the street below. He quickly removed his hands from Galla's body and he looked down in embarrassment, ashamed to have taken such liberty with the noble Galla Placidia.

Galla saw his uneasiness and she put her hand on his arm, "Thank you, Pontus, you are a good friend. I am indebted to you for your assistance. I will remember you."

Pontus looked at Galla and flashed a grateful smile. He was about the same age as Fortus and he had the same clear, honest eyes. Galla felt that the two must be very dear friends for Pontus to risk his career, and even his life, this way.

At that moment, a large rustic wooden cart drawn by a single mule rumbled up and stopped. The sole figure on board was swathed in a voluminous brown cape and hood. The figure reached up, pulled off the hood, and soft brown curls reflected the moonlight. It was Fortus.

Galla's heart filled with joy. She ran to the cart, bounded up the running board, and dove into his arms sobbing violently.

Fortus held her tightly and she buried her head in his cape. "It's all right, Galla, it's all right. I'm here now, everything will be all right."

Slowly Galla's heavy sobbing began to subside. She sat up and ran her hand over her face to wipe away the tears.

"Oh Fortus, I'm so sorry. I don't know what came over me. It's just been so long, I've missed you so much. I thought I'd never see you again . . ." and with that she began to cry again.

Fortus drew out a large square of cotton cloth and offered it to Galla. Once again, she regained her composure, smiling with embarrassment at her emotional outburst. She took the cloth and dried her eyes.

"Come on," he said, "let's go somewhere where we can talk. I'm afraid we might be discovered if we linger here."

Pontus had been standing by with his back discreetly turned so as not to witness the tearful reunion.

Fortus called to him, "Thank you, Pontus, dear friend. May God bless you."

"And you, too, Fortus. Go with God." Pontus smacked the rump of the old mule and it lurched forward drawing the noisy cart behind it.

Fortus guided the mule through the winding maze of dark city streets. Even though it was past midnight, the streets were crowded with carts headed for market and with drunken revelers headed to the next party. Lights beamed out from the open doors of taverns and gaudily dressed women beckoned passers-by.

Galla and Fortus rode silently, their cloaks drawn up over their heads to hide their identities. After about fifteen minutes, Fortus drew up the cart in front of an old brick building with a heavy wooden door. His servant boy Alcibiades ran out from the shadow of an alley and took the mule's reins from Fortus as he stepped down off the cart. Fortus walked around to the other side of the cart and helped Galla down from the seat.

"Good evening Alcibiades, it's good to see you again," Galla said to the boy. Alcibiades blushed with pleasure and piped, "Good evening my Lady, it's good to see you, too!"

Fortus and Galla laughed at the boy's enthusiastic sincerity. Alcibiades blushed even deeper and he dug the toe of his leather boot into the ground.

"Alcibiades, take the cart around to the back. Wait there until I call you," Fortus commanded the boy gently. Alcibiades drove the mule into the alley and disappeared into the darkness.

Fortus led Galla to the heavy wooden door, which he opened with a large bronze key. Once inside, Galla waited at the door while Fortus lit several small clay oil lamps. When the lamps were finally lighted, Galla could see that they were standing in an old bakery, one that had been out of service for many years if the dust and cobwebs were any indicators.

Fortus picked up two oil lamps. He handed one to Galla and placed the other in his left hand. He directed Galla past the big stone worktables and the huge brick ovens to a small door at the far end of the bakery. He opened the door and they passed into a long narrow corridor. Halfway down the corridor on the left side was another door. Fortus stopped, opened the door and went inside. Once again Galla waited for Fortus to light the clay oil lamps.

When the room was lighted, Fortus came to the door and held out his hand. He led Galla into the tiny room. Unlike the old, dirty bakery, this room was neat and clean. The walls and ceiling had been plastered and freshly whitewashed. The wooden plank floors had been carefully sanded and oiled. The furnishings, although sparse, were in simple good taste. Two leather camp chairs flanked a large trunk that served as a table. A highly polished desk and chair stood against one wall, and along the other wall was a small but comfortable-looking bed. The only decorations on the walls were a large vellum map with a maze of roads drawn in brown ink, and a simple black wooden cross. The effect was neat and orderly. Galla knew instantly that this must be Fortus' room--it reflected his austere military background and his dislike of excess.

Fortus pulled out a chair for Galla and she crossed the room and sat down. She had never been alone with a young man in his room before and she suddenly felt awkward and nervous. Fortus took out an earthenware pitcher and poured wine into two wooden cups. He looked up at Galla.

"If you'd prefer something else, I could call Alcibiades," Fortus offered, seeing her tension.

"No, Fortus, I'd like the wine. I think I could use it. I don't know what's come over me tonight, really . . . first a fit of hysteria and now a fit of apprehension at being alone with a man in his bedchamber."

"This isn't just my bedchamber, it's really all of my chambers. If I had somewhere more appropriate to go, I'd take you there. Perhaps you'd prefer to sit out in the bakery, would that make you more comfortable?" Fortus offered eagerly and with great sincerity.

Galla felt herself relax when she heard Fortus' heartfelt attempts to make her feel at ease.

"No, Fortus, I'm all right now. I'm very comfortable right here. I can't think of anywhere I'd rather be than in your lovely room. I thought you lived in the barracks with all those raucous and wild young men to lead you astray, and now I find you living here in solitude, almost like a monk," Galla teased, beginning to feel her old self again.

Fortus smiled and sat back in his chair. "Yes, just like a monk--chastity, poverty and obedience--and work, we can't forget work. I've never worked so hard in my life as I have since I was sent to Rome." Fortus looked down at his hands and Galla could see they were blistered and callused. She stood up and moved her chair alongside that of Fortus. She took his hands in hers.

"Has it really been that bad, my darling?" Galla looked up into his light blue eyes, a surge of pity rising within her.

"No, it hasn't been that bad," Fortus said reassuringly. "Other than the fact that I can't see you, I actually enjoy my work. I think I've made a valuable contribution by helping to strengthen the walls around Rome. You know, Galla, things are looking pretty bad up north. The Goths have a new chieftain named Alaric and he's driving a hard bargain with Rome. He's demanding to be paid off or else he threatens to move south."

"Yes, I know a little of it, Uncle Julius told me."

"Well, the situation is getting worse day by day. Alaric has attacked and taken one of our forts in the north. The Roman soldiers have revolted. They blame Stilicho and his gang. They say Stilicho is siding with Alaric. All I know is the Goths are at the northern border of Italy now and there's not much to stand between them and Rome."

"And Rome! Fortus, I had no idea. Why hasn't anyone told me? I deserve to know these things."

"Yes, you do deserve to know these things Galla. Are you aware that Stilicho has, only this morning, gone to Ravenna? He's hoping to find sanctuary there."

"Ravenna! Does Serena know this?"

"She must. That must be why she came to Rome, to seek protection from her network of social misfits--and to seek the comfort of the company of that boy Marcus that she keeps here in Rome," Fortus added bitterly.

"Serena told me that she was coming to fetch her daughter Thermantia. Julius said that Stilicho and Serena hope to marry Thermantia to Honorius."

"That would make sense," Fortus said thoughtfully. "It would give Stilicho the Imperial backing he needs to show the soldiers that the government of Rome is still behind him. It might be enough to rally the Roman troops behind Stilicho again. We'll need all the support we can get if we're going to fend off the Goths." Fortus was clasping his hands together so tightly his knuckles were white and Galla could sense the urgency of the situation.

"Do you mean that a marriage between Thermantia and Honorius might really help Rome?" Galla asked, beginning to see the connection between this sordid personal alliance and important government strategy.

"It might. I'm not sure. If the troops can be made to believe that all is well between Stilicho and Honorius, then we might have a fighting chance."

"Oh, Fortus, it seems so unfair that Rome's hope for security rests on the shoulders of a fragile little nun."

"Yes, I know, Galla, and I agree, but life isn't always fair. I dislike their plotting as much as you do, but if that marriage can save thousands, even tens of thousands, of Roman lives, and Germanic lives too, then so be it. Sometimes individuals must make sacrifices for the good of the many."

Galla had never heard Fortus speak so coldly, and she knew that he, too, found the idea of marrying an innocent nun to a depraved Emperor repugnant. She decided to change the topic. Their time was so short together, she reasoned, that there was no point spoiling it with a discussion of things they could not change.

Galla stood up and walked over to the large vellum map nailed to the wall. She studied the map for several minutes as Fortus watched her intently. Finally Galla spoke. "When I first came in, I thought this was a map of roads, but now that I've looked at it, I don't believe they are roads, but still I can't quite figure out what they are."

"Keep looking. See if you can guess," Fortus said with hushed enthusiasm. He stood up and walked over to where Galla was examining the map.

Galla ran her finger along the dark brown lines, trying to trace their paths.

"No, they're not roads," Galla thought out loud. "They have different levels and steps. Is it the plan of a new apartment complex or a barracks perhaps?"

Fortus smiled broadly, obviously very pleased to have Galla share his interest in the map.

"Keep working, you're getting close," Fortus moved a step closer to Galla, their arms now touching.

Galla tilted her head one way then the other as she tried to decipher the maze of twisting corridors. Suddenly, she turned to Fortus and exclaimed, "It's the catacombs! It's the plan of those old catacombs beneath Rome, isn't it?"

Fortus laughed with delight, "Yes, Galla, my darling, yes! I knew you could figure it out!" And he put his arm around Galla and squeezed her tightly, all the while beaming proudly at the map.

Galla looked up at Fortus beside her and observed his excited enthusiasm.

"Forgive me, Fortus," Galla said slowly, "I understand now that this is a map of the old subterranean burial grounds, but I don't quite understand why you're so happy about it. Those are dreadful, smelly, old tunnels, *I know*, we have to walk through one to get to our family chapel below our villa. It's a terrible place full of death and decay, not to mention things still living like spiders and worms. It's a disgusting place, how can you be so interested in it?"

Fortus looked up at the ceiling and laughed loudly, barely able to contain his happiness.

Galla drew back and looked at Fortus, concern written on her face. "Fortus, my friend, I think you've been overworked. I had no idea the strain you've been under. Come, sit down, have some wine."

Fortus looked at Galla and he could see her concern was very real. He brought his elation under control, but he continued to smile broadly. "Yes, Galla, they are dreadful, smelly, horrible things. They are everything you say they are, and worse. There are millions of bodies down there rotting away and being eaten by worms. There are hundreds of miles of those disgusting passageways, sometimes they are five stories deep connected with dark, dank, slimy stairways. It's absolutely the worst place I've ever been and I simply love it!"

Galla drew back in revulsion. She blinked in disbelief at her dear friend. Had he really gone mad? Had the strain of being removed from his post as Imperial palace guard affected his brain? Galla extricated herself from Fortus' embrace. She took his arms in her two hands and looked sternly into Fortus' eyes.

"Control yourself, Fortus. You're going to be all right. I'll ask Honorius to arrange a leave for you. Perhaps you could go to the seaside at Neapolis, it should be lovely this time of year. Now come, sit down, just relax."

Fortus, seeing that his guessing game had played itself out, wiped the tears of delight from his eyes and gained control of his emotions. "I'm sorry, Galla. I'm all right, really. And when I tell you what has made me appear mad, you might get a good case of madness yourself. I was hoping you would guess, but it really is so incredible that no one could be expected to guess. I didn't guess it for myself, either. Come on, let's sit down and I'll start at the beginning."

Fortus took Galla's elbow and led her back to the camp chair. She was still studying him with great concern and he could sense her uneasiness. He refilled the two wooden cups and they each took a drink. Fortus drew in a long deep breath and sat back in his chair.

"About a week ago, while we were working on the repairs to the north city wall, one of our workers fell into a deep hole. We lowered ropes and tried to help him out, but he was injured too badly to pull himself out. Then we tried lowering one of the other workers down to carry the man out, but the hole was too small for the two of them to get out together.

While we were all standing about, trying to decide if we should widen the hole to get the two men out together, a priest walked by and asked what the problem was. He said he had a solution and he asked Pontus and me to follow him. He led us into the cloister of his church and then into a tiny storage room. After moving some crates, the priest uncovered a trap door in the floor. He opened it and explained that it led to the old early Christian catacombs from the time of the Christian persecution. He led us down the stairs and to the place where the worker had fallen. We were able to carry the injured man out through the door in the storage room floor."

"Later that evening, when I had returned to my quarters, I was still living in the barracks then, I began to think about the tunnel that the priest had shown us. The more I thought about the tunnel, the more I began to remember stories about those tunnels that I had heard as a child. When I was young I had a morbid fascination with those spooky old subterranean dwelling places of the dead."

"As I recalled the old stories of spirits and hauntings, I was reminded of another thing I once heard about the catacombs. The memory is very hazy, I was only about six at the time. My father and I had accompanied Bishop Ambrose on a trip from Milan down to your country palace to see your father. One evening, after the service in your catacomb chapel was over, we were all dismissed and everyone returned to the palace except Ambrose and your father. I was in my stage of fascination with those old tombs and I didn't leave with everyone else. I stayed around to explore. I don't think I would have had the nerve to stay if Ambrose and Theodosius weren't close by."

"I remember that I was poking around, looking into recesses and imagining spirits, but I could still hear Ambrose and Theodosius talking together in the chapel. Although I wasn't really listening to them, I remember one thing they discussed that sounded interesting. I recall Ambrose expressing his apprehension about the Emperor of Rome establishing his household outside the security of the walls of Rome. And then I remember your father telling Ambrose not to concern himself, that the safety of Rome's walls was as close as those tunnels. I didn't understand what he meant at the time. I thought he just meant that if there were trouble, he and his family could hide in the chapel, which didn't seem very practical, even to a six year old. I didn't understand what he meant until less than a week ago."

"The day after the worker's accident, I went back to talk to the priest. He told me all about those subterranean catacomb tunnels. He even had a map of them, which he allowed me to copy," Fortus nodded at the map on the wall. "Since then, every hour that hasn't been spent working on the walls, I've spent exploring the catacombs." Fortus' eyes shone brightly and he leaned forward towards Galla. "I've found it, Galla. I've found it."

Galla looked at Fortus quizzically, "Found what? What have you found?" she said, her irritation beginning to show. "Come to the point, Fortus. What's this all about?"

"I've found the tunnel to your country palace chapel!"

"A tunnel to the chapel?" Galla stammered in disbelief.

"I've stood there myself . . . in your chapel."

"You've been in the chapel since you were sent to Rome?"

"Yes, I've been there, Galla, just to be close to you, and to pray."

Galla thought immediately of her father and how he loved to go to the old chapel to be close to his ancestors and to pray. She wondered where she was and what she was doing when Fortus was so close to her in the chapel below the palace.

"Fortus, that means we could see each other and no one would know," Galla said, her mood lightening.

Fortus stood up, walked over to Galla's chair and knelt beside her. "I was hoping you would say that." Fortus took her hand and kissed it. Galla leaned over and put her arm around Fortus and drew him to her. Fortus could hear her heart beat through the thin silken gown.

"Now I see why you love those filthy old tunnels so well," Galla said softly. "You're not mad."

"Yes, I am mad, mad about you, absolutely crazy in love," and with that, Fortus reached up and kissed her.

He leaned back and looked at Galla. "I thought I'd never do that. I thought I'd never be this close to you, really close I mean. Galla, I love you so, if you only knew . . ."

"I know Fortus, I love you too."

Fortus smiled, his blue eyes shining brightly. He sprang to his feet.

"And look, Galla! There's more! While I was exploring the tunnels, I found this." Fortus went over and moved the bed out from the wall. Concealed beneath the bed was a square cut into the floorboards. Fortus grabbed a rope handle and pulled the trap door open. Galla walked over and peered down into a deep stairwell.

Fortus explained, "It's a stairway to the tunnels. The people who used to run this old bakery must have been Christians. That's why I rented this dilapidated old place and moved in. I can access the tunnels anytime I like and no one will know."

He closed the panel, pushed the bed back into place, and sat down. Galla sat down on the bed next to him and he took her hands in his. "If you ever want to see me, Galla, you can leave a note in the recess over the chapel door. Alcibiades is having a great time running around those tunnels; he's just like a little gopher, as happy underground as above it. He'll check the chapel door every Sabbath to see if you've left a message for me." Fortus put his arm around Galla. "Whatever happens, Galla, whatever you need, you can count on me."

Galla looked up at Fortus, tears of happiness filling her eyes. Fortus put his arms around her, drew her close to him. He kissed her again, and again.

CHAPTER VI

The first rays of dawn were peeking over the treetops when Galla lowered herself over the wooden fence and down into the peristyle garden of Serena's villa. Galla scurried along the garden path and into the villa to her quarters. As she closed the doors to her bedchamber she let out a sigh of relief. No one had seen her. She undressed quickly and slid into bed. She knew she should sleep but she felt wide-awake. So much had happened, there was so much to think about.

The next thing Galla was aware of was Lastia shaking her gently.

"My Lady, my Lady, it's after noon and Serena is already awake. She wants you to join her for breakfast in her rooms before you both go to fetch Thermantia."

"Breakfast," thought Galla, "Past noon? How like Serena to take her first meal of the day when most people have already had their second. But then, who am I to talk? I'm just getting out of bed myself." She smiled and stretched.

Galla forced herself out of the soft bed and began to prepare herself to meet with Serena. Lastia prattled on and on, but Galla heard little of the maid's babbling, she was too absorbed in thoughts about the events of the previous night.

Galla paid little attention, too, as Serena droned on and on during breakfast about the previous night's dinner guests, listing each one's financial status and giving explicit details of their sex lives. Everything around Galla seemed so sordid and ugly, only Fortus and her love for him seemed pure and untainted by Rome's moral decay.

The trip to the convent took only a few minutes. When Serena and Galla arrived, a nun in a simple black habit escorted them into an antechamber. There they awaited Thermantia's arrival. The convent was quiet and peaceful. The only sounds were the cheerful singing of birds in the adjoining cloister garden and, in the distance, the sound of young girls' voices chanting hymns. It was as if there was no Rome outside, no noisy, teeming city of over a million souls. Here, inside the convent walls, one felt calm and at peace.

The door finally opened and a thin, plain girl entered. She was dressed in the simple black vestments of her order. It was several seconds before Serena and Galla recognized that the girl before them was Thermantia, and it was longer still before Thermantia realized who her two visitors were.

After an awkward introduction and reunion, Serena announced the purpose of her visit. "I've come to take you home. Hurry and get your things, we're ready to leave," Serena announced perfunctorily.

"Leave?" Thermantia looked completely blank. "Home?"

"Yes, dear, we're taking you home. Now get your things, go on, hurry," Serena commanded.

Thermantia looked like a frightened deer, her big hazel eyes wide with incomprehension and fear. She turned and ran out of the room.

It was nearly twenty minutes before she returned. Her hands were empty and she had changed from her habit into a plain hopsack dress. An older nun accompanied her into the room and was the first to speak, "Good afternoon, Your Highness, I am Mother Mary Anne. I understand that you are here to take Thermantia home for a visit. How long shall we expect her to be away?" the nun asked sweetly.

Serena gave the woman an irritated look and replied, "Thermantia will not be returning. We plan to have her live at the palace with us. I've missed my darling daughter too much, I can't bear to be apart from her any longer." Serena walked up to Thermantia and took her by the arm.

Thermantia was still in a state of shock. "Not coming back? But this is my home, my work is here, my sisters are here, I can't just leave," she stammered. Serena began to lead Thermantia out of the room, ignoring the girl's protestations.

Mother Mary Anne tried to step in Serena's path, protesting, "But, Your Highness, please reconsider . . ." but Serena pushed by, steering Thermantia by the elbow.

"Mother Mary Anne! Please, do something!" Thermantia pleaded.

The elderly nun shook her head sadly. "I'm sorry, my child. She's your mother and I cannot go against her wishes. We will pray for you. Go with God, my dear."

Serena headed for the door of the convent. She stopped briefly and said, "Where are Thermantia's things?"

"Things?" Mother Mary Anne inquired.

"Yes, her things, the things that she has here, the things that must belong to her."

"We have no things here at St. Mary's. Everything we have belongs to God."

"Oh, all right, never mind," Serena scoffed. "I doubt if there's anything she needs here anyway," Serena turned abruptly and strode outside with Thermantia and Galla.

Mother Mary Anne called after her, "Everything she needs she has with her--she has our love and the love of God." With that Mother Mary Anne closed the door.

The three women seated themselves on the Imperial litter and Serena ordered the slaves to take them post haste to the country villa.

The ride from Rome back to the country palace was silent. Serena sat looking stiffly forward. Thermantia rode with her head hung down, tightly clasping her rosary. Galla knew that she couldn't say what she wanted to say to Thermantia with Serena present, so she, too, remained silent.

When they approached the country palace, Galla saw that the entire building was lighted festively and many carriages, chariots and litters were lined up outside.

"I wonder what's going on," Galla thought out loud.

"We're having a party to welcome Thermantia home. It looks like many of the guests have already arrived. We'll have to hurry and dress," Serena replied.

"Shall I take Thermantia to my room and help her get ready?" Galla offered, hoping for some time alone with the frightened girl.

"No, thank you, Galla. My daughter will come with me. I have everything that she needs ready for her," Serena responded without looking at Galla.

The litter arrived at the palace door and the three women stepped down and walked into the palace.

The party was well under way by the time Galla arrived at the dining hall. She was in no hurry to watch poor Thermantia suffer in the midst of countless strangers, so Galla had taken her time dressing. When Galla entered the hall, she found all the dining couches occupied and many guests standing. "There must be hundreds of people here," Galla thought to herself. "This is quite a homecoming party."

Galla looked around for Serena and Thermantia but couldn't find them in the crowd. She managed to spot Julius, however, and she was happy to have this refuge in the crush of boisterous party guests. Galla walked over to the couch on which Julius was reclining and sat down on one corner. She gave her uncle a kiss on his cheek and picked up a wine goblet from the serving tray.

"Well, it's happened sooner than we expected, hasn't it Galla?" Julius said wryly.

"What has happened sooner than we expected, Uncle?"

"The wedding! The wedding between Thermantia and Honorius. That's why all these guests are here. You just spent two days with Serena, didn't she tell you?"

"No, she didn't tell me." Galla set down her wine goblet and put her hand over her forehead rubbing her temples distraughtly. "Uncle, isn't there something we can do--something to stop this fiasco?"

Just then, twenty trumpets announced the arrival of the guests of honor. Serena entered first. She was dressed in a wine-colored sheath and her hair was decorated with pink rose buds. Honorius followed Serena, wearing his formal Imperial toga of gold silk with embroidered purple bands. The last member of the little parade was Thermantia. She was dressed in a white wedding gown and on her head she wore a saffron orange veil, held in place by a crown of yellow roses. The veil covered Thermantia's face, but Galla could tell from the bowed head and trembling hands that the young girl was terribly frightened.

The trumpets blasted again and the ceremony began. Bishop Theophilus performed the brief rites and in a few fleeting moments, Honorius and Thermantia were pronounced man and wife. Galla was relieved when Honorius declined to lift the veil and kiss the bride. Serena took Thermantia by the hand and led her out of the hall. Honorius stayed on at the party, laughing with his friends and, as always, teasing his little Celtic slave boy. Honorius was still there drinking and laughing when Galla left the hall several hours later.

The next morning Galla awoke to find a note on her breakfast tray. Galla sat up and wrapped the blankets around herself; it was an unusually cold morning. Galla read the note. It was from Julius. He asked her to come to his quarters at her earliest convenience. Galla ate quickly, dressed, and headed for Julius' apartments.

She found Julius seated at his desk with his head bent over a stack of correspondence. He was deep in concentration and he didn't hear Galla enter. Galla whispered softly, "Uncle, I'm here." The elderly man looked up from his work. He looked especially old this morning, his gray hair hadn't been combed and his face was unshaven.

"My goodness, Uncle! Look at you! How late did you stay at that party last night?" Galla teased.

The old man didn't smile. "I left right after you did, but I was up all night nevertheless."

"Are you ill, Uncle? Is there something I can do?"

"No, I'm not ill Galla, not ill physically anyway, mentally is another matter. Sit down Galla," Julius indicated a chair next to his desk and Galla sat down.

"I've had some terrible news, Galla. I wish I didn't have to tell you, but this is something you should know." The old man paused, rubbed his eyes and sighed deeply. "I don't know if you are aware that, day before yesterday, Stilicho fled the palace and went to Ravenna."

Galla pretended she had not heard this bit of news that Fortus had already told her in Rome. "Oh?" she said casually.

"Yes, he sought refuge there. Ravenna is a city well protected by the surrounding swamps. It's practically impenetrable and Stilicho hoped he would be safe there from his enemies. Lord knows he had enemies. The Roman soldiers hated him because they thought Stilicho was siding with Alaric and the Goths. The Goths hated him because he wouldn't give in to their demands for land to settle on and grain for their storehouses," Julius paused and rubbed his eyes.

"Uncle, you're speaking of Stilicho in the past tense, like he's dead. Has something happened to Stilicho?" Galla asked, her concern mounting as each second passed.

"Yes, my dear, Stilicho has been murdered. When he arrived in Ravenna he sought refuge in a church, but by some ploy his enemies convinced him to leave the sanctuary of the holy place and once he was outside, they decapitated him."

Galla gasped and drew her hand over her mouth. A wave of disgust and nausea washed over her. When she could finally speak, she stammered, "What's being done about this? Is Honorius having the assassins hunted down? They must be caught and punished!"

"No," Julius sighed deeply, "Honorius is not having the assassins hunted down. The Roman soldiers are rallying behind the culprits and Honorius is afraid to offend the army. As if Stilicho's death were not sufficient, the army is demanding even more bloodshed. Galla, I don't know how to tell you this . . . there's no way to put this delicately. The troops have asked for Eucherius' head as well and Honorius has agreed to their demands. Eucherius has fled to Ravenna to seek refuge in some holy place but Honorius has ordered that he be hunted down and executed on sight."

Julius leaned on his desk, pulled himself up to his feet, and walked over to the window. "He may already be dead for all I know. The entire country is in a state of rebellion. Citizens loyal to Rome blame the Germanic tribes for Stilicho's murder and they are massacring every Germanic person they can find. The streets of every city in Italy are running with blood this morning. That wedding last night was a last, desperate attempt to show Romans and the Germanic tribes alike that Honorius wants peace with both sides, but it was too late. It may as well have never happened."

Galla felt dizzy and ill. She grasped the arms of her chair to steady herself. Julius walked over and poured a glass of water for her. Galla took the glass with trembling hands.

"Then poor Thermantia was sacrificed for no reason?" Galla blurted out.

"No, she wasn't 'sacrificed' as you call it, not yet anyway. She spent the night with her mother. Honorius was in council all last night. I've just now left him at the Senate."

Julius sat back down at his desk, picked up a large sheet of vellum bearing the Imperial crest and pushed it in Galla's direction. "There, that's your brother's handiwork. It's the official command ordering Eucherius' execution."

Galla pushed the document back towards Julius. "I don't want to look at it. This whole thing makes me sick. What can we do, Uncle? What should we do? Is it safe here at the country palace?"

"I believe it's safe here, for now anyway. Thank God they never married you off to Eucherius or you'd be in Ravenna right now, running for your life," Julius said, looking Galla directly in the eye. "Thank God you're here." The old man's hands trembled and tears rose in his eyes.

"Yes, thank God I'm safe. But why did God choose to help me? Why didn't He help Stilicho or Eucherius?" Galla stopped and pondered the question. "Uncle, do you think God really picks and chooses those He wants to help and those He wants to cast out? Do you think He even knows what went on last night? If He did, how could He allow it to happen?"

Julius sighed deeply and wiped the tears from his eyes. "Those are weighty questions, Galla. Man has been trying to answer those very questions since the beginning of time. I certainly don't know the answers. Maybe only God himself knows the answers. I do know that He is a great and powerful God, that He must know and see everything. But why He works the way He does is a mystery to me, but then I'm just a poor mortal, maybe it would be too much for me to know." Julius rubbed his eyes again and Galla could see how tired he was.

"Uncle, you should get some rest. We'll talk again at dinner this evening. Let's dine alone and not with Serena. Serena!" Galla gasped. "I forgot all about Serena! She must be half-mad, losing her husband in such an awful, brutal way--and now her son! Oh poor Serena!" Galla looked quickly at her uncle. "Or is it 'poor

Serena'? Is Serena in on this? Was she part of Stilicho's double dealings with the Roman army and the Gothic troops?"

"I don't know Galla. I do know that she couldn't marry her daughter to Honorius fast enough to save her husband's life. And it looks like there's nothing she can do to save her son. As for her allegiances, I can't say for sure, I can only surmise. You were at her villa on the Palatine Hill at Rome. What was your impression?"

Galla thought for a moment and said, "I really didn't see anything, except some pretty boy she's keeping in fine clothes, and that she's spending money like water on that villa of hers."

"Yes, money like water. Where do you suppose she's getting all that money? I know for a fact that she's not getting it from Honorius--nor could Stilicho's salary have paid for her tremendous expenditures."

"The Germanic tribes? Do you think the Germanic tribes are giving her money?"

"I don't know. They may very well be giving her money. I'd even go so far as to bet they are. What I'd really like to know, if they *are*, in fact, giving her money, what do they expect in return? It must be a pretty big favor if one can judge by Serena's lavish lifestyle." Julius tried to suppress a yawn but could not.

"Oh, Uncle, I'm sorry, I've stayed too long. We'll talk again after you've slept. I'll be in my rooms. Call me when you're rested." Galla leaned over the desk, kissed the old man's forehead, and left the room, her mind a blur of jumbled thoughts.

It rained on and off all afternoon and a cold breeze blew from the north. It was after dark by the time Julius sent for Galla. She arrived at the huge dining hall to find Julius sitting alone next to a lighted brazier in the corner.

"Uncle, why are you sitting here alone in this big cold room? You'll catch a chill." Galla walked over to where the old man was sitting and put her arm around him.

"I'm sitting here alone because everyone has left the palace, except you and me and a few servants. And I'm here in the Imperial dining hall because, well, because I just wanted to be here, that's all."

Galla sat down on a dining couch next to Julius and held her hands out to warm them at the small fire in the bronze brazier.

"So, Serena has left, too?" Galla inquired hesitantly, half hoping that her conniving cousin was at last out of her life and half hoping the events of the previous night had just been a vicious rumor and that the palace could go back to "normal," whatever that meant. As bad as things had seemed only weeks ago, the current situation was indeed much worse. Galla felt as if she were on board a big ship in a squall, each time she got a good footing, another big wave would come along and knock her off her feet again. She longed for the boat to stop rocking.

"Yes," Julius replied, "Serena has gone to Rome. She'll be safer there. She has an extensive network of friends there, both Roman and Germanic. I think she feels secure whichever way the political wind blows."

"Is Thermantia with her?"

"No. Thermantia is with Honorius at your father's old villa near Serena's palace in Rome. He's still trying to keep up the guise of unity between the Romans and the Germanic tribes. Honorius wants us to join him there," Julius said, watching Galla carefully to read her reaction.

"Leave the country palace to go to Rome? This is my home, I don't want to leave," Galla replied, an awful feeling of apprehension rising within her.

"Neither do I Galla. It's the last thing I ever thought I'd have to do--flee your father's favorite Imperial palace. I'm an old man, but I'm not blind. Even I can see the writing on the wall. The Goths will reach Rome within the week. They're all fired up about the Romans slaughtering innocent persons simply because they are Germanic. The Goths had hoped that their fellow Germanic tribesman Stilicho could negotiate some terms with Honorius. But now Stilicho's dead and Italy is rife with civil disorder. It's the perfect time for Alaric and his tribes to attack Rome."

"Uncle! It's happening too fast. It's like a horrible dream. I keep trying to wake up, but I am awake. I want to go back--back to when things were peaceful and orderly. I wish this would all just go away!" Galla buried her head in her hands.

Julius smiled, but his eyes revealed his sadness. He, too, would like to go back--back to when he was young and strong and could march out to defend his beloved city. He understood Galla's frustration. Their world was falling apart around them and all either one could do would be to sit and watch.

"You know as well as I, Galla, that no one can ever go back. What's done is done. The challenge is to accept what we've been given and to move forward. We've weathered a lot together, my dear, we'll get through this, too." Julius reached out and patted Galla's hand.

Eli entered the dining hall carrying a tray of broiled chicken and roasted nuts. She set the tray down next to Galla and Julius.

Galla was surprised to see Eli serving the dinner. "Eli, what are you doing serving us? Where are the dining hall attendants?"

"They've left, my Lady. They've all left, not just the dining room attendants, but everyone."

"Left? They can't leave! They are slaves, they have no right to leave without our permission!"

Julius interrupted Galla. "Honorius gave permission for the slaves to go with him to Rome. Only Eli, Anta, and my manservant Joseph have chosen to remain here with us. The others have all fled to the protection of Rome's walls."

Galla's eyes widened. "There are only the five of us here, alone in the palace?"

Eli looked at the floor and Julius nodded slowly. "Only the five of us, Galla."

Galla stood up and began to pace back and forth. Julius and Eli watched her silently. After several minutes, Galla returned to her dining couch and sat back down. She looked at Julius, "How long will it be before the Goths reach this area?" she asked without emotion.

"Three days, maybe four days at most."

"Very well. Tomorrow we will pack up what we can. We'll leave first thing in the morning day after tomorrow. I want to stay here as long as we can. Let's have dinner now, Uncle Julius. Those Goths have disrupted our lives enough without causing us to miss our dinner as well. Thank you, Eli, you may go now."

Eli turned and started to walk out of the room. Galla called to her, "Oh, Eli! Thank you. Thank you for staying. You are a good and faithful servant," Galla added quickly, "and *friend*." Eli smiled and left the room.

Julius poured two cups of wine and he and Galla began eating. It was a long time before either spoke; each was lost in personal memories and recollections.

Finally Galla broke the silence. "I think I'll put another coal on the brazier. It really is cold for this time of year." Galla picked up a pair of long copper tongs and lifted a chunk of charcoal onto the low brazier.

"Yes, it's unseasonably cold, all right. The soldiers returning from the north say that there is still snow blocking many of the passes through the Alps. It must be bitterly cold north of the Danube. You know, in a way, I really can't blame those Germanic bastards for coming south." Julius looked at Galla, "I'm sorry Galla. Sometimes the old army language slips out of me."

"Don't worry, Uncle, I've heard that word before. I think it fits the Goths perfectly. I wish they would stay within their own borders and leave us alone, even if it *is* cold up there. They have no right coming down into Italy. Italy belongs to Rome."

"Well, let's say I play devil's advocate for awhile," Julius proposed, watching Galla intently. "If I were a Goth, I wouldn't recognize any arbitrary boundaries. Who set them up, anyway? The Romans, that's who. As a Goth I know no boundaries or borders. We wander from place to place following game and searching for fertile lands to grow our crops. Just because someone puts up a wall doesn't mean I stop being hungry. You say Italy belongs to Rome. I say Italy belonged to the Etruscans first, and Rome took it from them. And now we Goths will take it from the Romans."

"But don't the Goths have any law, any government to control them? They pillage and plunder and no one among them seems to control them or to stop them."

"As a Goth," Julius responded, "I wouldn't know what you meant by 'government.' We are organized into tribes; we owe our allegiance to a chief, like Alaric. The fiercer the chief, the more power he has. We have no 'government' to provide us with armies, roads, currency and all that. We survive by our wits and our strength. We have some laws. We have one very sophisticated law called wergild. If a person in another tribe kills a person in one tribe, then the killer pays money to the tribe that lost its member. That stops additional killings as retribution. That way we won't keep fighting and killing. The whole matter is settled and we get on with things."

"Money for a person's life? How can you establish a value on a human life?" Galla asked.

"Oh, it depends on who the person is . . . an old man like me wouldn't bring much, a beautiful young girl like you would bring more, and a strong young warrior like Fortus would bring the most. The Germanic tribes place a high value on youth and strength."

Galla smiled at Julius. "I don't like you as a Goth. You don't make any sense. To me the Germanic tribes are just like animals, invading others' territories and taking what isn't theirs."

"It depends which side of the fence one is on. *You're* a Roman on the warmer southern side of the fence, so you say I'm invading. *I'm* a Goth on the colder, northern side of the fence and I say I'm migrating. The Romans have always encouraged the extension of the benefits of Rome and its citizenship to other peoples. Rome extended citizenship to all its provinces, and, working together, Rome created the greatest empire the world has ever seen. But now the Romans are saying, 'No more! That's enough!' And we Goths are left out in the cold, quite literally. Now Rome says it can't feed all the peoples it already has; they talk about unemployment and lack of resources to care for all the people. Can you blame us Goths for being angry when we are denied the same opportunity as everyone else?"

"Yes, I can blame you--I mean I can blame the Goths, Uncle Julius. Rome can't keep extending its benefits to infinite numbers of peoples. We have hundreds of thousands of citizens without work. Most of the ones who do work, work for the government. It's like a giant animal feeding off itself. It can't go on indefinitely. Many of those unemployed persons have turned to robbery, and even worse, just to feed themselves. Entire gangs rule the streets of Rome at night. One can't travel after dark for fear of their random acts of violence. And we simply do not have the money to expand our police units. And now that we frown upon sending criminals into the colosseum to fight to the death, we have thousands in prison and even more of them free on the streets. And you think we should allow the Goths, one of the most notoriously wanton of the Germanic tribes, to add to these problems by extending them citizenship with all the benefits it has to offer?" Galla demanded angrily.

Julius smiled. "I'm not certain what I think, Galla. I do know it's good to look at both sides. If we can *understand* an opponent, perhaps we can *deal* with that opponent. And remember that Plato advised never to exclude a group. If you exclude a group, then you don't know what it's up to. It's better to include everyone--that way you can keep an eye on them."

Julius winked at Galla and finished a date he had been eating. "I think I'll have another glass of this wine. It may be awhile before we taste another vintage this fine. Can I pour another cup for you my dear?"

"I don't know. Are you a Goth now, or a Roman?" Galla teased. "I don't accept favors from Goths."

"I'm a Roman . . . through and through," Julius smiled and filled Galla's cup.

"Uncle, have you heard any news of Eucherius?" Galla asked hesitantly, not certain she really wanted to know.

"No, no news yet. So far he seems to have escaped, or else Honorius would have sent word to me. Ravenna is an ideal city in which to seek refuge. It's a strategist's dream for defense . . . completely surrounded by water--the sea to the east, marshes to the west, arms of the River Po on the north and the south, and canals everywhere. If Eucherius is found and executed, it will be by a few men and not by an army. An army has never taken Ravenna. It's a beautiful city, too. You remember, don't you Galla?" Galla nodded affirmatively. "Your father spent a great deal of time in Ravenna. You were very young then. Do you remember the beautiful churches and villas?"

"Yes," Galla replied, "and I remember that huge temple of Apollo that my father always threatened to tear down, but never did. And I remember my mother being so upset with the bawdy shows presented in the amphitheater! She even went to speak before the council to try to stop those lewd performances, but the council did very little to prevent them. I also remember how you took me down to the harbor to see the Imperial fleet. I was so proud--proud to be my father's daughter--proud to be a Roman-- proud to have such a magnificent fleet of ships at our command."

"We still have that magnificent fleet," Julius responded. "Unfortunately it won't do us a damn bit of good to fend off the Goths. They have a powerful land force, but no ships. We're like the Athenians with their powerful navy--they were practically helpless when the Spartan army attacked them during the Peloponnesian Wars. From what I hear, though, the Goths are eager to get their hands on a few of those Roman vessels. Alaric says his people are starving and he's demanding that Honorius supply his tribes with grain from North Africa. Alaric threatens that if Honorius doesn't give them the grain they have demanded, the Gothic tribes will commandeer Roman ships and go to Africa and get the grain themselves."

"Is Honorius going to give Alaric and his people the grain they're asking for?"

"He's letting the Goths think he's going to, but, if the truth be known, Honorius doesn't have the funds to send an expedition to Africa to trade for grain. So he's stalling and buying a little time, hoping that something else will turn up."

"Is that all the Goths are asking for, just grain?" Galla asked.

"They say they want grain and lands upon which to settle, but the longer Honorius delays, the more of each the Goths demand. Alaric is now claiming that supernatural beings are ordering him to destroy Rome. The Germanic tribes are very superstitious and a story like that carries a lot of force. Who can argue against voices that only Alaric can hear?"

"I thought the Goths were Christians. How can Alaric say he believes in supernatural beings who tell him to destroy cities?"

"Many of the Goths are of the heretical Arian sect of Christianity that believes Jesus is divine but not one body with God. But the Goths haven't been out of those dark north woods long enough to give up all their primitive beliefs in many gods and goddesses. Much like many of our own Romans who, although professing to be true orthodox Christians, still make sacrifices to the pagan deities and look to fortunetellers to interpret omens. Old beliefs die hard."

Julius reached to pour another cup of wine but found that the wine was all gone. He shrugged his shoulders. "The pitcher is empty, perhaps it's a sign that the gods believe we've had enough." Julius smiled and Galla laughed. Even in the face of all these problems, Julius could maintain his sense of humor, exactly like her father. Galla admired that quality in the two men.

"Yes, it must be a sign from the gods," Galla said as she rose to her feet. "Rest well, Uncle. I'll see you in the morning." Galla leaned over and kissed the old man's cheek.

Julius said goodnight and Galla left the dining hall. She headed directly for her apartments, and, once there, she sat down at her writing desk. She pulled out a small square of papyrus and dipped her quill into the ink.

My dearest Fortus,
    In two days we will leave for our villa on the Palatine in Rome. I hate leaving the country palace, but I am happy to be closer to you. It looks as if we won't have to use those old catacomb tunnels after all. I'm grateful for that. As you know, the situation with the Goths is growing increasingly serious. Please take care--I couldn't bear to lose you. I will write to you from the Palatine villa as soon as we arrive.
With love and prayers,
        Galla

Galla rolled up the papyrus, dripped some melted sealing wax on the opening and pressed her Imperial seal into it. She picked up a heavy woolen shawl, put it around her shoulders, and headed for the chapel. She stopped outside the door of the tunnel to light a small bronze oil lamp. She opened the door. The familiar odor of death and decay filled her nose. She hurried down the steep stairs and along the narrow corridor. She had hoped to see a light in the chapel indicating that Fortus was there, but the chapel was dark and empty. She pulled a chair over to the entrance of the chapel. She climbed up on the chair and felt for the recess that Fortus had told her about. Thoughts of crawling things entered her mind as she ran her hand over the rough surface of the tunnel wall. She held the lamp up higher and she was finally able to locate the narrow slot carved into the wall above the lintel of the door. She placed the tiny scroll deep into the slot and climbed down off the chair.

Galla re-entered the chapel, set the little lamp on the altar, and returned the chair to its original position. An odd feeling came over her as she stood in the chapel. She knew she should be frightened, she always had been when she was down in these subterranean tombs, but somehow now she was no longer afraid. The flame of the oil lamp flickered and danced, giving animation to the paintings on the chapel walls. There were the four evangelists, hands lifted in prayer, eyes raised to heaven, looking so lifelike it appeared they could speak. And above her, in the dome covering the center of the chapel, was a depiction of the young Christ as a Good Shepherd, carrying a lamb over his shoulders. It was as if Jesus were looking directly at her. Galla fumbled for a chair and sat down, still staring directly overhead. She felt a sense of calm come over her. She felt for the first time what her father must have felt when he came to worship in this old chapel. She now knew, too, why Fortus had been drawn to this room. It was as if the burdens of the world had been lifted from her shoulders and she was at peace. Galla fell to her knees and prayed.

CHAPTER VII

The following morning, Galla arose early and began preparations for the move into Rome. She had never realized how many things she had accumulated during her short lifetime. Now came the difficult decisions about what to take to Rome and what to leave to the barbarian invaders.

Galla sat down at her writing desk and began to make out a list of her most treasured possessions. Without hesitation, she wrote at the top of the page, "Letters of Correspondence - State and Personal." With that she ordered Anta to begin boxing her collection of scrolls from her father, from her mother, from various important dignitaries and statesmen, and, of course, from Fortus.

Galla thought a long while before writing her second entry, "Jewelry." Although none of it had any great sentimental value, except the tiny bronze ring from Fortus, which she was wearing, jewelry was small, portable, and it had great intrinsic value. It could be sold if worse came to worst. Galla asked Anta to place her jewelry in a velvet pouch with a secure drawstring. Galla planned to carry that pouch on her own person for extra security.

The third category Galla listed was "Codices and Scrolls." She knew she couldn't take her entire library, so she listed only the most important or the most rare volumes. She began the list with the Bible her father had left to her--it was said to have belonged to the Emperor Constantine himself. Among the other volumes Galla asked Anta to pack were her ancient copies of Virgil and Homer, several works of Cicero and Cato in their own handwriting, and an ancient manuscript from Egypt bearing excerpts from Plato and Aristotle. Galla asked that the remainder of her library be carefully packed in wooden crates and hidden deep in the subterranean vaults beneath the palace.

Galla knew that it was impossible to take the furniture. Honorius had already sent men out with carts to carry the sculptures and valuable bronze lamps and fixtures to the villa in Rome. But most of the beautiful marble couches and delicately carved chairs and beds would have to remain. "At least those barbarians will be able to see how civilized human beings live," Galla thought defiantly, trying to rationalize the loss of so many precious pieces.

When her short list was completed, Galla began to pack her personal items of clothing and cosmetics. Eli came in several times, asking if she should pack certain kitchen and cooking items. She had already packed all the silver and gold plates, goblets, and serving items. Eli specifically requested to take the huge bronze cooking cauldrons. They were believed to be of Etruscan manufacture and Eli was convinced that the new cauldrons produced in Rome now could not compare in workmanship or durability to those made by the ancient methods of production. Galla told her old nurse to take whatever she needed, but the two old cauldrons were the only items Eli requested specifically.

"Poor Eli," thought Galla, "this move must be hard on her, too. She's lived here twice as long as I have." Galla wondered where there would be room for all of them at the city palace. It was a very old villa, built centuries ago, not by an Emperor, but by a wealthy senator who had elegant, but conservative, tastes. The villa was beautifully designed but it was not one-quarter of the size of the country villa where Galla now lived. Theodosius had preferred living in the country, away from the noise and stench of the city. He had used the city palace only briefly when matters of state kept him in Rome. Even his villa in Ravenna was much grander than the small palace on the Palatine Hill. Of all the many Imperial households, the city palace was the smallest and the most neglected. Galla wondered what life would be like in the city. She knew she would miss her long rides on Odysseus and her leisurely walks in the north valley she loved so much. Galla decided to take one last ride out to the old oak tree. She left the rest of the packing to Anta and headed for the stables.

It was late afternoon before Galla returned. A row of heavily laden carts and donkeys lined the drive along the front of the palace. Galla returned Odysseus to his stall in the stables and gave him a ration of oats, hay, and water. She noticed that a half-dozen of the other horses had been left, unattended, in their stalls. She gave them oats, hay and fresh water, too. In all the years that she had visited the stables, Galla had never personally fed the horses. She found it strangely satisfying to watch them now as they greedily munched their dinners, their large brown eyes revealing their gratitude.

Galla entered the service door of the palace and found Eli at work making dinner. It was hard for Galla to believe that this was the last dinner she would have at the villa, at least until the barbarians were driven out of Italy. Galla entered the kitchen and sat down at the big, worn, wooden worktable.

"I hope you're hungry," Eli said. "I want to use all of the food we have on hand that we can't take to Rome. I packed up the staples and the wines, of course, but there's a lot of fruit and things here that just won't keep."

Eli talked on and on and Galla's thoughts turned to all the happy hours she had spent in this big warm kitchen. Her father had loved the big kitchen, too, and he and Galla had many times surprised one another there in the middle of the night while searching out leftovers from the banquets. On those occasions, the two would sit at the old wood table and talk for hours. They were often there, still talking, when Eli came in to start breakfast. Of all the rooms in the palace, Galla loved this kitchen the most. She sat there now, rubbing her hand over the rough surface of the old table, recalling the past.

"I'd like to have dinner in here tonight," Galla told Eli.

"In here? In the kitchen?" Eli asked, not understanding Galla's feelings about the room. Eli spent most of the hours of her day working in this room. A treat for Eli would be to dine in the great hall and to be served on gold plates. As for Galla, it was the opposite this evening. Tonight she wanted to return to the days of her childhood--to sit at the old table and to use the heavy earthenware dishes that she and her father used on their early hour forays to the kitchen.

"Yes, in here," Galla repeated. "Do you think Uncle Julius would mind?"

"If that's what you'd like, then I'm sure he won't mind. I'll ask him when he wakes up from his nap," Eli said as she slipped a loaf of bread dough into the oven.

That evening Galla and Julius dined at the heavy wooden worktable in the kitchen. They sat atop the tall stools, ate off earthenware plates and drank out of clay cups. Neither one of them mentioned the approach of the barbarians or the pending move to Rome.

It was late in the afternoon of the following day that the little caravan of carts and horses arrived at the Palatine Hill. Honorius was still at the forum meeting with the Senate. Galla and her party were met by the housekeeper Gaia, who showed them to the rooms that Honorius had selected for them.

Galla was satisfied with her quarters. They were small, just two medium-sized rooms and a bath, but they were private. She even had a view of the city from one window. She decided to place her writing table there. It didn't take long for Galla to settle in, she had brought so few things with her.

While Anta was arranging the clothes, Galla decided to take a look at the villa. It had been over a year since Galla was last there, but nothing had changed. So much of the first century design remained that Galla felt as if she were walking through a museum. The plaster walls were painted with panels of illusionistic colored marbles in the fashion of the centuries before the birth of Christ. The mosaic floors were done in fanciful designs of Venus, Apollo and the other pagan deities. Theodosius had found the patterns objectionable, but not so much so that he was willing to spend money to have them replaced. The only renovation that Theodosius had undertaken on the old villa was to have one of the cubiculae off the small entrance atrium transformed into a family chapel. It was too tiny to hold more than a dozen persons, but the Emperor had the floors, walls and ceilings decorated with Christian motifs done in the latest mosaic styles from Constantinople. Galla sensed she might have need of the little chapel in the months to come.

Galla decided to go to the servants' quarters, which were in the back of the villa, to see how Eli was settling in. She found her old nurse already hard at work in the kitchen. Galla asked Eli if she had been comfortably situated and Eli explained that she had a very pleasant little room off the pantry, right next to the housekeeper Gaia's room. Eli and Gaia were busily replacing the existing antiquated kitchen and serving items with the more fashionable pieces that had been brought from the country palace.

Gaia ooh'ed and ah'ed over each new item, completely delighted to see the old kitchen filled with such beautiful new pieces. It was clear that Eli and Gaia were fast becoming friends and Galla was pleased to see Eli looking so happy.

Just as Galla was returning to her room, Honorius and his guards entered the villa. Honorius looked worn and tired. He brightened when he saw Galla. He strode forward and greeted Galla warmly.

"Galla! Welcome! I'm glad you decided to come. We've all been so worried about you, out there alone in the country. Thermantia isn't adjusting well to all this and I thought you might be able to help her." Honorius looked at Galla and shook his head wearily. "And maybe you can help me, too."

"Of course, Honorius. I'll help anyway I can," Galla answered. Honorius always confused her when he was nice to her. She knew exactly how to respond when he was mean and despicable, but when he was nice, she wasn't exactly sure how to react.

"Thank you, Galla. I hope you'll excuse me now. I've been in the Senate since dawn. I'm in desperate need of a bath and a massage. I hope you'll join me at dinner. We can talk then."

"Certainly, Honorius, I would be pleased to join you at dinner," Galla replied, still eyeing Honorius carefully to see if his courtesy was just a ruse to set her up as the brunt of a joke. But no joke followed and Honorius turned and headed off to his quarters.

It was then that Galla noticed that one of the guards accompanying Honorius was Pontus, the good friend of Fortus. Pontus glanced briefly at Galla, bowed his head slightly in salutation, and then quickly followed Honorius and the others down the corridor.

Galla arrived at the dining room that evening before Honorius. She was pleased to see Julius already reclining on a couch. Galla took the couch next to Julius and a servant poured a cup of wine for her.

"Uncle, I'm glad to see you weathered the long journey today so well."

Julius smiled at the compliment and said, "We old soldiers travel well, my dear."

"I didn't see you this afternoon, Uncle. Where are your rooms?"

"Honorius has provided me with a lovely little house at the back of the peristyle garden."

"A house? You don't mean that old gardener's shack, do you?" Galla asked, indignation towards Honorius rising within her.

"Yes, it was the old gardener's shack, but Honorius had it fixed-up. It's really quite nice now. I have three lovely little rooms and my own garden to walk in."

"But it's not even in the palace," Galla protested.

"And that's what I like best about it," Julius smiled, his eyes revealing his satisfaction with his new cottage. "I have all the benefits of the palace--the dining hall, the library, the *kitchen*," he emphasized the last word, "but none of the problems. I can get away whenever I want. I'm really very happy, Galla, I couldn't have asked for better arrangements."

Galla sipped her wine and thought how smoothly the transition from country to city had gone. She began to feel at ease. "Perhaps this won't be as bad as I thought," Galla told herself. "Perhaps this might actually be fun. Many people enjoy living in Rome. Think of all there is to do here--the hippodrome, the theaters, the museums and churches . . . I think I might actually like it here."

Galla was busy mentally planning her social itinerary when Honorius and Thermantia entered the room. Honorius had benefited from his bath and massage; he looked rested and more at ease. Thermantia, however, looked tired and drawn. She was always a very thin girl, but now she was positively gaunt. Honorius strode over to Galla and threw himself down on the dining couch next to hers. Thermantia stood where she was, wringing her hands, a look of worry on her pale face.

"What's wrong with you Thermantia?" Honorius bellowed. "Come over here and sit down. Don't just stand there looking like a frightened mouse!" Honorius sighed deeply and rubbed his forehead. "Come on! Come on! We're not going to bite you!" he said, softening his tone.

Thermantia took a few tiny steps forward, stopped, and began to wring her hands again.

"All right! All right! Go back to your rooms, then. See if I care. I thought for once you'd like to have dinner with your husband--and your sister-in-law. But if you want to run off and hide, go ahead." Honorius turned away from her and she ran out the door.

"Worthless little wench," Honorius muttered and he took a long drink of wine.

Galla was eager to change both the subject and Honorius' mood. "Uncle Julius was just telling me how much he likes his new quarters, Honorius."

"Oh?" Honorius looked first at Galla and then at Julius. "Good! I'm glad. Sorry we couldn't accommodate you in this old villa. I'm pleased you're here Julius; I could use your advice on some very pressing matters. I'd like for you to come with me to the Senate tomorrow."

Julius sat a little straighter and he smiled, pleased that Honorius wanted his advice. "Certainly, Honorius, I'll be happy to do whatever I can."

"The situation is getting worse by the hour," Honorius stopped suddenly and looked at Galla.

"It's all right," Julius said. "She knows all about it. Your sister is a very intelligent woman, and a very brave one I would venture to add. You can discuss the situation freely in front of her."

"If only my wife were intelligent and brave. I can't even discuss *dinner* in front of her without her going to pieces. Well, all right," Honorius glanced again at Galla. "As I was saying, the situation is getting worse by the hour. The Senate is still refusing to place me on the Eastern throne. They say it's against established policy. Meanwhile, the Germanic tribes see Arcadius' son--*a seven-year-old boy*--on the throne at Constantinople, and, to them, the situation looks ripe for the picking. Alaric is feeling so sure of himself; he's increasing his demands on Rome daily. Right this minute, he and his hoards are heading towards Rome, destroying everything in their paths, just like a plague of locusts," Honorius added bitterly. "He says if we don't give him what he demands, he'll burn Rome to the ground." Honorius took a drink of wine. Galla could see he was clutching the goblet so tightly that his knuckles were white.

"What offers have been made to him?" Julius asked calmly.

"The Senate has offered him the grain he demands, and a portion of the money, but it's not enough for Alaric. He's a complete idiot. He's got a brother with him named Athaulf who seems to be a reasonable man, but Alaric won't let this Athaulf lead the negotiations. Alaric wants all the power for himself," Honorius said with disgust.

"How familiar," Galla thought to herself as she watched her brother intently.

"Any news of Eucherius?" Julius asked solemnly.

Once again, Honorius' eyes flashed towards Galla.

Julius nodded, "She knows that, too. I've told her everything. I felt she had a right to know, in case she needed to make any decisions about where she should go, or what she should do."

Galla looked directly at Honorius, "I'm all right. Please, go on."

"Eucherius is dead. He knew my men were after him. He was running into a church when they caught up with him and killed him." Honorius rubbed his palm over his forehead. "I know I gave the orders, but the bastards could have let him reach the church. It would have bought us some time; maybe we could have spared him. Eucherius wasn't a traitor, he didn't have the brains for it, unlike that bitch of a mother of his." Honorius again looked at Galla.

"Yes, that, too," Julius said. "I told her everything."

"You're a brave one, Julius, or else very foolish," Honorius retorted. "Every time I told a woman anything, half of Rome knew it within the hour."

"Galla's not just any woman, Honorius," Julius said reassuringly.

"You really think she can keep a secret, do you?" Honorius asked Julius.

"Yes, I do. I would trust her with my life." Julius looked over at Galla and smiled. Galla was honored by the old man's confidence and faith in her.

"Well, then maybe you *can* be useful, Galla. I mean really useful. Do you think you could get close to Serena--attend her parties, go shopping with her?" Honorius asked.

"Yes, I don't see why not. Why?" Galla replied, her interest whetted.

"To keep an eye on her . . . to find out whom she sees and where she goes. I don't know exactly . . . just to get a feel for her attitudes and alliances."

Galla looked at Honorius. "Do you think Serena is a traitor?"

"I don't know for sure. That's what I want you to find out. The Senate is asking for *her* head, too." Honorius looked down to avoid Galla's eyes. "I'm not happy that I had to order Eucherius' execution. And I'm even more reluctant to have Serena killed. She's a woman. And our father cared deeply for her. I just don't want to order her death, that's all. Not yet anyway, not until we know for sure, one way or the other." Honorius paused. "If you were to help, you'd be placing yourself in grave danger if she really is a traitor," he warned.

"I'm willing to accept that risk. I'm glad for an opportunity to be useful. You and Julius get to go off to the Senate and be in the thick of things. I only get to sit idly by and hear of things second and third hand."

Honorius moaned, "Oh, to get to sit idly by and let others be 'in the thick of things' as you say. I'd trade places with you any day. No one's ever happy with their lot, are they, Julius?"

"Seldom, Honorius, seldom," Julius replied, pleased to see the two siblings sharing a civilized conversation with one another, even if it was about such an uncivilized subject. "Unity," thought Julius, "the only way we will pull through this is if we work together."

"I'll pay a call on Serena tomorrow," Galla offered.

Honorius smiled and pinched Galla's cheek. "Just see that you keep this to yourself. Don't tell anyone--and I mean *anyone*. Julius says you can be trusted. You don't want to make a liar out of

him, do you Galla? If you *do*, it might mean *all* our heads."
Honorius slapped her cheek lightly.

Honorius looked over at Julius, "Things have gotten pretty
bad if we have to depend on women for anything more than a romp
in the hay or a legitimate heir, wouldn't you say Julius?" Honorius
laughed hoarsely and began pulling apart a rack of roasted pork
ribs.

"Yes," Julius replied, "things *have* gotten pretty bad."
Julius winked at Galla and smiled his approval.

The next morning Galla wrote a brief note to Serena letting
her know that Galla and her household had moved to Rome. In the
late afternoon Galla received an invitation for a visit. By the
evening of the same day, Galla was, once again, sitting in the guest
quarters of Serena's palace waiting the appointed hour for dinner
with her hostess.

Shortly before eight, there was a knock at Galla's door.

"Come in!" Galla commanded.

The door opened and Serena's young friend Marcus entered
the room, closing the door behind him. He looked carefully around
the room. Then, seeing that no one else was there, he walked over
to Galla.

"Yes, Marcus, is something wrong?" Galla inquired in her
most officious tone.

Marcus did not speak.

"What is it Marcus? It must be very important. Gentlemen
do not go to ladies' quarters."

Marcus continued to stand in front of Galla, staring lewdly
at her, but not speaking.

Galla stood up. "I must ask you to leave or I will call the
guards," she said firmly and began to walk to the door.

Marcus grabbed Galla's arm and spun her around to face
him. "I wouldn't do that if I were you, Galla," Marcus whispered.
"And don't make a sound. I have some information for you, but
you'll have to agree to my demands first."

Galla jerked her arm free of Marcus' grasp. "How dare you
touch me? I am Galla Placidia, the sister of the Emperor Honorius
and if any harm comes to me, my brother will see to it that you are
severely punished."

"You may be the noble Galla Placidia, but you're still a woman and I know what you want. I saw it in your eyes the other evening. You're just pretending to be so prim and proper, but you're just like all the others."

"How dare you speak to me in this manner! Guards!" Galla began to shout, but Marcus put his hand over her mouth.

"Shut up! I want you to know I'm willing to play your game. I'll give you what you want and then you give me what I want." He took his hand from Galla's mouth.

"What do you have that I could possibly want?" Galla hissed as she wiped her mouth.

"Information," Marcus whispered. "Information that you and that brother of yours could use."

"And what do you want in return for that information?" Galla asked, feigning ignorance.

"You." Marcus said as he slipped his arm around Galla's waist.

"You're out of your mind!" Galla pushed the young man away once again. "What kind of information could you possibly have that would be worth that?"

"Information that could save the city of Rome--that's what. Don't you think you're a pretty small price to pay to save the city of Rome?" Marcus leaned forward and she could smell his heavy, wine-soaked breath.

Galla turned and took a few steps, then turned back. She was beginning to realize that the information she had come here to seek, might be seeking her out instead. She brought her temper under control.

"You say you have information that could save Rome. What proof do you have of this information or am I just supposed to take your word for it?"

Marcus smiled, tricked by Galla's sudden change in attitude.

"I can bring you proof--written evidence," Marcus said as he stepped closer to Galla, "but first I must have your word."

"My word?" Galla asked, still feigning naiveté.

"Your word. You must promise me that if I give you this information, you'll give me what I want," and he once again slipped his arm around Galla.

"How do I know that this information is really important? Perhaps if you tell me a little of it, you can convince me of its importance," Galla put her hand on Marcus' arm and smiled up at him.

"It has to do with a traitor in your family," Marcus drew Galla closer.

"A traitor? In my family? Impossible!" Galla pushed Marcus away with an expression of hurt and shock. "I don't believe you! You're lying to me!"

"I am not lying. It's Serena who's lying. Pretending to be a virtuous Roman and all the while siding with the barbarians!"

Galla struck a pose of surprise, her fingertips to her mouth. "That can't be. And even if what you say *were* true, I thought you cared for Serena. If you care for her, why would you tell me this awful thing?"

"Care for Serena? One might as well care for a hungry wolf. She was fun for awhile, but then I saw *you*." Marcus stared at Galla, looking much like a hungry wolf himself.

Galla smiled, "Do you like me? I mean really like me?" Marcus nodded and took Galla's hand. She continued, "Then bring me proof of what you say. If what you say is true--and if it's as important as you say it is--then I'll agree to your bargain."

Marcus reached down to kiss Galla but she quickly placed her finger over his mouth. "Not now. You must bring me written evidence first."

Marcus kissed Galla's finger and said, "You'll have your evidence within the week . . . and then I'll have you." Marcus beamed with self-satisfaction. "See you at dinner!" He turned and strode proudly out of the room.

Dinner that evening was much the same as Galla's recent dining adventure at Serena's villa. From the laughter of the guests and the gaiety of the entertainers, one would never have known that the hostess was in mourning for the very recent loss of her husband and the even more recent loss of her son. The only clue one would have to Serena's bereavement was the fact that Serena was, this evening, wearing black, but the gown was cut so low that few would have recognized it as a mourning dress.

Marcus and Serena once again shared a single dining couch. Galla watched Serena playfully placing grapes down her deep décolletage and Marcus eagerly retrieving them with his tongue.

"Pity the poor widow," Galla thought sarcastically. She marveled at the act that Marcus was putting on--no one could have guessed that only an hour before he had offered Serena's head on a silver platter to Galla. Now, here he was, laughing and playing with Serena as if nothing were wrong. "Janus-faced traitor," Galla thought.

It was then that Galla realized that perhaps it was *she* who was really the one who had been deceived. "What if he set me up?" Galla thought. "What if he just wanted to find out why I'm here? Perhaps Serena herself sent him." Galla was suddenly filled with uncertainty. "Oh well, no going back now. The die is cast. I'll have to play this one out."

Galla remained at the banquet for several hours, taking note of all the guests in attendance. If she didn't know an individual's name, she found a discreet way to learn it from another guest. Serena's guest list was varied . . . it included senators from the finest Roman families as well as Germanic officers of high rank in the Roman army. Stilicho had always prided himself on fairness to all peoples who promised allegiance to Rome.

"It was such a noble idea," Galla thought, "to have all peoples united under one law and under one government." She looked around the hall and saw guests of Roman, Celtic, Iberian, African and Germanic ancestry all laughing and enjoying one another's company. "This is how it should be . . . all peoples living together peacefully. How did it all go so wrong? The Germanic barbarian tribes are nearly on our doorstep. Why? And yet, look at all these guests, laughing and drinking as if there's nothing wrong!"

Galla shook her head in incomprehension. At eighteen Galla sometimes felt she knew all the answers, while at other times she felt she had barely scratched the surface of life's mysteries.

Galla finally left the party about midnight. Serena, Marcus,
and the others were still eating and drinking. Only Marcus seemed
to notice Galla as she left the hall, but he didn't bid her goodnight.

Once out in the hall, Galla looked about, hoping to see
Pontus waiting for her with a message from Fortus. But Pontus
was not there this night and Galla returned to her room
disappointed. She wanted to see Fortus and to tell him what
Marcus had said about Serena. "It will have to wait," Galla
thought. "Perhaps I'll know more later anyway."

Galla was awakened the next morning by the maidservant
who had attended her on the last visit.

"This is for you," Lastia said as she held out a small square
of paper.

Galla sat up in bed and rubbed her eyes as Lastia opened
the drapes to let in the daylight. Galla read the note.

> Galla dear,
>> I have to run an errand this morning and I would
>> like for you to accompany me. We will leave
>> within the hour.
>>> Serena

"She could have at least told me what the errand is," Galla
thought with irritation. "I don't know what to wear, or where we're
going. How like Serena to be so wrapped-up in herself." Galla
pulled herself out of bed and walked over to the window. It was
another cool, gray day and the dark clouds portended rain.

Lastia helped Galla wash and dress. Galla had a light meal
and then set off to find Serena. Much to Galla's surprise, Serena
was in the foyer waiting for Galla.

"How good of you to come, Galla. I'm sorry we didn't get
to visit last night, but you know how banquets are--very dull really.
But today we'll get a chance for a nice long visit. Come on, I'm
ready, let's go."

"Where are we going?" Galla inquired as they walked out
to the awaiting litter.

"Oh, we have a rather unpleasant task, I'm afraid," Serena sighed. "Honorius has sent word that Thermantia is very unhappy. He thinks it's best if she returns to the convent."

"Returns to the convent? But she's married," Galla protested.

"Yes, she is. But Honorius claims that the marriage was never consummated. He says that Thermantia was never cut out to be the wife of an Emperor. He says she should remain the bride of Christ." Serena bit her lower lip in agitation.

"I'm sorry, I just don't understand," Galla offered, sensing that the dissolution of this union must be a great disappointment to Serena.

"Neither do I. But I cannot oppose the wishes of my cousin the Emperor. And, moreover, I think it's what Thermantia wants, too. So be it. Obviously neither one of them gives a fig for what I want," Serena added bitterly.

"I wonder what Serena does want," Galla thought to herself. "First she lost her husband, then her son, and now her daughter is repudiated by the Emperor. That's a lot for one individual to bear. I almost wouldn't blame her if she *were* plotting against Rome. Honorius and the Senate have dealt her some strong blows recently. Yet, she is my father's niece--a Roman by birth--perhaps that's enough to cement her loyalty to Rome, if not to Honorius and the Senate."

They arrived at the city palace to find Thermantia standing on the steps. She carried no bags and she had on the same plain hopsack dress that she wore when she left the convent. When the four Nubian slaves set the litter down in front of the palace, Thermantia ran down the steps and climbed up onto the litter.

"To St. Mary's," Serena commanded. The ride to the convent was silent. Serena stared off to the side, avoiding Thermantia's eyes. Galla sat quietly, intently watching the sites of Rome pass by. Thermantia sat perched on the edge of her seat, her eyes straining for the familiar facade of the convent. When it finally appeared, Thermantia leapt off the litter before it stopped. She ran up to the convent door and pulled the rope to ring the bell. Within seconds, the door opened and Thermantia disappeared inside.

"To the dressmakers," Serena ordered, and the four powerful slaves set off down the street. It was then that Galla realized, on all the recent occasions that she had been with Thermantia, that she had not spoken one word to the girl. It was a very odd empty feeling. Galla was sorry that she hadn't spoken some kind words to Thermantia to let the girl know how much she cared. And now it was too late . . . Thermantia was once again with the Holy Sisters of St. Mary.

The remainder of the afternoon was spent ordering dresses, veils, sandals, and jewelry. Serena was well known to all the shopkeepers and they welcomed her warmly. It was obvious that money was no object to Serena; she never once discussed price with any of the merchants. Serena was like the sharks Galla once saw on a voyage to Constantinople. She remembered the sharks' growing intensity and excitement as they gobbled up refuse dropped from the ship. Serena was much the same, the more she purchased, the more she wanted. By the end of the afternoon, Galla had lost track of how many dozens of gowns, veils, sandals, boots, bracelets, necklaces, and crowns Serena had ordered. Serena had even insisted upon buying gifts for Galla, who had, at first, tried to refuse, but upon further consideration decided to accept and thereby enhance Serena's trust in her. Galla didn't like the feeling of deceiving Serena. She felt dishonest and guilty. But she knew her motive was noble--it was to protect and preserve Rome, and so she tried to put the unpleasant feelings behind her and to concentrate on the mission entrusted to her by Honorius.

At last Serena's buying spree spent itself out and the two women began their return journey to Serena's villa. Their litter was piled high with bundles and it was accompanied by several of the shopkeepers' slaves who followed behind, laden like donkeys with packages and boxes.

The afternoon's shopping had lightened Serena's mood and she chatted cheerfully as they rode along. Galla felt a strange sense of elation. She had never indulged in wanton expenditures before and she found it embarrassingly pleasurable. By the time the two arrived back at the villa, they were laughing and talking like the best of friends.

That evening's banquet was much like the others--scores of hungry and thirsty guests, dozens of musicians and entertainers, and food, course after course of exotic, and expensive, food. This evening, Serena had ordered the long pool in the peristyle garden to be filled with live fish. Each of the guests was given a net and sent off to catch a fish for dinner. Galla was amused to see dignified senators and aristocrats, down on their hands and knees, dipping their nets into the pool trying to catch the biggest fish. Several of the guests leaned too far over the pool and ended up swimming with the fish.

Serena was seated on an elegant throne-like chair at the opposite end of the pool from where Galla was standing when Marcus walked up behind Galla and tapped her on the shoulder.

"Shh!" he whispered as he placed himself between her and the other guests, blocking their view with his back. "I just want to give you this," he smiled his most charming, albeit smug, smile and handed Galla a scroll. "Put it under your shawl. Don't let anyone see it," he warned and walked casually away.

Galla quickly tucked the scroll under her shawl and into her belt. She walked to the far end of the unfinished peristyle wall. When Serena and her guests all turned to watch another guest fall into the pool, Galla dropped the scroll down between two large pieces of lumber and then she returned to the party.

Galla remained at the banquet, laughing and drinking with the other guests, until well after midnight. Even at that late hour, Galla was one of the first guests to leave the festivities. She bade her hostess a pleasant night and headed down the corridor to her rooms. Galla was still laughing at a humorous hunting story that one of the dinner guests had told her, when Pontus stepped from the shadow.

"Good evening, Your Highness," Pontus saluted and held out a small scroll sealed with blue wax.

The sight of the tiny chi-rho brought Galla back to her senses.

Pontus saluted again and before Galla could speak, he was gone.

Galla stood there without moving, suddenly ashamed of herself. "How easy it is to get swept up in all this," Galla thought as she looked around the marble corridor with its gold lamps and bronze statuary. How easy it is to get caught up in shopping and spending. And how easy it is to start staying later and later at those banquets." Galla thought of the lotus-eaters in Homer's poem and how Odysseus' men were tempted to eat the lotus blossoms, too. "This life style is like that exotic drug," Galla thought. "It tricks your mind into thinking it has something real to offer. It's only when I see this," she looked down at the tiny cross on Fortus' seal, "that I can see what is truly real." She clutched the scroll tightly and ran down the corridor to her quarters.

She knew now not to worry about Lastia--each night while their masters partied in the grand hall, the servants partied in the kitchen. When Lastia eventually stumbled drunkenly into the room, Galla feigned fatigue and told Lastia she could take the rest of the night off. As before, Lastia gladly accepted Galla's offer.

When Lastia had left, Galla sat down at the dressing table and opened the scroll.

> Galla, Darling,
>> I long to see you. If it is possible, please meet me as before. Do not take any chances. If you cannot meet me tonight, perhaps tomorrow night.
>>> Your loving Fortus

Galla changed into a warm dress and shawl. She opened the door and peeked out. The hallway was empty. Only the sounds of laughter and music from the dining hall could be heard. Galla pulled the shawl over her head and hurried out into the peristyle garden. The walk was still wet from where the unfortunate fishermen had fallen into the pool earlier.

Galla made her way to the far end of the enclosure and found Pontus waiting for her. She gestured to him to wait a moment. She went over to where she had hidden Marcus' document several hours earlier. She reached down between the boards, pulled out the scroll, and tucked it under her belt. In a few minutes, Pontus and Galla were on the other side of the fence where Fortus was waiting for them. Galla quickly climbed up on the old cart. She and Fortus waved to Pontus and drove off.

They didn't speak until they were safely inside Fortus' room at the old bakery.

"Galla, I've been worried about you. I'm so happy to see you," Fortus said as he put his arms around Galla and drew her close to him.

Galla was glad to have Fortus' strong, reassuring arms around her again.

"Fortus, I have so much to tell you . . . so much is happening . . . look!" Galla pulled Marcus' scroll out of her belt and held it up.

"What is it, Galla?" Fortus asked, slightly resentful of the object that had diverted Galla's attention away from him.

"I'm told it is written proof that Serena is in collusion with the Goths," Galla said with hushed excitement, pleased to show Fortus her cleverness.

"How did you get it?" Fortus asked, concerned that Galla was involved in this dangerous matter.

"That doesn't matter now. Let's read it and see what it says," Galla responded, purposefully avoiding any explanation of Marcus and the sordid agreement.

Galla took a seat and spread the scroll out on the old trunk. Fortus brought an oil lamp close and the two looked at the document.

"It's from Serena," Galla explained. "I can tell from her elaborate writing. See?" Galla pointed to several curvilinear flourishes at the end of each written line.

Fortus read the document out loud, "A. I have not received your latest payment. The fact that H. has refused to pay you does not concern me. If you want the information about the gates, you must send the payment at once. When the time comes, and you have the information, I will need a letter guaranteeing my safety. It must be signed by you. These are my demands. S."

Fortus let out a long sigh and ran his hand through his hair. "She's selling us out, Galla. A member of the Imperial family is selling us out!" Fortus sighed again and threw himself down on a chair.

Galla took the scroll from Fortus' hand and read it again, slowly, line by line.

"'A.' Who's 'A'?" Galla asked.

"It must mean Alaric, the Gothic chieftain."

"'I have not received your latest payment.' So the Goths *have* been bribing Serena, just like Julius suspected," Galla added. "'The fact that H. has refused to pay you does not concern me.' 'H.' must be Honorius. He himself told me that he was only going to pay a small part of the huge sum that Alaric is demanding. 'If you want the information about the gates, you must send the payment at once.' The gates? What do you suppose that means?" Galla looked at Fortus.

Fortus kicked the table with the heel of his boot and stood up. "*Our* gates! The gates of Rome! The gates we've been working on all these weeks trying to make impenetrable. She must have a spy--or spies--among us. She's planted someone among us to learn about the gates. It's probably one of our own troops. It would take only one man to leave a gate unbolted, or to turn his back at the right time while on guard duty, and Rome would be overrun by those barbarians." Fortus pounded his fist against the wall. "Damn her! Damn her!" he shouted, frustration and anger taking hold of him.

Galla rose to her feet, a feeling of fear and urgency rising within her. "What can we do? Whom should we tell?"

"We must go straight to the Emperor with this news. He'll have to act fast to silence Serena, or else Rome is lost." Fortus reached for his cloak and threw it over his shoulders. He looked up and saw Galla standing in the flickering light of the oil lamps, looking very frightened and very alone. He went over to her and put his arms around her. "You've done a wonderful thing, Galla. You may have saved the city. I know this will be hard for you . . . she's your cousin and she helped raise you, but you must think of Rome now. Rome comes first." Fortus placed Galla's cloak over her shoulders. He picked up the scroll and the two headed off to warn Honorius.

When they reached the Imperial palace, Galla and Fortus were surprised to find no guards outside the front entrance. Fortus pushed open one of the tall bronze doors and the two walked inside. The palace was dark and quiet.

"Guards! Where are the guards?" Galla demanded, her apprehension increasing. There was no response. Galla and Fortus walked through the entrance hall and into the atrium. They could see light coming from the door of the chapel. They walked over to the chapel and looked in. There, kneeling before the little altar, was Julius. They walked up to him.

"Uncle! What are you doing here? Where is everyone? We must speak to Honorius!" Galla blurted out without waiting for the old man to answer.

"Galla! Galla!" The old man struggled to his feet and embraced Galla. He began to sob. "We thought you were gone. We thought they had taken you. No one knew where you were. Honorius looked for you before he left, but no one could find you."

Galla interrupted, "Honorius has left? Where did he go?"

Julius began to get his emotions under control and he answered more coherently, "Honorius has gone to Ravenna. The Goths are at the gates of Rome. Honorius just made it out in time. He wanted to take you with him, but he couldn't find you. You weren't in your quarters at Serena's and no one knew where you were. Honorius didn't want to leave without you, but the Senate insisted." Julius was still shaking and Fortus led him to a chair and helped him sit down.

"I've been here praying, Galla, praying for your safe return. Honorius was convinced the Goths had you--to hold you for ransom. But thank God you're safe," Julius looked up at the altar and crossed himself.

Fortus and Galla were too stunned to speak. Honorius was gone and the Goths were at the gates of Rome. Perhaps even now Serena's accomplice was opening a gate for the barbarians to enter the city.

"Galla, we must go to the senators to let them know about Serena," Fortus said urgently.

"Senators? Serena?" Julius asked.

"Yes, Julius," Galla explained, "you were right. Serena is in collusion with the Goths. She's promised to give them access to Rome through one of the gates. That's why we're here--we came to tell Honorius. But since he's gone, we must wake up the top men in the Senate and let them know of her treachery. Perhaps we can stop her before it's too late."

Julius stood up and smoothed his rumpled toga. "The Senate is in session now, deciding what to do about the blockade the Goths have set up around the city. I'd like to go with you."

Fortus smiled his approval and Galla said, "Would you, Uncle? That's good. The Senate will listen to you, you're one of their most respected members." Galla put her arm around Julius and the three set out into the darkness.

They arrived at the impressive marble Senate building to find the lights aglow and nearly every seat filled. It seemed as if everyone was talking at once and the speaker on the floor couldn't be heard above the din. Galla, Julius, and Fortus entered by the ground floor door and they walked out to where the speaker was standing. The sight of the three individuals drew the attention of the crowd and little by little the din decreased. When all was silent, the speaker inquired as to the nature of their visit to the Senate.

Julius stepped forward. He was used to speaking before this august body of Roman citizens so he spoke first. "Fellow Romans, we have come before you on a matter of utmost urgency and importance. The noble Galla Placidia, sister of our revered Emperor Honorius, has uncovered a treasonous plot against our city. She begs to be allowed to speak here on the Senate floor."

The crowd began muttering and shuffling. Some openly expressed their objections to allowing a woman to speak before the Senate. The speaker voiced the opinion of his colleagues, "This is quite an extraordinary request," he said as politely as he could. "Perhaps the senator could speak for the noble Galla Placidia," he nodded towards Julius.

Julius stepped forward and spoke again, his irritation with his fellow senators reflected in his tone, "Yes, senators, this is an extraordinary request, but as you sit here, stubbornly forbidding a woman to speak before the Senate, the Goths are at the gates of Rome. The daughter of our beloved Emperor Theodosius, now called 'The Great,' wishes to share some grave and pressing information with you. I believe it is in your best interest and in the best interest of Rome itself that you permit her to speak."

Slowly, one by one, the senators nodded their heads in assent. Galla had never spoken to any large group before and now she was to speak before the foremost governmental body in the world. Fear gripped her. She felt she could barely breathe.

Julius returned to where Galla was standing and he beamed proudly at her, "This is your chance; show them what a woman can do."

Galla looked up at Fortus standing next to her. He nodded confidently at her, handed her Serena's scroll, and smiled. Galla dried her palms on the sides of her dress and then walked out to the speaker's area in the center of the Senate floor.

"Fellow Romans." Her voice sounded dry and faint. She cleared her throat. Several men began to snicker. Galla flashed them a defiant look. Anger began to take hold of her. How dare they laugh! She began again.

"Fellow Romans," she spoke in a clear loud voice, "I come before you with serious and distressing news. The nature of the news is made even more grave by the fact that it involves treachery by a member of the Imperial family." A wave of whispers washed across the auditorium. The room fell silent again.

"This evening, a certain document was delivered into my hands." She held up the scroll. "This document is written proof that Serena, widow of Stilicho and cousin of the Emperor Honorius, has conspired with the Goths to destroy the city of Rome."

Several of the senators leapt to their feet and shouts of protest could be heard across the hall. Galla waited for the men to control their reactions.

"Gentlemen, I, too, am distressed and outraged by this news. Serena is my father's niece and I was raised in her household. No one in this room can feel the gravity of this situation more than I. But we must all put aside our personal feelings and look at the facts!" Galla snapped open the scroll and held it up to the crowd.

The senators all began talking at once and several began to head for the exits.

"Senators!" Galla shouted. "I see some of you are making ready to leave. I would like to suggest that you remain in your seats. If word were to reach Serena of our knowledge of her deceit, it could only come from someone in this room. I know that none among you wants to be accused of conspiring with Serena." The men all returned to their seats.

"What do you want us to do?" one of the senators shouted to Galla. Another called out, "I say we lop off Serena's head, just like that traitorous husband and son of hers!" "Yes! Execute Serena!" several others chimed in.

Galla had not expected a call to execute Serena. Women were traditionally imprisoned or exiled where they could do no further harm.

"Senators!" Galla shouted to be heard over the crowd. "A matter as serious as execution should be decided only by the Emperor."

"The Emperor is in Ravenna! He's not here to make that decision," one senator responded. "You're the next in line here in Rome, Galla Placidia, you must decide!" another shouted and the others nodded and cheered in agreement.

The words fell on Galla's ears with a thud, "You're the next in line, Galla Placidia, you must decide!" "Next in line," Galla thought, "impossible! Surely there's someone else in Rome to make this terrible decision!"

She turned to look at Julius for advice. He lifted his eyebrows and nodded his head indicating his agreement that Galla was, legally, the highest person in the city of Rome at that moment. "Protocol requires that only a member of the Imperial family can rightfully order the execution of another Imperial person," Julius said gravely.

Galla looked desperately at Fortus to come to her aid. Fortus nodded his head and looked at her with pity. She was alone . . . a single woman in the midst of a hundred angry men calling for blood. The familiar words rang in her head, "Rome comes first. Rome comes first."

"What say you, Galla Placidia, will you order the execution of the traitor Serena?" a senator in the front row called out. The others began chanting, "Execution! Execution! Execution! Execution!"

"Senators, I hereby order the execution of Serena," Galla began, but the cheers of the bloodthirsty senators interrupted her. Galla shouted over their revelry, "I hereby order the execution of Serena, but not by beheading," the crowd quieted down and Galla continued. "Serena is to be given the opportunity to commit suicide as was considered noble by our ancestors. If she refuses, she is to be strangled until dead. I want no bloodshed. This is my order."

The crowd leapt to their feet and began chanting "Galla, Galla, Galla!" The room began to grow blurry and Galla felt faint. As she took a few steps towards Fortus, she felt her knees give way and then everything went black.

Galla awoke to find herself lying in bed. Julius and Fortus were seated beside her.

"Where am I? What happened?" Galla said as she tried to sit up.

"Shh. Shh." Fortus whispered. "Lie back down." He dipped a cloth in a bowl of water on the table and placed the wet cloth on her forehead. "You fainted, that's all. And it's no wonder. No one, man or woman, could have done what you did for Rome without feeling a great strain." He took Galla's hand.

The events of the night came rushing back to her. "Oh my God, Fortus, Serena! What's happened to Serena?"

"Hush, Galla, it's over. Serena is no longer a threat to Rome," Fortus said in a strained voice.

"Suicide?" Galla asked, hoping that Serena had taken the responsibility for her death into her own hands.

"Strangling," Fortus said softly. Galla let out a small cry. "You did what you had to do, Galla. You had no choice."

"But I've taken a life! God will never forgive me!" Galla stammered.

Fortus stroked Galla's hair. "Perhaps God used you to save many lives."

"Yes, Galla," Julius added, "God works in mysterious ways. It's not up to us to understand them all. You did the only thing you could do. We're very proud of you." Julius looked at Fortus who nodded in agreement.

"Yes," Fortus added. "The men in the barracks say all Rome is talking about you this morning. The senators are saying that watching you address the Senate was just like watching your father. Those old windbags are singing a different tune this morning." Realizing what he had just said, Fortus looked over at Julius. "I'm sorry, Julius."

"It's all right, Fortus. We senators *are* a bunch of old windbags. We need some young folk like you two to teach us something new once in awhile." Galla and Fortus smiled. "Just remember," Julius waved his finger in mock warning, "I said 'once in awhile.' I don't think this girl is up to a steady diet of this sort of thing."

"No! No, I'm not, Julius. You're right about that! I don't care if I ever stand on that Senate floor again," she yawned. Julius and Fortus tiptoed out of the room, and Galla drifted off to sleep.

CHAPTER VIII

Galla awoke to the clamor of voices and vehicles out on the street. She threw a blanket over her shoulders and went to see what was happening. Julius was at the front entrance of the palace standing just inside the open doors.

"Uncle! What's happening? What is all that noise?" Galla asked as she crossed the foyer.

"It is the sound of Romans, my dear Galla, fleeing their own city," Julius said with disgust.

Galla reached the open doors and looked out. The street in front of the palace was lined with carts filled to overflowing with family possessions. Alongside the carts walked persons of all ages, they themselves laden with bundles and cases.

"Where are they going? What will they do? The Goths are outside the walls of Rome! These poor people will be killed!" Galla said fearfully.

"Alaric is allowing anyone who wants to leave Rome to leave safely. He knows that the more persons who desert the city, the easier it will be for him and his men to defeat us when they do decide to attack."

Julius and Galla stood at the door of the palace, watching the unending line of Romans filing past. Finally Julius closed the doors. "I can't watch anymore," he said as he placed the bolt over the opening. "Fortus has been at his post on the north wall all day. He said he'd bring us news as soon as his watch is over. You'll probably prefer to be dressed when he arrives," Julius smiled.

Galla looked down and realized that she had been standing in her sleeping gown, in front of the Imperial palace, watching the procession of deserters. She flushed with embarrassment. "Yes, Uncle, you're right. No wonder no one acknowledged me out there. They must have thought I was a lazy servant girl who hadn't bothered to dress! I'll go change. I wouldn't want Fortus to see me like this!" With that, Galla flushed even deeper.

"Come to the library when you're ready," Julius said, trying to allay her embarrassment. "I'll wait for you there."

Galla arrived at the library dressed in a dark blue silk dress with a wide brocade belt. Her long auburn hair was held back from her face with blue ribbons and it cascaded loosely in soft curls over her shoulders and down her back.

"Well, no one would mistake you for a lazy servant girl now!" Julius said as he stood up and showed Galla to a chair. "Eli has heated some wine for us. Here, take some." Julius poured a tumbler of aromatic red wine and handed it to Galla.

"Fortus hasn't arrived yet?" Galla asked, trying to mask her eagerness.

"Not yet, but he should be here shortly." Julius cleared his throat and Galla could tell that something was on his mind.

"What is it, Uncle Julius? Is something wrong?"

"No, Galla, no. Nothing's wrong," Julius said reassuringly. He cleared his throat again and sat down.

"Fortus is a fine young man, Galla. He's honest, and intelligent, and devoted to Rome. One couldn't ask for a better soldier or a better friend." Julius paused.

Galla leapt to her feet, ran over to Julius and knelt down by his chair. "I was hoping you liked him, Uncle! He really is wonderful, isn't he?" Galla gushed, smiling brightly.

Julius put out his hand and stroked Galla's hair. "Yes, he *is* wonderful. He's perfect," Julius paused again, "except for one thing."

Galla looked up at Julius, the joy fading from her face.

"What? What thing?" she demanded defensively.

"He's not a member of the Imperial family. He is not of noble birth," Julius said hesitantly, knowing that Galla didn't want to hear these words. "He's not even a patrician."

Galla sprang to her feet. "Uncle! I thought you were a Christian! I thought you were above all this patrician-plebeian snobbery. Fortus is a wonderful person and I'm in love with him! I don't care what you say!" Galla felt tears rising in her eyes and she turned away from Julius. She had never before used this tone of voice with Julius. "I'm sorry, Uncle, but I thought you, you of all people, would understand." Galla wiped her eyes.

Julius stood up and walked over to where Galla was standing. "I do understand, Galla," he said with such sadness that

Galla could feel the pain he was experiencing. "I would give anything not to have to say this to you. I love you deeply and I'm very fond of Fortus." Julius took Galla by the hand and led her back to her chair. Julius sat down across from her.

"Honorius has no heir," Julius continued, "and Arcadius' son in Constantinople is only seven. That places a great burden on you Galla. You may be Rome's only hope for the continuation of the Imperial bloodline. An interruption in the chain of Imperial succession could lead to anarchy and even revolution."

"But what about *me*? What about Fortus?" Galla sobbed and pounded her fist on her lap.

"Fortus understands, Galla."

"What do you mean, 'Fortus understands'?" Galla demanded. "You haven't talked to him about this, have you?" Galla's eyes widened with fear.

"It was he who spoke to me about it, Galla. He wanted me to know that he has your best interests at heart--and Rome's best interests. He didn't want me to think he was an opportunist."

Galla fell back in her chair and covered her eyes with her hand. "He won't marry me then?" she asked tearfully.

"He loves you too much to marry you. He knows you are destined for great things and he doesn't want to stand in your way. That's unselfish love--the greatest kind of love." Julius reached over and took Galla's hand away from her eyes. Julius looked at Galla. "No one can stop you from loving Fortus. No one can even stop you from marrying him. It's a decision you'll have to make for yourself, Galla." Julius tucked a stray auburn curl back behind the blue ribbons Galla was wearing in her hair.

Galla scoffed, "It seems as if I'm making a lot of decisions these days, doesn't it? It's as if a month ago I was a child with everyone making my decisions for me and now I'm expected to be all grown up and to make decisions for the entire Empire."

"You don't need to decide anything right now, Galla dear. I just wanted to discuss this with you . . . before . . . before it was too late and things between you and Fortus had gone too far." Julius patted Galla's hand.

At that moment, there was a knock on the library door and Fortus entered. He could tell immediately that something was wrong. He walked over beside Galla and looked questioningly at Julius.

The old man stood up to welcome the guest. "Good evening, Fortus. I'm glad you're here. This niece of mine has it in her head that she's in love with you and I'm trying to talk her out of it."

Fortus smiled and sat down by Galla. "In love with me, eh? Did she really say that, Julius?"

Galla looked at the two men and wondered what other things they had discussed about her in her absence. "Yes, I *did* say that, and you know it, Fortus. But Uncle Julius wants to turn me into some kind of Imperial brood mare. He thinks all I'm good for is bearing little Emperors," Galla feigned a look of anger at Julius.

Fortus took Galla's hand. "Hopefully that will be a long, long time from now." He looked at her with his sea-blue eyes and she could feel the love he felt for her.

"Yes," she agreed. "And if we all pray very, very hard, perhaps Honorius will find a woman stupid enough to marry him and *she* can serve as the Empire's brood mare. I want no part of it. I just want to be left alone and to be happy." She squeezed Fortus' hand and thought how large and strong it felt.

"Here, Fortus, have some of this hot mulled wine," Julius offered as he poured a tumbler full. "Tell us the news. How are things at the wall?"

Fortus took the hot wine and sipped it. "Not good, I'm afraid. People are leaving the city like rats leaving a sinking ship. And not just Romans . . . Gauls, Celts, Iberians, all of them. It's disgusting. Rome gave them citizenship and how do they repay us? They run away at the first sign of danger."

"What about the Goths?" Julius queried.

"There are thousands of them out there beyond the walls. More of them arrive each hour. They have all their wives and children with them and they are setting up camps like they plan to be here awhile."

"Wives and children?" Galla asked with surprise.

"Yes," Fortus replied. "The Goths always take their families along on these forays. They could be gone years and they don't want to be away from the pleasures of home," Fortus said bitterly. "So there they all are, setting up tents and hanging out laundry. One would think we're in the middle of Germania rather than right here in Rome. When I left tonight, the Goths had campfires as far as I could see into the distance. I sure hope Honorius can get troops here in time. If not, there may be a bloody massacre!"

Galla tightened her grip on Fortus' hand. "I'm sorry Galla, I don't mean to alarm you. I should be more careful how I speak," Fortus said softly.

"Don't apologize, Fortus. It is I who should apologize. I don't mean to be so timid. I want to be brave, but, to tell you the truth, I'm beginning to feel very afraid," Galla confessed.

"You don't need to be afraid, not for awhile anyway," Fortus explained. "Alaric and his men don't have the skill or the equipment to besiege our walls. It appears his plan is to wait us out and to blockade supplies going into the city. The warehouses in Rome are fairly well stocked and we can hold out for quite some time. By then Honorius will have been able to gather enough forces to attack and destroy the Goths outside the city walls of Rome. As long as we're inside the walls, I believe we're safe."

"How long do you think our supplies will last, Fortus? Do you have any idea?" Galla asked.

"Well, the generals say we can hold out three months, four if we're careful. The problem will be controlling our own people and preventing them from looting the warehouses. Everything will have to be carefully rationed. We've already arrested some merchants for selling food at twenty times the normal price. There's always someone who will take advantage of a desperate situation. Fortunately, the Church has agreed to help distribute the food. If we all work together, we can hold out until Honorius can come to our aid," Fortus said reassuringly.

Eli entered the library and announced that dinner was ready. Galla, Fortus and Julius went to the dining hall where they supped on broiled pheasant and wild boar, confident that Honorius was, at that very moment, working to gather an army to free the city of Rome from its barbarian captors.

Days became weeks, and weeks became months, but still there was no sign of troops from Honorius. The Church and the army managed to stretch the supplies as far as they could, but at last the warehouses were nearly empty. The Romans began to allow their slaves to flee the city in order to avoid having to feed them. Most of those slaves joined the barbarians outside the walls, and the Gothic troops grew in number and strength each day. By autumn, many Christian Romans had reverted to pagan sacrifices in desperate attempts to appease the gods--any gods who would listen. Hunger and panic gripped the city of Rome.

One morning in early October, when Galla was just returning from St. Peter's Basilica where she had helped the priests distribute the last of the store of grain, Fortus and Pontus arrived at the palace. They were white with fear and they were panting hard from running.

"Galla! We must speak to you," Fortus said between gulps of air.

"Yes, certainly, Fortus. Come in. Let's go to the library. Eli! Eli! Bring water!" Galla led the two men into the library and bade them to sit down.

"Catch your breath, Fortus. My goodness, you're both white as sheets!" Eli entered with a pitcher of water. Galla poured two cups and handed one to each man. "Here, drink this."

"Galla, I . . . I don't know how to tell you this . . . but I must. Two men have just been arrested . . ." Fortus pulled himself to his feet and began wringing his hands furiously. "Galla . . . they were selling children . . . I had heard tales of people so hungry they were turning to cannibalism . . . but this morning we saw it . . ." Fortus retched and appeared as if he were going to vomit. "Galla! Children! They've all gone mad! The world's gone mad!" Fortus cried and fell to his knees, hiding his face in his hands.

Galla felt nauseated and dizzy. She reached for the arm of a chair to steady herself. Poor Fortus! To have seen such an awful thing. She looked at Fortus on his knees on the floor. "He's been so brave," she thought to herself. "He's been here for all of us, working himself to the bone night and day! And now to experience this!" She walked over, took Fortus by the shoulders and helped him to his feet.

"Fortus," she said steadily, "we must get food into the city."

"Food! There *is* no food! People are dying in the streets," Fortus gasped, tears filling his eyes. "They're even . . . children! My God, little children!"

"Fortus, listen to me!" Galla commanded in a raised voice. "I have an idea. I don't know, but it may work. I've been thinking about my father's country villa. The orchards should be ready to harvest now. If we could get there, there would be plenty of food-- not just at our villa, but at the neighboring villas as well."

Fortus looked dumbly at Galla. "You don't know what you're saying, Galla. We can't just walk out of the gates, through the Goths' camps, go pick apples and walk back through again."

"Not *through*," Galla countered, "*under*." She smiled.

Fortus stood staring blankly at Galla. Suddenly, a look of recognition flashed across his face.

"Under! Of course, under! We'll walk out under them! The catacombs! A brilliant idea, Galla! Pontus and I will go immediately," Fortus said and he turned to go.

"Wait! I'm going with you," Galla said.

"No, Galla, I can't let you take that chance. I won't let you," Fortus said firmly.

"It's *my* idea and I'm going. Since when did you start giving me orders anyway?" Galla said with firm resolve.

"Better let her go, Fortus," Pontus said, wakening out of his initial shock. "You've never won against her yet, I don't know why you think you'd win this time." Pontus slapped his friend on the back. Fortus smiled sheepishly and rolled his eyes.

"All right. Get your cloak. And we'll need some bags. The three of us will go out and scout around. For all we know the Goths have already picked the trees bare. Or, worse yet, they may be camped there. Nothing like the Emperor's country villa in which to spend the winter. We must be *very* careful. We don't want anyone to suspect what we're up to. If the Goths find out about the catacomb tunnels, all our fine strong walls will be useless. Go on, get your things," Fortus said, nodding to Galla.

Galla ran off and returned in a few minutes carrying her cloak and a stack of burlap bags. The three left the palace and headed for the old bakery. They went straight to Fortus' room, moved the bed, and lifted open the trap door. The familiar dank odor stung Galla's nose.

Fortus whispered, "Let me go first. I've gone to the villa before through these tunnels and I know the way. Here, take these oil lamps," Fortus said as he handed one to Galla and one to Pontus. "All right, follow me."

The three climbed down the narrow, steep staircase. When they finally reached the bottom of the steps, Galla could see that this branch of the catacombs had not been converted for worship like the tunnels under the country palace. In order to use his subterranean chapel, Theodosius had seen to it that the bodies of the deceased that were interred in the nearby burial areas were respectfully moved to other locations. The deep-tiered recesses along the walls of the palace tunnels were empty. But here, in this unused section of the catacombs, the bodies of the deceased still lay where they were placed centuries ago. Several of the tombs' panels had fallen, revealing the corpses along the walls. Galla gasped.

Fortus took her hand, "Don't look at them. Just look straight ahead and try not to think about it." Galla stood riveted to the ground. "Perhaps you should wait for us upstairs, Galla. There's no need for all of us to go," Fortus offered.

"No. No. I'll be all right. It was just the shock, that's all. Go ahead, I'll follow."

They started off down the narrow passageway. Galla tried to keep her eyes off the skeletons resting in the niches carved from floor to ceiling along each wall. She had never been surrounded by death this way and she was beginning to regret her demand to be allowed to accompany the two men. Galla forced herself to think of the children--those innocent Roman children--who were being slaughtered in the streets above her at that very moment. The thought made her angry and she resolved to continue on the dangerous journey.

Fortus stopped at the point where the first passage was intersected by a second. He held up his lamp and pointed to a small gouge in the wall. "Here. This is a marker. I've marked each turn in the path to the country palace. It's very important not to get lost down here. There are hundreds of miles of these passages, and they are several stories high. If you were to get lost, you might never find your way out, particularly if you ran out of lamp oil."

Pontus smiled and looked at Galla. "What do you think Your Highness? We have our very own Theseus here!"

"Yes, Pontus, I just hope *our* Theseus is not going to lead us through this labyrinth to be eaten by a Minotaur. You've done well, 'Theseus.'" Galla patted Fortus on the shoulder. She turned back to Pontus, "And Pontus, please don't call me 'Your Highness'! It makes me feel so *old*. Please call me Galla."

"Thank you, Your High-, I mean Galla. I'm very honored."

Galla turned back to Fortus, "All right, Theseus, lead on!" And they headed down the second corridor.

One hour passed, then two, then three, as they wound their way through the maze of passages and stairwells. Galla was growing cold and tired and hungry. The straight road above ground from Rome to the country palace was long enough, but this subterranean route was far more circuitous and lengthy than she had ever imagined. Galla stopped walking and leaned against the wall. "Can we rest a moment?" she asked.

"Of course, Galla. It *is* a long way, isn't it?" Fortus replied.

"Yes! And you say you've done this before? What possessed you?" Galla asked.

"You," Fortus smiled. "I did have great hopes for these tunnels," he said as he gave Galla a mischievous smile and winked. Galla blushed.

"We're nearly there," Fortus explained reassuringly. "Only a few hundred yards more. We'd better be very quiet now, just in case the Goths have discovered the stairs from the country palace to the chapel."

"I'm ready. We can go on now," Galla said, encouraged to learn that they were so close to their destination. She longed to be out of the dark musty damp tunnels and to breathe fresh air again.

They made one last turn and Galla found herself in the familiar palace tunnel. They reached the chapel door and stopped. Galla looked up at the slot above the lintel that was to serve as a hiding place for messages.

Fortus saw her glance and he smiled at her. "So much has happened since that day when we agreed to send secret messages to one another," Fortus thought to himself as he watched Galla.

Fortus stopped and took Galla's hand. "You two wait here. I'll go up and see what the situation is. If I don't come back for you in half an hour, assume the worst and head back to Rome as fast as you can."

Galla's heart raced. "Assume the worst?" she thought to herself. The trip through the catacombs seemed like an adventure when they first set out . . . like children exploring a cave. But now Galla was beginning to realize that the game was very real indeed, and very dangerous. For the first time in her life she felt complete and utter fear--not for herself, but for Fortus. She pictured the palace above them--she imagined it filled with Goths buzzing around like hornets--and Fortus was about to walk straight into their nest.

"Fortus! Wait!" Galla cried in a whisper. "Don't go! I've changed my mind. I can't let you go out there!" Galla grabbed Fortus by the arm.

Fortus saw her fear. He placed his hand on her shoulder and looked down into her soft brown eyes. "I have to go out there, Galla. That's what we came here for. We cannot let the people of Rome starve if there's a chance that we can find a way to get food to them. You must get a hold of yourself. I won't take any chances I don't need to take. Just remember, you are to wait here for thirty minutes. If I don't come back by then, you must return to the city immediately. Under no circumstances are you to follow me until I come back and say it's all right. Do you understand?" Fortus asked firmly.

Galla nodded her head, too terrified to speak. She reached up and kissed Fortus. He put his arms around her and held her close for several seconds, and then he released her, turned and disappeared up the stairs to the palace.

Galla and Pontus went into the chapel to wait for Fortus. They both knelt before the altar and prayed for Fortus' safe return. They were still on their knees praying half an hour later when they heard the sound of footsteps running down the stairs. Galla and Pontus leapt to their feet, their hearts racing with fear, their eyes on the chapel door. Pontus drew his dagger and stepped protectively in front of Galla. The sound came closer and closer and finally a figure appeared at the door. It was Fortus! Galla and Pontus ran to him and each put out their hands to touch him, as if to see if he were real or just a specter come to haunt them.

Fortus smiled, touched to see the affection the two showed for him. "I've got wonderful news!" he said excitedly. "The palace is unharmed and the orchard trees are heavy with fruit! I can't understand how the Goths missed this place. It must be that its location is so far west of the main road that the Goths passed by without seeing it! Come on, let's have dinner!" With that, Fortus led Galla and Pontus up the stairs and into the palace.

Galla felt a strange sensation upon seeing the palace again. It was just as she had left it all those months before. Nothing had been touched. It was as if she had never been away. It was as if, in the midst of all the insanity and confusion, one thing had remained unaffected and constant--her father's palace.

"Come on!" Fortus interrupted her musings. He ran out into the orchard and Galla and Pontus followed. Night had fallen and they were hidden by darkness. There, in the dim moonlight, Galla could see the branches of the trees bending down under the weight of the ripe fruit. Fortus reached up and picked a large red apple and handed it to Galla. She bit into the cool crisp fruit. Never, in all the years that she had eaten fruit from this orchard, had an apple ever tasted that good. It was sweet and juicy and delicious.

When the three had had their fill of the delectable fruit, they began to fill the burlap bags they had brought along. "We'll take as much as we can carry tonight," Fortus explained, "and then tomorrow I'll choose fifty or sixty of our best and most trusted troops to come out and begin relaying this fruit into the city."

Galla watched Fortus as he spoke. He was standing silhouetted against the night sky and the moonlight played over his handsome features. Galla thought, "How brave, how kind, how wonderful he is." Several months ago Galla believed she loved Fortus as much as was humanly possible. Tonight she knew differently.

CHAPTER IX

The fruit from the orchards staved off starvation in Rome for several weeks. There were no more verifiable reports of cannibalism, but the approach of winter and the absence of any word from Honorius in Ravenna presaged the return of the heinous crimes. The Senate in Rome, seeing no alternative, finally decided that they would try to meet the demands of the Goths. The state coffers were empty, so all available precious metal objects in Rome were ordered melted down and either minted into coins or formed into bars in order to pay off the barbarians and secure the release of the city from the Gothic blockade.

Within days, the public spaces of Rome were emptied of their beautiful bronze statuary. The Senate appealed to each and every Roman to contribute precious jewelry and artworks. Even the Church was prevailed upon to part with cherished religious objects. Finally the money was raised and a treaty was drawn up between Rome and the barbarians. On the day of the first snowfall, the Goths packed up and moved a hundred miles north to Etruria. The city was freed from its barbarian noose and supplies were quickly brought in to relieve the hunger and suffering of its inhabitants.

On the morning of Christmas Eve, Galla was reading in the library when Eli entered carrying a small scroll sealed with dark blue wax. Galla smiled at the familiar chi-rho and she thanked Eli. Galla opened the scroll and read the neat, clear handwriting.

Galla,
Since the withdrawal of the Goths, our time on duty has been reduced. I have arranged to have this evening and tomorrow free that I might spend this holy time with you. Will you do me the honor of allowing me to accompany you to the services at St. Peter's Basilica this evening? I will await your reply.
Your devoted Fortus

Galla stood up and walked over to the writing desk. She quickly wrote a reply inviting Fortus to come to the palace at his earliest convenience. She sealed the note, called for Eli, and instructed her to have the note delivered to Fortus.

Galla returned to her chair but she didn't pick up the book she had been reading. Instead she sat, looking at the fire in the brazier, and thinking of Fortus. She had seen him so seldom in the past few months; she missed him dearly. It would be good to have some time with him.

Eli returned to say that she had found an errand boy and that she had sent him to deliver the note to Fortus.

"Eli," Galla said, "tonight is Christmas Eve. I'd like to have a special dinner. What do we have in the pantry?"

Eli sighed and shook her head. "Not much, my Lady, even without the barbarian blockade, supplies are hard to come by this time of year. The routes over the Alps are already snowed in, so the only supplies we can get must come from the south. Even much of what comes up from the south goes to the Goths up in Etruria, from what I hear."

"Goes to the Goths? What do you mean, Eli?" Galla asked with surprise.

"Well, we've been waiting on a shipment of pepper from the port at Brandisi, but now we're told the Senate sent all three thousand pounds of it to Alaric and those barbarians up north!" Eli said indignantly.

Galla let out a sigh, "I'd hoped the money would satisfy them, but I don't think they intend to be satisfied. I think they intend to sit up in Etruria like leeches and to continue to drain Rome's lifeblood. Well," Galla sighed again, "this is the first time Fortus has been able to come for a visit in over a month. Do the best you can. I want to give him a nice dinner. I'm sure the food in the barracks has been awful, what there has been of it." Eli nodded her understanding and left the room.

From the festive glow of the oil lamps and the cheerful animated conversation, no onlooker would have guessed that the evening's dinner consisted of bits and pieces that Eli managed to gather that afternoon. Galla looked at each dish as Eli served it and she marveled at her old nurse's ingenuity. There were pears soaked in brandy, a hearty stew of rabbit and root vegetables, and even a venison pie. Fortus ate with such enthusiasm that he had to stop occasionally to apologize for his poor manners. It was clear that he appreciated his hostess' excellent dinner and Galla was glad to see him enjoying himself.

Julius, too, seemed in exceptionally good spirits. He was happy to have Fortus' male companionship. Julius saw the men in the Senate nearly everyday, but what he really enjoyed was talking to the soldiers, the men on the front lines like Fortus. It reminded him of his youth when he, too, was a soldier in the service of Rome.

After dinner, Galla, Fortus and Julius went to St. Peter's Basilica to celebrate mass. The basilica was built nearly eighty years earlier but careful maintenance had kept it looking like the day it was dedicated by the Emperor Constantine as both a place of worship and as the sacred burial site of St. Peter, the apostle of Christ.

As they mounted the front steps, Galla remembered how her father had loved this Holy place. Theodosius had always admired the simple, austere brick exterior and how it contrasted with the brilliantly lit interior of the basilica. Theodosius said it should be the same with a good Christian--simple and plain on the outside, with the brilliant light of the love of God on the inside. Galla, too, loved this old basilica. She liked the way the thick walls shut out the outside earthly world, and how once inside, she felt like she was in a different, spiritual world.

This evening, the interior of the basilica was not as brilliantly lit as in other years. Candles and lamp oil were in great demand now and their prices were too dear for the impoverished Church. Nor was the basilica as full of worshippers as it had been in earlier, happier years. Thousands of Rome's Christians had fled the city before Alaric's blockade.

Many of the Christians who had remained in Rome after the blockade had reverted back to pagan practices to worship the ancient gods in desperate hopes of freeing Rome from the barbarian hoards. Even on this Christian Holy day, there were thousands in Rome who were celebrating the ancient pagan deity Mithras in hopes of attaining everlasting life through baptism in the blood of slaughtered oxen. Galla shuddered to think how this Aryan mystery religion, banned by her father nearly twenty years before, continued to hold power over so many of the merchants and soldiers.

Galla and her two escorts walked down the long central nave and took their places in the Imperial box in front of the altar. Pope Innocent I led the mass himself this evening and he was assisted by many members of the ever-increasing hierarchy of the Church. The voices of the men's choir echoed and reverberated off the high walls and open timbered ceiling. The scent of incense filled the room and the flames of the oil lamps flickered and gave animation to the frescoed murals on the walls.

The mass was longer than usual this year as the Pope prayed over and over to God to bring peace and prosperity back to Rome. Finally, the worshippers filed up to the altar to partake of Holy Communion, the bread and the wine, symbols of the flesh and the blood of Christ, the promise of life-everlasting in His Name.

When the service was completed, the congregation remained in their seats until Galla passed by. The homage paid to her by the parishioners always made Galla feel uneasy. "We are here to pay reverence to God, not to me," she thought to herself as she left the warm light of the basilica and went out into the cool, crisp night air.

Galla's carriage was waiting by the front of St. Peter's and she, Julius and Fortus headed in that direction. When they were but a few yards from the carriage, a man stepped directly into Galla's path, causing her to stop abruptly.

"Good evening, Your Highness," the man said boldly.

Galla immediately recognized Marcus, Serena's haughty young friend.

"Good evening, Marcus." Galla replied coldly. "May God bless you this Holy night." And with that Galla tried to continue on her way, but Marcus once again stepped in front of her.

"Perhaps Her Highness has forgotten about our . . . our . . ." Marcus stopped, searching for a neutral word, "about our *business* agreement." Marcus looked directly at Galla and she could see his determination.

"No," Galla replied, "I have not forgotten our business agreement." Galla looked quickly at Fortus, eager that he not detect any problem. "Come to the palace next week and we'll discuss the matter further." Galla nodded politely and Marcus stepped out of her way, bowing deeply.

"Until next week, Your Highness," Marcus said smugly and sauntered away.

Once in the carriage, Fortus could contain his curiosity no longer. "What was that about, Galla? What business dealings could you have with Marcus?"

"Oh, you know Marcus, do you? Where do you know him from?" Galla asked casually, hoping to change the subject.

"I know *of* him--his reputation anyway--and what I hear isn't good. He's a notorious opportunist, for one thing--he bends whichever way the wind blows. After Serena was out of the picture, this Marcus fellow took up with Attalus, a real scoundrel."

Seizing the opportunity to draw the conversation onto another topic, Galla interrupted, "Attalus. I believe I've heard that name before. Who is he again?"

Fortus played directly into her hands. "Attalus is Prefect of Rome, but if the truth be known, he's really a friend of Alaric, the barbarian chieftain."

Galla began to find the topic of Attalus of more than simply diversionary interest. "The Prefect of Rome is a friend of Alaric, that despicable Goth?" she asked with concern.

"Yes. Alaric has been busy making friends in Rome. He's making promises to whomever will listen."

"What can Alaric possibly promise anyone in Rome?" Galla inquired.

"Well," Fortus continued, "as incredible as it may seem, considering we are supposedly under a truce with the Goths, Alaric still has aspirations to rule Rome one day and, as Emperor of Rome, Alaric can offer political appointments, military positions, things like that."

"Emperor of Rome! Alaric? A Goth? Surely no one *believes* anything like that, do they?" Galla said with alarm.

"Some people do . . . scoundrels like Marcus and Attalus do anyway. Those are two very dangerous men. I don't like to see you involved in business dealings with either one of them," Fortus warned.

Galla looked down to avoid Fortus' eyes. She had never thought of Marcus as anything but a rather presumptuous pretty young boy--she had certainly never considered him dangerous. And she certainly never expected to see Marcus again after that night at Serena's villa. "Surely Marcus must know that I never intended to honor that devil's bargain," Galla thought to herself. "I'll just talk to him, that's all. Surely he'll listen to reason."

Galla looked back up at Fortus. "It's nothing for you to concern yourself over, Fortus. It's just an insignificant business deal, that's all. I can handle it. And then I promise to have nothing more to do with him," she smiled.

Fortus looked at her with concern. "If you need any help, let me know, all right?"

"Yes, Fortus, certainly. It really is nothing, nothing at all." Galla turned to Julius who had been listening silently. "It really was a lovely mass this evening, wasn't it, Uncle?" and the topic of conversation turned to the worship service and Christmas.

When Galla awoke the next morning, the city of Rome was dusted with snow. The sky was clear and blue. She and Fortus planned to ride to the hippodrome and to exercise their horses there. It had been months since Galla had ridden Odysseus and she was eager to get started. She dressed quickly in a warm woolen tunic, ate a small piece of bread with olive oil, and headed for the lane behind the palace where Fortus was standing by their horses waiting for her. The air was cold and Galla could see the horses' warm breath turning white in the frosty air.

"Good morning!" Galla called to Fortus as she exited the palace. "Have you been waiting long?"

"No, I just got here. Cold, isn't it? The horses are a bit unsure of the snow, so we'll have to take it slow until we get to the hippodrome." Fortus leaned his shoulder on Odysseus's side, put his arms down straight and laced his fingers together. Galla placed her foot in the little step he'd made and he lifted her up on Odysseus' back.

"I must be getting old," Galla joked. "You never helped me up on a horse before!"

"Well, you'll be nineteen next week. I figure it's about time I start treating you like a lady instead of one of the boys," Fortus quipped as he leaped up upon his horse.

The two set off along the busy streets to the hippodrome. It was December 25th, but the streets of Rome were still crowded and noisy. Even the snow couldn't muffle the din of the city. Galla was glad when they finally reached the arena and she could let Odysseus gallop freely.

She and Fortus had been riding in the arena for about an hour when Galla noticed a small cluster of men watching them from up in the stands. Galla galloped over to Fortus and said, "Don't look up now, but I think we're being watched," and she rode away, pretending not to notice the men in the stands.

A short while later, Fortus rode up alongside Galla and the two walked their horses side by side.

"Well, well. What a coincidence." Fortus exclaimed sarcastically. "It's your young friend Marcus again . . . and this time he's with that Attalus fellow."

"What are they doing here?" Galla wondered out loud, drawing on all her willpower to refrain from looking up at the men.

"I don't know," Fortus said slowly, "but I for one have had enough riding for today. Shall we return to the palace?"

"Yes," Galla answered, happy to be away from the menacing Marcus.

Galla and Fortus rode back through the busy streets to the palace. The day was growing slightly warmer and the snow was melting into little rivulets between the paving stones. Merchants and beggars called out to the two as they rode by. Galla was relieved when they were both back, safe within the palace walls.

Julius was waiting for them in the dining hall where Eli had placed a steaming pot of pork sausages with carrots and parsnips. Galla and Fortus joined Julius and the three began devouring the hot meal. Galla was carefully picking the parsnips out of her bowl of stew and setting them to the side, when Fortus addressed Julius.

"Julius, we saw that man Attalus at the hippodrome today. What do you know about him?"

Julius was busy picking up Galla's discarded parsnips and popping them into his mouth--after the famine of the blockade,

Julius had determined that nothing would ever be wasted again, not even parsnips. He didn't respond immediately to Fortus' inquiry.

Fortus rephrased his question. "Julius, have you ever heard anything about that new Prefect Attalus?" Fortus asked again.

"Yes. Yes. I've heard about him . . . just rumors, nothing for certain. I wouldn't want anything I say to go any farther than this room." Julius paused and looked up at Fortus and then at Galla.

Galla and Fortus both stopped eating and nodded their understanding.

"Well," Julius continued, "it's all just speculation, you know. And it's rather complicated. I've heard that the barbarian Alaric plans to depose Honorius."

"Yes," Fortus responded, "I've heard that, too. Alaric has some crazy notion that he can make himself Emperor of Rome, but what does that have to do with Attalus?"

Julius lifted his eyebrows and took a deep breath. "It seems that Alaric realizes that a Gothic chieftain has little chance to seat *himself* on the throne of Rome, so Alaric has devised a plan to depose Honorius and to make this Prefect Attalus the new Emperor. It appears that Alaric believes that this Attalus would make a good puppet that Alaric could manipulate for his own greedy goals."

Galla and Fortus both stared at Julius in dumb amazement.

"Yes," Julius said, "that's the word in the Senate. But remember, it's just a rumor. There are lots of rumors going around Rome these days."

Julius picked up a sausage with his knife and bit off one end. He looked at Galla and Fortus who had not changed their expressions of utter disbelief. Julius shrugged, "Well, you asked. Don't look at *me* that way. I'm not deposing anybody. I'm just reporting what I hear at the Senate."

Galla picked up her wine cup and took a long drink. She looked at Julius. "Uncle, I don't understand. How does anyone think that Alaric, of all people, can depose Honorius and set up his own Emperor instead? The very idea is utterly ridiculous!"

"Well, not too ridiculous, Galla," Julius responded, "considering your brother's actions these last few months. The

Senate has sent messenger after messenger to Honorius in Ravenna, but as of yet, we have not received one word in return. He's incommunicado, whether by choice or by force, we can't say for certain. One thing *is* certain, for the last several months, Rome has been a ship adrift at sea without a captain. The people are calling for a new Emperor. Honorius has no son and neither do you. Arcadius' son is too young to rule his *own* half of the Empire, let alone *this* half as well. There is no one inside your family who could rule, no *male* anyway, so the Senate is beginning to talk about looking outside the family."

Julius looked down to avoid Galla's eyes. "I'm sorry, my dear, you know how I feel. I wouldn't want to see your family ousted from power for all the world. If only Honorius would *do* something . . . I just don't understand." Julius took a sip of wine and shook his head sadly.

Galla stood up from her dining couch and began to pace the floor. Julius' words raced through her mind. Finally she stopped pacing and faced Julius. "Why Attalus? What makes Alaric, or the Senate, or *anyone* for that matter, think this Attalus would be a good Emperor?" Galla asked.

Julius smiled, "Oh, I don't believe anyone thinks Attalus would be a *good* Emperor. And that's exactly why they want him to be Emperor. A *good* Emperor would be intelligent, a *good* Emperor would work hard for the best interests of Rome, a *good* Emperor would care. With Attalus, they wouldn't have to worry about any of those things. They would simply tell him what to do and he'd do it--for the right price, of course. And no one would have to worry about this Attalus fellow getting any of his own ideas. *That's* why Attalus seems to be the popular choice, by both the Romans *and* the Goths. Both sides believe he is the ideal *compromise*," Julius added sarcastically.

"*Compromise!*" Galla shouted. "*Compromise!* They can't compromise Rome!" Galla threw herself back down on her dining couch and pounded her fist on the arm. "If only I could rule!" Galla moaned with frustration.

"Ah, well, now you've hit on it, Galla," Julius laughed bitterly. "That's what many of them are afraid of--that you not only *could* rule, but that you *will* rule." Galla looked up at Julius, her face revealing her incomprehension. "Yes, Galla, that's what the Senate fears . . . that you might take the reins of government yourself. They fear it not so much because of your gender, but because of your politics. You're an old fashioned Roman. Did you hear yourself when I uttered that word 'compromise'? You can't stand the sound of that word--neither could your father--and neither can I! But that's what the Senate wants now--compromise. They're sick of all this business with the Goths. They want a formal, official treaty with the Goths, but Honorius won't sign it--or can't. Either way, the Senate wants peace, and they don't think you'd give them that." Julius stabbed another sausage with his knife.

Galla picked up a carrot and began chewing on it thoughtfully. "Do you think the Senate would ever let a woman rule, providing she had the right political leanings, of course?" Galla asked.

"They might," Julius answered. "They're watching Constantinople right now. Arcadius' son Theodosius is only seven and too young to rule, but his sister Pulcheria is older and she's a force to be reckoned with, I'll tell you. She's younger than you Galla, but she has the officials at Constantinople dancing to her tune. The senators here in Rome are afraid you'll take a lesson from Pulcheria and that you'll try to usurp Honorius' position before they find a more, shall we say, *agreeable* replacement."

Galla remembered her niece Pulcheria. When Galla visited Constantinople as a young girl, she was forced to play with the young Pulcheria. Galla recalled the occasions with displeasure. Pulcheria was a selfish, whining little brat who always insisted on having all the toys. It wasn't hard for Galla to imagine Pulcheria as a headstrong young woman, threatening harm to her little brother if she couldn't always win the game.

"So, the Senate is afraid of me. Ha! I can tell them one thing, I'd rule a damn sight better than that selfish, spoiled brat Pulcheria!" Galla hissed.

Both Julius and Fortus looked up at Galla and raised their eyebrows. Neither one of them had ever heard Galla utter a word of profanity and this outburst startled them. Julius laughed, "You've been around us army men too much, I'm afraid, my dear. Our bad habits are rubbing off on you."

Galla smiled sheepishly. "I guess they are. This whole thing just makes me so mad, that's all," Galla paused. "Well, this is no fit topic for Christmas Day. Let's talk about something more amusing. Tell me about the celebration you two have planned in honor of my birthday. I hope it's worthy of the future Empress of Rome," Galla teased and laughed. Julius and Fortus laughed with her and the conversation turned to the party planned for the following week.

The day of her nineteenth birthday finally arrived and Galla awoke early, eager with anticipation. Even at this early hour, wonderful smells were emanating from the kitchen. Galla sat up in bed and breathed deeply, trying to guess what delectable dishes were already cooking on the broilers and in the ovens.

Anta brought in a small platter of toasted bread spread with soft cheese and placed it on the table next to Galla's bed. Galla ate quickly, slipped out of bed, and walked into her bath area where Anta was filling the tub with water from heated kettles.

"I still don't know what to wear today, Anta," Galla said, exasperated that she couldn't come to a decision. "I have all those beautiful clothes, but none of them seems perfect for today," Galla sighed.

Anta stopped pouring the hot water; her face flashed a happy smile. "Look, my Lady, look!" Anta ran from the room and returned carrying an exquisitely woven woolen gown. Anta smiled broadly.

"Anta! It's so beautiful! The colors are like a fabulous sunset over the sea--yellow, orange, red--I've never seen anything so beautiful."

"And look, my Lady!" Anta held up a matching shawl, edged with long fringe.

"Anta! It's lovely! It must have cost a fortune! Who sent it?"

Anta shrugged her shoulders and shook her head. "I don't know, my Lady. A delivery boy brought it early this morning. He said he didn't know who sent it. He was just told to deliver it to Her Highness, Galla Placidia."

Galla walked over and took the beautiful shawl from Anta and held it up in the morning light. It was woven so finely; it felt like a soft cloud. She examined the fabric--the threads had been dyed individually and then woven into a pattern of colorful bands of shaded colors.

Galla smiled, "Well, now I know what I'll wear today! It's the most beautiful shawl I've ever seen . . . and the dress--look how the colors are shaded, lighter yellows across the breast and the hips, darker reds at the shoulders and the waist. Whoever wove this beautiful gown certainly knows how to show off a woman's figure to its best advantage."

Galla held the dress up to her body, imagining how she would look in the magnificent garment. "Yes, Anta. I've decided. *This* is the dress I'll wear for my birthday celebration today. I can't wait for Fortus to see me in it! This will take his breath away." Galla handed the gown and shawl back to Anta. "Hang them up carefully, Anta. I want them to be perfect for the party."

Galla bathed and Anta did her mistress' hair in the latest of fashions with full round curls piled high atop her head. Then Galla slipped into the beautiful new gown and placed the soft shawl over her shoulders. Anta laced fine gold sandals onto Galla's lovely narrow feet. Galla picked up the polished bronze mirror and surveyed the results. She was very happy with what she saw. The sunset colors of the gown and shawl looked beautiful with her red hair and amber eyes.

"Well, I guess I'm ready," Galla said somewhat nervously. "I hope this is a wonderful party--one that I'll always remember!" With that, Galla left her rooms and headed for the dining hall where the guests were already gathering for the day's festivities.

When Galla arrived at the dining hall, she paused briefly at the door. Morning sunlight bathed her figure and reflected off her auburn hair. The effect was as if she were sunlight itself. The guests all stopped talking at once and turned to stare at the radiant creature at the door. Galla saw their stunned reaction to her beauty and she suddenly felt very embarrassed.

"Good morning, my friends, welcome to our home," Galla said somewhat awkwardly, trying to break the spell that she had cast over the guests in the room.

Julius was the first to speak. "Galla, my dear, you have never been lovelier . . . nineteen becomes you. May you always be as beautiful as you are at this moment." Julius walked over to Galla, took her hand, kissed it, and then held it high above her head. "Ladies and Gentlemen, I present to you Her Highness, Galla Placidia Flavius!"

With that the crowd cheered and applauded. Galla smiled broadly, pleased to receive such an enthusiastic ovation from Rome's leading citizens. Galla walked into the room and began greeting her company. Julius had drawn up the list of distinguished guests. Among them, Galla recognized several of the senators before whom she spoke that fateful night in the Senate. They greeted her with warm respect. One by one, Galla welcomed her guests and bade them to enjoy themselves.

When she had, at last, reached the end of the large hall, she saw Fortus and Pontus standing by a potted rose tree in the corner. Galla walked quickly over to where the young men stood and she began to give Fortus a welcoming hug, but Fortus stepped back imperceptibly.

"Not here, Your Highness, the guests would not approve," Fortus smiled and lifted his eyebrows as his eyes scanned the room.

Galla looked back over her shoulder and then turned back to Fortus. "Yes," she sighed, "you're probably right. Well, I'll owe you a hug then," she smiled mischievously.

"Gladly," Fortus replied with a broad grin, "I'll hold you to that debt."

Galla blushed and turned to Pontus. "Pontus, what you must think of us, behaving in this manner."

Pontus smiled and said, "I think it's wonderful that two persons can care so deeply for one another. You are both very fortunate. May I extend my best wishes to you on this special occasion, my Lady? And thank you for including a humble soldier in your festivities." With that Pontus bowed deeply.

"There he goes again, Fortus," Galla quipped, "all that 'my Lady' and 'Her Highness' business again." Galla turned to Pontus and her look became serious. "Pontus, I would like to think we are *friends*, *equals*, so please call me Galla. You have already done more for me than I can ever hope to repay. Please do call me Galla, I want to be friends."

Pontus smiled, "All right then, 'Galla' it will be. I want to be friends, too. It's easy to see why Fortus loves you so dearly."

Fortus was so touched to see the two persons he loved most getting along so well, he reached out his arms and embraced them warmly. As suddenly as he had made the impulsive gesture, he regretted it. He looked up to see if anyone had noticed and he caught the icy stares of two men looking directly at him. It was Marcus and Attalus.

Fortus dropped his arms and stepped back from Galla and Pontus. He looked at his two friends and, still smiling, said, "Don't look now, but we're being watched. Laugh like I'm telling you a joke." Galla and Pontus laughed on cue. "Good," Fortus continued, "just act casual. There are two very interesting guests over there--no! Don't look! I don't want them to know that we know they're watching. It's that despicable Attalus and his little dark shadow Marcus."

"Attalus and Marcus!" Galla exclaimed, her eyes widening, "What are *they* doing here? Surely Julius didn't invite *them*!"

They probably invited themselves," Fortus replied. "All of Rome knows it's the birthday of the noble Galla Placidia. There are festivities going on all over the city. Those two probably just came without an invitation, after all, who would turn away Attalus, the Prefect of Rome, or the handsome Marcus, son of a prominent senator?" Fortus scoffed.

"Oh no!" Galla pouted. "I did so want this party to be perfect. I'll only be nineteen once, you know."

Pontus laughed, "Oh, I don't know about that, my sister has been nineteen for three years now, but still she has no suitors!"

Fortus threw Pontus a cautionary look.

"It's all right Fortus," Galla said warmly. "It was a good joke, Pontus. Fortus is worried that I'm insulted because I'm nineteen and I have no suitors. The only person I *want* to marry, I'm told I *cannot* marry," Galla looked at Fortus. "So I'm very happy to be without a suitor. If I can't have the one I want, then I will have no one." Galla smiled. "Tell me about your sister, Pontus. If she looks like you she must be *very* lovely. I'm surprised a sister of yours wasn't married off at a very early age!"

Pontus blushed at the compliment. "She is pretty, very pretty. Her name is Claudia and if she'd had a dowry, she could have been married many times. But our parents died when we were very young. I joined the army a year ago when I was seventeen. I'm saving all I can to give her a dowry. She's taken care of me since our parents died and she deserves a life of her own now." Pontus stopped speaking, afraid that he'd talked too much.

"Claudia. What a beautiful name," Galla exclaimed, touched to see Pontus' affection for his sister. Galla's brothers could have provided a grand dowry and allowed her to marry at any age, but they were conniving and selfish and declined to do so. And here was this young soldier, selflessly saving his meager salary to give his sister a proper marriage. "You choose your friends well, Fortus." Galla said. "One can always judge a man by his friends." Galla looked up proudly at Fortus and then at Pontus. "Please go on, Pontus."

Pontus continued, "When I first met Fortus, I thought he'd make the perfect brother-in-law, but then he told me about you. And then I *met* you, and, as lovely as Claudia is, she can't compare to the noble Galla Placidia," Pontus blushed.

"I think Pontus here has a bit of a crush on you, Galla, just like *all* the men in Rome," Fortus laughed and Pontus blushed even deeper.

"I'm very flattered," Galla said sincerely. "Pontus, you must bring Claudia to visit us. Perhaps we can have a little party for her, introduce her to some young men. If she's as pretty as you say she is, she may not need your hard-earned soldier's pay. You can save that for your own bride."

The trumpets sounded and luncheon was announced. Julius had arranged for braziers to be lighted to warm the large peristyle garden, so, even though it was nearly January, the guests could dine outdoors among the greenery and fragrant winter roses from the greenhouse. The guests filed out into the lovely manicured garden where tables were piled high with culinary delicacies--wild boar with raisin wine sauce, pheasant stuffed with figs, tureens of vegetable stew, and trays of honey cakes and brandied apples . . . and wine--pitchers and pitchers of wine.

When all the guests had been served and their wine glasses filled, Julius stood up and proposed a toast. "To the noble Galla Placidia, descendant of Constantine the Great, daughter of Theodosius the Great, sister of the Emperor Honorius, and, God willing, future mother and grandmother of great Emperors of Rome! We salute you and we drink to your good health!"

The guests all raised their wine glasses and shouted in unison, "To your Health!" and they drank their glasses dry. With that the feast began.

Galla giggled and blushed at the toast to her health, pleased to be saluted by the highest persons in Rome. It was only when she turned to Fortus that she regained her composure. He had not drunk from his cup; he sat staring blindly at the ground, the muscles in his temples revealing his tension.

"Fortus, what's wrong?" Galla asked with concern.

"Oh, Galla! I'm sorry," Fortus looked up and smiled in an attempt to hide his sadness. "To your very good health!" and then he, too, drank the contents of his wine glass.

"Was it Julius' toast?" Galla asked. "That business about future mother and grandmother of Emperors? Don't let that bother you, Fortus. Julius is a very wise man, but even *he* cannot predict the future." She smiled warmly and Fortus' melancholy passed.

"I don't believe I told you how lovely you are today, Galla. Your gown is almost as lovely as you are yourself. I don't think I've ever seen anything quite like it. Where is it from?" Fortus asked.

"I don't know," Galla replied. "I had hoped *you* knew," she smiled. Fortus looked blank. "It's not from you, then," she said with a degree of embarrassment on behalf of Fortus. "It must be from Julius then," Galla said quickly. "It arrived this morning without a note. It really is lovely, isn't it?"

"Yes," Fortus agreed, picking up a corner of the shawl and examining the excellent craftsmanship. "I don't believe I've ever seen a fabric that finely woven, and in such brilliant colors. It would take more than a poor soldier's pay to purchase a valuable garment such as this." Fortus dropped the corner of the shawl he was holding. "Pontus and I brought you those pheasants they are serving today. That's where we've been the last two days, out in the countryside hunting. I know it's not much, just pheasants," Fortus apologized, avoiding Galla's eyes.

"Oh Fortus, but you knew I *love* pheasant. How thoughtful of you and Pontus. It's so cold this time of year! You two must have frozen out there in the countryside. It was a great sacrifice for you to make on my behalf. Thank you so much!" And she took a bite of the broiled pheasant on her plate. "It's wonderful really. It's been so long since we've had pheasant--before those awful Goths came. I'm sure all the guests are enjoying it," Galla said enthusiastically.

Just then Julius walked up and Galla said, "Isn't the pheasant delicious, Uncle Julius? Fortus and Pontus brought it."

"Yes," Julius replied, "I was in the kitchen this morning at dawn when they arrived. They brought a whole cart full of them, enough for all the guests. We are truly grateful to you two young men for helping us to entertain our guests in such a splendid manner. Thank you, Fortus."

"You're welcome, Julius. Galla was just showing us her beautiful new dress. It's very lovely. Doesn't it become her well, Julius?"

"Yes, Uncle," Galla gushed, "I don't know how to thank you. It must have been very expensive. You shouldn't be so generous, really."

Julius interrupted, "I wish I could take credit for the gift of the lovely gown, but I've never seen it before. It really is striking and it suits you perfectly. You look like Aphrodite herself in it!" Julius laughed, and then grew serious. "So, you don't know where this valuable gift came from? That's odd, for surely it must have cost a small fortune. Quality like that doesn't come cheap."

"You're right, Julius," an unfamiliar male voice replied. "It did cost a small fortune."

They all looked up to see Attalus standing in front of them, with Marcus at his side. Julius, Fortus and Pontus all quickly rose to their feet, half out of instinctual courtesy, half out of a desire not to be looked down upon by these two unwelcome intruders. Galla remained seated, frozen with apprehension.

Attalus continued, "But I figured the cost of the gown was inconsequential when I considered the worth of the recipient."

Attalus bowed deeply, took Galla's hand, and kissed it before she could withdraw it. "Many happy returns of the day, Your Highness."

"I am at a disadvantage, sir," Galla replied coldly. "I do not believe we have been introduced."

"My name is Attalus. I am Prefect of Rome, and, as such, I am your devoted servant." Attalus bowed a second time, leaning forward to look Galla directly in the eye as she sat stiffly in her chair.

"Then, am I to assume this gown was a gift from you, sir?" Galla said in her most formal tone.

"Yes, Your Highness, I ordered it from Parthia especially for you. I see I chose well. You and the garment are well matched in beauty."

Galla did not smile. She stood up and looked at Attalus, her chin held high. "If you will forgive me, sir, I was under the impression that the dress was a gift from a close family member. Since that is not the case, it would not be proper for me to wear it any longer. I cannot accept such a valuable gift from a . . . a . . . *stranger*." Galla emphasized the last word slightly. "If you will excuse me, I will go and change immediately."

Galla turned to leave, but Attalus stepped in front of her. Fortus and Pontus each took a step forward, prepared to defend Galla from Attalus' unwanted advances.

"Your Highness," Attalus said in a softened tone, "if you feel you must return the dress, then do so, but please do so later. Do me the honor of wearing it the rest of the day. To do otherwise might draw the attention of your guests and cause me great embarrassment."

Galla turned and looked directly at Attalus, "It is *you*, sir, who have caused *me* great embarrassment. I will return the dress at once. Please allow me to go to my chambers."

Fortus and Pontus took another step towards Attalus who then stepped away from Galla, bowed deeply and said, "As you wish, Your Highness."

Galla left the five men standing there as she exited the peristyle garden and went to her rooms to remove the now despicable dress. Galla felt that as long as she was wearing that man's dress, it was if his hands were all over her.

Without stopping to explain to the confused maidservant Anta, Galla entered her room, took off the shawl and dress, and went into the bath to wash herself before returning and putting on a dark blue silk gown. Galla pointed to the brightly colored shawl and dress lying on the floor. "Anta, please fold those carefully and set them by the front door. See that Prefect Attalus takes them with him when he leaves," Galla ordered.

Galla returned to the party just as the entertainment was about to begin. She purposefully avoided returning to the place where Attalus and Marcus were still talking. She scanned the large peristyle and finally spotted Fortus and Pontus seated in the far corner, watching the acrobats from Africa. Galla spent the remainder of her party with her two friends, as far away from Attalus, and from Marcus, as possible.

When the party was finally over and all the guests had left, Galla returned to her rooms, sat down at her writing table, and began to remove her jewelry. "Anta?" Galla called. "Anta? Are you here?" There was no reply and Galla assumed that Anta and the other servants were enjoying a well-deserved party of their own in the kitchen with the leftovers from the banquet. Galla removed the ribbons from her hair and unwound the long curls.

As she began to brush her long hair, she sensed the presence of someone else in the room. "Anta? Is that you?" Galla asked, continuing to brush out her long, thick hair. Still, there was no reply. Galla stopped brushing her hair and listened. She heard a rustling sound and she turned around to look. Within a split second, someone grabbed her and put his hand over her mouth. Galla turned to see the offender. It was Marcus. Galla struggled to free herself but Marcus held her tighter.

"Don't scream or I'll break your arm!" Marcus whispered, twisting his hand harder around Galla's wrist. Galla dug her teeth into Marcus' hand, which was covering her mouth. He drew it away quickly and blood poured from his palm.

"Why you little . . . listen to me Galla, you may think you're so high and mighty, but if you don't *give* me what you promised, then I'll *take* it!" Marcus bent Galla's arm harder and pushed her onto the bed. She screamed as he began to tear at her dress.

The door burst open and Fortus and Pontus ran into the room, daggers drawn. Marcus drew his dagger and held it to Galla's throat. "One move from either of you two, and I'll use it, I swear I will," Marcus hissed.

Fortus and Pontus stopped in their tracks, afraid for Galla's life if they took any further action to help her.

Marcus yanked Galla off the bed by her arm and steered her over to the open window, still holding the sharp dagger against her throat. Marcus stepped out the window, dropped the heavy bronze grate down over the opening, and ran off into the darkness.

Fortus and Pontus raced out after him, leaving Galla collapsed on the floor in tears. She could hear the shouts of men outside. "Fortus, oh Fortus!" she thought fearfully. Several minutes passed before Fortus came back in through the open window. Galla was still on the floor, holding her neck.

Fortus swept her up into his arms, carried her over to the bed, and laid her down gently, propping her head up with a pillow. "Are you all right, Galla?" he asked. She nodded, still in shock. "Pontus has called the guards. Marcus won't get away. Thank God we waited."

"Waited?" Galla asked weakly.

"Yes, we waited down the street and watched all the guests leave. We never saw Marcus leave and we figured he was up to something. I never thought he'd be so brazen as to pull anything like this though." Fortus looked at Galla and stroked back her hair. "Are you all right, my poor darling?" Fortus said with concern.

Galla covered her face and began to cry. "Oh Fortus, I'm so ashamed. It's all my fault. It's all my fault," she sobbed.

"No, Galla, no. It's not your fault! You did nothing wrong. Marcus is a criminal and he'll pay for this, you'll see."

"No Fortus, it's *my* fault. I made a promise. I didn't mean to keep it, I just wanted the information, that's all," Galla said shaking with sobs. "Someone could have been killed. Oh Fortus, I'm so sorry." Galla wrapped her arms around Fortus and cried violently.

When she had calmed down, Fortus unwound her arms from around his neck, he leaned back and he looked deep into her eyes. He asked firmly, "What promise, Galla? Explain what you mean."

Galla looked up fearfully at Fortus. "Oh Fortus, I can't tell you, you'll hate me! You'll never speak to me again."

"I could never hate you, Galla, not if you're honest with me. What happened here tonight is *not* your fault, regardless of *anything* you said or did. Marcus is the only one who is to blame. Now, tell me."

Galla recounted the whole story for Fortus who listened patiently and sympathetically.

When she was finally finished, she sighed and said, "Please don't tell Uncle Julius, Fortus. He'd be so ashamed of me."

"Ashamed, no," Fortus replied, "perhaps a bit disappointed that you'd do something so foolish. We can *all* learn a valuable lesson from this . . . only promise what you plan to deliver." Fortus kissed her on the forehead and smiled.

There was a knock on the door and Pontus entered. "Did they find him?" Fortus asked hopefully. Pontus shook his head and looked discouraged. Fortus turned to Galla, "We'll stay here outside your door tonight, Galla, darling. If you need anything, just call."

Fortus got up to leave, but Galla took his hand. "I'm sorry, Fortus, really I am."

"Nothing to be sorry about, Galla, we all live and learn. You were only eighteen when you made that silly mistake. You're nineteen now and *much* wiser." Fortus smiled, winked at Galla, and left the room.

CHAPTER X

Months passed, but the culprit Marcus was not seen again in Rome. Rumor was that he had fled to Ravenna and had sought sanctuary there. There were also rumors to the effect that Honorius was gradually rebuilding his armies. He still steadfastly refused to acknowledge the treaty with the Goths that the Senate had drawn up in the last months of 408. Alaric and his tribes were growing restless up in Etruria and the Senate in Rome feared a renewal of the blockade of the city if Honorius didn't confirm the treaty.

The rains had once again nudged the tiny buds on the trees into full blossom and a soft warm breeze heralded the onset of summer. Galla and Julius had kept busy in the spring by planting a large vegetable garden in the unused peristyle at the back of the city palace. They were in the garden, on their knees, digging weeds out of the rich black earth, when Eli came out to announce lunch.

Galla stood up and rubbed her back. "Oh! I'm stiff from bending over," she moaned. "It must be old age."

Julius looked up and gave her a sarcastic look. "They just don't make young people like they used to. Back in my time, we worked twenty hours a day in the fields."

Galla laughed. "Oh, Uncle, you never worked a day in the fields in your life!"

"Well, no, but I *wanted* to. I just never had the time, that's all. It's good finally to have the time," he said as he dug out one more large weed and slowly stood up.

Galla sighed, "It seems like all we have anymore is time, too much of it if you ask me. I'm getting bored."

"Well, if you're getting bored, perhaps we should begin planting that vacant lot on the other side of the wall over there. If the Goths do return and blockade the city, we'll have plenty of carrots, anyway. And parsnips!" Julius added with a grin.

Galla gave her Uncle an impatient look. "Everyone in Rome is planting every available square inch. I don't think the Goths *will* come back and we probably won't be able to *give* this produce away. Besides," she sighed again, "I'm tired of working. I want to do something fun. Things are just so dull around here with Fortus and Pontus gone all the time."

Julius looked at Galla and smiled. "'Dull.' You're in one of the most exciting cities in the world and you say it's dull. Why don't you go visit the libraries or some of the ancient sites?"

"I've done all that," Galla said with irritation, "and besides, it's so boring alone. Fortus is too busy with his new commission to spend much time with me, and I hate going to those places alone."

Julius nodded, "I know Galla, I haven't been much company either, I've got so much work to do in the Senate. What you need is a new friend--a girl your own age--someone who won't be off working all the time."

"Uncle! What a wonderful idea! And I know just the girl. Claudia! You remember Fortus' friend Pontus, don't you Uncle?" Julius nodded and Galla continued, "Pontus said he has a sister named Claudia. She's just three years older than I and she isn't married, either. Oh, it would be lovely to have a *girl* to talk to . . ." Galla looked up at Julius quickly and said apologetically, "I'm sorry, Uncle, I *love* talking with you, but there are just some things that girls like to talk about that . . . well . . . that . . ."

Julius chuckled. "Yes, I know all about 'that . . . that . . .' and I agree. You need another young girl to talk to and to do things with. Have you met this young . . . um. . ."

"Claudia, her name is Claudia," Galla said. "No, I haven't. Last winter I told Pontus I'd have Claudia to one of our parties but we haven't had a party since then."

"Well," Julius said with enthusiasm, "then we shall have one now. No time like the present." Julius secretly hoped that the thought of a new party might serve to displace the memory of Galla's last party that ended in such disaster.

"May we?" Galla asked excitedly. "That would be wonderful. And it would give me something to do," she looked over at the garden, "something *fun* to do, for a change."

"Yes, something fun," Julius agreed. "Young people should have something fun to do on occasion. When you're older, there's so little fun . . . you should take advantage of it while you're young." Julius put his arm around Galla. "We'd better go in to lunch now, my dear, or Eli will have a fit. She doesn't like it when we're late. It always pays to keep the cook happy--that's something I learned in the army. It's a good rule." Galla laughed and they went into the palace.

After lunch, Galla hurried to her rooms to begin planning the party. Galla decided that, for the very first time, she would plan the party entirely by herself. She would select the date, draw up the guest list, decide the menu, and order the entertainment. "It's about time I became the mistress of the household. I'm not a little girl anymore and I've got to take over these responsibilities one day, so why not now?" she thought to herself as she sat down at her little writing desk and began to plan the festivities.

She began by deciding the date--the summer solstice. The date had ancient pagan connections, but they could ignore the antiquated sacrificial rites and simply celebrate the first day of summer. "I hope this summer is warmer than last," Galla thought as she recalled the cold and damp of the past summer. Next Galla drew up the guest list--Fortus, Julius, Pontus, several other young men from the barracks, the usual senators and generals and their wives, and, of course, Claudia, the guest of honor.

Galla decided she should begin by inviting Claudia, to be certain that she would be able to attend on that date. It wouldn't do to have a party without the guest of honor present. Galla brought out a nice piece of vellum and wrote out an invitation in her very best penmanship. She rolled it up, sealed it with hot wax and stamped her Imperial seal onto it. She called Eli and asked her to find a delivery boy to take the scroll to Claudia. Then Galla began work on the menu and the entertainment.

It was late afternoon before Galla completed her initial preparations for the party. When someone else planned a party, it didn't seem to matter much if the broiled duck was served in orange sauce or lemon sauce. Now that it was her *own* party, and now that such decisions would reflect her *own* good taste, it mattered very much in which sauce the duck was served. Everything mattered more now. She wanted this to be the most memorable party ever, and she wanted to show all Rome what an excellent hostess she could be.

That night at dinner Galla delighted Julius with her explanations of the various party plans. Not only had Galla never *planned* a party before, she had never *paid* for one either. Several times during the discussion Julius had to stop Galla to inform her that certain of her proposed plans were not within the current palace budget. Julius was pleased that Galla didn't allow these financial constraints to dampen her enthusiasm.

After dinner, Galla and Julius went into the library. It was a cool evening and Julius' manservant Joseph lit a fire in a brazier. Then, just as Joseph was lighting a small bronze oil lamp next to Julius' favorite reading chair, there was a knock on the door.

"Come in," Julius commanded.

The door opened and Fortus entered with Pontus following behind him.

"Welcome! Welcome!" Julius struggled to his feet. "We were just wondering what to do with our evening. Now we are four. Perhaps we could play a board game. Can I offer you each a nice cup of this excellent wine?" Fortus and Pontus nodded gratefully. "Sit down, sit down," Julius continued. "This is quite a coincidence, isn't it Galla?" Julius looked at Galla and then at the two young men. "We just spent the whole of dinner talking about you two."

Fortus laughed, "I don't think we're interesting enough to talk about through an entire dinner, do you Pontus?" Fortus looked at Galla and smiled, "You must have been at a loss for conversation."

Galla replied, "Oh, no! We had much to talk about. I have wonderful news! I'm planning a party. It's in honor of your sister Claudia, Pontus. I sent her an invitation and I'm waiting for her reply."

Pontus looked down awkwardly, "I'm her reply. You see Your High . . . Galla," Pontus corrected himself, "Claudia knows neither how to read nor write. The aunt who raised us after our parents died was very conservative. She didn't believe girls needed an education, other than to learn how to cook and to keep house. While I was at school, Claudia stayed at home, learning what my aunt called the 'Household Arts.' When Claudia received your invitation, she came to me to have me read it to her." Pontus paused. "She's very flattered and grateful for your thoughtfulness, but I'm afraid she says she'll have to decline."

"Oh," Galla said with disappointment. "Is it the date? If she has other plans that day, we can choose another date that would be better for her."

"No. It's not the date. It's just . . . just . . . well, she has nothing to wear and she says she'll feel out of place in such fine company. I told her how wonderful you are," Pontus looked down with embarrassment. "But she's shy. I hope you'll forgive her."

"Of course I forgive her, Pontus. But I won't *excuse* her. I have dozens and dozens of gowns that I haven't worn in ages. I insist on giving her one so she can come to the party. Tell me about her. How tall is she?" Galla asked in a tone that Pontus recognized as more of a command than a question.

"Well, she's about your size, except not as tall," Pontus said, feeling awkward to be discussing such personal matters in front of the noble Galla Placidia.

"Good!" Galla said. "And is she fair or dark? I want to chose something that will flatter her complexion."

Pontus cleared his throat. "Well, she's fair, very fair. She has hair the color of . . . of . . ."

"Of flax," Fortus finished Pontus' sentence.

Galla looked at Fortus. "You've met her, then, have you Fortus? Tell me more. What color are her eyes?"

"They're blue," Fortus replied without hesitation.

"Blue," Galla said. "How clever for you to have noticed, Fortus."

Fortus heard the slight sarcasm in Galla's voice and realized that he had perhaps been too observant in regards to Claudia's appearance. He decided to let Pontus do the rest of the talking.

"And her complexion, is it very light? Galla looked at Fortus who simply shrugged his shoulders.

"Yes, very light," Pontus replied, realizing the delicate position in which Fortus had placed himself. "It's kind of you to lend her a dress. I think she'd really love to come. She just wants to look nice."

"Of course she does," Galla said, her tone softening. "That's perfectly natural. Every woman wants to look pretty. You wait here, I'll go chose something lovely for her." Galla smiled at Pontus and then gave Fortus a sidelong glance. "Any more *details* I should know about Claudia before I select a dress, Fortus?"

Fortus lifted his eyebrows and shook his head trying to look as innocent as possible. "No, nothing more. I don't recall another thing about her."

"Good," Galla teased, seeing that her jealousy was unfounded. "See that you don't remember anything else, all right?" She smiled and left the room.

"Whew!" Fortus whistled.

Julius smiled. "Let that be a lesson to you two young men. Just when you think you're on solid ground with a woman, you find yourself on thin ice." The three men laughed. "How about another glass of wine?" Julius offered. Fortus and Pontus accepted gratefully.

"Julius," Fortus began, "have you heard any news from Ravenna? Has Honorius agreed to sign the treaty yet?"

Julius shook his head. "No, no word. We just hear rumors, that's all. I'm sure Alaric and his people hear them, too. I *do* know that Honorius has managed to gather quite an army again." Julius sighed deeply. "No treaty and a large army . . . it doesn't look good." Julius rubbed his hand across his forehead.

"Any news about the Goths?" Fortus asked.

"We've had reports that they are building up their forces again, too. After the blockade, many of Alaric's people moved on. You know, most of them don't want war. They don't care about politics. They just want a full belly and a tent over their heads. It's this Alaric who has all the big political aspirations."

"I've heard there's another Gothic leader named Athaulf. What do you know about him?" Fortus inquired.

"That's Alaric's brother. From what I hear, he's a good man, reasonable, levelheaded. But you know those Goths and their tribal system, fanatics really. They pledge their loyalty to the one leader and they'll follow him off the edge of the earth. Those Germanic tribes are all the same . . . just like sheep blindly following the leader off a cliff . . . no minds of their own. Too bad this Athaulf isn't their leader; we might have a chance negotiating with him, but that won't happen, not as long as Alaric is alive."

Julius took a long sip of wine. "It's good, isn't it?" Julius asked, holding up the wine goblet. Fortus and Pontus nodded their agreement and Julius refilled their cups. "Funny thing about this fine wine," Julius continued, "it's from Germania of all places! Ironic, isn't it? That an unruly gang of cut-throats like the Goths can come from an area that produces a fine wine like this!" Julius smiled sardonically.

"It is excellent wine. I don't believe I've ever tasted better," Fortus commented. "Julius," Fortus said hesitantly, "have you heard anything more about the Prefect Attalus and his plans?"

"Only what we already knew--that he's a real social climber. He's got half the Senate fooled into believing he's got a brain. Those old windbags, as you call them, Fortus, are easily fooled. 'Most of them don't have any brains of their own," Julius said bitterly. "Most of them don't have any backbone either. They're afraid of Alaric and most of them would do anything to appease him and prevent another blockade or even an all out war."

Julius stood up, walked over to the brazier and put another chunk of coal on the fire. "I've learned to take things one day at a time," Julius said as he returned to his seat. "Not like the old days. But then you young folk don't want to hear about the old days."

Just then Galla re-entered the room carrying a stack of clothes. "I just couldn't decide," she said, "so let Claudia decide for herself. Take them all to her, as a gift from me. She'll have to shorten them, but then she's skilled in the 'Household Arts,' isn't she? At least she learned something practical, unlike me. I can't remember the last time anyone asked me to recite Homer in Greek, or to conjugate a verb in Gothic, but there are many times that I've wished I could sew!" Galla handed the stack of dresses and shawls to Pontus who accepted them gratefully. "I'm very eager to meet Claudia," Galla said enthusiastically. "I simply can't wait for the party!"

Time passed quickly and the day of the party arrived before Galla had completed all her preparations. "Oh, Anta!" Galla worried as she quickly dressed the morning of the party, "I still have so much to do! The guests will be arriving by late afternoon and I still have to oversee the decorations in the dining hall."

"The men are already at work on the decorations, my Lady," Anta consoled, "and Eli says everything in the kitchen is going fine."

"Well, I'd better go check, just to be sure," Galla said as she raced out the door. Entering the kitchen, Galla found Eli, Gaia, and all the kitchen staff hard at work. Galla walked from table to table, inspecting the various dishes that were being prepared. Then Galla went to the dining room where Julius' manservant Joseph was directing the decorations of garlands of laurel leaves with clusters of pink roses. After seeing that all the interior decorations were going well, Galla went out into the peristyle garden to oversee the last minute touches on the exterior decorations.

Galla was directing the placement of a large vase of flowers, when Julius entered the garden. "Hello, Uncle!" Galla called out. "It's a lovely day for the party, isn't it?" she said happily.

"Yes, Galla, a lovely day," Julius replied. "Eli sent me out to fetch you, she has lunch ready in the alcove off the kitchen. We'll be out of everyone's way there. I nearly got run over twice this morning just walking from my quarters to the library. Come in now, let's have lunch." Julius put his arm around Galla and they went inside to the little alcove. The simple table was set and Eli had left a tray of cheese and fresh fruit.

"Galla," Julius began as the two were seating themselves, "there's something I want to talk with you about."

Galla knew Julius well enough to recognize that his tone of voice meant that what he had to say wasn't good. Galla sighed, put down the cheese she was holding, and looked at Julius. "Please, Uncle Julius, no bad news, not today. Can't it wait until tomorrow?" she pleaded.

"No, it can't," Julius said firmly. "You'll know soon enough anyway, but I thought if I told you first, then you could prepare yourself."

Galla sighed deeply again and said, "All right, what is it?"

"There will be an extra guest at the party today . . . one who's not on your guest list." Julius stopped and cleared his throat. "It was unavoidable, simply unavoidable. I had to say he was included when the senators asked. I had no choice." Julius fumbled with some grapes but didn't eat one.

Galla's mind raced through a list of persons whom she would find unpleasant to have at her special party. It stopped on one name. "Oh, no, Uncle. Not Attalus!"

Julius nodded sadly. "The senators all wanted to know if he would be here. To say that he was *not* invited would have been a great insult to him and, I'm afraid, it would have made your position here in Rome even more difficult than it already is, my dear."

"But Attalus, of all people. Why does *he* have to come and spoil my day?" Galla pouted.

"Neither he nor the Senate perceives his attendance as spoiling your day. As a matter of fact, they perceive his desire to attend your party as a compliment to you and your ancestors." Galla flashed a look of disgust at Julius. "Yes," Julius continued, "the fact of the matter is that the Gothic chieftain Alaric is demanding that your brother Honorius be deposed. Alaric, with the consent of many in the Senate, has proposed to make Attalus the Emperor of Rome."

Galla felt as if she were going to become ill. "Can't I even have *one* day," she thought to herself, "just *one* day to myself? Must my entire life be manipulated and pushed and pulled?" She put her hands over her ears to block out the sound of Julius' voice.

Julius reached over and patted Galla's knee tenderly, then he reached up and took her hand from her ear. "Not hearing what I have to say will not alter the situation, my dear. You've always wanted to hear the truth before."

Galla dropped her other hand limply down into her lap. "Oh, all right, go on," she moaned.

"You're going to hear all this at the party, Galla, and I just want you to be prepared. We don't want anyone to think we are ignorant of current events, do we?" Galla shook her head and Julius went on, "There's a very good chance that Alaric and the Senate may get their way. Honorius still has many supporters, I among them, but we simply cannot get him to sign that treaty. As long as Honorius hides in Ravenna and refuses to deal with the problem with the Goths, Attalus' chances of becoming Emperor grow greater and greater each day."

"So? Even if Attalus *does* become Emperor, I don't see what it has to do with today and my party," Galla objected.

"Attalus has no real grounds to overthrow Honorius or to establish himself as Emperor. He's been Prefect of Rome, but he's not of Imperial blood . . ." Julius looked at Galla, "although he could *marry* into the Imperial family and thereby establish his legitimacy."

Galla sprang to her feet, a look of horror mixed with disgust on her face. "Not *me*! They're not thinking of marrying *me* to that Attalus, are they? Oh, Uncle, tell me it isn't true!" Galla begged.

Julius stood up and put his arm around Galla. "All they're doing at the moment is talking, nothing more than talking. I've heard people talk for years and never take any real action. I've found the best thing to do is to let them talk. No use arguing and getting upset until they've made a decision and they're ready to act. In the meantime, we'll let them talk, odds are they'll talk themselves right out of it."

Julius helped Galla back into her seat and he, too, sat down. "Besides," he chuckled, "you're not the only fish in the marriage sea, it would appear. Some of the senators have suggested a union between Attalus and Pulcheria over in Constantinople." Galla looked up hopefully and Julius went on, "If Attalus is as greedy as I think he is, he may not settle for marrying solely into the Western Empire, he'll want to marry into the Eastern Empire and then rule the East and the West." Julius cut off a slice of cheese and handed it to Galla. "So you see, my dear, there's nothing to worry your pretty head over today. I invited Attalus here as an outward showing of our good will . . . to refuse him would upset him and it might force his hand. People often want most what they can't have. Let Attalus believe he can have you, and then, perhaps, he won't want you as desperately."

"Oh, all right, Uncle. As usual, your point is well made, and, as usual, I am glad you were honest with me," Galla smiled. "It's a good thing you warned me that Attalus would be here today.

If his arrival had caught me unprepared, who knows *what* I would have done . . . probably doused him with wine!"

"Oh no! Galla," Julius responded, "never douse an unwanted guest with wine . . . wine is too valuable. Douse them with something cheaper, like beer!" Galla laughed and they changed the topic of conversation to the more pleasant subject of the pending festivities.

After lunch, Galla returned to her rooms to begin getting ready for her party. She had a massage with oil of lavender from Gaul and then she bathed in perfume of heather from Britain. After Anta had completed her exquisite coiffure, Galla dressed in her finest gown of blue silk. Fortus liked blue and Galla wanted to be especially beautiful for him today.

At the appointed hour, Galla stood in the entrance hall and received her guests . . . noted senators, generals, public figures, clergymen, and, of course, her close friends. As arranged, Fortus and Pontus were to arrive last and to bring the guest of honor, Claudia, with them. Galla wanted the great hall to be full and all the guests settled when she introduced her special guest.

Finally, Fortus and Pontus arrived. "Good afternoon," Galla greeted them warmly, "and welcome!" Galla looked about expecting to see Claudia. "Where is your sister, Pontus, is she not with you?" Galla asked with some alarm.

"Yes, she's just taking an extra breath of air. I think she's a bit faint with apprehension. A visit to the Imperial palace to meet the noble Galla Placidia is enough to make anyone faint at heart," Pontus explained.

Just then Claudia appeared at the door. Galla had expected Claudia to be very pretty, but she had not expected the exquisitely lovely young woman who now stood before her. Galla took Claudia's hands and welcomed her warmly. Galla then stood back and appraised her guest.

"Claudia, your brother said you were pretty, but his vision was dulled by brotherly love. You are truly beautiful!" Galla said sincerely. Claudia blushed with pleasure. Galla recognized the light golden gown that Claudia was wearing. Claudia had shortened Galla's gown in front to match her own shorter stature, but she had left the back of the hem long, so it trailed out gracefully behind her as she walked. Rather than belting the gown at the waist, as was the fashion of the time, Claudia had gathered the voluminous folds of the dress with flowing gold ribbons and tied them just under her bosom, accentuating her full breasts. The gold ribbons were the only accessories Claudia wore. Her milk white arms and throat were bare. She wore her smooth blonde hair long and simple, cascading in gentle waves down her back. The air around her smelled of fresh roses. The overall effect was of an ethereal golden angel floating in a sea of light. Claudia smiled, revealing beautiful pearl white teeth.

"Thank you for inviting me, Your Highness. My brother speaks of you often and it is a pleasure to meet you," Claudia said in a sweet, even voice as she curtsied deeply. Her cheeks were flushed with pink and her clear blue eyes shone with pleasure.

Galla thought to herself, "I see how Fortus remembered the color of her eyes . . . only a blind man could have missed their lovely pure cornflower blue color."

Galla wrapped her arm around Claudia's and said, "Let's go into the dining hall now. I can't wait to see the faces of the guests when they behold you my dear Claudia. You are truly a vision!" They turned and had begun walking to the dining hall when a loud voice stopped them.

"Greetings," the voice boomed, "Greetings one and all!" Galla turned back to see who had so rudely interrupted her carefully planned entrance into the dining hall. It was Attalus. He was striding towards her with one arm extended, prepared to take the liberty of kissing Galla's hand. Galla placed her other hand on Claudia's arm and looked at her unwelcome guest.

"Ah, Prefect Attalus, how good of you to join us. The guests are assembled in the dining hall. Please go in and make yourself comfortable. We will be in shortly," Galla said, stopping where she was immediately in front of the entrance to the dining hall.

Attalus was obviously very pleased that Galla remembered him and he took it as a sign of friendliness. "You're looking lovely today, Your Highness. And who is this charming young lady you have with you?" Attalus leered down at Claudia.

"This, sir," Galla replied coldly, "is our guest of honor whom I was just about to announce."

"Wonderful! Wonderful!" Attalus boomed out. "Let's not waste another moment! Let's go in!" With that, Attalus swept Galla and Claudia through the double doors and into the dining hall. All eyes turned to the doorway where Galla stood, Claudia on one side and Attalus on the other. The guests cheered the arrival of their hostess. The supporters of Attalus cheered the loudest, believing that he was serving as host of the day's festivities. Galla had no choice but to introduce her guest of honor and, as she did so, Attalus walked around to the other side of Claudia. When Galla finished her speech of introduction and said, "Ladies and Gentlemen, I present to you Claudia, the guest of honor," Attalus proudly led Claudia forward, as if he were, in fact, the formal host of the party. Galla was left standing by the doors, alone.

Fortus and Pontus had followed Galla into the dining hall and they witnessed Attalus' maneuver. They quickly walked up to Galla and stood at either side of her. They smiled and looked out at the crowd. Without looking down, Fortus muttered under his breath, "You have to give him credit, he's good at what he does, even if what he does *is* despicable."

"Yes," Pontus replied, "any general would be proud of a brilliant maneuver like that."

"Gentlemen," Galla said, smiling and speaking through her clenched teeth, "I am in dire need of a glass of wine." Galla took Fortus' arm and the three crossed the large hall nodding to guests along the way. When they reached the table at the far end of the hall, a servant poured goblets of wine for them. Galla took a long drink. Over the rim of the cup she watched Attalus introducing Claudia to the various guests.

"Shall I go fetch Claudia away from Attalus?" Pontus offered.

"No, Pontus, I don't want to embarrass Claudia by letting her know she's been a pawn in Attalus' game. It would spoil her day. She doesn't know who that awful man is and it looks as if he's actually amusing her."

Galla watched as Attalus entertained Claudia. It was the first time that Galla had really looked at Attalus. He wasn't bad looking . . . a man in his late thirties, tall, with dark hair and dark eyes. She wondered why the sight of him repulsed her so much. To many women, he would appear as an attractive catch, but to Galla, he represented treachery and a threat to her Imperial lineage. She thought to herself, "This man could put an end to the bloodline of Constantine the Great and my father, Theodosius the Great. If he usurps Honorius' position, all that will be ended, unless . . ." Galla felt a wave of nausea, "unless I marry him--or unless Pulcheria does," her thoughts brightened when Galla remembered that there was that alternative. "I'll pray," Galla continued thinking to herself, "that Attalus is as greedy as he appears to be and that he won't settle for *just* the Western Empire."

The musicians from Dacia began to entertain and Galla realized that she had been ignoring her guests. "It is, after all," she thought, "*my* party and Attalus or no Attalus, I'm going to enjoy myself." Galla turned to Fortus and Pontus and began talking with them about their new commissions defending the Salarian Gate of Rome. After awhile, Attalus returned Claudia to Galla's presence.

Uncle Julius saw the opening and he cleverly whisked Attalus away on pretense of discussing urgent business. Galla was glad to have Claudia to herself and to have the opportunity to get to know her. The two young women learned they had much in common. Galla liked Claudia immediately. She found Claudia to be an intelligent girl with pleasing manners and a simple, direct charm. It was clear that the two were fast becoming good friends.

The party proved to be a great success. The first course of oysters in cumin sauce was served in the dining hall. When it was completed, the guests moved out into the peristyle garden for the remainder of the feast. Tables had been placed at intervals around the circumference of the garden. A different group of delicacies was to be found on each table--seafood on one table--wild game on another--domestic fowl on another. The guests were invited to wander about the garden and to serve themselves whatever they desired. Servants strolled among the guests, refilling glasses and taking away discarded plates.

It was a warm evening and the flowers in the garden were in full bloom. At dusk the servants lit oil lamps that floated on the surface of the long reflecting pool. Several groups of musicians took turns entertaining the guests. There were no dancers or acrobats; Galla had decided that type of entertainment was not proper in a Christian household. None of the guests seemed to miss the absence of such entertainment and, from the sound of the chatting and laughter, they all appeared to be enjoying themselves immensely.

It was well after midnight when the last of the guests finally departed. Julius had already retired, but Galla, Claudia, Pontus and Fortus remained in the garden enjoying one another's company. At last, Pontus and Claudia said their good-byes and left. Galla and Fortus remained alone in the garden. They were seated at one end of the long reflecting pool and the brilliant stars in the night sky were mirrored in the still water. Galla shivered.

"Are you cold?" Fortus inquired. "Here," he said as he wrapped Galla's shawl over her shoulders.

"That's better, thank you," Galla smiled at Fortus and nestled under his arm. She sighed with deep satisfaction. "It was a lovely party, wasn't it?"

"Yes, a lovely party," Fortus agreed, happy to be alone with Galla.

"The way it started out, I thought it was going to be a disaster," Galla said with relief.

"By the way," Fortus sat up straighter and turned to look at Galla. "What was old Attalus doing here anyway? Did he come uninvited again, like he did to your birthday party?"

"No. He was invited. Julius invited him," Galla answered and then explained to Fortus all of the unpleasant dealings going on with Alaric and the Senate. She even told Fortus about Attalus' desire to marry her . . . or Pulcheria. "I've made up my mind to pray that it's Pulcheria, if it happens at all." Galla paused.

Fortus took Galla's hand and said, "You know, when you were going to be betrothed to Eucherius, I rationalized it to myself. After all, Eucherius was a member of the Imperial family, and a marriage between you and him seemed to make sense at the time-- big tub of lard and all. But Attalus is a nobody. He doesn't even deserve to be Prefect, let alone Emperor of all Rome! I can't rationalize that. It just makes me plain angry." Fortus squeezed Galla's hand.

"Well, hopefully it will never happen," Galla said consolingly, "not with Attalus, anyway." Galla wrapped her hands around Fortus' powerful arm. "Fortus, when I *do* get married, if I *have* to, that is, what will you do?"

"Oh, I don't know," Fortus replied. "I haven't thought much about it. It's not a pleasant thing to think about."

"But you'll have to do something. What do you think it will be?" Galla asked.

"I imagine I'll just continue on in the army. I like my work. It's all I know, really," Fortus shrugged.

"I mean *personally*," Galla prodded. "You'll get married, too, won't you?"

Fortus laughed sadly and shook his head. "No. I don't think so. I love *you*. Just because you have to marry for reasons of state doesn't mean I'll stop loving you."

"Oh, but Fortus, you must marry one day. You'll need a wife to take care of you and children for your old age. Certainly you'll marry one day."

Fortus sat silently watching the stars sparkling in the night sky. "I'll never love anyone but you, Galla."

Galla sighed, "Who says you have to *love* someone to *marry* them? Look at me! I have to marry whomever the Senate decrees. Will they ask me if I'm in *love*? No. You know, Fortus, marrying because of love is really a luxury . . . only the very rich can afford it . . . or the very poor. Most people marry because of convenience or because it's arranged for them. You're independent. You can choose your own wife. What about Claudia? She's a lovely girl! She'd make an excellent wife."

"Yes," Fortus said, "she would make an excellent wife. She's beautiful, intelligent, hard working, a devoted Christian . . ." Fortus paused.

"And?" Galla asked, suddenly wishing she hadn't brought up the subject of Claudia.

"And, she'd be a perfect wife. No man could ask for more than Claudia has to offer. Any man would be fortunate to marry Claudia," Fortus said sincerely. "Claudia has everything any man could desire."

Galla drew away from Fortus and looked up at him, her large amber eyes reflecting her feelings. "Then why don't you marry Claudia?" she asked sadly.

"Because I don't *love* Claudia. I love *you*, you little matchmaker." Fortus laughed and kissed her on the forehead.

"But Fortus, I don't want you to spend your life alone just because I have to agree to a marriage of state," Galla continued, but Fortus stopped her and kissed her on the mouth. She pulled back and began again, "Promise me if I have to marry that you'll marry Claudia." Fortus kissed her again. She pulled back and looked at him. "Now, Fortus, I'm serious!"

"I'm serious, too." Fortus smiled and kissed Galla a third time.

"Now stop that and listen to me!" Galla insisted but Fortus only kissed her again.

"Well, at least promise me that you'll *think* about marrying Claudia. Promise me that if I have to get married that you'll *consider* marrying Claudia."

Fortus began to kiss Galla again but she placed one finger over his mouth and she looked directly into his eyes. "I won't let you kiss me again until you promise me you'll consider marrying Claudia one day."

"All right, all right, I'll consider it," Fortus laughed.

"Promise me!" Galla ordered.

"I promise," Fortus smiled and he kissed Galla again.

CHAPTER XI

Over the next few months, Galla and Claudia saw one another often and they grew to be close friends. They enjoyed riding horses, visiting the ancient sites, and attending mass at St. Peter's Basilica. Fortus and Pontus would join them on occasion, when their military duties permitted, but usually the two girls contented themselves with their own company.

On one crisp autumn morning, Galla arrived at the Pantheon to meet Claudia. Galla was early, so she decided to look in the shops that lined the lane adjoining the ancient monument. She was browsing through a leather goods store when she overheard two men talking excitedly in the back room.

"No! It can't be!" one of the men insisted.

"But it's true! I tell you it's true!" the other man argued. "I heard it in the forum only an hour ago!"

"But no one can depose an Emperor just like that. Who does this Attalus think he is? Honorius won't take this sitting down. There may be civil war!"

"Ha! Honorius is a spineless worm. What has he ever done for Rome? What has he ever done for *us*? Nothing, that's what. He let us starve last year and he didn't lift a finger to help. I say good riddance. We need some new blood to face up to Alaric."

Just then the two men came out of the back room and into the shop where Galla was standing, eavesdropping on their conversation. The two recognized Galla immediately and they were taken aback to find the sister of the deposed Emperor standing in their shop.

"Your Highness! This is an honor," the one man stammered.

Galla turned and walked quickly out of the shop, leaving the two men staring blankly after her. Galla made her way back to the entrance of the Pantheon where she was to meet Claudia. Just then she saw Fortus, Pontus and Claudia hurrying across the large square in front of the temple. Galla ran over to meet them.

"Fortus," Galla said excitedly, "I just heard that Honorius has been deposed! Is it true?"

Fortus nodded his head. "Yes, Galla, it's true. Come on, let's all go into the Pantheon where we won't be on public display." Fortus took Galla's arm and led her quickly across the square. Several passers-by had recognized Galla as the sister of the unfortunate Honorius and a crowd was beginning to form.

Fortus led Galla and their friends up the steep steps of the podium, across the deep porch, and into the huge circular temple. The ancient building was empty and Galla was relieved to be away from the crowd outside.

"Come, sit down Galla," Fortus said as he directed her to a marble bench along one wall.

"I don't want to sit down!" Galla said with irritation. "I want to hear what's happened! Is it true? Has my brother been deposed?"

Fortus bit his lip and ran his hand through his hair. "Yes, Galla, it *is* true. Alaric has set up his blockade again. He has demanded that Honorius be deposed and that Attalus be put in his place as Emperor!"

"But the Senate! The Senate won't let this happen," Galla said desperately.

"The Senate expected this. They were already prepared for it. They don't want the city to have to go through what it had to endure last year at this time. They have no choice. Honorius didn't do a thing to help the city of Rome last year and since then he's only made things worse. He's refused to ratify the treaty and he's building up his army."

"But he's the rightful Emperor! He's the son of Theodosius . . ." Galla began to cry and Fortus put his arm around her.

"I know," Fortus said softly. "He *is* the rightful Emperor. He has many people still on his side. He also has amassed a large army. He may be able to reclaim his position."

Galla looked up hopefully at Fortus. "Do you think so?" she said between sobs.

Fortus hugged her tightly. "Anything is possible in this crazy world." Then Fortus smiled and said, "All we've heard are rumors. Let's go back to the palace and talk to Julius. He hears the official news from the Senate. Perhaps he can tell us more about what's really going on."

Galla smiled faintly and dried her eyes. "Yes, let's go back to the palace and ask Julius. There's probably no truth at all to this vicious rumor!"

When Galla and her three friends arrived back at the palace, they went straight to the library in hopes of finding Julius there. Julius was there as they expected, but he was not alone. Attalus was with him.

"Good morning, Galla," Julius said in his most officious tone. "You have a visitor." Julius nodded to Attalus who had risen to his feet and who was now bowing deeply.

"Perhaps we should go . . ." Fortus offered and turned to leave.

"No!" Galla commanded. "Stay. Please, everyone, be seated." Fortus, Pontus and Julius helped Claudia to a seat and then they, too, sat down. Only Galla and Attalus were left standing. Attalus pulled out a seat for Galla but she refused.

"I prefer to stand," she said coldly.

"Then so shall I," Attalus replied.

"To what do we owe the honor of this unexpected visit, *Prefect* Attalus?" Galla emphasized the word Prefect.

Attalus smiled and looked smugly at Galla. "Perhaps you have not heard the news, Galla. I am no longer Prefect. I am *Emperor*," Attalus drew out the last word for dramatic effect.

"I heard an ugly rumor to that effect, but I thought it was mere gutter swill," Galla said, her proud Flavian chin held high.

Attalus took a step closer to Galla and he gave her a long appraising look. "I haven't come here to exchange insults with you, Galla Placidia. I have come here to offer my friendship and protection."

Galla turned her back to Attalus and took several steps away from him, but she said nothing.

Attalus continued, "It is understandable that you are upset, Galla. This is, for you, an unfortunate turn of events. I hope you will see that, for Rome, it is the only available option. We must do what's best for Rome."

Galla spun around and hissed, "How *dare* you tell me what is best for Rome! *I am Rome!*"

Attalus picked up his cloak and threw it over his shoulders. "As I said, Galla, I didn't come here to fight with you. I came to offer my friendship and assistance. When you have had time to think this all through, you may see the value of that offer. In the meantime, as I've already discussed with Senator Julius, you may remain here in the palace and I will see that your monthly stipend continues. I want you to be inconvenienced as little as possible by this turn of fate." With that, Attalus bowed deeply and left the room.

Julius quickly closed the door behind Attalus. He knew Galla wouldn't wait for Attalus to be out of the palace before she vented her anger. Julius didn't want to cause any additional animosity by allowing Attalus to hear the insults that Galla would undoubtedly hurl as soon as he was out the door. Julius and the others sat silently, waiting for the tirade they were expecting. But Galla said nothing. She walked over to the window and silently watched Attalus ride off down the street, accompanied by four of her Imperial guards.

She let out a long deep sigh, turned back and looked at her friends. "I know it's early, but I could use a glass of wine. How about all of you?" Galla walked over to the library door, opened it, called for Eli, and ordered wine and lunch brought to the library. Her friends watched her in amazement. She seemed so uncharacteristically cool and calm.

"Galla," Julius said hesitantly, "are you all right, my dear?"

"Yes, Uncle, I'm perfectly all right. I am a little chilly though." Galla went over and put another coal on the brazier. Galla sat down, folded her hands in her lap, and smiled at her friends. "Well, Honorius has been deposed. This is probably the worst thing in the world that could possibly happen to me, but suddenly I feel very free!" Her friends looked at her quizzically. "Yes! I feel free! All my life I've had this heavy Imperial Eagle hanging over my head, dictating what I can and cannot do. But now it's gone! It got up and flew away and now I'm free. Free to live my own life any way I want!"

Eli came in with a pitcher of wine and a tray of cold meats and cheeses.

"Please, help yourselves," Galla offered jovially. "I feel like we should be having a party." Everyone remained seated, motionless and silent. "Well, what's wrong with all of you?" Galla asked. "Aren't you happy for me?" Galla took a long drink of wine.

Just at that moment, the Imperial physician Ptolomy entered the library.

"Ptolomy! What are you doing here? Is someone ill?" Galla asked.

"I sent for him, Galla," Julius responded. "I thought you might be distraught. I thought we might have need of a physician."

"Well, you were wrong! I'm perfectly all right. I'm perfectly ecstatic!" Galla laughed and drank another cup of wine. "The first thing I want to do is to go on a trip. I haven't been out of Italy in years. I'd like to go to Greece . . . or to Egypt! You've been to both of those places, Uncle, which one do you recommend?" Galla asked as she poured another glass of wine for herself.

"I'm afraid it's not that easy," Julius answered softly.

"What do you mean, 'not that easy'?" Galla demanded. "I'm a free woman now. I can go anywhere I want." Galla finished another cup of wine and staggered over to a seat. "Ptolomy! You're not drinking! Have a drink with me, and that's an order! Oops! I can't order anyone anymore, can I? Well, have a drink anyway, Ptolomy! Tell me, Ptolomy, where would you go on a vacation . . . back to Egypt, I imagine."

"Galla," Julius interrupted, "I think it's best if you remain in Rome for awhile . . . to give the appearance of calm and order. The people will look to you for direction."

"To me? Why me? I'm just one of the common folk now. My bother is no longer Emperor, so I'm no longer a member of the ruling Imperial family! I don't owe anybody anything!"

"You are a Flavian, Galla, a member of a very old and a very distinguished Imperial family."

"Where?" Galla shouted. "Where do you see that name written on me? Is it here on my face? Is it on my arms? My legs?

Where is it written? I will wash it off and forever be rid of that name!"

Julius walked over and sat down next to Galla. He put his arm gently around her shoulders. "It's not on the outside that it's written, Galla, it's on the *inside* . . . it's in your *blood* . . . *Flavian* blood . . . and it's in your *heart* . . . You can't wash away who you are on the inside anymore than we can stop the sun from setting. You're a Flavian, Galla, it's part of you . . . just as you are part of Rome and its future . . ."

"Oh Uncle!" Galla sobbed, the wine catching up with her, "I don't want to be a part of Rome! I want to be free! I want to live my own life."

"I know, Galla, I know. But you're a Flavian and you've got that Flavian destiny built into you. And you've got that Flavian strength built into you, too. It won't fail you when you need it most."

Ptolomy mixed a soothing potion and he handed it to Galla. She tried to refuse it, but Julius insisted. After Galla had swallowed the potion, Julius said, "You know, this reminds me of one time when your father decided that *he* no longer wanted to be a Flavian or an Emperor, for that matter."

"My father?" Galla said with disbelief.

"Yes. He was just a little older than you are now and he decided that he, too, wanted to be free of all the Imperial duties and obligations. He had met a beautiful girl and he had fallen in love with her and he wanted to marry her. But the Senate and the Church said no, he couldn't marry her. They called her a heretic. Theodosius was beside himself with anguish. At that moment, he, too, hated the sound of his own name. He wrote the Senate saying that he had abdicated and he ran off to marry the girl."

Galla's eyes widened, "What happened?"

"Well, it took him several days to get to where the girl lived and in those several days he had a lot of time to think . . . and to pray. He said by the time he had arrived at the girl's home, God had given him the answer. He knew he had to continue on as Emperor and to continue on serving Rome."

"What about the girl?" Galla asked.

"The girl? Oh, he eventually worked it out and he married her. That girl was your mother."

"And what about his abdication?"

"Oh, he had given his letter of abdication to me to deliver to the Senate after he had left Rome. I forgot to give it to them." Julius smiled. "I'm telling you this, Galla, because I don't want you to act in the heat of the moment . . . give it time . . . think about it . . . and pray. Put your trust in God . . . He will work it out."

Galla sighed deeply. "Thank you, Julius. I know you're right. I'll think about it . . . and I'll pray." Galla yawned.

Ptolomy whispered, "The potion takes effect quickly, Your Highness, perhaps you should retire to your quarters.

"'Your Highness,'" Galla echoed, "'Your Highness.'" Eli came in and helped Galla to her quarters. They could hear Galla repeating "Your Highness . . . Your Highness" all the way to her rooms.

When Galla awoke much later that afternoon, her head throbbed. "Oh, Anta," Galla mumbled as she struggled to sit up in bed, "what have I done? What have I said?"

Anta helped Galla to her feet and began to dress Galla in a fresh gown. "Your Uncle Julius and the others are worried about you, Your Highness. They are waiting for you in the library."

"Your Highness." The words reverberated in Galla's head. "Oh," Galla thought to herself, "I've made a fool of myself, haven't I? I've let that upstart Attalus rattle me." Galla slipped her feet into the sandals that Anta was holding. "Now is not the time to lose control," Galla thought with resolve, "now is the time for clear thinking. Rome has had many worse usurpers to the throne than this fledgling Attalus and Rome has made it through. We can make it through this, too. But I must get a grip on myself. I must not lose control again."

The throbbing in Galla's head began to lessen. She wrapped a light shawl over her shoulders and headed for the library. She arrived to find Julius, Fortus and Pontus seated around the desk, deep in conversation.

"Where is Claudia?" Galla asked as she entered the room.

"We thought it best if Claudia returned home before the curfew," Julius responded as he stood to greet her.

"Curfew?" Galla inquired.

"Yes," Julius continued, "the rumors have been confirmed. The Goths are heading south towards Rome again. Several thousand are already camped outside our walls. I'm afraid we're in for another long winter like last year."

Galla sighed deeply and Fortus seated her in a chair at the desk. The three men looked at Galla apprehensively.

"You needn't look at me that way. I'm all right, just a bit of a headache, that's all." She smiled sheepishly then added, "You needn't worry about me. I won't fall apart again, at least not on account of that pretentious Attalus."

Julius patted Galla on the back and then resumed his seat at the desk. "It was Attalus about whom we were just speaking when you came in Galla." Julius paused and scratched his head hard as if trying to scrape up the right words.

Galla sighed, "Then the rumors about Attalus are true, too, aren't they? The Senate has deposed Honorius and placed Attalus on the throne." Galla placed both her elbows on the desk and held her forehead in her hands. Her head began to throb again.

"Galla," Julius said in a calm, steady voice, "I've thought long and hard about this and I believe that the Senate had no choice. We've waited for over a year for Honorius to move against the Goths. Meanwhile, the Goths have gained in strength and in number. If the Senate does not reach some sort of compromise with the Goths, I'm afraid Rome will not be as lucky as it was last winter."

"Lucky!" Galla uttered with disgust. "What could be worse than what happened in Rome last year?"

Julius looked directly at Galla and said, "Rome could be destroyed. The Goths could overrun the city, and the city, with everyone in it, could be laid to ruin." Julius did not break his direct stare at Galla and Galla recognized the urgency in his voice. Julius continued, "Within the past year, Rome has lost over half her population. At this very moment, the roads are filled with Romans fleeing the city. Even the Pope himself has given up hope and he has fled to Ravenna to protect himself against the barbarian onslaught. We have no Emperor and now we have no Pope to lead us. The state coffers are empty. I don't see what else we can do

Galla. I'm afraid we must support the decision of the Senate. We must save Rome at all costs, even if it means accepting Attalus as the Emperor. We must bring order to Rome, it's the only way Rome can survive." Julius dropped his steady gaze and he sat back in his chair with a deep sigh.

"Yes, Uncle," Galla said slowly. "I see your point. I agree. Rome must come first. We must do whatever we can to save the city--our monuments--our churches--our *people* . . . How can I help? What can I do?"

Julius sat up, leaned over, and took Galla's hands in his. "You *are* your father's daughter," Julius said with proud affection. "As for what you can do to help, I'm not sure. Perhaps it would be best if you went to Ravenna and joined Honorius there. At least you'd be safe."

Galla smiled and scoffed, "You don't really mean that, Uncle Julius. You know that I would no sooner leave Rome than you would. No, our place is here. It's our duty to remain in Rome and to encourage others to remain also. If we all leave Rome the city doesn't stand a chance. I may be a woman and perhaps I cannot take up arms against the barbarians, but at least I can show them what it is to be a true Roman."

Julius smiled and shook his head. "As much as the 'Uncle' in me would like to see you safely ensconced in Ravenna, the 'Roman' in me is proud to know you're willing to stay here in Rome. Perhaps when the people of Rome hear that the noble Galla Placidia intends to remain in Rome, they will think twice about deserting the city."

"What else can I do to be of use?" Galla asked. "It hardly seems enough just to sit by when there must be much to do."

"Well," Julius replied, "there *is* something you could do, but I'm afraid it's very distasteful."

"What is it?" Galla asked.

"The Senate is planning a celebration tomorrow to announce the appointment of Attalus as the new Emperor," Julius looked up to catch Galla's eye but she was staring at the goblet in her hand. Julius continued, "If you could bring yourself to attend the festivities, to feign your support for the Senate and for the new

Emperor, I believe you could do much to alleviate the fears of the citizens."

Galla sat silently for several moments. "All right, I'll attend their charade, providing the three of you accompany me. I don't want to be alone with Attalus. I don't trust him and what he might do. And I don't trust myself and what I might *say*," she smiled.

Fortus was the first to accept Galla's conditions. He, too, wanted to be present when Galla was in the company of the unscrupulous Attalus. When all the arrangements for the following day had been discussed, they bade one another goodnight. It was long past curfew, so Julius arranged for Fortus and Pontus to spend the night in his small cottage in the garden. Fortus would have preferred to stay alone with Galla for a while longer, but Julius wisely steered Fortus towards the garden and Galla and Fortus resigned themselves to a goodnight wave from a distance.

By the time they arrived at the forum the next day, the festivities were well under way. Fortus and Pontus wore their finest dress armor and Galla beamed with pride as she watched the crowds part for these two handsome young Imperial soldiers. Julius had brought out his formal toga and he looked every bit the dignified Roman senator that he was.

Galla, on the other hand, had taken great care to look as plain and as unattractive as possible. She wore her hair in a tight bun atop her head, her dress was loose and shapeless, and she wore a voluminous shawl over her head and body. Even with these efforts to disguise her comeliness, Galla's natural grace and stately presence shone through and she was recognized wherever she walked. Rumors had spread that the new Emperor Attalus was planning to marry the noble Galla Placidia and everyone was eager to get a look at the prospective bride.

The forum was filled to overflowing with Romans happily celebrating the appointment of the new Emperor. As Galla surveyed the surging crowds, she found it difficult to believe that over half a million persons had already left the beleaguered city. She wondered with amazement at how the government had ever managed to control so many citizens and how the state had ever brought order to so many diverse peoples. She thought briefly of Alexander's dream of a *cosmopolis*--a universal city--one united state with all peoples speaking one common language. What a glorious dream. Rome had nearly achieved that dream . . . they had come *so* close. As Galla watched the thronging masses here in the forum, she prayed that somehow, someway, she could bring that dream to life again.

Just as Galla and her escorts were entering the huge forum of Trajan, two Imperial guards approached her and saluted stiffly. "Galla Placidia, you are hereby requested to join the Emperor Attalus on the Imperial dais in the Basilica Ulpia." The guards saluted again then and, without waiting for a response, they strode off into the crowd.

Galla looked at her friends and sighed, "Well, I suppose I have no choice . . . the *Emperor* has commanded me." She headed in the direction of the Basilica Ulpia at the far end of the forum of Trajan.

Once inside the mammoth old building, the clamor of voices and shuffling of feet increased to an insufferable din. It seemed as if everyone were talking at once. There, in an apse on one side of the huge hall, was a raised platform with several chairs flanking a grand throne in the center. Several persons were already seated in their places and Galla walked the length of the basilica towards the platform. Before she reached her destination, a familiar voice boomed out behind her.

"Galla! Galla! How good of you to come. We are very pleased and honored to have you here today!"

Galla turned and saw Attalus striding towards her. He was wearing the official Imperial toga of gold with purple bands-- colors reserved for members of the Imperial family only. Attalus did not notice Galla's icy glance at his attire. He held out his hand to her and he smiled warmly. Galla, too, extended her hand, allowing Attalus to kiss it briefly.

As Galla followed Attalus up the steps and onto the dais, she sensed that something was different about him today. He seemed calmer, more in control . . . more . . . more like an Emperor. Attalus stopped in front of the Imperial throne and he gestured to Galla for her to take the chair immediately to his right-- a position of special honor. When everyone had taken their places, the trumpets blew, the crowds fell silent, and the ceremony began.

Since the Pope was no longer in Rome, the duty of announcing the new Emperor fell to his Archbishop who respectfully proclaimed the Church's blessing on the new appointment. Then the State took its turn at approving the new Emperor as the first Consul announced the Senate's confirmation of Attalus. Last, it was the People's chance to express *their* approval and the crowd roared their support of Attalus as the new Emperor of Rome.

Within minutes, Honorius had been officially deposed and a new Emperor, an upstart from the provinces, had been named to the most important governmental position in the Western world . . . the Emperor of the Roman Empire. Galla's head swam and she felt disconnected from the events around her. It was as if she were a tiny droplet of water being carried along with the surging tide of history. The crowds swarmed over the dais, eager to touch the new Emperor. They swiftly lifted Attalus to their shoulders and carried him out of the basilica and into the forum. Galla was pushed aside by the throngs of celebrants as they hurried out of the hall. She suddenly found herself alone on the dais at the end of the empty basilica. She stood listening to the shouts of the crowd outside in the forum.

"Galla," Julius' voice broke the silence of the hall, "Galla, perhaps that's enough excitement for one day. Perhaps we should return to the palace now and you can rest."

Galla nodded silently and she allowed her three friends to lead her home.

CHAPTER XII

The next few weeks were filled with hectic attempts to stave off another barbarian blockade of Rome. The Goths were once again encamped outside the walls of Rome and their demands for grain, land, and money, increased daily. Their new puppet Emperor Attalus did not fulfill their expectations or their demands.

No one was certain whether Attalus *would* not or *could* not supply the grain that Alaric and his people demanded. Some speculated that Attalus felt his primary allegiance was to Rome and that was why he hesitated to send forces to Africa to secure the grain the barbarians demanded. Others believed that Attalus' lack of action on behalf of his Gothic friends was due not to his love of Rome, but simply to his lack of funds. In short, no one was certain where Attalus' allegiances lie.

On one day, Attalus agreed to allow Honorius to abdicate, provided he were mutilated first as a sign of his dishonor. And another day, Attalus sent considerable revenues to Ravenna to help the beleaguered Honorius and his forces. Not long after the day that Attalus had celebrated his appointment as the new Emperor, he found himself losing the support of both the Romans and the barbarians.

Galla was kept apprised of the events of those weeks and of the vacillations of the new Emperor. Each day she expected to receive some word from Attalus, but weeks passed and no communication from the new Emperor arrived. Galla was unsure whether to be happy or to be worried by the lack of attention, however she didn't allow herself to dwell on Attalus or his erratic behavior. She knew there was too much work to be done to prepare the city for the long winter under another barbarian blockade.

Fortunately, many Romans had also learned a lesson from the previous year's tragic events. The government had filled the storehouses with provisions. Many individuals had planted gardens and had begun to keep chickens, goats, and other farm animals on their properties.

Galla was now pleased to see the hard work that she and Julius had expended last summer in their own garden pay off in much needed fruits and vegetables. Most of the produce from their garden had been preserved or pickled and stored away in root cellars. Even now, in mid-December, the garden still gave forth turnips, rutabagas, and an occasional onion or carrot.

Galla was out in the garden, pulling out the last of the parsnips, when Eli came out with a scroll that had just been delivered.

"A messenger just brought this for you, my Lady," Eli said as she held out the large vellum scroll.

Galla stood up and wiped her hands on the heavy cotton apron she was wearing.

"My Lady!" Eli scolded. "You don't need to be out here working in the dirt like a common farmer. Let the servants do this!"

"Yes, Eli, I *do* need to be out here working in the dirt. I think I'd go mad if it weren't for the work here in the garden and at the church. Julius is at the Senate all day everyday trying to make some progress towards a settlement with the Goths. Fortus is at his post at the Salarian Gate sixteen hours a day. Even Claudia is busy overseeing the distribution of grain to the poorhouses and orphanages. I *must* have *something* to do. This waiting is driving me crazy." Galla wiped her forehead with the back of her hand.

Eli looked down at the scroll, "Perhaps this is what you've been waiting for," she said as she handed the scroll to Galla.

Galla took the scroll and saw a large mass of purple sealing wax impressed with the Imperial eagle. She sighed, "I think I'll go inside to read this. It looks too important to be read standing in fresh manure. Or, perhaps, if it's from whom I think it is, this scroll would find good company in the dung," Galla added with sarcasm. Eli chuckled.

"Eli, please bring some fresh water and some fruit to the library. I'll wash up and I'll be there in a moment.

Galla arrived at the library freshly washed, but she had not taken the time to change from her gardening clothes. She removed the dirt-stained apron, sat down on a leather chair, and picked up the scroll. Galla paused, postponing what she knew would be important news. Eli entered, set down a pitcher of water and some freshly sliced fruit, and left the room. Still Galla sat with the unopened scroll in her lap. Finally, very slowly and with great care, Galla broke open the Imperial seal and unwound the large scroll.

> To Galla Placidia Flavius - Greetings.
> His Highness, the Emperor Attalus,
> requests the honor of your company
> tomorrow evening for dinner at
> his villa.

"That's it?" Galla thought, "That's all? No signature, no explanation? Just an order to appear? How like an upstart to forgo the proper formalities. These ill-bred provincials!"

Galla stood up and paced the room. She was outraged that Attalus would keep her waiting week after week, and then just order her to dinner without an explanation or a word of apology. She felt like a neglected pet, one that is always kept waiting until it suits the owner's whim to bring it out and play with it. She suddenly thought of Odysseus and how he must feel, waiting patiently in his stable, day after day, for Galla to come to exercise him, or groom him, or just pat his nose. Galla was filled with remorse for neglecting her faithful horse and she decided to go for a ride. Without changing her clothes, Galla headed for the stable.

Galla set out on Odysseus without any destination in mind but she soon found herself riding alongside the massive walls of Rome, heading for the Salarian Gate. When she arrived at the Gate, she dismounted and asked the soldier standing guard where she could find Fortus. Before the sentence was out of her mouth, Fortus was standing beside her.

"What is it? What's wrong?" Fortus asked.

"Oh, nothing's wrong," Galla said sheepishly, realizing the fear her sudden and unexpected arrival had caused in Fortus. "I was just out riding and somehow I ended up here," she explained.

Fortus breathed a sigh of relief.

"Fortus, how did you get here so quickly? I only just now arrived." Galla asked.

"My duty is to watch everything that happens here at the Salarian Gate, outside *and* inside. I saw you riding up so I came down off the wall. I thought something was wrong when I saw you and how you are dressed."

Galla looked down at her muddy gardening dress and smiled. "Oh, I forgot to change, that's all. You see, I received word from Attalus and . . . and . . ." Galla's voice trailed off as she looked around at several curious soldiers gawking at them.

Fortus saw the gathering crowd, too, and he took Galla by the arm and led her over to a small tavern across the street from the gate. He tied Odysseus to a post in front of the tavern door and he gave a small coin to the tavern boy to watch the valuable animal. Fortus then led Galla into the musty little tavern.

"What'll it be?" a big woman shouted from across the room.

"Two glasses of wine and make it your good vintage," Fortus ordered.

"That'll be cash only," the woman warned.

"Yes," Fortus responded, "cash only." He looked down at his common soldiers' attire and then at Galla's soiled gardening dress and he laughed. "I guess we don't look very trustworthy in our working clothes." Galla smiled.

The heavyset woman lumbered across the room, set two earthenware mugs of wine down on the wood table, and held out a dirty palm. Fortus placed the coins in her hand and she lumbered off again without a word.

After Galla had taken a sip of wine, Fortus inquired as to the contents of the correspondence that Galla had received from Attalus.

"He wants me to come to his villa for dinner tomorrow evening," Galla said without trying to conceal her irritation.

"That's all? He didn't give you any indication of why you should come or what he wishes to discuss?"

"No," Galla said between sips of the dark red wine. "He didn't even write the note himself, he dictated it and didn't sign it. If I thought he had manners, I would consider this an insult, but I think the fool is entirely devoid of any proper upbringing. He's simply ignorant."

"And stupid," Fortus added. "His actions of the last months have alienated his followers on both sides of the political fence. He can't decide which way to jump. He's an idiot," Fortus fumed.

Galla had rarely heard Fortus use such disparaging words; he normally was very careful how he spoke. But in this case, Galla had to agree with Fortus' assessment of the provincial usurper to the Imperial throne. Attalus was keeping all Rome, all the Empire, in suspense while he played his feeble game. Galla knew, too, that Fortus was angry that this upstart held *her* future in his treacherous hands. She understood that Fortus was frustrated to be so powerless against this new undeserving Emperor and his whims.

Galla reached out and took Fortus' hand. He looked up at her with his clear sky blue eyes.

"Be careful," Fortus warned. "I don't trust this Attalus. I believe he's in league with the devil himself."

"I will be careful, Fortus. You needn't worry about me. Besides, it's a dinner party and there will be many people there. He wouldn't *dare* try anything in front of the guests. I'll take Julius' manservant Joseph along with me and I'll have him wait and take me home early. After all, there *is* a curfew now and even Imperial dinner parties can't last past curfew."

Just then Pontus entered the tavern. He smiled broadly at the sight of Galla and strode over to the table.

"Pontus! How good to see you!" Galla greeted him warmly.

"Hello, Your . . . Galla! I heard you were here and I just wanted to pay my respects. Claudia sends her regards, too. We've missed you these last weeks." Pontus then turned to Fortus and said, "When I heard Galla was here, I asked the commander if I could be permitted to take the rest of your watch at the gate so you could see Galla back to the palace. He said it would be fine. I know you two haven't had much time together and I thought you might like to . . . to . . . be alone." Pontus looked down with an embarrassed smile.

"You thought right," Galla interrupted. "How kind and thoughtful you are Pontus, dear friend."

"Yes," Fortus added, "you are a *dear* friend indeed. I'll take your watch tomorrow so you can go see your sister Claudia -- I'm sure she misses you, too."

"Thanks! I'll do that. Well, I'd better get back to the wall before the commander changes his mind. It's good to see you looking so well Galla. May God go with you."

"And with you, Pontus. Give my love to Claudia. Ask her to come see me when she can."

Pontus left the tavern and Fortus ordered two more glasses of wine and a small loaf of freshly baked bread. He and Galla sat there through the remainder of the afternoon. In the early evening, Galla and Fortus walked back to the palace leading Odysseus behind them. The first warning bells of curfew were ringing when Fortus finally started back to his post at the Salarian Gate.

The next evening, Julius' manservant Joseph accompanied Galla the few blocks to the villa of Attalus. Joseph waited in the foyer as two Imperial guards escorted Galla down a long corridor and into a small room. The guards closed the tall bronze doors and Galla looked around the room. She was alone. A fire was lit in a bronze brazier in one corner and several oil lamps gave forth a warm glow. The shutters were closed and the curtains drawn, so the lamplight was the only light in the room. Galla wondered if she were early since the other guests had not yet arrived. Or perhaps the other guests were already assembled in the main dining hall and her host was waiting to announce her arrival and to present her personally to the assembled company.

Just then the tall bronze doors opened and several servants entered carrying serving trays with pitchers of wine and platters laden with delicacies. They set up the tables, arranged the food and drink, and then stood at attention. One of the younger serving girls smiled directly at Galla. The girl wore a tiny cross around her neck and Galla returned her smile. The girl blushed with pride to be acknowledged by the noble Galla Placidia. Attalus entered shortly after the servants had completed their tasks. He did not address Galla at once, but instead he inspected the tables carefully.

"Good. You may go," he ordered. The servants scurried out of the room and closed the heavy doors behind them.

Still, Attalus did not speak. He stood across the room and looked appraisingly at Galla. Finally, Galla could stand the silence no longer. "Good evening, Attalus. I hope you will understand that I am somewhat confused. It was my belief that I was invited to a dinner *party* . . . a party with many guests. Am I now correct in assuming I am the *only* guest?" Galla looked directly at Attalus.

"Yes, Galla, I thought it would give us a chance to get to know one another better." Attalus walked over to where Galla was standing and pulled out a plush chair for her, indicating that she should be seated.

"Prefect Attalus," Galla said coldly, "this is highly irregular. If you had been raised in the proper circles you would know that a young woman does not dine alone with a man." Galla ignored Attalus' gesture for her to be seated.

"It is not 'Prefect' Attalus, Galla, as you well know. It is *Emperor* Attalus, and I am not just *any* man, Galla," he said, his voice growing louder with each word, "I am the Emperor!" he shouted.

Attalus took a few steps away from Galla and took a deep breath. "Listen, Galla," he said, his voice softening, his tone lowered, "why are you making this so difficult? All I have asked is to be friends. If I had any other designs on you, I'd just *do* it, I wouldn't need your permission, or anyone else's. Like it or not, Galla, I *am* the Emperor. Now, please be seated and let's see if we can start this evening over again." He pulled the chair closer to Galla and indicated for the third time that she should be seated. Galla reluctantly sat down. Attalus stepped over to the serving table and poured two goblets of wine.

Galla watched Attalus as he carefully selected and poured the wine. She was once again struck by his confident manner. She knew she irritated and insulted him and she admired how he managed to control his temper. She was also reminded that he was not unattractive. He had a good, solid muscular build, dark wavy hair, and dark luminous eyes. This evening he was dressed in a long tunic of fine soft brown suede. As he handed her the gold goblet, she noticed that he smelled nice, too, like sandalwood. Why did she, then, find him so despicable? As he leaned over to sit down on the chair across from her, Galla noticed a gold chain around his neck from which was suspended the gold Imperial Eagle . . . symbol of the Emperor of Rome. "*That* is why I hate him," Galla thought angrily as she stared at the pendant.

Attalus had followed her icy stare and he smiled. He reached up, slipped the pendant and chain over his head and placed it on the table. "Let's not let this get between us, Galla, not tonight anyway," Attalus said gently as he covered the Imperial Eagle with a napkin. "Tonight I want us to get to know one another, without titles, without family names, without politics. Do you think that's possible, just for *one* night?" Attalus asked softly.

"I don't know if it's possible," Galla replied, her tone also softening, "but I'll try, for *one* night, anyway."

The conversation turned to horses, the vegetable gardens, Rome's remarkable monuments, and various other neutral subjects. Whenever the topic skirted political issues such as the Goths, or Ravenna, or African grain, Attalus carefully maneuvered the conversation on to other subjects. Over several courses of delicious food and fine wine, Galla began to see the man behind the Imperial seal. It was obvious that he was an upstart and a social climber. Galla wondered how much of his success had been of his own making or of others.

As the servants cleared away the dinner things, Galla began to wonder about the time. She felt that the hour must be getting late. With the shutters closed and the curtains drawn it was difficult to tell the time. During several lulls in the conversation, Galla remarked about the hour and indicated that she was ready to go, but Attalus assured her that the servants would notify them when the first curfew bells rang.

Finally, Galla decided it really must be time to go. She stood up and thanked her host. Attalus stood also. He took Galla's shawl from her arm and he gently placed it over her shoulders, allowing his arm to rest across her back for a few seconds more than was proper. Attalus opened the doors and went out into the corridor to talk to the servants. Galla could hear their conversation in the hall and she went out to see what was wrong.

"I'm afraid something terrible has happened, my Dear," Attalus said looking distraught. "The servants forgot to notify us and now the curfew is in effect. I'm afraid it's impossible for you to return home this evening. You will have to spend the night." A tiny flicker of satisfaction flashed across Attalus' eyes and Galla realized she had been deceived.

"He tricked me," she thought to herself angrily, "all that small talk and gentleness . . . it was all a ruse!" Galla glowered at Attalus, "*You're* the Emperor . . . *you* issued the curfew . . . well, you can just revoke it!" Attalus threw back his head and laughed at Galla's anger.

Galla pushed past Attalus and headed down the hallway towards the entrance to the villa. "Curfew or no curfew, I'm going *home* this evening. Joseph! Joseph!" Galla called out.

Attalus said, "He's not here. Joseph returned home before the curfew. So you see, my Dear, it really *is* impossible for you to return to the palace this evening." Attalus smiled and reached for Galla's hand.

Galla leapt back out of his reach. "You deceiving upstart!" Galla said coldly, "How *dare* you hold me here against my will."

"Be careful of how you use your words, Galla. Remember, I *am* the Emperor. The words you utter could be interpreted as treasonous. The penalty for treason is death. As for your *will* . . . that strong will of yours is what got you in this situation tonight. I was warned that you were a difficult and headstrong girl. Frankly, Galla, I have neither the time nor the inclination to persuade you to see things my way. What I need is an Imperial wife to secure my position here in Rome. You have made it painfully clear to me since our first meeting that such an alliance with you is out of the question. You left me no other choice."

"Choice? What choice? You have no choice. I'd rather die than marry you!" Galla fumed.

"That won't be necessary, my Dear. After tonight, it won't really matter whether or not you marry me officially. It's the *unofficial* appearance that really matters. By morning all of Rome will know that the noble Galla Placidia, bastion of virtue and Roman womanhood, spent the night, the *entire* night, with the Emperor Attalus." He paused and smiled at Galla. "So you see my Dear, by morning we'll be married in the eyes of the *people* and it's the *appearance* of marriage that really matters. In the morning, you can choose to remain here as my wife in a position of respect and honor, or you can choose to return to your villa . . . a ruined woman, devoid of virtue and reputation. Guards! Show my *wife* to her quarters. See that the doors are securely locked."

The two guards led the stunned Galla down the hallway to a large sleeping chamber. They ushered her into the room and then locked the doors behind her. Galla stumbled over to a chair and sat down. Her thoughts were a confused jumble. She hovered between anger and fear.

"Julius!" Galla thought, "He'll be so worried. And Fortus! Poor Fortus! What will he think? What will he think of *me*?" Galla stood up and began to pace the room. She stopped suddenly as a new fear crossed her mind. "What if Attalus returns?" she thought as her heart raced faster. "What if he doesn't intend to leave me alone tonight?"

At that moment, Galla heard the sound of metal against metal and she turned to face the door. She gasped with fear and stepped behind a chair. The door opened slowly and silently, each moment of delay causing Galla's heart to beat faster. Galla closed her eyes tightly, not wishing to behold the sight of the detested Attalus.

A small high voice penetrated the throbbing in Galla's ears. "Will my Lady be wanting anything tonight?" the young servant girl asked nervously. Galla opened her eyes to see a pale, thin girl of about fifteen standing before her. It was the young girl whom Galla had acknowledged earlier that evening in the dining room.

Galla released her breath with a sigh. "No, no thank you," Galla responded, feeling somewhat foolish to have let her imagination run away so.

The girl did not move, but stood searching the room with her eyes. "I'll turn back the bed for Your Highness," the girl offered in a nervous voice. She walked over to the bed and turned back the linen bed covers. "Shall I help you undress?" the girl said in a firmer tone, nodding towards the door. Galla glanced at the open door and then back at the girl, wondering why the young servant seemed so anxious.

The girl stepped quickly to the door, closed it, and hurried back to Galla. Then she pulled a necklace out from where it was hidden under her dress and held it up for Galla to see. It was the small wooden cross that Galla had seen her wearing earlier.

"What do you want?" Galla inquired. The girl signaled her to be silent, took her by the hand, and led her over to a large trunk in the corner of the room. The girl smiled nervously, opened the trunk, and pushed back the blankets that were stored there. She rapped on the flat bottom of the trunk. Galla heard a hollow, empty sound. Her heart raced. "Could it be? Could it really be?" she thought as the servant girl emptied the contents of the trunk and pulled up the bottom panel. The familiar dank odor of the catacombs wafted up into the room.

Galla looked at the girl in amazement and the girl looked down nervously. "But this is too dangerous a thing for you to do!" Galla whispered anxiously. "If Attalus finds out what you've done, he'll have you killed!"

The young girl smiled with a look of serene composure. She grasped her necklace in her hand. "Do not worry about me, Your Highness, I will be protected. I overheard the Emperor discussing his plans for you, Your Highness. I believe that man is the devil himself. You must go and go quickly." The girl handed a bronze oil lamp to Galla and lit the heavy wick. "Go, Your Highness, may God go with you!"

"And with you, my Dear!" Galla responded as she took the lighted lamp and descended down the worn steps into the dark abyss of the catacombs. Galla looked up to see the heavy trunk panel close and to find herself alone in the cool damp darkness. She tried to imagine the expression on Attalus' face when he found her missing the next morning . . . or would he return to her chamber tonight? A man as unprincipled as Attalus might try anything. She knew she'd better hurry and leave the vicinity of his villa as quickly as possible just in case her escape route was discovered.

Galla held up the oil lamp and started down the narrow tunnel. It was then that Galla realized that she had no idea where she was going. Fortus' words echoed in her ears, "hundreds of miles of tunnels, several stories deep, if the oil lamp runs out . . ." Galla's heart raced. Only a short while earlier she had told Attalus she'd rather die than marry him. Now she knew, that if she weren't careful, that her threat just might prove true.

Galla stopped and carefully imagined the villa of Attalus above her. She tried to picture in which direction she would head to find Fortus' room in the old bakery. After careful consideration she retraced her steps back past the way she entered and she started to head down a different passageway. Suddenly she heard voices above her. It was Attalus shouting orders to his guards. He must have returned to her room and discovered that she was missing. Galla knew she could waste no time and she ran down the nearest tunnel.

As she passed the first intersection of two tunnels, Galla held up her lamp and carefully scanned the corners of the intersection for the marks that Fortus had used to find his way through this labyrinth of passageways. There were no marks there. Galla continued on . . . two intersections . . . three . . . still no marks to lead her to the old bakery. Galla began to panic. The catacombs were frightful enough when Fortus was there to lead her, but now, alone in these halls of death, Galla was filled with terror. Her terror was compounded as her gaze fell upon the rows and rows of corpses on the narrow shelves from floor to ceiling.

She ran on blindly, stopping only where two tunnels met to search for Fortus' markings. Suddenly Galla heard voices behind her, and then the pounding of men's heavy boots. She stopped to listen. Were the sounds coming from above the catacomb tunnels or from within them? Galla hid her oil lamp in a crevice and looked back down the long dark tunnel. A faint light flickered in the distance and the sounds of men's voices grew louder.

Galla knew instinctively that the light from her oil lamp would give away her position. She spied one of the open tombs along the bottom of a wall. She knelt down, pushed aside a pile of dried bones, crawled in and lay down. Then she blew out her lamp. Galla held her breath as the sounds of the men came closer and closer. As they approached, Galla could see the light from their oil lamps illuminate the shelves around her, which were filled with decomposing bodies and skeletons. Galla lay motionless among the death and decay.

Suddenly the men reached the area where Galla lie prone in the narrow crevice along the bottom of the wall. She watched as they ran past . . . soldier's legs with heavy nailed boots, and then a flash of a brown suede tunic--it was Attalus. She could hear him frantically ordering the arrest of the chambermaid and shouting at the men to run faster, faster.

In a flash they were past her. Soon the men, the sound, and the *light* disappeared down another tunnel. Galla released her breath and crawled out of the narrow crevice. She pulled herself back up onto her feet. She stood still, hoping her eyes would adjust to the darkness, but there was no light, none at all, and Galla was left in total darkness. For a split second she thought she should call out to bring the men back, but then she gathered her courage and decided to continue on.

As she worked her way through the total darkness, she carefully examined each intersection for Fortus' markings. She made her way carefully along the maze of tunnels and staircases. Her hands grew scratched and sore from running them over the rough tufa walls in search of the tiny arrows that Fortus had carved into the walls of the tunnels in the vicinity of his old bakery. From time to time her hands fell upon a decomposed corpse or onto a crawling insect.

One hour passed, then two . . . or was it that long? Galla began to lose her sense of time along with her sense of direction. Her nerves were at their end and Galla began to be overcome with weariness and desperation. Just when Galla was about to give up hope, her hand felt a familiar arrow carved in the tufa wall. Galla turned down the tunnel in the direction of the arrow and she continued slowly along the corridors, cautiously following each signpost in the absolute darkness.

At last she reached what she thought must be the staircase to Fortus' room. She felt her way up the slimy worn steps and tapped weakly on the heavy trap door. There was no response.

"Oh no!" Galla thought, "Fortus must still be at his post. Or . . . what if I've misinterpreted the signs? What if this is the wrong door . . . or not a door at all?" Fear gave her new strength and she pounded harder on the door. She thought she heard someone stirring above so she gave a third hard knock on the door.

She heard a muffled voice say, "Alcibiades, is that you? What on earth are you doing down there at this hour?" With that the heavy trap door swung open and the tunnel was filled with light. Galla had to look away . . . her eyes blinded by the light after so many hours in total darkness.

"Who is it? Who's down there?" Fortus demanded sternly.

"It's me," Galla sobbed, too tired to finish climbing the treacherous stairs. "It's Galla."

"Galla!" Fortus bounded down the stairs, lifted Galla into his arms and carried her up into the warm fresh air.

"Galla, how did you get here? What were you doing down there?" Fortus began asking as he seated Galla on a chair. He poured a cup of cool water for her and he explained that all of Rome was out searching for her. Attalus had put out an order for Galla's arrest for violation of the curfew. Fortus said that it was nearly dawn and that he had just now come in from searching for her.

Slowly Galla recounted the night's events to Fortus. When she had finished, Fortus shook his head with disbelief and anger. "That Attalus is a worse scoundrel than any of us imagined," Fortus stormed. "When the Senate hears of this, he'll lose what little support he has left there. We received news this evening that Alaric and the Goths officially withdrew their support of Attalus just yesterday. No wonder he was so desperate to create the illusion of an Imperial alliance last night. He knew that by morning, he might be deposed if he couldn't get a foothold any other way."

Fortus sighed deeply and threw himself onto a chair. He looked at Galla and saw how tired and drawn she appeared. "Galla, you need to rest. I'll have Alcibiades bring you water for a bath and something fresh to wear . . . I hope you don't mind one of my nightshirts . . . I'm afraid I'm fresh out of silk gowns just now."

Galla smiled weakly and said, "Do you think Alcibiades might be able to find some bread and maybe some cheese? I feel as if I walked the length of Rome last night."

"Bread and cheese it is. You wash, eat, and get some sleep. I'm going to the palace to consult with Julius. We may need to go to the Senate, so don't worry if I'm gone awhile. You'll be safe here. Julius and I have to find a way to get Attalus to cancel his orders for your arrest. Now," Fortus leaned over and kissed Galla's forehead, "you try to relax and regain your strength."

Fortus headed for the door, but Galla stopped him. "Fortus," she said softly, "I love you."

Fortus smiled and said, "I love you, too, Galla, more than you'll ever know." With that he left the room, closing the door quietly behind him.

Fortus returned in the late afternoon. He looked haggard and discouraged.

"What is it? What's wrong?" Galla asked when Fortus entered the room.

Fortus set down the bundle of fresh clothes for Galla that he had brought from the palace. He ran his hand through his hair and sighed deeply.

"They won't do it, Galla. The Senate refuses to lift the arrest order that Attalus issued last night. Fortus flung himself down on a chair and propped his feet up on the old trunk. "We've been everywhere and we've spoken to anyone who would listen."

"That lying Attalus," Galla hissed, "That lying upstart!"

"It's not just Attalus, Galla, but Alaric, too." Fortus said with disgust.

"Alaric? The barbarian chieftain? What does *he* have to do with all this?" Galla queried. "I thought he and the Goths had withdrawn their support of Attalus."

Fortus stood up, walked over to the bed and sat down next to Galla. He put his hand gently on her arm. "Galla, these men are grasping at straws . . . trying anything they can to hold on to some power in Rome. They feigned the withdrawal of their support . . . to make the Senate think Attalus is loyal to Rome." Fortus paused and swallowed hard. Fortus put his arm around Galla and said, "Oh my darling Galla, these are men without scruples, without honor, without God." Fortus' voice quivered and he paused again to bring his emotions under control. "Attalus and Alaric have decided that the one bargaining chip they may have with Honorius is you, his sister. And what's worse, the Senate backs them."

"Me?" Galla looked up with fear.

"Yes, they think that if they have you then Honorius will be forced to follow their demands."

"Ha!" Galla laughed sarcastically. "Honorius doesn't give a twig for me! He'd love nothing better than to see me out of the picture!" Galla stood up and began to pace the room.

"Well, yes and no, Galla. When Honorius was Emperor, he wanted to prevent your marriage to protect his right to the throne. Now that he is no longer Emperor, you're his hope for choosing the *new* Emperor--someone whom he can select, marry to you, and then he can rule through his appointed puppet Emperor. As long as Attalus and Alaric have you in *their* custody, *they* control whom you marry. He who controls *you*, controls the Imperial lineage of Rome . . . the *legitimate* Imperial lineage, that is."

"Well, why all this game-playing then? Why doesn't Attalus just *command* me to marry him?

"Because Alaric has forbidden Attalus to marry you. Alaric is unhappy with the way Attalus has handled his new position as Emperor. Attalus still hasn't gotten Alaric the grain from Africa and, on top of that, Attalus has even sent funds to Honorius and the Roman army in Ravenna. Attalus isn't the little puppet that Alaric thought he'd be. Rumor is that *Alaric* wants to be the next Emperor."

"Alaric!" Galla uttered with disbelief. "A *Germanic* barbarian? Emperor of Rome? Never! Rome will *never* have a Germanic barbarian as Emperor!" Galla stopped pacing and faced Fortus, a look of incomprehension on her face. "We won't let that happen, will we?"

Fortus shook his head and shrugged his shoulders. "Anymore, I'm not certain what will or can happen. The way I see it, we'll just have to ride the tide of events and take each day as it comes. I think it's best if we just go about our daily activities and draw as little attention to ourselves as possible. Julius has convinced the Senate to allow you to be under house arrest . . . that means you don't have to go to a prison, you can stay at home in the palace. Julius has given his oath that you will not try to flee. The Senate has even agreed to allow you a certain number of visitors," Fortus said as he took Galla's hands in his, "so Pontus, Claudia and

I can still see you from time to time," Fortus smiled and kissed each of her hands.

"House arrest . . ." Galla mumbled, "Galla Placidia Flavius under house arrest by order of an upstart Prefect and a Germanic barbarian! Oh Father! What has become of your Little Acorn? What has become of Rome?"

Fortus stood up and put his arms around Galla and held her close. After a few minutes he said, "You'd better change into some fresh clothes. They are expecting us back at the palace. Julius is worried sick about you. He'll only rest when he sees you safely back within the palace walls." Fortus kissed Galla on the forehead and left the room.

CHAPTER XIII

Galla returned to the palace under full house arrest. She was permitted visitors, however with the city under blockade by the barbarians once again, Galla's friends had little time to spare. Many Romans who had eagerly accepted her invitations to dine in happier years, now avoided Galla's extension of friendship. Only Julius, Fortus, Pontus and Claudia remained unflaggingly loyal to Galla. It was they who regularly joined Galla in the little chapel of her palace for Sunday worship, since visits to St. Peter's to celebrate mass were forbidden to Galla under the conditions of the house arrest. Galla looked forward to her Sunday worship services with her dear friends and to their leisurely lunches afterwards during which Galla would hear the news from outside the palace walls.

The Christmas season came and went without the customary festivities this year. Galla and her small circle of friends celebrated her twentieth birthday without the public fanfare of former years. Galla watched from the palace windows as the spring rains were replaced by summer sunshine. And still there was no word from Honorius in Ravenna.

On one unusually chilly Sunday morning in late July, Galla and her friends assembled in the library for lunch following their private worship service in the palace chapel.

"Every week I think about having lunch in the dining hall," Galla commented as she, Julius and Claudia entered the library, "but it's been so cold and that big hall is very drafty. It's cozier in here." Galla walked over to the brazier and placed another coal on the fire. "I wonder what's keeping Fortus and Pontus? It's not like them to be so late. Did Pontus say anything to you this morning Claudia?" Galla asked as she seated herself on a dining couch.

"Pontus didn't come home last night, Galla," Claudia replied with a slightly apprehensive tone. "None of the soldiers returned home after their watches yesterday."

Galla turned to Julius, "Do you know what's happening, Uncle Julius?"

Julius nodded slowly and set down the loaf of bread he was slicing. "Yes, Galla, I know. Or at least I *think* I know; one can never tell what's fact from what's rumor anymore." Julius paused and took a sip of wine. "Bits and pieces of news have been trickling down from the north the last few days. It appears that Honorius has condoned an attack against the Goths. If that's true, it will have dire consequences for us here in Rome. Alaric already has us surrounded with troops, but thus far he has not thrown all his strength against us. If Honorius has, indeed, attacked, or even *condoned* an attack, then it's very likely that Alaric will force a complete blockade of the city and perhaps even lay siege."

Galla sat quietly, mulling over Julius' words. Just then, the library doors opened and Fortus and Pontus strode in, still in the uniforms of their guard watch.

"Here!" Julius said, rising to greet the two men. "Here are the ones who can shed some light on the situation. Welcome, gentlemen, welcome. Please sit down. Have something to drink. You're just in time for lunch." Julius poured two goblets of wine and handed one to each man as he was seated.

Galla could tell by her friends' attire and the fact that they still carried their helmets with them that Fortus and Pontus had come straight from their watch on the wall at the Salarian Gate.

Julius waited for the two to be seated and to catch their breath. Then he inquired, "What news have you heard about the battle in the north? Has the rumor been confirmed that Honorius ordered an attack on the Goths?"

Fortus nodded, "Yes, a messenger arrived before dawn this morning. How the man got through the barbarian camps, I'll never know." Fortus took a long sip of the cold wine. "Honorius' troops have attacked a band of Goths. I don't know what Honorius was thinking . . . to attack one faction when there are Goths spread out over half of Italy. I gave him more credit for military strategy. He's had two years to amass an army large enough to wage a full war against the Goths, but instead he decides to fight piecemeal . . . with the city of Rome at the mercy of Alaric."

Fortus paused again and took another, longer sip of wine. "Honorius has played directly into Alaric's hands. A Roman attack on Germanic soldiers is exactly what Alaric needed to fire-up his troops. There will be no stopping an all-out war now," Fortus said angrily.

"War!" Claudia cried, "Oh Pontus!" She ran to her brother's side.

Pontus smiled and patted her hand gently. "We're not sure there will be war, Claudia, but it does look likely. But you're safe behind the walls of Rome."

"Yes, I may be safe, but what about you?"

"Fortus and I will be fine, too. We're guards at the wall, not foot soldiers or cavalrymen. We won't be asked to go into the field."

Pontus' words seemed to calm Claudia's fears and she returned to her seat on the couch next to Galla.

Galla, however, was not so easily appeased. She had spent her entire life in the midst of military and political activity. She sensed that the current situation was more critical than Pontus cared to admit to his sister.

"What's next?" Galla asked.

Fortus stood up and walked over to the window. "The Goths have cut off all communication and supplies from the city. No one or no thing can pass in or out of the walls of Rome. That messenger this morning is perhaps the last person to pass through the gates of Rome for a long, long time."

Galla sat watching Fortus as he stood before the open window. Light washed over his tall, muscular body and bathed his silhouette with a golden glow. She was struck, as she so often was, by how handsome, how competent, how strong he was. Seeing him in his Roman military uniform, framed by the tall window, Galla felt as if no harm could come to her or to Rome with men such as this to protect them.

During the ensuing weeks, the Goths tightened their stranglehold on Rome. Famine once again plagued the city. During the previous blockades Galla had been able to assist in the relief efforts. Now, under house arrest, Galla was forced to remain in the palace and her frustration with her position of impotence grew daily. The streets of the city were filled with looters and thieves, preventing the comfort of further visits from her dear friend Claudia. Even Fortus and Pontus were forbidden to leave their p

Late one afternoon in mid-August, Galla was reading in the library. Julius was away at the Senate and the servants were taking their afternoon rest. The house was unusually quiet and Galla's mind wandered off her book and to the last time she had seen Fortus, when he was standing in front of the window, looking radiant and handsome. She often thought of him just as he looked that day, so strong and confident. She longed to see him again and wondered how many more days would pass before he could leave his post and come to visit her.

Galla was startled out of her daydreams by the sound of the tall bronze library doors being swung abruptly open. She turned to see six Imperial guards stride through the doors, swords drawn. The guards looked around the room suspiciously.

"Who are you? What right have you to enter my private quarters without my permission?" Galla bellowed.

"They don't need your permission, my dear."

Galla recognized the familiar voice of Attalus as he walked into the room. He was followed by the culprit Marcus who had fled Rome following his attack on Galla the night of her nineteenth birthday party.

"Attalus! Marcus! You have no right to enter my private apartments without my consent. The Senate agreed."

Attalus and Marcus stood smirking at Galla. Attalus stepped forward and reached for Galla's hand. Galla pulled her hand behind her and stood staring defiantly at the two intruders.

"Galla, Galla, Galla," Attalus sighed. "When will you learn? For someone who's so very pretty, you're awfully dumb," Attalus said bluntly. Marcus chuckled at this insult to Galla. "We've come to bring you terrible news." Attalus paused for dramatic effect. "The Goths have entered Rome."

"That's impossible!" Galla countered. "The Goths can't possibly scale our walls!"

"Oh, they didn't scale our walls. They were *admitted* . . . admitted through the *Salarian* Gate," Attalus added firmly.

"The Salarian Gate! How? Who would do such a thing?" Galla gasped, her heart leaping to her throat out of fear for Fortus' safety.

"It appears there was a traitor at the gate," Attalus smiled wryly.

Galla flashed a look at Marcus as she quickly recalled Serena's traitorous liaison with Alaric and the Goths. Marcus gave Galla a smug, superior look.

"Yes, a traitor," Attalus continued. "I believe you know the cowardly scoundrel. He's a Roman guard, a *former* Roman guard, by the name of Fortus." Attalus paused to see what impact this would have on Galla.

"Fortus! Fortus is no more a traitor to Rome than I am!" Galla hissed.

"That's exactly why we're here. We believe you *are* a traitor to Rome. We have proof that you know this Fortus--that he's visited you, right here in this villa."

Galla stood stunned, riveted to the floor.

Attalus and Marcus exchanged self-satisfied smiles. Marcus took a few steps towards Galla, glaring hatefully into her eyes. "I told you not to cross me, Galla. I told you that I'd have my way." Marcus lifted the edge of Galla's shawl but she jerked it away and stepped back. "You still don't get it, do you Galla? You still think you're in charge, don't you? Well, my pretty one, you're in for a *big* surprise," Marcus grinned.

"Guards!" Attalus commanded, "Place this woman under full arrest. Take her to my palace."

Two guards stepped forward and took Galla's arms. Galla struggled to free herself but the guards tightened their grip.

Marcus and Attalus stood laughing as the guards pulled Galla from the library and out into the atrium. Just then the front doors to the palace burst open and Pontus rushed in. Before he knew what was happening, four of Attalus' guards had him surrounded.

"Galla!" Pontus cried out, "Don't believe them! Fortus is not a traitor. It was *they*," Pontus screamed, pointing his hand directly at Attalus and Marcus. "*They* allowed the Goths to enter the city!"

"Yes!" Galla called out, "Yes! I know who the *real* traitors are!" She scowled at the vile traitors before her.

Attalus ordered the guards to throw Pontus into the prison, "Take him away!"

"Pontus!" Galla screamed after them, "Tell Fortus I know-- tell him I know he's not a traitor!" With that Attalus drew back his hand and slapped Galla squarely across the face.

"Shut up, you little bitch! Keep your mouth shut!" and he gave her a second hard slap across the side of her face.

"I will, Galla, I will," Pontus called out as the guards drug him out of the palace.

"Come on, let's get her out of here before anyone else drops by," Attalus quipped. "Guards! Guards! Take her to my palace!"

With that the guards pushed Galla out of the front doors of her palace. It was as if all hell had broken loose in the city and the devil himself was on the loose. The streets were teeming with chaos and confusion as both Romans and Goths pushed past her in all directions. Screams of horror filled the air. Everywhere was hysteria and panic.

As the guards led Galla down the streets she could see fires burning across the city of Rome. People were running past her in terror. Women and children huddled in corners, shawls drawn over their heads to hide them. Mutilated corpses littered the streets. Every so often Galla caught a glimpse of a filthy Gothic barbarian carrying off a Roman woman, or hacking to death a Roman child. Galla felt as if she would faint but somehow she managed to keep walking, the sounds of anguish and slaughter ringing in her ears.

When they reached the villa of Attalus, Marcus pulled open the bronze doors and the guards pushed Galla into the atrium. Attalus and Marcus followed, closing the huge doors and bolting them securely. The din from the street lessened and the villa was calm and quiet.

Attalus, Marcus, and the guards started to lead Galla across the open atrium when a deep voice boomed out, "So! I thought I'd find you here!"

Galla and the others turned to see the source of the unfamiliar accent. There, standing hidden in the shadows of the wall were a dozen or so Goths. The largest among them stepped out of the shadows and towards Attalus.

Galla had never seen a human being that large before. He towered over Attalus and the guards. He was dressed in a sheepskin loincloth and his hair was spiked out in greasy points. He wore a gold torque around his neck and he carried both a long sword and a heavy club. His voice sounded like gravel under a metal chariot wheel.

Attalus put out his hand and approached the monster, "Alaric! How good to see you again," Attalus said in a thin, nervous voice.

"Humph," Alaric growled, "is it?" He stalked past Attalus and approached Galla. "Who's this?" he demanded loudly.

Attalus cleared his throat and stuttered, "This . . . this is Galla Placidia, sis . . . sister of Honorius." Attalus paused. "I thought we should bring her to somewhere safe with all this fighting going on."

Alaric turned to face Attalus and he peered down on the trembling would be Emperor. "Is that what you were planning?" Alaric said in his thick Gothic accent.

"Yes," Attalus insisted. "Yes, we were just protecting her."

"Then you won't mind if I take over from here?" Alaric said gruffly.

Attalus stopped and threw a defiant look at Alaric. "Galla Placidia is in my charge. I have her under house arrest by order of the Senate of Rome."

Alaric smiled revealing black stained teeth. "You must not have looked outside my friend. As of today *I* am in charge of Rome and *I* make the rules."

Alaric reached for Galla's arm, but the two Roman soldiers stood steadfast. "Men!" Alaric roared. Suddenly dozens of Goths appeared from every room surrounding the atrium. Each was a full head taller than the Roman soldiers and each was heavily armed. The two Roman soldiers holding Galla looked at Attalus.

"Let her go," Attalus said quietly.

"Let me go?" Galla stammered, "Let me go? You parade around as the Emperor of Rome and yet you're just going to turn me over to this barbarian?"

"It appears that I have no choice," Attalus said as he glanced at Alaric and his men. Alaric laughed and ordered his men to seize Galla. Two massive Goths grabbed Galla's arms.

"Stop it! Stop it! I am Galla Placidia, daughter of Theodosius and sister of Honorius, the true Emperor of Rome!" Galla screamed as she struggled to free herself.

Alaric chuckled and translated Galla's protests into Gothic for his men to appreciate the joke. They all laughed heartily.

"Take her to my camp and lock her up. Tell Heda to watch after her," Alaric commanded.

One of the huge Goths picked up Galla and flung her over his shoulder. Another tossed a blanket over her. Galla kicked and screamed in protest.

"Silence her!" Alaric shouted.

Galla felt a crashing blow to her head and everything went black.

PART II

CHAPTER I
410 A.D.

A flash of daylight and the sound of women's voices brought Galla slowly back to consciousness. She lay very still, listening carefully to the sounds around her, trying to determine where she was without drawing attention to herself. She heard two women chattering away in Gothic. Their accents were different from the clear, precise Gothic that Stilicho had taught her, but still Galla could make out most of the women's conversation.

"There she is, the little Roman bitch," one of the women said with contempt.

"Shh, she'll hear you!" the other warned.

"Look at her! Do you think that little Roman princess understands Gothic? She only understands luxury and pampering. She doesn't understand our language or anything about us."

Galla opened one eye just wide enough to see the women seat themselves on short stools and begin milking two cows. Galla saw she was lying on the floor of a large barn. The women continued chatting as they filled their buckets. When they finished milking the cows, they got up to leave. One of the women came over to Galla and kicked her roughly. Galla opened her eyes and struggled to sit up to defend herself. The woman laughed hoarsely. She threw down a wooden cup and nodded at the cows. The two women turned and left the barn, closing the door tightly behind them.

Galla rose slowly to her feet. She was stiff from lying on the hard floor of the barn. She began to pick off the sharp straw from her thin silk dress. She tried to figure out what time of day it was and how long she had been unconscious. The barn had no windows and the only light that entered was from the cracks around the doors and in the rock walls. Galla recognized that this was a Roman barn; Goths had neither the time nor the inclination to build fine, permanent architecture like this. The Goths were always on the move and the few structures they did build were of sticks and hides.

"I must be in the barn of a Roman country house. Oh! The poor owners who built this fine barn, what has become of them?" Galla thought as she remembered her own fine country villa in which she grew up. "These Goths are only consumers, never producers. Even when someone else has created something fine and lasting, these Goths just use it and destroy it."

Galla brushed the last of the straw off her dress and stood wondering what her next move should be. She went to the barn door and placed her ear against the opening, hoping to hear some sounds to let her know what was going on outside, but she could hear nothing. She reached out and gently tried the latch on the door. It didn't budge.

The lump on Galla's head began to throb and she felt weak and dizzy. She pulled out one of the short milking stools and sat down. She glanced at the wooden cup lying on the floor. Galla knew she should be hungry but she could not bring herself to drink warm cow's milk, not out of that filthy cup on the barn floor anyway. Galla resolved to wait until someone brought her something proper to eat -- something clean.

Galla sat and waited, listening attentively for any sounds from outside. The hours dragged on as Galla watched the tiny slivers of light from the cracks in the barn door as they marched their way across the floor. The bands of light had crossed the floor and were beginning to fade into darkness before Galla heard any sign of life outside the barn. At first Galla heard only faint voices, but the voices grew louder. Then she heard the heavy pounding of horses' hoofs and the shouts of many men.

Galla's heart leapt with fear. "Perhaps it's a battle," Galla thought suddenly. But then she heard laughter intermingled with shouting and women's voices raised in cheers. "The Gothic warriors must be returning back to their camp for the night," Galla thought. Her first instinct was to feel relief that there were other living persons close by, but then she began to think about whom those persons were--Germanic barbarians--and fear began to take over.

Galla stood up and started to pace. She knew she must get control of herself. If the Goths saw her fear they would surely use it to their own advantage. Galla knew that her greatest advantage was what it had always been--her nobility. She would show them what it was to be an aristocrat, a *Roman* aristocrat. Even the vilest barbarian would have to respect the daughter of Theodosius and the sister of Honorius, the true Emperor of Rome.

Galla decided, too, that she would not reveal all she knew--not all at once anyway. She decided to let them believe she knew no Gothic. Perhaps, then, they would talk freely in front of her and she might learn something she could use to her advantage.

The barn doors opened and in walked a large ruddy-faced blond woman. She signaled for Galla to follow her and she left the barn.

Galla's heart quickened. All the tales of barbarian brutality that she had heard in Rome raced through her mind. She swallowed hard, smoothed her hair and gown, and walked straight and tall out of the barn.

Evening was descending upon the Italian countryside. Galla could discern hazy figures in the distance and campfires burning. The heavy blond woman stopped by the door of the farmhouse and waited for Galla to follow. She signaled impatiently for Galla to hurry. Galla quickened her pace and followed the woman into the farmhouse. Once inside the entry hall, the woman pointed to a chair, indicating that Galla should be seated. The woman crossed a large atrium and disappeared into another room. Galla was alone. She briefly contemplated dashing out the door and running for help. Then the vision of the Goths' campfires returned and she knew it was unlikely that she could make it through the barbarian camps. "Besides," she thought to herself, "I don't even know where I am. I don't know which direction to run."

The faint smell of roasted meat filled the air and Galla suddenly realized she was famished. She thought of the dirty wooden cup on the barn floor and regretted that she had not helped herself to some milk. She knew she had to keep up her strength. She remembered her father stressing the importance of supplying food to the Roman troops. "Soldiers can't fight with empty stomachs," he always said. Galla's stomach began to rumble and she knew that she, too, could not fight if she allowed herself to grow weak from hunger.

The large blond woman returned and signaled once again for Galla to follow her. She led Galla into an expansive dining room that was filled with men wearing little but thick leather belts and loincloths. When Galla entered the room the men fell silent and all turned to gaze at her. The blond woman saw their leering glances, shrugged with disgust, and left the room.

"Galla Placidia," a familiar rough voice said in Latin with a thick Gothic accent, "Welcome."

Galla turned to see Alaric entering the dining room. She was once again impressed by his massive size. She had never seen another man that tall or that broadly built. He was no longer wearing the sheepskin loincloth that he wore when she had first seen him. He now wore a loose shirt open at the neck and leather trousers with high-laced boots. Galla had seen Germanic men before, but Honorius had passed a law forbidding their native barbarian attire, and now all men in Rome, citizen or other, were required to wear the accepted Roman tunic.

Alaric walked over to the huge table and sat down. He pulled out the chair next to him and said to Galla, "Come sit. Eat." The men in the room moved aside as Galla walked across the room and took the seat next to Alaric. Once again Galla was surprised by the barbarian practice of dining while seated in chairs rather than reclining on dining couches. Romans often took their informal, early meals of the day at tables, but formal evening meals were nearly always served on serving tables to guests reclining on couches.

"Here." Alaric grunted as he set a heavy pitcher of frothy beer in front of Galla. "Drink."

Galla looked around for a cup expecting Alaric to notice and to pass one to her. She saw the men reaching eagerly into a high pile of cups, plates, and knives thrown onto the center of the large table. Alaric was busy talking to some of the men and Galla realized that she'd better get her own cup or she might miss another meal that day. She reached into the pile in the center of the table and drew out a cup and a knife. She poured a cup of the dark brown foamy liquid. It smelled musty and tasted sharp and bitter. She winced. Several of the men noticed her expression of displeasure and they laughed. Alaric turned and laughed, too.

"Not like your fine Roman wine, is it? Wine is for women, beer is for men. Weak things make you weak. Strong things give strength." With that Alaric lifted his mug and downed the contents. He belched loudly.

Galla refrained from returning the insult Alaric had just paid the Romans. "Weak," she thought to herself. "You'll see how weak we are when the Roman troops come to rescue me!"

Alaric turned back to his men and began speaking Gothic again. He spoke very fast in a broad flat accent and Galla only caught a word here and there. She could tell Alaric was explaining to the men who she was and one by one the men leered at her. Galla felt uncomfortable in her thin silk tunic and she wished she had a shawl to cover her bare shoulders.

The heavy blond woman entered the room again carrying a huge platter of roasted lamb. Galla had never liked lamb . . . she pitied a poor animal whose life was cut so short. But tonight the smell of the freshly roasted meat overcame her and she reached eagerly for some as the tray was passed around the table.

"Heda! Bring some more beer!" Alaric commanded. The woman nodded and left the room.

The conversation ceased as the men noisily devoured their dinners. Galla tried to ignore the sounds of slurping and belching as the Goths attacked each course. Galla noticed how much food there was and thought of the famine in Rome. Her resentment of the barbarians increased but did not diminish her appetite.

Part way through the meal a tall muscular young man entered. He had long dark hair, which contrasted with his emerald green eyes. He was dressed in trousers like Alaric and the two nodded at one another as the newcomer seated himself at the far end of the table. The young man was followed by a beautiful woman with long pale blond hair. Galla was reminded of Claudia's flaxen hair . . . only this woman was much taller and had a strong, muscular frame. Her gray eyes scanned Galla carefully.

"Letta, bring me some beer," the young man said to the woman. She gave another cold glance at Galla and left the room.

"So, Athaulf," Alaric boomed across the table, "where have you been? You nearly missed dinner and we have a special guest this evening." Alaric spoke in his thick Latin and Galla knew it was purposefully so she could understand his words.

The young man looked briefly and without expression at Galla. "I've just returned from the city," Athaulf said in precise Gothic. He then turned to Galla and said in flawless schoolbook Latin, "Welcome, Your Highness, it is an honor."

Alaric laughed hoarsely as if Athaulf's words were meant in jest, but something in Athaulf's eyes revealed a certain sincerity.

"Thank you," Galla said, careful to remain true to her plan to speak and acknowledge only Latin. She nodded respectfully at Athaulf. Although she hated each and every Goth for the atrocities they had perpetrated against her people, Galla knew that she should make as few enemies as possible while a captive in their camp.

The beautiful Letta returned again with a pitcher of beer for Athaulf. She leaned over the young man and gave him a kiss on the cheek. Athaulf smiled up at her and patted her cheek fondly. He reached up and spoke a few words into her ear. Letta threw an angry glance at Galla, turned, and left the room.

"So what do you think of our pretty caged bird, eh brother?" Alaric said in Gothic as he nodded at Galla.

"Watch what you say, Alaric, perhaps she can understand you," Athaulf warned.

"She can't understand me. Besides, even if she could, would I care? I don't watch my words in front of Roman riffraff," Alaric said with contempt. Galla carefully maintained her look of complete incomprehension.

"I'd hardly call her riffraff, Alaric," Athaulf replied, still speaking Gothic. "She's the sister of Honorius. If we want to get anything from her brother, we'll have to treat her well."

"Be damned!" Alaric slurred, the heavy beer thickening his tongue. "I'll do what I damn well please with her!" Alaric took another sip of beer. "Athaulf, you're worse than a woman, you're so soft. Sometimes I can't believe we sprang from the same womb," he added with disgust.

"I'm just using my brain, Alaric. That's something you should use more often, rather than some of your other organs!" Athaulf said jovially. "After all, what kind of bargaining chip will we have if she's damaged goods?"

Alaric growled, "Who's to say she's not damaged already?" Galla gripped her cup so tightly that her knuckles turned white. She did not dare look up from her plate on the table. "Oh, to Hell with you," Alaric stammered as he staggered to his feet. "I'm going to bed. You keep away from her, you hear? Don't go getting any ideas." He pointed at Galla, "That's the little lady that's gonna' make me Emperor of Rome," he slurred as he stumbled out of the room.

Galla finally looked up to see if Alaric had left and her eyes met Athaulf's steady gaze. Athaulf nodded slightly, held up his cup to Galla, and took a long sip of beer. Galla glanced back down.

"Heda!" Athaulf called out.

Heda entered the room and Athaulf instructed her to show Galla to a room in the villa. Heda protested that the barn was good enough for Roman prisoners, but Athaulf stood up and ordered her to be silent.

Galla watched the young Goth as he spoke with the woman. He was tall and sturdily built, yet not so massive as his brother. Athaulf had finer features and he wore his long dark hair loosely over his shoulders, free of the grease the others used to spike up their hair. And his mannerisms were more civilized too, Galla thought, than the other crude barbarians she had seen that night.

Athaulf turned to Galla and said softly, "Heda will show you to a room." Galla was impressed with his ability to switch from Gothic to Latin without an effort.

"Thank you," Galla said in Latin as she rose and walked over to where Athaulf was standing.

"See that you don't try to leave, Your Highness. Alaric has given strict orders that anyone who tries to escape be executed on the spot, no questions asked. He will not make an exception to that order, even for you. Do you understand?" Athaulf looked down at her with his emerald green eyes.

Galla nodded, "I understand."

Heda then led Galla down the hallway to a small room in one wing of the big Roman farmhouse. The room was bare--no bed, no blankets, nothing remained but the hard wood floor. Heda smirked at Galla's forlorn expression. Heda tossed her head proudly and strode away, leaving Galla alone in the dark room.

Galla walked over to the tiny window and looked out over the countryside. The Goths' campfires burned far off into the distance and she could hear the sounds of drunken singing and muffled laughter. She saw the pretty blond girl Letta standing by the barn. After a short while Athaulf came out and the two walked off together into the darkness.

CHAPTER II

Galla awoke the next morning before dawn. She heard shouts and the sounds of horses. She got up and looked out the tiny window. The courtyard was filling with horses and carts. Everyone seemed to be talking at once. Over the din Galla could hear Alaric's gruff voice shouting orders. "Pack up . . . you there! Hurry! Move that cart over there . . ."

The door to Galla's room swung open and Heda signaled Galla to follow her. Heda led Galla out into the courtyard where hundreds of Goths were busy packing crates and loading up carts. Heda directed Galla to a cart piled high with cages filled with cackling chickens. Heda nodded at the cart but Galla could not understand what she wanted. Finally Heda pushed Galla onto the cart and shouted at the driver to move out. The driver slapped the reins across the oxen's backs and the two heavy beasts lumbered off. In a few minutes they became one more cart in a river of carts, all moving in a steady flow across the Italian countryside.

Galla looked up at the sky and saw the rising sun was on her left. "We're heading south," she thought. "South! That must be away from Honorius and his troops in Ravenna. Perhaps Honorius has sent his troops southward to rescue me and these barbarians are retreating."

Galla watched as the long line of barbarians grew in length and width. She had no idea that so many of these Germanic tribes had invaded Italy. It was one thing to *hear* about them, but it was quite another thing to actually *see* the thousands of Goths moving across the landscape.

Several hours passed before the long caravan slowed to a stop. The sun was high in the sky and the day was uncommonly warm, even for August. The driver pulled the cart up alongside a shady tree next to a narrow creek. He climbed down off the cart, went over to a bush and relieved himself.

Galla turned away in disgust. "Animals! They're just like animals! No! They're worse," Galla thought indignantly. "Animals don't know any better. These are human beings . . ." she paused in her thoughts and looked back at the man lacing up his trousers, "or are they?"

Galla stepped down off the cart, went over to the creek, and splashed some water on her face. She longed for a bath and fresh clothes. Galla stretched. It felt good to be off of that rocking cart. She wondered why the Goths weren't taking the smooth roads; it would be so much more comfortable. Galla shook the water from her hands, went over and sat down under the shady tree. Suddenly she was aware of Alaric's raspy voice. She turned and saw Alaric riding a fine black stallion alongside a cart carrying several women, Heda and Letta among them.

"Stop here!" Alaric barked after he surveyed the shady spot beside the stream where Galla was sitting. Alaric dismounted and the cart drew to a stop. The women stepped off the cart and began unpacking baskets of fruit and cheese. The women occasionally threw Galla a resentful glance. Finally one of the women said something to Alaric.

Alaric shouted at Galla, "Go! Help! What are you, some kind of princess?"

Galla stood up and walked over to help the women unload the cart and set up lunch. Just as they were about to eat, Athaulf rode up on a beautiful chestnut mare. He dismounted using a metal loop suspended from a seat atop the horse. Without thinking, Galla went over to examine this unusual horse trapping. Athaulf saw her interest and he explained in Latin that the metal foot loop was an Asian device called a stirrup. It allowed one to mount and dismount more easily, and to maneuver the animal more efficiently.

"Stirrups! Stirrups!" Alaric interrupted. "Who needs these fancy foreign things? Those are for women! Look at you Athaulf, even your horse is a woman!"

Alaric wondered why no one was laughing at his joke and then he realized that he had been speaking Latin. He quickly translated his clever remark into Gothic and the crowd howled with delight.

Athaulf laughed, too, and walked over to where Letta was waiting for him, leaving Galla standing alone by the horse.

When lunch was over, the women packed up and the caravan set off again, bumping slowly over the rugged terrain. It was well past nightfall before the carts drew to a halt again. Galla climbed down from the cart and brushed the chicken feathers from her soiled dress. This time she didn't wait to be ordered to help the women. She walked over and began to unpack their cart. The women smirked at her feeble efforts to assist with the heavy crates. As the men assembled the tents, the women killed several of the chickens, plucked them, and dropped them whole into pots of boiling water.

When the chores were completed, Galla sat down on a log by the roaring fire. Her back ached from the long ride and from unloading the wooden crates. The Goths began to help themselves to the soup. Galla looked around for the pile of plates and knives like at the Roman farmhouse the night before, but she could find none.

Alaric was busy talking to some men and he didn't notice that Galla was without a bowl and knife. Athaulf noticed Galla's dilemma and he ordered Letta to find a cup and knife for Galla. Letta stubbornly refused, but Athaulf spoke more firmly. Finally Letta got up, dug through some boxes, found a cup and an old knife and tossed them over to Galla.

"Thank you," Galla said in Latin, but Letta just glowered at her and sat back down next to Athaulf.

When the meal was finished, Galla noticed that the Goths rinsed their bowls and knives in the river and then placed them in leather pouches they wore suspended from their heavy belts. Galla had neither pouch nor belt, so she rinsed her bowl and knife and placed them in the cart where she assumed she would ride again the next day.

After the dinner things were put away, the men gathered by the campfire and passed a jug around, each man taking a long sip in his turn. Most of the women wandered off to their tents with their children. Finally the jug was empty and the fire burned low. One by one the men wandered off to sleep. Galla watched as Letta led Athaulf to a large tent made of heavy branches covered with goatskins. Letta held up the flap door of the tent and Athaulf entered. She tossed Galla an icy glance, entered the tent, and dropped the flap behind them.

Galla found herself alone by the dying firelight. She shivered in the cool night air and looked around for a place to sleep. She decided to try sleeping propped up under a big tree. She was afraid to lie down on the grass among all the crawling insects. She sat down with her back against the rough bark, wrapped her arms around her knees for warmth and placed her head on her arms. Just as she was drifting off to sleep something startled her awake again. Galla looked up to see a tall figure looming over her. Galla gasped.

"Have no fear, Your Highness. It is I, Athaulf. I came to bring you this." He knelt down on one knee, carefully unfolded a burlap blanket and placed it gently over her. His face was close to hers and his green eyes shone in the moonlight.

"Thank you, Athaulf, you are very kind," Galla stammered wishing she could think of something else to say. He continued looking deep into her eyes as if searching for something . . . then he rose and returned to his tent. Galla watched as he walked across the open field. As he approached his tent, the flap opened and Letta stood silhouetted against the open door. Athaulf entered the tent and Letta closed the flap behind him.

Galla sat in the darkness thinking about Athaulf. This was the man whom Julius and Fortus said would make a better leader than his headstrong brother Alaric. Now Galla could see for herself why many in Rome wished for Athaulf to become chieftain of the Goths.

Galla's thoughts turned to Julius and Fortus. "Poor Julius," Galla thought sadly, "he must be *so* worried. And Fortus! What has become of him? Is he rotting in some foul prison . . . or . . . or worse?" Galla refused to allow herself to think of what worse things could befall her dear Fortus. She looked over at the tent and imagined Letta lying safe within the strong arms of Athaulf. Galla's heart ached and she longed to be with Fortus again, secure within his gentle embrace.

The next day was much like the first, as was the following day, and each of the days after that. The Goths continued to head south. Each evening the cooking pots were filled with livestock stolen from the surrounding farms. Each night the Goths passed the jugs around and drank to oblivion. Even when the Goths found an empty farm and a good strong farmhouse for shelter, they still slept in their makeshift tents. The Goths cared little where Galla chose to sleep and she often sought the comfort of a room in an empty farmhouse.

One evening after the supper things were put away and the men were taking their turns with the jug, Galla slipped off into the big farmhouse to look for a place to sleep. The barbarians had stripped the place bare as usual, but this time they had overlooked one room, and Galla found a bed that had not been burned in the evening's fire.

"A bed! A real bed!" Galla thought as she entered the room. She hadn't slept on a bed in weeks and she raced over and sat down on the soft feather mattress. "Ahh," she sighed out loud as she sank into the deep down.

"Do you like it?" a voice came from the hallway. Galla looked up and saw Athaulf standing in the doorway. "Do you like the bed?"

"Yes," Galla said slowly.

"I had the men leave it for you," Athaulf explained. "I've noticed how you've sought shelter beneath roofs whenever you can, and I remembered that you Romans love beds," he said as he entered the room and looked around. "Strange, I don't understand why you like those things. I tried it once, it hurt my back." He smiled.

"I guess it's just a matter of what we're used to. Sleeping on the ground hurts my back," Galla replied.

Athaulf nodded. "May I?" he said pointing to the bed. "I see my men didn't leave a chair."

Galla moved to one end of the bed and Athaulf seated himself on the other end as far away as possible from where Galla was seated. As always, she was amazed at his command of the Latin language. Other than a tiny hint of an accent, one would think that he had been born in Rome itself.

"Yes," Athaulf said, "I guess it *is* a matter of what you're used to. Like this room, you feel safe here. I don't like to be closed-in inside rooms. I can't hear what's going on outside, I can't pick up scents in the air, I can't feel what's going on outdoors. I don't feel safe inside."

"But what about where you live back home, don't you have houses, real houses?" Galla asked.

"Home?" Athaulf looked blank.

"Yes, home, where you live, where you came from," Galla explained.

"Ah, home, yes, I know what you mean. You Romans are an unusual lot. You live in one place and seldom leave it. You call that 'home.' We Goths are home wherever we are, wherever we're together. We live where we are, like here," Athaulf said simply.

"But surely you're going to go back where you came from someday," Galla replied.

"We didn't come *from* anywhere, we just came," Athaulf laughed.

"I mean where you were born, where your family is," Galla said beginning to show her frustration with the conversation.

Athaulf smiled and said, "I don't know where I was born. We Goths don't mark places and name them like you Romans do. I was born somewhere in the north where it gets very cold in the winter, or at least that's what my mother told me. She died a few years ago. The only family I have is here with me now," Athaulf shrugged.

"Like Alaric? I heard in Rome that he is your brother."

"Yes," Athaulf nodded, "he's a great warrior and a great chieftain."

"And Letta, is she your wife?" Galla asked slowly.

"Letta is my . . . my property. I won her in a battle. She belongs to me."

"Oh," Galla said awkwardly. "I thought you Goths were Arian Christians. I thought you believed in holy matrimony . . . that you took wives in marriage."

"We do. Many of the men in our tribe are married. Their wives are here, and their children. We marry when we are ready. Until then, we find other companionship. It's not good for a man to be alone."

"So, you're not going to marry Letta?" Galla asked but quickly withdrew her question. "I'm sorry, that was rude. I shouldn't have asked so personal a question."

Athaulf gave her a sidelong glance. "No, I won't marry Letta." He stood up without any further explanation. He walked over and stood before Galla. He picked up one of her long curls in his massive hand. "You have hair the color of fire," he whispered. He dropped the curl, turned, and walked out of the room.

Galla walked over to the window and watched Athaulf stride away from the farmhouse over to where the men were seated around the fire. She heard Alaric's raspy voice bellow out, "Where have you been? We've been looking everywhere for you! You've been with her, haven't you? You stay away from her! She's mine! You hear me, Athaulf? She's mine!"

Galla saw Athaulf say something back to Alaric but he spoke too quietly for Galla to hear. Athaulf took several long drinks from the jug then he walked off and disappeared inside his tent.

Galla reclined on the soft bed and propped up her head on the pillow. She wondered what it was about this Athaulf that affected her so. She was somehow drawn to him. It wasn't the same type of feeling she had for Fortus. She grew up with Fortus and she felt she knew everything about him . . . they were so alike. And here was Athaulf, a Gothic barbarian, as different from Galla as night from day. And yet she felt inexplicably attracted by him.

A sudden pang of guilt pierced Galla's heart. "Oh Fortus, darling," Galla thought, "forgive me. You may be lying in a filthy jail cell and here I am letting my imagination run away like a silly schoolgirl. I feel nothing for this Athaulf except gratitude. He's been kind to me. He's the only one who seems even remotely human around here. It's only natural that I feel friendship towards him, even if he is a Goth."

Galla grasped her hands together and prayed, "Dear Heavenly Father, thank You for providing me with a protector during these trying times. Please help Athaulf to see the error in his Arian heresy and to recognize Your son Jesus as Christ. And, Dear God, bless and keep our beloved Fortus. Give the Senate the wisdom to know the truth from the lies so that they will free this innocent man. Bless, too, oh Father, Uncle Julius, Pontus, and Claudia. Keep them safe from harm. And, if it please You, oh Heavenly Father, please bring us all together again safely under the veil of Your Divine Love. Amen."

CHAPTER III

The weeks wore on as Alaric drove his people relentlessly down the Italian peninsula. Usually word of the approach of the plundering barbarians preceded their arrival and the towns and villages were often deserted by the time the Goths arrived. Many Romans were not so fortunate, however, and the vicious Goths fell upon them without warning, pillaging, raping, burning, looting, and killing without mercy. Wherever they went, the Goths left a trail of death and destruction. Galla was forced to witness the brutal destruction of her countrymen and her land as the nefarious tribes traversed the length of Italy.

One day, late in the autumn of 410, the Goths reached the southern tip of Italy. When the Goths arrived at the strait across from Sicily, they set up camp. Galla had discerned from the bits and pieces of information that she could gather, that Alaric planned to sail to Africa to secure the grain that Honorius had refused him. Alaric ordered several small groups of men to go out to steal boats, any boats they could get their hands on, from small fishing craft to Roman galleys. Alaric was in a hurry to cross over to Sicily before winter set in and the seas became too rough to cross over to the island.

Galla noticed that the Goths took more time and trouble than usual setting up their camp. She speculated that they planned to leave some of their people here, perhaps the women and children, while the rest went on the expedition to Sicily and then on to Africa. Galla wondered if Athaulf, too, would sail for Africa. He was the only one among the Goths who had been kind to her and the thought of his leaving troubled her.

As usual, Galla helped unload the crates and set up the camp. She unpacked the few bundles of possessions that she had managed to accumulate from cast-off items of the Goths and from deserted Roman farmhouses along the way. She was sorry to see that the Goths had chosen a campsite far away from any Roman town or villa. There was no sturdy house to provide shelter for her, a fact that concerned Galla greatly particularly with the approach of winter. A cold wind blew from the north and white-capped waves dotted the strait to Sicily.

The days were short this time of year and darkness fell before the camp was completed. Alaric and most of the men were off on looting parties, but Athaulf remained behind to direct the camp preparations. Athaulf approached Galla while she was filling a large kettle with water.

"No house here for you, eh?"

"No," Galla replied, "No house here." Galla looked around the barren landscape.

"I'll build one for you," Athaulf smiled.

"*Build* one? It's not easy to build a house."

"It can't be that hard. Tell me what to do, and I'll build a little house for you," Athaulf looked at her with enthusiasm.

"Well," Galla said as she placed the kettle on the fire and wiped her hands on her apron, "it takes bricks and cement, I guess."

"All right, bricks and cement. How do we make them?"

"Make them?" Galla asked.

"Yes, we need bricks and cement. We don't have any bricks or cement, so you'll have to tell us how to make them."

Galla thought long and hard, and then admitted sheepishly, "I don't *know* how to make them. I always took them for granted. They were just there."

She shrugged her shoulders and thought of the many things she used every day that she would be unable to make herself. She looked at the bronze kettle over the fire. "I guess I never thought about it. I guess there are a lot of things I don't know how to make."

Galla had spent the last months feeling quite superior to the Goths because she came from a society with so many advantages-- aqueducts, baths, fountains, and *houses*. Now she realized that she was just the recipient of those technologies, not the creator. She was suddenly humbled.

Athaulf saw the perplexed expression on her face, "No matter. I know how to build tents. Tomorrow I'll build you a good Gothic tent. A Gothic tent is better than a Roman house we can't build," he laughed.

Galla smiled, partly at his joke and partly at the kindness he was once again showing her. "Thank you, Athaulf. I will be grateful for a fine Gothic tent." Galla reached out and shook Athaulf's hand. Galla then tried to withdraw her hand but Athaulf continued to hold on to it.

"Look," he said as he held her hand out flat with the palm up. He ran his finger over the calluses on her palm. He looked down sadly into her eyes. "I'm sorry," he said. Then he dropped her hand, turned and walked slowly away.

When Galla awoke the next morning, Athaulf was gone and only the women and children remained in camp. Galla seated herself by a crop of trees next to the edge of the sea and looked out over the strait to Sicily. "Surely," she thought to herself, "surely Honorius will not let the Goths cross over to Africa. Surely *this* will get Honorius to act and to send an army to rescue me." Galla watched thin columns of smoke rising from the island across the strait. "What an odd time to have cooking fires," Galla thought and dismissed the unusual sight.

As the sun reached high noon, Galla heard the sound of men's voices in the camp. She returned to find Athaulf and several men hard at work building a brick wall.

"Look!" Athaulf said proudly. "We found some bricks and some cement. There isn't enough to build an entire house, but we'll be able to build two walls. The rest will be a tent. We will *compromise*. Isn't that how you say it?"

"Yes," Galla smiled, deeply touched at Athaulf's efforts, "a compromise, and an excellent idea." Galla thought back to all the years of strife between the Romans and the Goths. If only they could have reached a compromise before, she wouldn't be standing here on the edge of the earth with a cold north wind blowing in her face.

Letta walked up and uttered a few angry words to Athaulf who told her to go back to their tent. Letta passed by Galla and spit at her. Athaulf walked over, took Letta by the arm and chastised her in Gothic. "No, Letta, that won't make things better. It will only make things worse. If you want to stay with me, you must treat this Roman with respect, the way she has treated you."

Letta yanked her arm away from Athaulf's grip and stalked away.

"'This Roman,'" Galla thought about Athaulf's words. "Is that how he thinks of me? Not as a person, but as his enemy, a Roman?" Galla had been so busy thinking of the Goths as *her* enemy, that she never stopped to think that they, too, thought of her as *their* enemy.

By nightfall, the two brick walls were completed. Athaulf had built the walls on the north and east sides of the small shelter to keep out the worst of the winter winds. It would take a day or so for the cement to dry before the other two walls of sticks and skins could be added, so the men ceased their work for the day. The workers climbed down the shallow cliff to the sea where they bathed in the cold waters of the strait.

After dinner Galla returned to the little crop of trees overlooking the coast. She spread out her sleeping blanket and arranged her few meager possessions. She sat looking out over the strait towards Sicily, watching their fires burning brightly. She wondered if they had any idea that the barbarians were just a few miles off their coast. She heard a rustling in the bushes and Athaulf appeared.

"Here, I brought you this," Athaulf said, handing her a jug of wine. "I found it today." He sat down next to Galla and poured two cups full of the deep red wine. He took a sip. "It's good," he commented. "It's sweet." Then Athaulf knit his brows and lowered his voice in imitation of Alaric's gruff accent, "Something for women!" he mocked.

Galla threw back her head and laughed. Athaulf said, "You are even more beautiful when you laugh. I imagine when you are at home you laugh often," he said with a tinge of sadness in his voice. "You must have many friends."

"Yes," Galla replied and the faces of her friends appeared in her mind's eye. She took another sip of wine and thought about what her friends were doing that evening. Galla sighed deeply.

Athaulf picked up one of her hands and held it gently in his. "I'm sorry it has to be like this, Galla. I've spoken to Alaric about letting you return to Rome, but he refuses. He still thinks your brother will bow to his demands in exchange for your safe return."

"What do *you* think, Athaulf?"

"I think your brother is a very stubborn man. I don't think he will ever give in to Alaric."

"I'm beginning to doubt it, too," Galla sighed.

Athaulf looked out across the strait to Sicily. "Perhaps if our expedition to Africa is a success . . . perhaps if Alaric gets the grain we need there . . . he may let you go when he no longer needs you."

Galla, too, looked out towards Sicily, and for the first time she found herself supporting the Gothic cause. After all, all they wanted was some grain and some land on which to settle. Rome's provinces in Africa had plenty of grain and Rome's empire had plenty of land. Why shouldn't these poor people share in Rome's bounty? Wasn't that part of the Roman task--generosity to the conquered?

The fires dotting Sicily's coastline caught Galla's eye again. "They certainly have many towns, don't they?" Galla commented.

"You mean the fires? No, those aren't towns. Their towns are all built several miles inland to protect them from pirates. The fires you see are along the beaches. The people are praying to their idols to bring terrible winds to destroy our fleets as we cross the strait."

"Praying to their idols? I thought the Sicilians were Christians," Galla said with surprise.

"Oh, they *are* Christians, when it suits them. But now they think the problem is too big for only one invisible God and they have created a graven image to help them."

"Fools!" Galla said with disgust. "Don't they know there is only one true God? What they are doing is blasphemy!"

"Your Christian faith gives you much comfort and strength, doesn't it, Galla?"

"Yes, Athaulf, it does. I'm sorry you don't know Christ as I do. He is my shepherd, my protector."

"Oh, I believe that Jesus existed," Athaulf protested. "I simply do not believe that he is God. I believe he was created by God and therefore he is inferior to God."

"Then you've missed the point of Christ's coming. God sent His Son to save us, but to be saved we must believe He is the Son of God. Don't you see?"

Athaulf shook his head. "I only believe in a higher being-- someone or some thing had to create all this," Athaulf gestured to the sea and sky. "I don't believe that ordinary men can become gods."

"Jesus was no ordinary man. He was . . . *is* the true Son of God."

Athaulf smiled at her perseverance. "When I *see* it, I will *believe* it," he said.

Galla looked at him and smiled. "When you *believe* it, you will *see* it," she replied.

Within the week, the Goths were ready to set sail on the first leg of their journey to Africa. The ships were loaded and the Goths all assembled on the beach to bid goodbye to the first contingent of ships. Alaric and Athaulf wished the departing men well and helped push the vessels out to sea. They stood on the rocky beach a long time, watching as the ragged armada of assorted boats headed off for Sicily. When the boats were well off the shore, the Goths who remained behind began the long climb back up the cliffs to the camp above. Athaulf, Alaric, and the men strode on ahead as the women and children struggled along behind.

By the time they reached the summit of the rocky cliff, a stiff wind was blowing and it was obvious that the ships were having trouble staying their course. Before long the stiff wind became a gale. The Goths watched helplessly from the cliffs as, one by one, their tiny vessels disappeared beneath the towering waves.

Men hung their heads and women wailed with anguish. The women who still had men on shore ran to them and threw their arms around them, shouting words of praise to God for sparing their men folk. Galla looked over at Athaulf and saw Letta hanging tearfully on his arm. Galla knelt down and prayed for the souls of the dead men. Several of the Goths joined her but most simply walked away. When Galla looked up from her prayers, she saw Athaulf kneeling close by. Letta was not beside him.

CHAPTER IV

The disaster to the fleet was a devastating blow to the Goths. They had walked the long length of Italy in hopes of crossing over to Africa via the short sea route. Their only other hope of reaching Africa was from the tip of Spain, a journey of countless miles and, since they marched so slowly, perhaps years. The Goths remained in their camp for several days and argued over what they should do. Some men suggested that they stay where they were camped and try to build a second fleet. Others voted to march straight to Ravenna and face Honorius and his forces there. Still others argued that they should have gone to Spain in the first place--that the strait of Gibraltar was the only safe place to cross over to Africa.

Galla listened as the men tossed around suggestions and insults. She was glad she had never disclosed that she understood the Gothic language. Galla hoped that the Goths would return north to Rome and thereby give the Roman forces a good chance to attack the Goths and to rescue her. From the first day of her abduction Galla had made up her mind that she would endure her captivity with the Goths, but as weeks stretched into months she was growing weary and her patience was wearing thin.

One evening, after a long and particularly heated discussion among the Goths, Alaric finally rose to his feet and shouted at the men to be silent. "I am your chief. I have listened to you and I have heard your words. Now it is up to *me* to make a decision." The men watched Alaric anxiously. "We are tired," Alaric continued. "We have marched all the way here without a long rest. Our women are thin and some of our children have died. We cannot go on this way. We must rest, we must rebuild our strength."

The other men nodded and began to talk. "Silence!" Alaric commanded. "We cannot stay here," Alaric said as he glanced around at the rocky coast. "There is nothing for us here. We cannot go south--the seas will not permit a winter crossing." Alaric paused and eyed his men, "We must go north."

Several men cheered and Alaric again ordered silence. "I want you to listen carefully to what I have to say," Alaric's eyes burned with intensity. "I'm tired of waiting on that old woman in Ravenna. I'm tired of these Romans thinking they can tell us what to do. Attalus has failed us. We made him Emperor but he, too, turned soft, like everything Rome touches! It's time Rome had a *man* to lead them!"

Alaric paused and everyone hung on his next words. "There is only one way to control a headstrong woman and that is to beat her into submission. *I* will be Emperor and *I* will beat this Rome into submission!" The men all rose to their feet and cheered wildly.

When the first shouts of approval died down, Athaulf stood up and approached his brother. "It's a good plan, my brother," Athaulf said slowly, "a fine plan. But how do you intend to become Emperor? It won't be easy."

"Easy!" Alaric scoffed. "Easy! Has Rome softened you, too, little brother?" Alaric slapped Athaulf's face and laughed sadistically. "*This*! *This* is how I intend to become Emperor of Rome!" Alaric strode over to Galla, grabbed her arm and dragged her to her feet. "This! This is our ticket to prosperity," Alaric shouted as he pushed Galla towards the crowd. "The winter solstice is in three days. On that day I will wed this little Roman pork chop . . . and then we'll all eat off the fat of Rome!"

The crowd burst into a frenzy of celebration. They began to dance around the fire, chanting wildly. Galla saw Letta staring at her through the frenetic crowd. Letta smiled coldly and then she, too, joined the ecstatic dance.

The revelry lasted until dawn. Galla could hear the last of the celebrants returning to their tents as the first light of day crept over the rugged coastline. Galla lay awake in her little shelter wondering how her life had come to this terrible point. She thought briefly of running to the rocky cliffs and throwing herself off, but she knew in her heart that suicide was not an option for a true Christian. Only God can give life and only God can take it away.

Galla stared at the walls of her little house and examined Athaulf's crude workmanship. All night long Galla had expected

Athaulf to come to comfort her, to offer a solution, but it was morning now and still he had not come. "No," Galla thought to herself, "I'm alone this time, really alone. Athaulf may be kind, but he is, after all, a Goth and Alaric is not only his brother, but his chief as well. Even Athaulf cannot help me now. Only God can save me from this terrible fate."

Galla's thoughts turned to her other suitors--Eucherius, Attalus--somehow they didn't seem so objectionable now, not when compared to this vulgar giant of a barbarian. Galla wondered if she should try to escape. "It might be better to be killed trying to get away than to be forced to marry that Gothic animal!" she thought hatefully. "But even if I succeeded and Alaric didn't find and kill me, what would I do out there alone? Where would I go? The Goths aren't the only bands of marauding brigands out there now." Galla moaned, rolled over and buried her face in her hands.

"Get up!" Galla turned to see Heda standing in the makeshift doorway motioning her to stand. "We're leaving." Heda turned and left, dropping the flap of the tent behind her. Galla quickly gathered together her meager possessions and boarded the usual wooden cart. As the carts and wagons began moving out of the camp, Galla caught a glimpse of Athaulf riding away on his horse. She turned back to look at the camp. She watched her little house grow smaller and smaller as the cart carried her northward.

In the evening of the second day, the Goths stopped and set up camp alongside a little river. The following day would be the winter solstice and the Goths began the preparations for the wedding celebration. Galla sat by the fire and watched as they constructed a large canopy and draped it with garlands of foliage. Several lambs were slaughtered, skinned, and set to roast over low fires. The wedding festivities would begin at dawn and last until the following day. Galla had witnessed several barbarian weddings during her sojourn with the Goths. She imagined that the wedding of the chief of all the tribes would be the most elaborate and the most unrestrained. From all across the countryside small bands of Goths arrived. Each group brought gifts to the bride and groom. The pile of gifts and loot grew higher with each passing hour. At dusk the music and dancing began.

Galla had not seen Athaulf since the morning he rode off when they left the camp at the strait. "Maybe he's gone for good," Galla thought forlornly. "Perhaps he objects to Alaric's plan and he's gone off to join another band of Goths. Well," she shrugged, "he couldn't do anything for me even if he *were* here," Galla thought as she watched Alaric and his men open a barrel of ale.

Alaric was in an especially raucous mood that evening. He consumed an enormous quantity of the ale and ordered Heda to open another barrel. He finally got up and announced crudely, "I've got to piss." And he wandered off into the brush.

The revelry continued and it was a long time before anyone noticed that Alaric had not returned. When some of the celebrants expressed concern about the whereabouts of the bridegroom, the others only laughed and jibed, "He's probably run off! He's probably changed his mind about marrying that Roman bitch!" The crowd laughed and continued their merriment.

Dawn arrived and still Alaric had not returned. Some of the men formed a search party and set off to look for their chief. They returned less than an hour later, bearing the lifeless body of Alaric on a makeshift litter. The men said they found him at the bottom of a ravine. They surmised that he must have stumbled into the ravine in the darkness. His neck was broken. They carried the litter over to the camp and placed it under the wedding canopy. Women began to wail and the men hung their heads in sorrow.

Later that day, the Goths diverted the waters of the little river next to which they were camped. They dug a deep hole in the river bed, placed Alaric's body in the hole, covered him with the treasures that the guests had brought as wedding gifts, and filled in the grave with soil and rocks. Then the river was returned to its normal course. The slaves and captives who had helped to bury the chief were then killed and left as carrion for the wild animals and birds.

The Goths were now left without a chief and bitter fighting began among them. Several extended families broke away from the main tribe and wandered off on their own. After a week of fierce infighting among the various factions, Athaulf returned. He didn't offer an explanation of where he'd been, nor did his people ask. When he was told of Alaric's untimely death, he merely nodded and avoided Galla's eyes. None dared to challenge Athaulf's claim to leadership of the tribe, in part because he was the rightful inheritor of the position and in part because he was unarguably the most accomplished warrior among them. Whatever sibling rivalry had spurred Alaric to make his disparaging remarks about Athaulf's manhood, their fellow Goths acknowledged Athaulf as the finest fighter of their tribe. So it was decided . . . Athaulf was the new chief of the Goths and his first decision was to move north to Rome.

That evening Athaulf came over to where Galla had spread her blanket. He sat down next to her but he didn't speak. They sat together for a long time, watching the Goths around the distant campfires. Finally Athaulf reached into the leather pouch he wore hanging from his belt. He pulled out a large silver ring and handed it to Galla. "It belonged to my mother. I want you to have it." Athaulf said quietly.

Galla took the ring and placed it on the first finger of her right hand. This ring was larger and more crudely carved than the tiny bronze ring she wore from Fortus. This ring was decorated with an elaborate interlace pattern reflecting the wanderings of the migrating tribes themselves. Galla looked at the two rings on her hand. They were only inches apart in space but they were worlds apart in culture and in symbolism. One was heavy and rough, the other sophisticated and fine.

Athaulf, too, studied the two rings on Galla's hand. He stared at the tiny bronze ring bearing the chi-rho cross. "It's from a friend in Rome," Galla explained, although Athaulf hadn't asked.

Athaulf sat quietly, looking at the ring. Finally he looked at Galla and said, "I can arrange his release from prison." Galla's eyes widened with surprise. Athaulf looked back down at the ring again. Athaulf said quietly, "It was Marcus who arranged for the Goths to enter through the Salarian Gates, not your friend. I can send word to the Senate. They will arrest Marcus and free your friend."

Athaulf looked up to see Galla's reaction. Her eyes were filled with tears of happiness. Athaulf looked down sadly. "If I do this, Galla, you must promise that you will stay here with me; that you won't try to return to Rome or to him." He stared fixedly at the ground, the muscles in his temples flexing strongly.

Galla drew a quick breath and stared disbelievingly at Athaulf. "But, I don't understand, Athaulf. Would you force me to stay here against my will?"

Athaulf stood up and stared at the sky. His face was strained and he swallowed hard. Galla stood also, took his hand and looked up entreatingly into his eyes. He looked down at her and she could see tears sparkling in his emerald green eyes. Athaulf drew her to him, clasped his arms fiercely around her and said, "I would rather tear my heart out and send it to Rome than send you back to him. I'm sorry, Galla, but I cannot let you go, not now. Not now that I . . ." He clasped Galla tighter and buried his face in her hair.

Galla's mind raced and she thought of Fortus laying in a filthy jail these many months. How could she allow him to rot in prison for a crime he did not commit? But never to see Fortus again, how could she bear it? Galla felt as if her heart would tear in two but she knew what she had to do. "All right, Athaulf, I promise."

Athaulf held Galla out in front of him at arm's length. He looked deep into her eyes. "You must write him. You must write him to say this is your decision so he won't come after you once he's free."

"Yes, Athaulf, I'll write him. I just want Fortus to be free. What he thinks of me is not important."

Athaulf called out and ordered vellum and ink for Galla so she could write to Fortus. Athaulf then left Galla alone. Galla sat down under a large tree and thought for a long time before she took up the quill and wrote.

My dearest Fortus,
I hope this letter finds you well and safely out of prison. We both owe a great debt to Athaulf for arranging your release. Speak well of him in Rome. I have chosen to stay with Athaulf. Perhaps, through him, I can help bring peace to our two peoples. I send my love to Julius, Pontus and Claudia. May they bring you much comfort and joy,

especially Claudia. Do not fear for my safety, I am in good health and I am well provided for. May God bless you and keep you, now and forevermore.
Galla

Galla reread the letter. "Yes," she thought to herself, "this is best. Even if I were to return to Rome, Honorius or someone else would just marry me off to the highest bidder. This way Fortus can get on with his life and find some happiness of his own. I don't think I was born for happiness. I think God must have other plans for me. Perhaps, through Athaulf, I can *do* something for Rome, instead of merely serving as an Imperial carrot to potential suitors."

Galla finished rereading the letter and signaled to Athaulf that she was finished. Athaulf came over and read the letter. Galla could see he was struggling hard with his decision, torn between wanting to keep her with him and knowing he should let her go. "Galla," Athaulf began in an unsteady voice, his eyes revealing the torture in his soul.

"It's all right, Athaulf," Galla interrupted. "I've thought it over. I think it's best if I stay." Athaulf searched her eyes. "I want to stay, Athaulf."

Athaulf took her hand and kissed it gently, gratitude and love shining in his eyes. He turned and walked back to his tent where Letta was standing waiting for him. Athaulf entered his tent, closed the flap, and left Letta standing outside. Letta never again slept in Athaulf's tent.

CHAPTER V

The route they took north was far to the east of Rome. Galla was unsure if this circuitous route was due to the availability of prosperous farms in that area, or if it was to keep her as far away from Rome as possible. Once they passed Rome, the tribes again moved to the west of Italy for fear of encountering Honorius' troops from Ravenna in the east.

The Goths moved like a plague of locusts, leaving nothing but death and destruction in their path. As always, Galla wondered how Honorius could let these people devastate his own country. Galla also wondered what the Goths would do once they had pillaged and plundered all of Italy.

As the Goths journeyed northward, Athaulf continued the negotiations with Honorius in Ravenna. Oftentimes responses were sent from a man named Constantius, a newcomer to Honorius' court. It appeared that Constantius was making every effort to thwart Athaulf's attempts to bring peace to the two peoples. At the same time Constantius was interfering with treaty negotiations, he also began to bargain for Galla's release.

One evening after dinner, Athaulf handed Galla a large scroll bearing the Imperial seal. "What do you think of this?" Athaulf asked. Galla read the scroll. "Do you know this Constantius?" Athaulf asked.

"Yes, I know of him. He was a friend of my cousin Serena."

"Tell me about him," Athaulf asked.

"I really don't know much about him," Galla replied. "He was Serena's friend, and Stilicho's. Back then he was some kind of businessman, trade or something like that. I didn't know he was with Honorius in Ravenna." Galla looked at the Imperial eagle on the seal. "He must be pretty high up in Honorius' circle to use this," she pointed to the seal.

"What do you think about the letter? What do you think he really wants?" Athaulf asked, carefully watching Galla's expression.

Galla looked back at Constantius' letter. "It looks to me as if we have one more pretender to the throne. Everybody and his brother wants to be Emperor of Rome," Galla said with contempt as she stood up and threw the scroll into Athaulf's lap. "He's very generous, isn't he?" Galla scoffed. "He's offering you all of Aquitane if you hand me over to him." Galla turned to look at Athaulf. "It sounds like a good bargain for you and your people-- one Roman prisoner in exchange for an entire land in which to settle."

Athaulf stood up and walked over to Galla. "Why do you think this Constantius has asked for your return when Honorius, your own brother, has never asked for your release?"

"Because my brother cannot marry me," Galla said with disgust. "Honorius is all too happy to have me here with you, instead of married to a would-be Emperor."

"That's what I thought," Athaulf said slowly. "What do you think we should do?"

Galla looked at Athaulf, surprised that he was asking her opinion on these matters. She picked up a long stick and began poking at the fire, stirring up the embers. "I wouldn't trust him if I were you, Athaulf. What guarantee would you have that he would really give you the land in Aquitane, providing it's his to give?"

Athaulf smiled, "I agree, Galla. I don't think we can trust this Constantius, either. What would you do now, if you were me?"

Galla looked up at Athaulf with surprise. "What would *I* do if I were *you*?" Galla laughed.

"I mean it, Galla. If you were the chief of this people, what would you do now?"

Galla finished poking at the fire and sat down on a big log. She stared at the flames as she thought about the options. "I'd try to find a place where my people could live peacefully--somewhere they could build a life for themselves."

"Ah," Athaulf said as he lowered himself down onto the log beside her, "that's a Roman speaking, not a Goth. You speak of peace and of building. The Goths don't know those words." Athaulf glanced over to the big campfire where the men were drinking and telling bawdy stories. "Look at them," Athaulf nodded at the group of drunken tribesmen. "Do you think they're interested in peace or in building snug little houses? They're only interested in their stomachs and their groins!"

"But you're their leader," Galla reasoned. "*You* can *lead* them to peace." Athaulf laughed but Galla continued, "You *can* lead them to peace. Oh, not all at once, but little by little." Athaulf stopped laughing but he continued to give her a bemused smile as she carefully described her ideas for bringing peace to the wandering tribes.

"First of all, you need to begin to establish order--you need to make some laws. Once you have laws, the people will know what they can and cannot do. That way you get the people to do what's best for the group." Athaulf laughed again. "Well, you asked me," Galla retorted, "so I'm telling you. That's how Rome became great . . . through her laws . . . through her order," Galla said angrily.

Athaulf saw Galla's irritation and he became serious again. "Yes, Galla, I know of Rome's great laws . . . innocent until proven guilty . . . jury of one's peers . . . all that. But Rome has had a thousand years to develop those laws. I need to decide what to do *now*. How should I respond to this would-be Emperor Constantius?"

"Don't deal with him at all," Galla advised, "to do so would be to acknowledge that he has power. Only negotiate with Honorius. That will keep Constantius in the background and perhaps he'll tire of striving for the Imperial throne."

"Perhaps it's not just the throne he's after," Athaulf said as he picked up one of Galla's soft red curls.

Galla watched the firelight play across Athaulf's rugged features. He was an extraordinarily handsome man, not by Roman standards of sophistication and refinement, but by Germanic standards that valued brute power and animal instincts. His long, dark, flowing hair covered his shoulders and framed his square-jawed face and long straight nose. His body was large, but muscular and lean. Galla reached up and touched his high cheekbones with her fingertips. Athaulf took her hand and held her palm to his lips, a look of lust and longing in his green eyes. Then he quickly rose to his feet, "Good night, Galla," he said, dropping her hand. "I should go now." He turned and strode off into the darkness.

The seasons changed one by one as the Goths foraged the length of Italy, but still no agreement was reached between Athaulf and Honorius. Galla lost track of the months as one day spilled into the next. She fell into the easy flow of nomadic life . . . following the movements of herds of game and flocks of birds . . . measuring time by the cycles of the moon rather than by the months on the calendar.

Athaulf slowly brought a degree of peace to his people. He encouraged the Goths to hunt more and to pillage less. He countered talk of war and looting with discourses on the benefits of barter and trade. Some of the more bellicose members of the tribe split off on their own, accusing Athaulf of having gone soft from consorting with his Roman captive. Most of the Goths, however, welcomed their new, more placid lifestyle.

When Galla complained that she missed her library of fine books, Athaulf showed her how to "read" the countryside around her. Galla learned to identify the tracks of various animals and to unlock the medicinal potential of assorted plants. Little by little, her memories of Rome were supplanted by her new experiences with the Goths. Little by little, time numbed the sharp pain she felt when she thought of Fortus and of Rome.

The Goths' more peaceful behavior encouraged openness in the communication between Athaulf and Honorius. Couriers from both sides traversed the considerable distance between the Gothic camp and Ravenna. It was from Honorius in Ravenna that Athaulf learned of yet another pretender to the Imperial Throne . . . one Flavius Claudius Constantinus, known as Constantine. This individual had plotted long and hard to usurp the title of Emperor. Constantine had, in the process, gained control of Britain, Gaul, and Spain. In little more than a few years, Constantine had garnered power over a good portion of the Western Empire. It was from Honorius, too, that Athaulf learned of the decisive defeat of Constantine by Constantius, the Roman suitor to Galla. This splendid military victory, and Constantine's consequent execution, added greatly to Constantius' reputation and power both in

Ravenna and Rome. Once again, Constantius moved aggressively to secure Galla's release.

Early in 412, Athaulf decided that he had had enough of the futile negotiations with Honorius. Athaulf and his people left Italy, taking Galla with them. The journey over the Alps was more difficult than any of them had expected. Winter was over, but snow still blocked the usual routes through the mountains and a bitter cold wind slowed their progress. Many times the Goths begged to turn back and return to the sun and warmth of Italy, but Athaulf marched doggedly forward. By the time the Goths had traversed the frigid regions of the Alps, summer had arrived in their destination--Gaul.

When at last they reached a broad plain that was skirted by forests and traversed by a shallow river, Athaulf gave the order to set up camp. "Finally," Galla thought to herself as she unloaded her little cart, "I thought we would never stop."

Athaulf gave orders as Galla and the others began to set up their tents of branches and goatskins. Out of the corner of her eye Galla watched Athaulf as he skillfully assembled the small shelters. It was a warm day and he wore only a leather loincloth. His tall muscular frame shone bronze in the summer sun. Athaulf glanced in Galla's direction and he caught her appraising stare. Athaulf smiled and walked over to where Galla was standing. "Tomorrow I will build a little house for you," he offered. "We have no bricks or cement, but we have plenty of good rocks," he added as he surveyed the surrounding landscape.

"I'm getting used to my tent," Galla commented, but Athaulf interrupted, "No, tents are for Goths, houses are for Romans."

Galla was disappointed to think that after everything they had been through that Athaulf still thought of her as a Roman and not, at least in part, as one of his people. She had endured the same hardships, the same long walks, the same biting cold, and the same hunger. She had hunted and fished and cooked alongside the others.

"Will you always think of me as just a Roman?" Galla asked sadly.

"No, you are not just a Roman. You are Galla Placidia, the daughter of the great Emperor Theodosius and sister of the not-so-great Honorius," Athaulf teased.

Galla had to smile at Athaulf's jovial mood. "I'm serious, Athaulf, I would like you to think of me as one of you now." She secretly felt a pang of guilt that she had never disclosed to Athaulf that she understood Gothic. Perhaps if she spoke the people's language, they would accept her more. But after all this time, to disclose her lie now, she feared she would only gain the animosity of the people and of Athaulf.

One of Heda's sturdy little girls toddled over to Athaulf and asked to be picked up. Athaulf lifted the hefty two-year-old into his arms. "Why would you want to be one of us, Galla?" Athaulf asked, his tone growing serious. "Certainly you wouldn't prefer to be this little wild Goth than the most noble woman in Rome?" Athaulf said with a slightly indignant tone.

"Yes," Galla responded, realizing that she had kindled Athaulf's fierce loyalty towards his people, "I would. That little girl will grow up free and unencumbered by matters of state. She'll marry a boy of her own choosing from the tribe. She'll get to move around and see many countries . . ." Galla paused for a second, just long enough for Athaulf to add, "And she'll never have a permanent roof over her head, nor will she ever know where her next meal is coming from." Athaulf set the little girl back down on the ground and she toddled away. Galla and Athaulf stood watching as she clumsily made her way back to her mother.

"Oh, Athaulf!" Galla said as she turned to look at him, "If I'm going to live with these people, I want to feel a part of them and for them to feel I'm a part, too. They still look on me as an outsider, and you . . . well, I never know if one day you'll pack me up and send me back to Honorius. I want to belong somewhere, Athaulf. Don't you understand?"

"You do belong, Galla. You belong here." He took Galla's hand and placed it on his bare chest over his heart. "You do belong." Athaulf leaned down and, for the very first time, he kissed Galla.

CHAPTER VI

The Goths remained in Gaul for the remainder of 412 and well into 413. Their little settlement grew as other Gothic tribes joined their midst. Some of the more farsighted of the Goths cleared and planted some fields with wild grain. Much of the grain they gathered had to be used for food rather than for seed, therefore the Goths' efforts at farming were severely hindered. Honorius had still not sent the grain he had promised, so by the autumn of 413, Athaulf made the difficult decision that he and his people must once again attempt to sail to Africa to secure the grain they so desperately needed to settle and to farm.

Night was falling as Galla returned from bathing in the river. She was seated on a low chair next to a small campfire, combing her long auburn hair. Galla did not hear Athaulf approach and she was startled when she looked up and found him gazing down upon her.

"Oh Athaulf, you startled me," Galla laughed, embarrassed that she'd been surprised. "What are you doing back?" she asked. "I thought you were off hunting with the men."

"I was," Athaulf replied as he sat down on a bench across from Galla. He sat looking at her from the other side of the low fire. "You grow more beautiful each day," he said softly.

Galla laughed, "Now, you didn't return from the hunt just to tell me that. What is it? Why did you return? Did you have success so soon?"

"No," Athaulf said slowly, "no success." He poked the fire with a long stick and several tiny embers rose into the sky. "The elders and I have been talking. We've decided not to wait until spring to sail to Africa." Galla looked up with surprise. Athaulf continued, "We've decided that we should go right away."

"Right away?" Galla queried. "But I don't understand. It will take months to travel back to the strait at Sicily." Galla immediately recalled the tortuous journey across the frozen Alps and her face reflected her dismay at the thought.

Athaulf continued poking at the fire. "No," he said. "We don't intend to go back through Italy. We'd have to pass by Ravenna again and I don't want to take any chance that Honorius and Constantius might . . . well . . . I just don't want to take any chances, that's all."

"You don't mean that you intend to go all the way to Gibraltar, do you? That's just as far . . . it would take months . . . and the Pyrenees in winter!" Galla shuddered.

"No, not to Spain, either," Athaulf replied and then sat silently, staring into the fire.

"Well then, *where*?" Galla demanded, angry that she was to be uprooted again, just when the tribe was beginning to settle and to farm peacefully. "Oh, Athaulf, I don't want to leave here. The people seem so happy. For once in their lives they're feeling secure." She looked up sadly at Athaulf, "I thought *you* were happy here."

Athaulf stood up and sighed deeply. "Honorius has given us no choice. We'll never be able to settle peacefully if we don't get the grain we need to plant crops . . . real crops to feed all of us, not just a few families." Athaulf walked around the fire and sat down next to Galla. "Galla, we can barely subsist on what we grow now. We need to have more than just enough to reach from hand to mouth. We need enough to fill warehouses--to trade and to sell. The only way we'll ever be really independent, really 'civilized' as you call it, is to produce more than we can consume. That way we could trade with others for things we don't have . . . like cement and bricks. If we could produce *excess* grain we can sell it and we could begin to *pay* individuals to do things . . . like to serve as judges, or police, or teachers. If we had excess grain we could sell it and *build* things . . . like aqueducts, senate buildings, *houses*," he paused and looked up at Galla, his eagerness reflected in his emerald eyes.

Galla was sincerely touched to see his enthusiasm. She knew his words were really *her* words. She had spent long hours with Athaulf, discussing the benefits of law and a strong central government. She had been particularly adamant that the Goths could not go on endlessly destroying everything in their path. Even if there were sufficient Roman towns to sack for *this* generation of

Goths, what about their children and their children's children? No, Galla had warned, the Goths must cease their pattern of plundering and pillaging and begin to support themselves from their own labor. Galla saw that Athaulf had taken her words to heart and that he was now taking a first step towards Gothic independence. She realized he needed her support in this difficult step. Galla resigned herself that she would have to leave her little stone house by the stream.

"If not to Italy or to Gibraltar, then where will we go?" she asked calmly.

Athaulf looked away from Galla and said flatly, "To Marseilles."

"Marseilles!" Galla gasped. "Marseilles is a Roman city! You don't--you *can't*--mean you intend to sack another Roman town, not after all we've talked about." Galla stood up and began to pace. "Athaulf, *please*," Galla began to plead.

"Sit down, Galla," Athaulf said firmly, but Galla continued to pace. "Sit down!" he finally ordered in a loud voice.

Galla tossed him an angry glance as she threw herself down onto a chair. She crossed her arms and stared at him defiantly.

"We're going to Marseilles," Athaulf repeated. "And no, I don't intend to 'sack' the city as you say. All I want from them is part of their fleet. If they give us the boats we need, we'll leave the city and its population unharmed."

"And what if they don't?" Galla interrupted angrily, "What then? Go back to rape and murder? Athaulf! Look at your people!" Galla pointed out across the fields where the Goths were settled around their campfires. "You've made so much progress, you can't turn back now."

"Hush, Galla. I don't intend to turn back now; I intend to go forward and to get my people the grain they need to establish farms and cities," he said and paused. Then he looked directly at Galla, "But I'll need your help."

"*My* help? You want *my* help to raid a Roman town?" she said in shocked disbelief.

"I already told you we're not going to raid Marseilles if we can possibly avoid it. Besides, we don't have the means to assault their massive walls. I want to enter the city peacefully and talk to an individual by the name of Boniface who seems to be in charge there."

"Oh, you think the Romans in Marseilles are just going to open the gates and let the Goths walk into their city?" Galla said sarcastically.

"I think they'd open the gates for one very important Roman if *she* were to ask to speak with Boniface."

"*Me*? You want *me* to be a traitor to Rome?"

"No, not a traitor. I want you to help save Roman lives. We'll go to this Boniface and negotiate. We'll tell him that, in return for the ships we need, we'll guarantee the safety of his people." Athaulf took Galla's hands in his, "Galla, can't you see? I'm trying to reach a compromise with my people. The elders in my council all want to lay siege to the city of Marseilles. They want to *take* what they want regardless of the death and destruction that is caused. I'm trying to avoid that. I want to get the ships we need without the bloodshed. Will you help me?" Athaulf asked as he looked entreatingly into her eyes.

Galla did not answer immediately. Finally she asked, "Do you promise me that no Roman blood will be shed?"

"Yes, Galla, if you help us and we can enter the city peacefully, I'll guarantee that no Roman blood will be shed."

"All right then," Galla sighed, "I'll help. But remember, I'm only doing this so you can get the boats you need."

Athaulf put his arm around Galla and hugged her tightly. "The boats *we* need, Galla . . . you, I, and our people."

The next day Galla wrote a letter to Boniface in Marseilles asking to meet with him and his council. She explained that Athaulf and his council would accompany her and that the subject of the meeting was the procurement of a small fleet of ships. The letter was sent ahead by messenger and a small party of Goths began the four-day journey to Marseilles. The majority of the Goths remained behind to tend to the fields and to protect the camp. If Galla and her party were successful in their negotiations with Boniface, they would send for the remaining Goths to join them in Marseilles.

On the evening of the fourth day, Galla and her party arrived at Marseilles and set up camp outside the city walls. Galla remembered how she felt when the Goths surrounded Rome and now here she was on the other side of the wall, setting up camp and lighting cooking fires. She wondered what the inhabitants of Marseilles were thinking. Would they believe that the Goths had come in peace or would they think of how the city of Rome was brutally sacked by the Goths in 410?

Galla looked out over the port of Marseilles and to the Mediterranean beyond. She thought of the arduous and difficult crossing from here to Africa. The Goths would most likely cross to Corsica and then on to Sardinia before attempting to traverse the wide stretch of sea to Africa. She recalled the day she stood on the low cliffs overlooking the strait to Sicily as the sea devoured the Goths' tiny vessels. She prayed that this time God would allow them safe passage and that this wandering could finally come to an end. Galla slept fitfully that night--her sleep broken by bad dreams and the sound of waves crashing against the shore.

The next morning, Galla and her party of Goths presented themselves at the gate of Marseilles. They were met by a contingent of Roman guards who led them to the council hall in the main forum. There they were asked to await the arrival of Boniface and his council members. It was some time before Boniface and his men arrived. When they did, Galla was surprised to see that they each wore the uniform of the Roman legion. Galla's heart missed a beat when she saw the familiar garments. She thought instantly of Fortus and the last time she had seen him-- he was standing in front of the library window, silhouetted against the light, looking so strong and handsome in his soldier's uniform.

"Good morning, Your Highness, and welcome," a tall man said as he strode forward, saluted, and then bowed stiffly. "Allow me to introduce myself. I am Boniface. Please, be seated. I am at your service." He bowed again and pulled out a chair for Galla at the head of the council table.

"Thank you," Galla replied politely. "Allow me to introduce to you the Chief of the Goths. This is Athaulf," Galla said as she took her seat.

Boniface gave Athaulf a cold stare and nodded to the seats along the side of the table to Galla's right. Boniface then took the seat at the other end of the table opposite Galla's position and his men took their places along his right, so that the Romans sat facing the Goths at the council table.

"Well, Your Majesty," Boniface began, "your letter said that you are interested in purchasing some ships."

"My letter said that we're interested in *obtaining* some ships," Galla said as she gave Boniface her sweetest smile. "You see, at the present we are not in a financial position to *purchase* any ships. We intend to use the ships to travel to Africa to obtain grain. When we return, we will reimburse you for the use of your ships."

"If you have no funds to purchase ships, how do you intend to purchase grain in Africa?" Boniface said in a most condescending tone.

"I don't intend to purchase the grain. I intend to collect the grain that has been promised to these people by my brother, the Emperor Honorius," Galla maintained her facade of sweetness and innocence.

"Ohhh," Boniface drawled, "the grain the Emperor promised, I see," he smirked. Boniface leaned back in his chair and gave Galla a long, appraising look. "Your Highness," Boniface continued in his condescending tone, "I have received no word from Ravenna that the Emperor has ordered any release of grain from Africa."

Galla could feel her anger rising as Boniface spoke to her in this superior tone. She stood up, leaned on the table, and addressed Boniface officiously, "My *brother*, the *Emperor*, has repeatedly promised these people grain from Africa. The Goths have waited and waited. Their patience is wearing thin. To continue to refuse them that which they have been promised may very well prove dangerous. I urge you to provide these people with boats so that they may peacefully proceed to Africa for the grain that is rightfully theirs!"

Boniface slowly rose from his seat at the far end of the table. "That sounds very much like a threat, Galla Placidia. Have these filthy barbarians corrupted you so that you are now a traitor to Rome?"

Galla stood up straight and replied, "How dare you accuse me of being a traitor to Rome! I came here today offering you peace--offering you a chance to bring about a settlement between these people and Rome. And you have the audacity to call *me* a traitor!" Galla drew in a long breath and tried to regain her composure. "I'm only asking for a few ships, ships that will be returned to you when the expedition is completed. These people want peace. They want to settle and they need grain to plant crops."

"Ha!" Boniface bellowed. "Plant crops! The Goths? You *are* insane, just like your brother says you are. No wonder he's asked us to detain you here until he can send for you. Guards!" Two heavily armed guards stepped forward towards Galla.

Within an instant, Athaulf and his men drew their weapons, leapt upon the table, and faced the terrified Romans who were still planted in their seats. Only Boniface and the two guards were standing. With a single nod from Athaulf, the Goths disarmed the guards. Galla gasped at the instinctive and well-orchestrated maneuver by the Goths. Athaulf nodded at Galla indicating that she should head for the door while they held off the Romans.

"You won't get away with this, you filthy barbarians!" Boniface snarled.

Galla ran towards the door as Athaulf and the other Goths backed slowly out of the room. The Romans remained glued in their places, their faces reflecting their terror. Once outside the council chamber, Galla, Athaulf, and the Goths made their way quickly towards the gates of the city. Behind them they could hear the shouts of alarm being raised across the city.

When Galla and the men reached the city gate, they turned to see if all members were accounted for. Galla saw Athaulf a few paces behind her. He signaled for her to continue out the gates. Just then, Boniface appeared at the end of the street behind Athaulf. Boniface was brandishing a large dagger. Without thinking, Galla called out in Gothic to warn Athaulf. Stunned to hear Galla speaking Gothic, Athaulf paused momentarily before turning to face Boniface. The split second delay gave Boniface the opportunity to throw his dagger. Athaulf turned and the dagger plunged into his chest. Galla screamed in horror. The Goths instantly surrounded their wounded leader. They lifted Athaulf to

their shoulders and carried him through the city gates. When Galla
looked back, Boniface had disappeared down the street.

The Goths who had remained at the temporary camp
outside the city gates had heard the alarm that rose inside the city.
They advanced, fully armed and ready, towards the city walls, but
the Romans did not send out any soldiers to meet the Goths in
combat. The huge city gates slammed shut and silence fell across
the countryside.

"Prepare to depart," Athaulf commanded as his men
carefully laid him on the ground. "Send a messenger ahead to
warn the others back at the main camp."

"But you're wounded," Galla protested. "You can't travel."

"We can't stay here," Athaulf replied. "The Romans will
surely attack as soon as their troops are rallied. There are only a
few hundred of us here and they must have thousands of soldiers
within those walls." Athaulf paused and gasped for air. "We must
go back to our camp in the north," he gasped again and clutched
his chest.

The Goths gathered only their weapons and their horses;
everything else was left behind in order that they could travel as
lightly and as quickly as possible. Within minutes, the Goths were
moving northward. A huge wooden cart carried the injured
chieftain. Galla sat next to him, witnessing the excruciating pain
caused by each rock and rut in the path of the heavy old cart. She
marveled at how bravely he endured the agony of the long and
arduous journey. Occasionally one of his men would ask if
Athaulf needed to rest, but the wounded leader always ordered
them to keep moving.

After two days and two nights of continuous travel, they
arrived back at the camp. Word of Athaulf's injury had preceded
them and they were met by a contingent of elders and concerned
tribesmen. They carried their unconscious leader into his tent and
gently laid him on his bed. Galla ordered hot water and clean rags.
She cleansed and bandaged the inflamed wound.

Athaulf drifted in and out of consciousness for three days,
often mumbling incoherently. Galla managed to get him to
swallow a few spoonfuls of soup and to take sips of beer to ease
the pain. The tribes people offered to watch over Athaulf so Galla

could rest, but she steadfastly refused to leave his side. On the morning of the fourth day, the fever broke and Athaulf began to breathe more easily.

"What day is it?" Athaulf mumbled dryly as he blinked his eyes open.

Galla thought for a moment, and then replied, "I don't know. I'm not sure. I'll go ask." Galla started to stand up, but Athaulf took her arm and drew her back down into the chair beside his bed.

"No, don't go," he said. "It's not important what day it is. It's only important that I'm still here." He ran his hand over his forehead as if checking to see if he were, indeed, still alive and whole. Suddenly he tried to sit up. "What about the Romans? Have they attacked?" he asked urgently, as details about the ill-fated trip to Marseilles began to return to his memory.

"No, no!" Galla soothed his fears. "The Romans have not attacked. They haven't yet left the city walls. The elders think perhaps the Romans will not attack at all." Galla finally convinced Athaulf to lie back down and to rest quietly. Galla explained to him about the journey back to camp and his long illness while she cleansed and bandaged his wound.

Athaulf lay quietly as he watched Galla skillfully nursing his injury. When Galla completed her tasks, she stood up to go fetch some broth and beer for him but he detained her once again. "No, wait, don't go," he pleaded, "not yet." He pulled her down onto the chair again. "I kept my promise, didn't I?" he smiled.

"Your promise? What promise?" Galla queried.

"That I wouldn't spill any blood," he looked quickly down at the fresh bandage that Galla had just applied, "any *Roman* blood, that is." He grinned up at Galla.

"Yes," Galla sighed, "you kept your promise, but you nearly got killed. Oh Athaulf, I was so worried." Galla held back a sob that was welling-up inside her and she looked away from Athaulf so he could not see the tears in her eyes.

Athaulf reached out and took Galla's hand in his. "Galla, there at the gate . . . you spoke Gothic. Where did you learn those words? How long have you known Gothic?"

Galla blinked back the tears and she turned to face Athaulf. "Always," she said in her perfect schoolbook Gothic. "I've always understood Gothic. Stilicho taught it to me when I was a little girl," she continued in Gothic.

Athaulf looked at her incredulously. "Then you've understood us from the start? You understood everything we were saying?" he asked in his native tongue, no longer needing to formulate his sentences into Latin. "Why didn't you tell me?"

"If you were captured by the Romans," Galla asked, "would you let them know you understood Latin?"

Athaulf laughed quietly and shook his head. "You are really a remarkable woman," he said as he pr⁄ lly beamed up at her. "Why did you finally decide to speak Gothic to me?"

"I didn't decide. It just happened. I saw Boniface standing there with his dagger drawn and I had to warn you. It just came out in Gothic."

"You saved my life," Athaulf said.

"No," Galla interrupted, "I put you in grave danger. If I hadn't interfered, you wouldn't have been wounded. If only I had spoken Latin . . . but I was so afraid . . . afraid he'd kill you . . . all I could think of was to warn you . . . I'm so sorry," Galla sobbed and she leaned over and put her arms around Athaulf. "I didn't know until that moment how very much I love you," she cried and laid her head upon his chest.

Athaulf put his arms around her and held her tight. "Oh Galla, my darling, how long I've waited to hear you say those words! And now . . . to hear you say them . . . and to say them in Gothic. Oh my love," Athaulf lifted Galla's head from his chest and he kissed her.

"I do love you Athaulf," Galla cried, "I love you very, very much."

CHAPTER VII

In the late afternoon of the following day, a messenger from Marseilles arrived at the Goths' camp. He carried a large vellum scroll, which he delivered to Athaulf personally. Still too weak to sit up to read the message, Athaulf ordered the messenger to wait outside while Galla read the letter aloud.

> To Athaulf, Chief of the Goths,
> You are hereby ordered to surrender
> Her Highness Galla Placidia by noon
> tomorrow. If this demand is not met,
> we will attack at dawn on the following
> day. If you surrender Galla Placidia as
> ordered, you and your people will be
> permitted to remain on the land you
> now occupy. The messenger will
> await your reply.
> > Signed,
> > Boniface
> > Marseilles

Athaulf laughed wryly. "Who does this Boniface think he is to give orders to me? Just *let* him attack at dawn! We'll show him who is the better foe!"

Galla stood up, went over to the door of the tent, and looked out over the countryside. Sounds of children's laughter filled the air. She turned back and looked sadly at Athaulf.

"I must go," Galla said solemnly. "I cannot allow men to be killed on account of me . . . on account of us. Look! Galla stepped aside and pointed out the door to the tents and fields. "These Goths are my people now . . . and the Romans are my kinsmen . . . how can I stand dumbly by and allow them to kill one another? God will not forgive me if I permit this tragedy to occur. I must go."

Athaulf struggled to raise himself up on one arm. He could tell from Galla's composure that her mind was set. "All right, Galla, we *won't* fight. But we won't let you go, either. It's time we moved on anyway. We don't have enough grain here for another summer and the men are eager to try a new location. We'll head west to Spain. That's where we should have gone in the first place. Unless . . ." Athaulf paused and looked at Galla, "unless you *want* to go back to your people."

"No, I don't want to go back to my people, I'm with my people, I'm with you," Galla smiled, walked over and sat down next to Athaulf. "Do you think the people will agree? Are you sure they'll follow you?" Galla asked with concern.

"I'll hold a council meeting tonight. I'll let the people decide for themselves what they want to do. Isn't that what they do in Rome? Let the people vote?"

Galla smiled, "Ideally, yes, but even in Rome, it doesn't always work out for the best. What if your people vote to stay, what then?"

"Then you and I will go on alone. I'm sure some of the men and their families will follow." Athaulf picked up Galla's hand and kissed it tenderly. "We've come too far to be parted now . . . I love you too much," he smiled. "Call in the messenger and I'll give him my reply."

The messenger re-entered the tent and Athaulf said, "Tell Boniface that we will release Her Highness Galla Placidia when the moon is at its fullest. Tell him that our gods forbid us to release prisoners at any other time."

The messenger gave Athaulf a look of incredulity. Athaulf picked up the bag of spices and herbs that Galla had used as a poultice for his wound and he handed it to the man saying gravely, "Carry this with you. It will protect you from evil spirits and witches." The man gingerly took the bag, gave Athaulf and Galla a confused look, and hurriedly left the tent.

Galla turned to Athaulf and asked, "What was all that about? Full moons, gods, witches? What were you talking about?"

Athaulf laughed loudly. "Did you see the expression on that man's face? Wait 'til he goes back to Marseilles with that tale.

If the Romans want to refer to us as 'barbarians,' then we'll give them a few barbaric things to think about . . . like witches and hobgoblins." Athaulf laughed wickedly and tickled Galla's waist. She laughed and pushed him away.

"But I don't understand," she countered.

"Oh, I just made all that up. It will buy us some time. It's three weeks until the full moon. The Romans think we're all a bunch of pagan tree-worshippers, so why not let them? It's worked before. It may work again. That will give us a three-week start ahead of Boniface and his troops . . . *if* he decides to pursue us. If he doesn't, well so much the better." Athaulf smiled slyly at Galla. "Come here you little barbarian tree-worshipper, let me cast a spell on you!" Athaulf teased as he drew Galla to him and kissed her.

That evening, Athaulf held a council meeting in his tent. He was unable to sit at the council table himself, so he appointed his friend, the aged and respected Candidianus, to sit at the table in his place. Athaulf directed the meeting from his bed. All of the elders and the heads of the various clans were in attendance. Galla was also present but as she was not permitted to participate; she sat quietly in her chair by Athaulf's bedside.

As in every Gothic council meeting, tempers flared and insults were hurled with great velocity, but, little by little, compromises were made and agreements were reached. By dawn it was decided that the Goths would head for Spain.

The next day the Goths packed up and began the long journey. Athaulf was not yet strong enough to sit on horseback so he rode in a cart with Galla. He appointed his faithful assistant Candidianus to head the procession and to lead the tribes to their destination. Speed was of utmost importance, not only to outrun Boniface should he decide to attack, but also to reach the Pyrenees before winter set in and a crossing would be more difficult. The Goths traveled as fast as their numbers would allow and by early-December they had reached Narbonne on the Mediterranean coast of Gaul. Since no sign of Boniface was seen or heard, the Goths decided to remain at Narbonne to celebrate the Christmas season and to welcome in the New Year of 414.

The Goths established a temporary camp alongside the shore of the azure blue sea. The wind was brisk but not cold and

Athaulf benefited from the sunshine and the sea air. Galla was pleased to have Athaulf restored to good health again and the two shared slow walks along the rocky shore and easy rides on horseback across the grassy meadows.

One evening, as the fires were being lighted for the evening's meal, Galla and Athaulf returned from a long ride. When they arrived at camp, Candidianus met them and signaled to them to dismount.

"Good evening, Candidianus," Athaulf shouted merrily as he slid adeptly off his horse, "how are you this beautiful evening?" Athaulf smiled broadly, happy to be well and active again.

"Fine, fine," Candidianus replied hastily. "We have a message from Ravenna . . . from the Emperor himself! I thought you'd like to know right away."

Galla dismounted and Athaulf signaled her to follow them into the tent. Once inside, the three took seats around a small fire that had been lit in the round hearth in the center of the tent. Heda brought in ale and cheese. Athaulf helped himself and Galla to huge mugs of cold ale and generous slices of yellow cheese.

"Well?" Candidianus asked, sounding somewhat annoyed, "aren't you going to read the dispatch?"

"Yes, yes, I'm going to read it, but not on an empty stomach. We had a long, hard ride today, didn't we Galla?" Galla nodded and bit into the thick wedge of cheese. "You know," Athaulf continued, "that girl can really ride! I've seen few men who could ride as well as Galla can--and none better!"

"But Athaulf," Candidianus interjected, "perhaps you didn't hear me. I said the message is from the Emperor himself! It's a message from Honorius! Aren't you going to open it?" Candidianus could barely contain his curiosity about the contents of the letter. He stood up and began to pace the floor, wringing his aging hands in anticipation.

"Sit! Sit, my friend," Athaulf patted Candidianus' bald head and gave the elderly man's round belly a friendly poke, "that letter can wait. After all, we've waited *years* to hear from Honorius. He can wait a few minutes for us to quench our thirst." Candidianus sat down with a short sigh of exasperation.

Galla, too, was eager to open the message from Ravenna. It had been over six years since she had any word from her brother and she was curious to know what finally prompted a response from him. She sat quietly, alternately sipping the ale and nibbling on the cheese, but her eyes never left the large vellum scroll with the purple Imperial seal.

Finally Athaulf finished the ale and the cheese, but instead of opening the scroll, he called for Heda. "When's dinner?" Athaulf asked her when she entered the tent, "I'm starving!"

Heda smiled and patted Athaulf's broad shoulder. "It's good to see you feeling like your old self again, Athaulf. I know you'll be all right now when I hear you bellowing for your dinner. We'll eat in about an hour. I'll bring more ale and cheese in the meantime." Heda left the room.

Galla could contain her curiosity no longer. She walked over and picked up the heavy official scroll. "Athaulf, please, I can't stand it. I simply must know what's in this letter!"

Athaulf laughed, "All right, open it. *You* read it. After all, he's *your* brother!"

With trembling hands, Galla unwound the thick scroll. She recognized her brother's broad penmanship immediately. "It *is* from Honorius! I recognize his writing! I can't believe it, after all these years." Galla fumbled for a chair and sat down. In a quavering voice, she read aloud,

Greetings to the Chieftain Athaulf,
Rome sends its regards to you and to my sister,
Her Highness Galla Placidia. We have good news
from Africa. The tyrants who have impeded
the exportation of grain from Africa have been
caught and executed. Their heads are on
display at Carthage. We can now provide the grain
that you have requested. You will receive your
first shipment shortly. In the meantime, prepare
Her Highness for her return to Rome.
We hope to celebrate the New Year with her in Ravenna.
His Imperial Majesty,
Honorius Flavius

Galla finished reading the letter and Candidianus sprang to his feet. "Great news! Oh happy message! We have our grain and Galla can be restored to her people! Thank God for His infinite kindness!"

Galla and Athaulf sat numbly without speaking.

"Well?" Candidianus asked, "Aren't you happy? Isn't this the answer to our prayers?"

Athaulf stood up, walked over behind Galla's chair and put his hands on her shoulders. "No," Athaulf replied, "this is not what I've prayed for."

Heda re-entered the tent carrying a tray of cheese and ale. She was met with a strained silence. She set the tray down and, sensing the tension in the air, she left without speaking.

Candidianus searched Athaulf's face for an indication of what the chieftain was thinking. The elder had known Athaulf for many years and he felt a deep compassion for what the young man was now suffering. He watched as Athaulf paced the tent, his face set in deep concentration.

"Athaulf," Candidianus said softly, breaking the brittle silence, "are you in love with Galla?" Athaulf looked up and nodded silently. Candidianus continued, "Do you plan to marry her?" Athaulf nodded again.

Galla looked at Athaulf. A strange feeling of fear and uncertainty washed over her. "Marriage!" Galla thought tremulously. "Marriage to Athaulf, chief of the Goths!" She had never given the subject a thought. It was too absurd, too un-Roman. She knew she loved Athaulf, but marriage . . . no. She had never allowed herself to contemplate the idea. And now Athaulf, the Gothic chieftain, and Candidianus, a Gothic elder, were discussing the prospect, not as a possibility, but as a distinct probability.

Athaulf saw Galla's look of bewilderment and apprehension. He walked over and knelt before her. Taking her hands gently in his, he said softly, "Galla, my darling, I didn't want it to be like this. When I dreamed of the day I'd ask you to marry me, I thought it would be a joyous occasion, somewhere beautiful-- beside a stream or a lake." He paused and sighed deeply. "Galla, I can't offer you what you had at Rome. I can't give you security or stability, or even a beautiful palace in which to live. All I can give you is myself and my love. If that is enough for you, will you marry me Galla?"

Tears stung Galla's eyes as she struggled to control her emotions. "Oh Athaulf! It's not what you can give . . . it's . . . it's . . . I need to think . . . I need time to think."

Athaulf nodded slowly and rose to his feet. "Yes, Galla, I want you to think about it, too. I want it to be *your* decision . . . a decision you make *freely*."

Galla stood up and put her arms around Athaulf. "Oh, Athaulf, I love you. Whatever I decide, I love you. Nothing will ever change that." Galla hugged him tightly, and then she turned and left the tent.

Galla spent the next week alone, her thoughts focused on the future. Most of her time Galla spent in the seclusion of her tent deep in concentration and prayer. Late in the evening of the fifth day, Galla heard a voice at the door of the tent. "May I come in?" the voice inquired. It was Candidianus.

"Come in, Candidianus! Come in! Welcome," Galla replied, eager to have someone with whom to discuss her thoughts. Candidianus was the most respected among the elders of the Council. He was known for his wisdom and sense of justice. "Please, sit down, Candidianus," Galla said, offering the old man the best chair. Candidianus seated himself and Galla returned to her chair at her desk.

"We've seen very little of you this week, Galla. I trust you are well," the old man began diplomatically.

Galla laughed, "Oh, I'm well physically, but mentally I'm very confused. Look!" Galla exclaimed as she lifted a huge stack of papers on her desk. Candidianus looked at her quizzically. "They're lists," Galla explained. "Lists of the pros and cons of marriage," she added in a somewhat bitter tone.

"Ah, lists," Candidianus repeated, nodding gravely, "very wise . . . very wise indeed. Important decisions should not be made carelessly. They should be given careful consideration. Well, what do your lists tell you, Your Highness?"

"That the brain and the heart have very little in common," Galla laughed as she threw down the stack of papers.

Candidianus smiled and nodded, "How true! Well, tell me, what do those two strangers have to say?"

Galla sighed, "Well, my *brain* says that I shouldn't marry Athaulf . . . that he's a Goth and I'm a Roman, and that he's an Arian Christian and I'm an Orthodox Christian."

"And what does your heart tell you, Galla?" Candidianus asked gently.

"My heart tells me to marry Athaulf . . . to forget Rome . . . to forget our differences . . . Oh Candidianus, I *love* him!" Galla buried her face in her hands.

Candidianus stood up, walked over to Galla and patted her gently on the shoulder. "My dear, I have something you should read--something for your brain that might ease your troubled heart. Wait here and I'll go fetch it." Candidianus left the tent and returned shortly carrying a large book. He placed the tome in Galla's lap and resumed his seat in the chair. Galla ran her hand over the jewel-studded silver cover.

Candidianus explained, "It's a book by Bishop Augustine of Hippo, perhaps you've heard of him."

"Yes, Augustine was a friend of my father's, they met in Milan. My father was very impressed with Augustine and respected him deeply." Galla opened the book and leafed through the pages.

"Augustine has written this book in response to the Goths' attack on Rome in 410." Galla looked up at Candidianus, her eyes revealing her surprise. He continued, "It's called *The City of God*, and in this book Augustine says the attack on Rome was God's punishment for man's sins. Augustine believes that God wants to establish a Christian state here on earth, in the City of Man. He writes that a Christian state, like the Christian Church itself, can help lead man to salvation and to the City of God in Heaven."

"A Christian state," Galla repeated.

"Yes, an *Orthodox* Christian state. Augustine is very clear that we must help pagans and other heretics to see the truth of God's Word."

"But," interrupted Galla, "I thought you and the others were Arians. Augustine always said that Arian Christianity is a heresy. He told my father that Arianism was a heresy when my father wanted to marry my mother!"

Candidianus smiled, "Yes, Augustine does believe that Arianism is a heresy. A heretic is anyone who does not believe that Christ is the true Son of God, that He is truly divine and of one substance with God. Augustine has convinced *me*, and I believe he can convince Athaulf, too . . . with your help."

"Athaulf?" Galla replied with a sigh. "Oh, I've spoken and spoken to him about the true Christian faith, but I don't think he listened."

"I believe he listened more than you know. Last week I found him reading this," Candidianus pointed to the volume in Galla's hands.

"And?" Galla asked eagerly. "What did he say?"

"He hasn't said anything, not yet. He went off hunting by himself. He said he'd be back on Christmas Eve. That's in three days. It appears that while you've been here thinking, he's been somewhere out there doing some thinking, too."

Candidianus stood up, moved his chair closer to Galla's, and sat down next to her. "Galla, I believe this book is divinely inspired. I believe God is sending us a message. He wants us to create a *new* state here on earth in the City of Man. He wants us to forget our old man-made states of Romans and Goths. He wants us to create a Christian state that will fight for good against evil . . . a state that will lead men towards salvation and God."

"A Christian state," Galla mumbled, "not Roman, not Goth, but Christian . . . a new state . . . with God at its head . . ." A sense of purpose and destiny washed over Galla and she felt as if all the pieces of her life were coming together into one, coherent whole.

"Could this be why God led me to this place, to this point in time?" she thought to herself. "Am I part of some divine plan rather than an insignificant pawn in a game of politics?" A tingle of excitement ran down her spine.

"Candidianus," Galla hesitated, "do you think Athaulf is thinking of creating a Christian state, too? I mean an *Orthodox* Christian state?"

"Yes, I do. I think that is why he gave me this book to read. I've already shared it with several of the others and even our head priest. This Augustine is an intelligent man. His writings are filled with power and conviction. I think this book will change the thinking of practically anyone who reads it. Surely," he said lowering his voice, "surely, God has spoken to Augustine." Candidianus stood up. "Good night, Galla. I'll leave you alone with Augustine's book. Let's see if it has the same effect on you that it's had on the rest of us."

Galla stood also and walked the old man to the door of her tent. "Thank you, Candidianus. Thank you for sharing this book with me. I appreciate your kindness and your friendship. God bless you."

"And you, too, Your Highness," Candidianus replied as he left the tent.

Galla returned to her desk and sat down. She opened the cover of the huge book and began to read. When she looked up again, the sun was rising in the east.

The Goths marked Christmas Eve that year with special celebrations and feasting. The camp was decorated with pine boughs and holly brought down from the north. Galla helped Heda mull the sweet Christmas mead as the other women baked honey breads and berry pies. Several of the men returned to camp about noon carrying a huge buck destined for the fire pit. In the late afternoon, Galla noticed that Athaulf had not yet returned to the camp. Galla completed her task of decorating oranges with cloves and she went into her tent to dress for the evening's festivities. Shortly after dark, the musicians began to play and Galla left her tent to join the others. Still there was no sign of Athaulf.

At midnight, the Goths ceased their festivities and they gathered on benches before the temporary altar under the tall trees that was to serve as their place of worship that night. Galla thought briefly of the celebration at St. Peter's in Rome that Julius and the others would be attending that very night. It all seemed so far away, in time and in distance--Rome, St. Peter's, Julius, and Fortus. She tried to picture her friends as they entered St. Peter's Basilica for midnight mass--Julius, perhaps a little older, not quite so straight and tall--Fortus, handsome and strong as ever in his soldier's uniform--and Claudia, beautiful and proud as she walked by Fortus' side . . .

"Sit here Your Highness," Candidianus interrupted Galla's imaginings. Galla took the seat that the old man indicated as her thoughts returned to the makeshift open air church in the Goths' camp in the south of Gaul. When the priest began the service, Galla's thoughts drifted off again . . . this time to a tiny manger in the little town of Bethlehem.

When the service was over, the Goths filed slowly past the altar and towards their tents. As Galla passed the altar, she was surprised to see Athaulf standing in a crop of trees nearby. Galla ran over to him, happy to see him returned safely.

"Athaulf! I'm so glad to see you! I was beginning to worry about you. Candidianus said you'd be back by Christmas Eve, and when you weren't here . . ."

"You worried about me?" he said in his gentle, teasing tone, smiling down at her.

"Well, yes . . . I know you can take care yourself, but things do happen out there."

"Yes," Athaulf replied, "things *do* happen out there . . . and something has happened to me. Come, let's sit down and I'll tell you all about it." Athaulf led Galla over to the bench in front of the altar and they sat down.

"Galla," Athaulf began in an excited tone, "I've been to Arles."

"Arles! That's a great distance from here. Why did you go to Arles?"

"To see the Bishop there . . . to talk to him."

Galla smiled, "To talk with him about Augustine and the City of God?" she asked hopefully. "Candidianus told me that you read Augustine's book."

"Yes," Athaulf replied. He paused and looked seriously at Galla. "I was baptized, Galla, in the Rhone River, by the Bishop at Arles." He hugged Galla tightly, "Thank you, Galla. Thank you for helping me to find Him, the true Lord."

"Oh Athaulf, I'm so happy for you, for your people . . . for us!"

Athaulf picked up a bundle he had been carrying and he placed it in Galla's lap. Galla unwound the string and opened the package to find dozens of yards of beautiful saffron-colored silk. Athaulf said hesitantly, "It's for a wedding dress, my dearest, if you'll have me. Will you marry me Galla?"

Galla paused for a moment and she looked into his emerald eyes. "Yes, Athaulf, I'll marry you."

"Have you really thought about it Galla? Do you make this decision freely and without reservations?"

"Yes, Athaulf . . . freely . . . and gladly."

News of the pending alliance between the Roman princess and the Gothic chieftain spread quickly across the Empire. For the majority of the populace, both Roman and Goth, the news was a welcome sign of potential peace between the two groups. For a small minority of persons, Honorius and Constantius among them, the news was an unwelcome threat to their power and their plans. As the Goths in Narbonne prepared to celebrate the royal marriage, the Romans in Ravenna began to increase the ante of grain and money they were willing to gamble in order to secure Galla's release into Roman hands. It was clear to everyone involved that he who held Galla, held the future of the Empire. In blatant disregard of Honorius' frantic and belated offers of grain, money, and land, the Gothic chieftain Athaulf married the Roman princess Galla Placidia on the first day of January, in the year 414, just one week after her twenty-fifth birthday.

The wedding ceremony was held in formal Roman fashion, but the subsequent celebrations were a colorful mix of Roman and Gothic traditions, reflecting the diverse composition of guests who came to share in the joy of the happy young couple. The festivities lasted late into the night and it was nearly dawn before Athaulf and Galla were able to sneak off, unnoticed, to the marriage tent.

Once inside the tent, Athaulf whispered to Galla, "Shh . . . follow me." He picked up a small bundle from the floor, led Galla past the elaborate, flower-strewn bed and out a slit in the back of the tent. There, two horses stood saddled and waiting. "Follow me," Athaulf said once again in a hushed tone as he helped Galla up on a horse. Athaulf mounted his horse and the two rode off into the woods.

After about an hour, Athaulf finally drew his horse to a halt and he dismounted in front of a small cabin. He helped Galla down from her horse and led her into the snug little house. A fire burned brightly in the fireplace and a jug of fine Roman wine stood chilling in water on the table. Athaulf poured a goblet of wine for Galla and one for himself. He smiled at the bewilderment of his new bride.

"You're wondering where we are, aren't you?" Athaulf laughed. "You've been to our Gothic weddings . . . you've seen what they do to newlyweds on their first night alone! Well, I wasn't going to let those drunken revelers interrupt our first night together. Tonight is just for the two of us . . . *alone*."

Athaulf put his arm around Galla and held her close. Galla withdrew from his grasp and took a long sip of the cool wine. Athaulf looked at her, searching for a clue to her feelings.

"Is something wrong, Galla?" Athaulf asked softly.

"No . . . well, I don't know . . . I'm, I'm nervous . . . and I don't know why. Oh Athaulf, I'm sorry . . . look at me, I'm shaking . . . I feel so silly."

"No, Galla, you're not silly. It's only natural," he said tenderly. "There's no hurry. I can wait until you're ready. We're tired now anyway. We've been up since this time yesterday. Look, the dawn is starting. Let's get some sleep." Athaulf led Galla to a bed in the corner, he tucked the sheets around her, and then he kissed her gently.

Galla watched silently as Athaulf crossed the room to another bed. He undressed quickly and slid under the covers. It was a long time before Galla could hear his rhythmic breathing indicate that he was asleep. Daylight peeked in around the heavy curtains and cast a soft gray light across the room.

Galla lay still, trying to understand her emotions. Just yards away was the man she loved--her husband. She looked again at Athaulf sleeping a few steps away from her. She could see his broad chest rising and falling under the thin sheets. The early morning light played across the strong muscles of his arms and accentuated his high cheekbones and long, dark hair. Galla rose from her bed, walked over to where Athaulf lie sleeping, and looked down upon this man whom she had married . . . the man she loved so dearly. She unfastened the pins at the shoulders of her wedding gown and the dress fell silently to the floor. She paused for one brief moment, then lifted the sheets and lay down next to her husband. Several dawns passed before Galla and Athaulf returned to their tent at the camp.

CHAPTER VIII

When news of the wedding reached Ravenna, Honorius' revenge was quick and vicious. The Emperor's first retaliation against the Goths was a complete blockade of the supply and trade routes. Honorius then ordered his armies to attack any and all Goths in southern Gaul on sight. When Galla and Athaulf returned to their camp following their brief honeymoon, they found the entire camp in a state of pandemonium.

"What's going on here?" Athaulf shouted as he dismounted his horse. "What has happened?"

"As if *you* don't know," snarled Sarus, one of the minor Gothic chieftains, as he loaded his cart with his meager possessions.

"What do you mean, Sarus? Know *what*? What's happened?" Athaulf demanded as he looked down upon the short, muscular man.

"You and that *woman . . . that's* what's happened! Now all Rome is out to get us! They're slaying us in the fields as we plow. While you're off with your Roman whore, the Romans are killing us like flies!"

Athaulf drew back his hand to hit Sarus but the latter only smiled defiantly. "Oh yes, Athaulf, go ahead and hit me! Show all the Goths where your allegiance lies--between her legs, that's where!"

"Get out of here you filthy swine," Athaulf hissed, his hand still poised to strike. "Finish packing your things and leave!"

"Oh, I'll leave all right! You couldn't get me to stay, not with that vile Roman wench here. Nothing's been the same here since she came. First that bull dung about plowing and planting, and now the whole blasted Roman army is out after our hides. I'll go all right . . . as far away from her and her kind as I can get! And anyone who's a *real* Goth will go with me!" Sarus turned to face the crowd of men who had gathered. "What say you, men, are you Goths or Roman ass-kissers? Who's with me?"

Several of the men cheered at Sarus' challenge and stepped behind him.

"All right then," Athaulf shouted. "Anyone who wants to go with Sarus is free to go. Take your shares of the supplies and get out!" Athaulf lowered his arm and walked away from Sarus and the men, his broad shoulders heaving with suppressed anger.

Galla had not yet dismounted and she sat stunned upon her horse. Athaulf walked over and helped his new bride off her horse. "This is quite a warm welcome we've received, huh Galla?" Athaulf said sarcastically as he led Galla towards his tent. They entered the tent and found Candidianus waiting for them inside.

"Oh Athaulf! I'm so glad you've returned," Candidianus said excitedly as he rose from his chair to greet them. "We didn't know where you were. We looked everywhere for you!"

"I was on my *honeymoon*," Athaulf said with irritation, "which, I can see, has come to an abrupt and unpleasant end, it seems." Athaulf cast a cold glance in the direction of his altercation with Sarus.

"Oh Athaulf," Candidianus began, but paused to acknowledge Galla, "and Your Highness," he nodded, "Honorius has ordered the Roman army to slay all Goths on sight. He's cut off our supply lines. Our people are either starving or lying dead in their fields."

Galla fumbled for a seat and sat down, her eyes wide with disbelief. "But I don't understand," she countered. "What possible motive would Honorius have to wreak this terrible havoc? He couldn't possibly care that I married Athaulf. He has ignored me for all these years. What has possessed him?"

"I think it's actually Constantius who's spearheading this rampage," Candidianus said as he stepped closer to Galla. "I think *he's* the one who's stirring up all the trouble. He's acting like a scorned lover. If he can't have you no one will."

Athaulf walked over and put his hand on Galla's shoulder. "I know what you're thinking, Galla, but this is *not* your fault. If this Constantius had plans for the throne of Rome, he can just forget them. You're *my* wife now, and God and the rest of the world know it! Just let this Constantius play out his jealous rage. Our plans are bigger and more important than he could ever imagine. Great changes take great chances . . . and this is one chance we'll have to take."

Galla looked up and saw the firm resolve in Athaulf's eyes. "Yes, Athaulf, I agree. We must hold the union between our peoples together. It will just take time, that's all," Galla smiled weakly. "But in the meantime, what can we *do*? How can we prevent more bloodshed?" Galla glanced between Athaulf and Candidianus.

The older man shook his head sadly, "You're the chieftain, Athaulf, and I don't want to tell you what to do, but I think we'd better get across those mountains and into Spain just as quickly as we can. No Goth is safe in Gaul, not with those murdering Romans on our tails." Candidianus stopped abruptly and looked hesitantly at Galla.

"It's all right, Candidianus," Galla said firmly, "they *are* murdering Romans if they attack innocent persons in their fields. And I agree," Galla shot a quick glance at Athaulf, "I think we should go to Spain."

Athaulf looked at Galla, searching for any sign of fear or apprehension but he found none. "It will be a difficult and dangerous journey this time of year. The passes will be filled with ice and snow," Athaulf offered, giving Galla a chance to rethink her decision.

"The Pyrenees couldn't be a greater challenge than the Alps in the dead of winter," Galla stated calmly.

Athaulf looked at his new wife with pride and respect and said, "Whoever says Romans are soft, hasn't met my wife! Eh, Candidianus?" Athaulf smiled broadly.

"Nor have they met the Roman *army*," Candidianus added in a more serious tone. "I suggest we prepare to leave at once."

"Yes, call the others and we'll hold a meeting. Those who wish to come with us are welcome to; those who wish to stay here in Gaul may stay. It's not my place to challenge the hand of fate," Athaulf paused briefly and glanced down, "or the hand of God."

The arduous trip over the Pyrenees took its deadly toll on both the Goths and their prized animal stock. The bitterly cold winds blew relentlessly day and night. Before two weeks of the treacherous journey had passed, three of the Goths' young children and seven of their elder members had succumbed to the freezing cold. By the end of the month, half of the livestock had died. The Goths, never ones to waste resources, fed upon the fallen animals and used their hides for protection against the piercing cold winds. By the time the ragged band of refugees reached the rolling hills of Spain, they had lost over fifty of their kinsmen and three-quarters of their animals.

The Goths settled just outside the city of Barcelona. The long arm of the Emperor did not reach as far as Spain, at least not with any menacing force. The Goths set up their camps and a few among them even began to prepare some of the flat valley basins for spring planting. Galla once again began the difficult and tedious task of setting up her meager household and instilling some order into her fragmented life.

"I think it's even prettier here than Marseilles," Galla called across to Athaulf as the two stretched the cowhide roof across the tent poles. Athaulf smiled back at Galla but a touch of concern darkened his green eyes. Galla's face was pale and she seemed to lack her former vitality. Athaulf worried that the long journey over the Pyrenees had weakened his wife and he hoped that the warm Spanish sun would help her to regain her former vigor and good health.

"Whew!" Galla breathed. "I'm tired. When this tent is up, I think I'll sleep for a week." She drew her hand across her forehead and she took another deep breath.

"Rest now, Galla," Athaulf said. "I'll get some of the men to help. I always tell you that you don't need to do all this work. You always try to do too much."

"I know," Galla said as she dropped one of the ropes and sighed, "I just feel like I should be useful, like everyone else is." Galla dropped the other rope. "I think I'll take you up on your offer this time, though. Would you ask some of the others to help? I think I'll go rest awhile."

Athaulf watched as Galla walked slowly away . . . gone was the long stride and the light spring that usually marked her step. Athaulf stopped working and thought of all his kinsmen who had perished during the long trek over the mountains. A dull pain tugged at his heart and a sudden lump of fear rose in his throat.

What if he were to lose Galla? He forced his thoughts back to his work, intent that the shelter be completed before nightfall so that his wife could rest protected from the damp night air.

By the next morning, Galla's condition had worsened. She was violently ill and too weak to leave her bed. Athaulf sent to Barcelona for a doctor, a *Roman* doctor if there was one. Athaulf didn't want to entrust Galla's life to the questionable care of the ancient Gothic midwives. Word came back from Barcelona that there was a Roman doctor in the town and that he would come out to have a look at the Gothic Queen within a day or so. He finally arrived in the late afternoon of the third day. Athaulf waited anxiously outside the tent as the doctor examined Galla.

The aged doctor emerged from the tent and smoothed his fine white tunic. "Why didn't you tell me that the patient was the Noble Galla Placidia, sister of the Emperor?" he scolded. "I would have been here sooner!"

"It would be best if as few persons as possible know of her presence here," Athaulf responded. "Tell me, how is she?" he asked anxiously.

"How long have you been married?" the doctor asked in his cold professional tone of voice.

"How long?" Athaulf looked rather confused at this unexpected question. "Four months, why?"

"That's long enough!" the doctor said matter-of-factly.

Athaulf's concern was now turning to irritation with the doctor's evasive manner. "Long enough? What are you talking about? I want to know how my wife is! What's wrong with my wife?"

"There's absolutely nothing wrong with your wife. She's as well as can be expected in her condition. Now if you don't settle yourself, *you'll* be the one who needs treatment." The doctor looked down to hide his bemused smile at the younger man's dawning revelation.

"Her 'condition'?" Athaulf looked wide-eyed at the doctor who could no longer contain his joy at being the one to announce this momentous event.

Athaulf stood dumbfounded, his palm held to his forehead. "I'm going to be a father?"

"Yes!" the doctor laughed, "You most certainly are!"

"I'm going to have a son," Athaulf said excitedly.

"Well, perhaps," the doctor smiled, "but it's been my experience that half the babies born are girls, so I'd say you have a fifty/fifty chance of having a boy. There's nothing wrong with a girl, though, I can tell you. I have three of my own. And if your daughter looks anything like her mother, she'll really be a prize!"

"Yes, yes, of course . . . a daughter, like Galla," Athaulf thought of Galla and turned to go into the tent.

"Wait, my boy," the old man paused, "excuse me, I mean Your Highness," the doctor fumbled for the correct words to address the Gothic chieftain.

"'My boy' is fine, doctor. I'm glad a Roman in your position could think of me that way, considering . . . 'My boy' is fine, or Athaulf if you prefer," Athaulf said jovially.

"Athaulf," the doctor said in a friendly tone, his voice growing serious, "you must take care of her. She *is* a Roman you know," the doctor looked at Athaulf and caught the younger man's appraising stare. "What I mean is, she's not built of the same material your Gothic women are. Your women are admirable, even formidable creatures; few Roman men could match their likes. They're built for this sort of thing . . . they can walk all morning, have a baby at noon, and be ten miles farther down the road by nightfall. But Roman women, the aristocracy, the *nobility*, well, they're different. Her Highness Galla Placidia is a Flavian. Her father Theodosius, God rest his soul, was one of the finest, most Christian men ever to rule Rome. But as breeders, well, it appears God had other plans for the Flavian bloodline."

"What do you mean?" Athaulf queried, his joy turning into concern.

"I'm just saying to take good care of her . . . keep her warm . . . don't let her walk too much . . . give her plenty of good food." The doctor took Athaulf by the hand and looked him in the eyes, "I'm only an old physician from a backwater Roman province, but I see a great future in what's happening here. That child might be just what the Empire needs, what we *all* need, to bring stability and peace. I want to give this child the very best chance we can," tears welled-up in the old man's eyes and he looked quickly away. "I'll be out every week . . . and I'll bring fresh produce and milk and whatever else I can."

Athaulf shook the doctor's hand firmly, touched by the old man's insight into his own feelings and dreams. After thanking the doctor profusely and ordering Heda to see that the elderly man was given something to eat and drink before he returned to the city, Athaulf went nervously into the tent to see his wife.

Galla was seated on the bed, propped up on feather pillows. Her face was flushed pink and when Athaulf approached her, she looked down shyly. Athaulf sat down on the bed and took Galla's hand. "Galla, darling, did the doctor tell you?" he asked gently.

"The doctor didn't have to tell me, I already knew," Galla looked up at Athaulf to see his reaction to this momentous news.

"You already knew?" Athaulf laughed.

"Yes, I knew before we left Gaul."

"But why didn't you tell me?" Athaulf asked with dismay.

"Because if I told you, you wouldn't have let me walk over those mountains. And we needed to come here. So I waited to tell you until we were here . . . until I was certain that everything was all right."

Memories of the long, arduous journey through the deep snow in the rugged pass flashed through Athaulf's mind and fear for what might have happened gripped his heart. He reached out, held Galla tightly and buried his face in her hair. "Oh Galla! Oh Galla!" was all he could say.

The days passed and Galla slowly regained her strength. The bright sun of southern Spain warmed the earth and Galla's spirits. The seeds in the fields burst open with new life and the buds on the trees blossomed into flowers that promised new fruit. As spring progressed into summer, Galla felt that she, too, was bursting with new life.

"Oh!" she laughed as she lowered herself down onto a chair, "I'm huge! I'm certainly not a 'Little Acorn' any more."

"'Little Acorn'?" Athaulf asked as he handed Galla a bunch of grapes.

"Oh, that's what my father used to call me, his 'Little Acorn.' It was a nickname he called me." Galla's thoughts traveled back through the years to the face of her beloved father Theodosius.

"Well, 'Little Acorn,' you're about to sprout a new branch of the family tree," Athaulf teased as he seated himself on the ground next to Galla and placed his head against her swollen belly. "And I can hear the little branch now--thump, thump . . . thump, thump."

Galla put her hand on Athaulf's head and ran her fingers through his long, thick dark hair. She marveled that this giant of a man, a chieftain and ferocious warrior, could be so gentle and so loving. She knew that he wanted this child as much as she did, and not just for matters of state, but for matters of heart. This child was a symbol of their love and devotion for one another. This child would carry on their plan of a united peoples under one government, the government of Christianity. Athaulf and Galla had talked endlessly of their dream of creating a single City of God here on earth. And now this child, half Roman and half Goth, would bring their dream to fruition. Galla leaned back in her chair and smiled contentedly. "God," she thought, "has surely led me here to fulfill His plan."

"Galla," Athaulf said softly, "I've been thinking about the baby's name."

"So have I," Galla replied. "What do you think we should call it?"

"Well, if it's a girl, I'd like to call her Galla, after you and your mother."

"Oh, I don't know," Galla replied. "I was thinking of Julia. It's a very old Latin name; it goes all the way back to the founding of Rome. And it's the feminine of Julius, in honor of my Uncle Julius."

"Julia." Athaulf repeated. "I like the sound of that. And it goes well with Galla. People will say to me, 'Where are your wife and daughter?' And I will say to them, 'Galla and Julia are at the palace.'" Athaulf said in an exaggeratedly officious voice.

Galla laughed, "'At the palace'? Oh? Are we going to have a palace?" she teased.

"Oh, several," Athaulf continued in his officious tone, "one for each day of the week. And Julia will have several tiny palaces of her very own."

"And what happens when she outgrows her tiny palaces?"

"Oh, we will build new ones for her. The old ones would be dirty by then anyway."

"Ah, I see. Athaulf, I think you're spoiling her already! And besides, what if Julia turns out to be a boy?"

"Well, he'll have to be very big and very strong . . . with a name like Julia it's likely that he'll get into a lot of fights."

Galla laughed and her belly shook, disturbing the baby who kicked in protest.

"Oh! Don't laugh, Galla! You've disturbed Princess Julia!"

"Well, that little Princess just might be a Prince . . . and we can't call him Julia. Seriously, Athaulf, have you given any thought to a name for a *son*?"

Athaulf lifted his head off Galla's round abdomen and he looked up at her with his clear emerald eyes. "Yes, Galla, I am hoping, if it's a boy, that we would call him Theodosius."

"Theodosius!" Galla whispered.

"Yes, I know I might be a bit presumptuous that any son of mine could carry such an honored and revered name . . ."

"Oh Athaulf," Galla interrupted, "it's a wonderful idea! I'm so pleased you suggested it. It's my fondest wish to have a son named for my father! Yes, *Theodosius* it will be!" Galla paused. "But what about *your* father, Athaulf? Shall we name our child after him, too?"

"No, Galla, but it's thoughtful of you to offer. My father was a great chief, don't get me wrong, but he was not a Christian, not even an Arian Christian, and he lived by the old ways. I want our son to live by our new ways."

"Well, then, how about Theodosius Germanicus, to symbolize the union between the Romans and the Goths?" Galla suggested, her eyes shining brightly.

"A fine idea, Galla, a very fine idea . . . Theodosius Germanicus, Emperor of the new City of God."

CHAPTER IX

Although the Roman army continued to persecute and slay the Goths in Gaul, the Goths who settled in Spain were allowed to live in relative peace. The fields outside Barcelona proved fertile and the Goths' first harvests were abundant. Late summer turned to autumn as Galla anticipated the pending arrival of her first child.

"I don't think this baby will ever come!" Galla moaned as she tried to pick up her shawl off the ground.

"Be patient," Heda consoled, "the baby *will* come in its own sweet time. Here," Heda said as she retrieved the shawl and handed it to Galla.

"Thank you, Heda, you're such a good help. I don't know what I'd do without you."

"Oh! What would any of you do without me? I swear you'd all whither up and blow away," Heda fussed as she stirred the huge iron pot full of venison stew. "Now where's that Athaulf gone off to now? The stew's been ready for half an hour and the men aren't here to eat it."

"Well *we're* here," Galla gestured to the women and children who were waiting patiently for the dinner to be served. "Let's go ahead and eat. I'm starved."

Just as Heda was dishing out the savory stew to the last child in line, the men appeared at the campfire.

"Well, here you are, *finally*," Heda drawled out the last word for emphasis. "Better get your bowls or this will all be gone before you've had your fill. We couldn't wait for you men. Athaulf, that wife of yours needs to be fed on time," Heda scolded as she filled Athaulf's bowl with the steaming stew.

"Yes, Heda," Athaulf smiled at the old lady's ire, "you were right to start without us." Athaulf thanked Heda for the stew, walked over to where Galla was seated at a wooden table, and sat down. "I'm sorry we were so long," Athaulf apologized as he broke off a piece of the loaf of dark bread that Galla handed him. "We've been in a meeting," he explained.

"A meeting?" Galla asked as she poured a tumbler full of dark brown ale for Athaulf.

"Yes. We've been discussing the problem in Gaul. The Romans are continuing their persecution of the Goths there and hundreds of our clansmen have been killed. Now the Goths are beginning to retaliate by killing any Roman who enters their territory. It's all going back to the way it was before," Athaulf paused to sip the ale, his green eyes deep in thought. "I've had an idea, Galla. I didn't mention it to the men because I wanted to discuss it with you first."

Galla set down her cup and gave Athaulf her undivided attention, flattered as she always was when he asked for her advice.

"We must do something to stop this carnage in Gaul. I don't think an appeal to either Honorius or Constantius in Ravenna would help . . . they're dead set on destroying us all." Athaulf paused and looked straight at Galla. "There is one other individual who might--and I say *might*--be able to help . . . Attalus."

Galla started to open her mouth in protest, but Athaulf raised a finger to silence her. "Now just hear me out. I have a plan. If I . . . If the Goths were to appoint Attalus as Emperor of Gaul and we promised to accept his rule, perhaps *he* could talk some sense into Honorius and Constantius. You see, Galla, with Attalus as Emperor of both the Goths *and* the Romans in Gaul, he might be able to bring peace. It's worth a chance anyway. I don't see how it could make things any worse."

Galla tore off a chunk of the coarse bread and chewed it thoughtfully. Athaulf began to eat his stew, patiently allowing Galla time to consider his plan. Galla recalled the upstart Attalus and his treacherous attempt to trap her into an unwilling union. She recalled also that Attalus was a pliable opportunist. He was just the individual to lean whichever way the wind blew. Right now, the wind seemed to be blowing in the direction of Gaul. Finally Galla spoke, "All right, I agree. It can't make things worse and maybe it can even help."

"Thank you for supporting me Galla. I value your confidence. I'll send word first thing in the morning. I have no doubt that he'll accept." Athaulf continued eating his dinner and the conversation turned to the harvest and to the pending birth of their child.

Several weeks passed and Galla's waist grew along with her apprehension. The Roman doctor visited each week and brought fresh produce from the port. Each week he had to allay Galla's fears.

"But doctor," Galla complained one morning, "you *can't* go back to Barcelona today! The baby is due any moment."

"Your Highness, the baby won't arrive for several weeks yet. It's only the first week of September. It will be two, maybe even three more weeks before we have to worry about that."

The doctor finished examining Galla and he stood up to leave. "Now, Your Highness, don't worry about a thing. Just get plenty of sunshine and rest." The doctor replaced his instruments in his bag and headed for the door just as Athaulf entered.

"Well, Doctor," Athaulf smiled, "how are our patients today?" Athaulf walked over and patted Galla's midriff.

"Her Highness is doing just fine," the doctor replied. "I was just telling her to get some sunshine. There won't be many of these lovely early autumn days. She should get out of this stuffy room and enjoy the fresh air."

"A fine idea! Come, Galla, let's go outside and take a walk. I want to show you the new colt that my chestnut mare presented us with last night. He's a fine fellow." Athaulf helped Galla to her feet and the two walked outside and bade farewell to the doctor.

Athaulf and Galla walked hand in hand through the olive orchards to the makeshift paddock where the mare and the little colt stood basking in the bright morning sunshine. Athaulf and Galla sat for over an hour watching the antics of the newborn as he tried to run on his spindly long legs. Galla studied the mare caring for her newborn, cleaning him and watching over him. She wondered what it would be like to be a mother and she hoped she would take to motherhood as naturally as this young mare had.

Finally, as the sun stood straight overhead in the sky, the scent of freshly baked bread and broiled chicken reached the paddock and Galla realized how hungry she was. Athaulf helped Galla struggle to her feet and the two walked slowly back to camp.

Just as they were beginning their lunch, Heda approached appearing very distraught and nervous.

"Athaulf, there's someone here to see you. I told them to wait in your tent," Heda said in a low whisper.

"Tell them to come out here if they wish to see me. I'm having my lunch. They can join us!" Athaulf offered cheerfully. "It's much too fine of a day to be indoors."

I think you should see them inside," Heda said, her voice still lowered and quavering. Heda glanced nervously at Galla who was paying no attention.

"Nonsense, Heda! I'll see them here or not at all! Now go tell them to come out here!"

"Very well, if you say so," Heda mumbled as she headed off to fetch the visitor. When she returned she had a tall blond woman with her--it was Letta.

Athaulf and Galla looked up with a start. They had not seen Letta since they left Italy over two years before. Now Letta stood before them, wringing her hands and fidgeting apprehensively.

"Sit down, Letta," Athaulf said coolly without bothering to rise from his chair. "Have something to eat. Then tell us why you are here."

Letta quickly pulled out a bench and sat down as Athaulf directed. Heda poured a cup of ale for her and gave her a plate of chicken. Letta ate as if she had not eaten in days. Athaulf and Galla quietly continued their meal, waiting for the woman to take her fill. When she was finally finished, Letta looked up at the couple, somewhat embarrassed to have eaten so greedily.

"I'm sorry for my manners," Letta apologized. "I haven't eaten in three days. I've come a long way--all the way from the west base of the Pyrenees."

"Why have you come *here*?" Athaulf asked in a reserved tone.

Letta looked cautiously around and seeing no one within earshot, she replied, "I came to warn you. Sarus is in Spain. He's bringing an army to attack you!"

"What?" Athaulf stood up and leaned over the table. "What are you saying? I haven't seen Sarus since our argument in

Gaul. Sarus left our band in a huff ages ago! You can't possibly mean that little malcontent intends to challenge me!"

"Yes," Letta looked up at Athaulf fearfully, "and he has an entire army with him."

"How did Sarus get an army? Who would follow *him*?" Athaulf demanded angrily.

"The *Romans*, that's who," Letta said defensively, resenting the tone that Athaulf was using with her and tossing a dark look at Galla. "That Attalus you appointed as Emperor of Gaul has taken it into his head to eliminate his competition, and that means you! Attalus has given Sarus a contingent of Roman soldiers and he's armed Sarus' own forces as well. They're marching towards Barcelona at this very moment!" Letta stood up and faced Athaulf across the table.

"How do *you* know all this?" Athaulf queried, his tone softening a little.

"I know it because . . . because . . ." Letta looked down at the table, "because Sarus is my husband."

Stunned, Athaulf lowered himself down into his chair. "Your husband! Then why have you come to warn *me*?"

"Because I couldn't stand by and let him kill you. Oh Athaulf! He's driven mad with envy over you. He's jealous that I once belonged to you. He's jealous that you married a Roman princess. He's jealous that your people love you and they're loyal to you." Letta paused and began to sob. "I couldn't let him kill you, I couldn't." Letta collapsed onto the bench, her face buried in her hands.

"Here Letta, have something to drink," Athaulf pushed a cup towards her. Letta regained some of her composure and managed to take a sip of ale.

"Well, well, well," Athaulf repeated as he mulled over the shocking news. "So Sarus is on his way to attack us. Well, we can't let him face us on our own fields, so we'll have to meet him half way. Men!" Athaulf shouted, "Prepare for battle!"

Galla sat stunned, random words ringing in her ears . . . "Sarus, Attalus, army, attack, battle . . ."

Athaulf leaned down and kissed Galla's forehead. "You stay here, Galla, I'll come see you before we leave," he said quickly. When Galla looked up, he was gone.

Galla and Letta now sat facing one another across the table. Letta looked nervously about, acutely aware that she was now the enemy, or at least the wife of the enemy, in an alien camp.

"I'd better go," Letta said timidly as she faced Galla.

"Where will you go?" Galla asked, suddenly realizing the very grave danger into which this woman had placed herself.

"I don't know," Letta said looking around in bewilderment. "I didn't think that far. I only knew I had to get here. Perhaps I can go to Barcelona . . . or Tarragona . . ."

"No!" Galla said firmly, "You'll stay here. After what you've done for us, it's only decent for us to repay you with sanctuary here."

"But I'm Sarus' wife!"

"You're a Goth, and a friend who just may have saved our lives." Galla stood up, walked around the table towards Letta. The latter realized only then that Galla was pregnant.

"Oh!" Letta moaned and wrung her hands, "I miss my baby!"

"Your baby?" Galla asked.

"I left my baby," Letta cried.

"Left him, where?" Galla said with alarm.

"With his father! I knew Sarus wouldn't mind if *I* left, but if I took his son, he'd hunt me down and kill me! Oh," she wailed, "my baby!"

Galla sat down on the bench next to Letta and held the sobbing woman in her arms. When Letta had finally cried herself out, Galla took her to Heda's tent and put her to bed. Galla then returned to the fireside to wait for Athaulf.

Athaulf returned in the late afternoon. He reported that the men were ready to move out. Galla and Athaulf bade one another a sad farewell and by evening he was gone.

The following days were a seemingly endless chain of waiting and watching. The women who remained at the camp did their best to complete the harvest and to begin planting the winter crops. Galla spent her days watching the horizon, searching for a sign of the returning men and praying that the baby would not arrive without a father there to greet it.

Galla's prayers were answered and Athaulf returned, safe and whole, after two weeks of bitter fighting. The rebel Sarus had been captured and executed and his followers were sold into slavery. Only Letta's child and a young servant boy named Dubius had been spared from the vengeance of Athaulf's warriors.

On the morning of the last day in September, Galla's labor pains began. Athaulf sent a messenger to Barcelona to fetch the doctor and Heda began gathering cloths and basins of hot water. By the time the doctor arrived in the late afternoon, Galla had reached a state of exhaustion.

"Keep her calm," the doctor ordered, "put some cold cloths on her head." In spite of his attempts to appear calm and cool himself, the doctor was as anxious and excited as the rest of the camp. News had spread far and wide of the approaching birth of a new heir to both the Gothic and Roman states and spectators were arriving from miles away. Each new arrival offered advice and suggestions of what to do for the mother-to-be.

"Well, if you ask me, I'd say cover her with garlic and coriander," offered one woman.

"This is a baby, not a stew," countered another.

"I say make the mother stand up and walk around. That way the baby will just drop out," suggested still another.

"Oh, like a ripe apple from a tree, eh?" quipped a fourth woman. "If you ask me, I say she should drink a cup of rose tea. Rose tea makes the delivery go faster."

Finally Athaulf could stand the clamor and din no longer and he ducked inside the tent to check on his wife's condition. Galla was lying flat on the bed, her face bright red with fever and the blankets soaked with perspiration. Athaulf rushed over and took her hand. She did not acknowledge his presence.

"What are you doing in here?" the doctor asked as he returned with a basin of fresh water. "Men aren't supposed to be at the delivery."

"*You're* here, and *you're* a man," Athaulf argued.

"Well, I'm the doctor, I'm supposed to be here."

"Well I'm the father and . . . well, I want to be here," Athaulf said with grave concern as he observed his wife's labored breathing. Athaulf dipped a cloth in the water basin, rang it out and placed it on Galla's forehead. She looked about disoriented and groped around with her hands.

"I can't find him," she mumbled. "Where is he?"

"Where's who, Galla? Who are you looking for?" Athaulf whispered softly.

"Julius. He's supposed to be here. Go look for him. Maybe he's down by the old oak tree. Tell him I need him."

"All right, Galla, I'll tell him. Now you just relax and don't worry about a thing, I'm here."

Galla's eyes focused on Athaulf's face and a smile indicated her recognition, but just as quickly it faded and she was off looking for Julius and the oak tree.

The hours dragged on and Athaulf drifted in and out of sleep while seated on the chair next to Galla's bed. Shortly after midnight, a loud cry awoke the entire camp, followed by the plaintive wail of a newborn baby.

"It's a boy!" the doctor announced proudly, "A beautiful boy!"

Athaulf took the tiny infant in his arms and marveled at the miracle he had just experienced. Here in his arms was a perfect little person, ten tiny toes, ten tiny fingers, and a voice that could be heard all the way to Rome.

Gradually Galla regained consciousness and she began to look around the room . . . there was Heda . . . and the doctor . . . and Athaulf . . . "But what is he holding?" she wondered to herself.

"He's here," Athaulf said with a broad smile.

"Who's here?" Galla asked as she wiped here eyes.

"Our son!" Athaulf announced proudly as he placed the tiny bundle he was holding into Galla's arms.

"Our son! Oh, Athaulf, he's here. He's really here!" Galla quickly unwound the little bundle and checked over each square inch of the tiny newborn.

"He's all there," Athaulf laughed, "I already checked. And look!" Athaulf held out a finger and the tiny baby grasped it firmly. "See how strong he is! Just like his father!" Athaulf added proudly.

"Yes," Galla sighed contentedly, "just like his father!" She smiled up at Athaulf and he leaned over and kissed her forehead.

"And what are you going to name this strong little man?" the doctor inquired.

"Theodosius Germanicus," Galla and Athaulf replied in unison.

The news of the birth of a son to Galla and Athaulf was greeted with mixed emotions across the Empire. Those farsighted individuals who dreamed of a united Roman and Gothic peoples celebrated the news as a sign of good fortune and hope. Those who remained stubbornly and solely allied with Rome viewed the birth as an ill omen and a portent of war.

Nothing, however, could lessen Athaulf's and Galla's happiness with their new son. They neglected all their other duties in order to spend each moment with their precious child. Galla even refused to send the infant out to a wet nurse, which was the custom among the aristocracy at the time. Instead, Galla delighted in nursing her son herself and feeling the very special bond that grew between mother and child. The weeks passed and the happy couple doted upon their beautiful new son.

"Look, Athaulf, look how thick his hair is becoming. It's so lovely and dark like yours," Galla cooed as she cuddled the tiny infant at her breast.

"And he has beautiful amber eyes like his mother," Athaulf said softly, stroking the baby's tiny back. "Tomorrow I'm going to take him to the council to introduce him."

"Oh Athaulf! Do you think you should? He's so little yet!"

"He's a month old, it's time he takes his rightful place next to me at the council table," Athaulf replied, his face beaming with pride.

"Well, let's see what the doctor says, he's coming out from Barcelona this afternoon. If he says it's all right, then I'll agree," Galla said as she shifted the baby to her other breast. "He really is wonderful, isn't he?"

"Who? The doctor?" Athaulf said half-jokingly. "You think more of the doctor's opinion than of mine," Athaulf teased.

"No, I don't," Galla reassured Athaulf, "I just don't want to take any chances with this precious one, that's all."

"Neither do I, Galla, my darling. We'll wait and let the doctor decide."

The doctor arrived in the late afternoon. He was riding on a cart piled high with produce, fresh seafood, and gifts for the new baby. It looked as if all Barcelona wanted to contribute to the new baby's health and happiness.

"Hello! Hello!" the doctor called out cheerfully. "Look what they've sent along with me! If there had been any more, I'd have had to bring two carts." The doctor climbed down off the cart and shook Athaulf's hand.

"It's good to see you, Doctor. Thank you for coming," Athaulf said heartily as he walked the doctor into the tent.

"Glad to . . . glad to . . . wouldn't miss seeing this young man for all the world . . . after all, all the world's talking about him," the doctor said as he set down his bag and the pair of scales he was carrying. "So, how's the new mother?" he asked, picking up Galla's arm and feeling her skin temperature.

"I'm fine, doctor, regaining my strength each day," Galla smiled. She turned to the infant and held him up, "Look who's here, Theodosius, it's your doctor! He's come to see you," Galla sang in a little voice.

"Yes, let me have a look at you, Theodosius, and see how you're progressing," the doctor said as he picked up the baby and placed him on the scales.

Athaulf laughed, "It always looks like you're weighing apples when you put him on that scale, doesn't it, Galla?"

"Yes, and I'll take a dozen more apples just like him," Galla said proudly. "Doctor, isn't he the best, the most beautiful apple you've ever seen?"

The doctor didn't reply immediately, and then he said, "Hum? What? Apple? Oh, yes, yes, beautiful apple all right . . ." the doctor paused again and studied the scales. "I'm concerned about his weight. He didn't gain weight for two weeks and now he's lost some," the doctor said as he adjusted and then readjusted the scales.

Athaulf stood staring at the scales and Galla offered, "He's just a very active baby, that's all, he's always wiggling and squirming."

The doctor gently lifted the tiny baby off the scales, laid him on the table and began to examine him, all the while saying nothing. A heavy silence filled the room.

Finally Galla broke the silence, "Perhaps it's me . . . perhaps it's my fault, maybe he's not getting enough milk."

"I don't think that's it, Your Highness, but I guess it wouldn't hurt to try a wet nurse, at least for a few feedings each day," the doctor said cautiously as he continued to look at the baby.

"Athaulf, get Heda. See if there's a woman in the camp who can nurse Theodosius . . . a *healthy* woman," Galla said anxiously.

Athaulf left and returned a few moments later with Heda.

"Yes, there are several new mothers here who could help," Heda considered, "but they are also nursing one or two of their own at the same time, except . . . "she paused.

"Except?" Galla said hopefully.

"Well, except Letta. She's just about to wean her little Frel. She'll have plenty of milk . . . if she's willing."

"Bring her here, Heda. We'll ask her if she's willing to help," Galla said slowly, knowing how Letta felt about Athaulf and how the woman might react to their request.

Athaulf walked over and sat down on the bed next to Galla. He put his arm around her and drew her close. He tried to imagine how Galla must feel . . . learning her only child was not doing well . . . and finding that the best hope of helping him might lay with another woman--*that* woman. "You are remarkable," Athaulf whispered hoarsely into Galla's ear.

Letta entered the tent and the doctor told her about little Theodosius' problem. Letta cast a nervous glance between Galla and Athaulf. She picked up the tiny baby off the table and replied, "I'll bring him back when he's had his fill." And Letta left the tent.

"I'll be back in two days," the doctor said as he packed up his things. "In the meantime, don't worry. Every baby is different. They each have their own growth pattern."

Two days passed and the doctor returned as he promised, but little Theodosius had not improved. Now his parents never left his side. They each took turns watching him while the other slept. After that, the doctor returned daily to monitor the tiny infant. One Sunday the doctor brought the priest from Barcelona.

"Hello, Father, welcome." Athaulf said hesitantly, "To what do we owe this honor?"

The priest cleared his throat and looked awkwardly about, "I . . . I've been asked to perform a baptism for your son, Sir."

Galla overheard the word "baptism." She flew to Athaulf's side and grasped his arm. "A baptism! No! He won't be baptized until he's older . . . when he understands," Galla said frantically as she looked between Athaulf and the priest. She could feel Athaulf's body tense and straighten as he drew in a deep breath. Athaulf put his arm around Galla and he held her tightly. He carefully searched the tense faces of the doctor and the priest.

"Galla," Athaulf said in a choked voice, "prepare little Theodosius for his baptism while we help the Father prepare for the ceremony."

"But Athaulf," Galla cried, "not now . . . he's too young . . . we should wait!"

Athaulf looked at Galla and she could see tears welling up in his eyes. "I think it's best we do this now, Galla. Would you like me to help you dress him?" Galla nodded and tears spilled over her cheeks.

At noon on the first of December, Theodosius Germanicus, age two months, was dedicated to the Lord in baptism. By nightfall his little soul was with God.

CHAPTER X

It was an unusually cold and damp winter in the south of Spain that year. Galla and Athaulf endured the empty hours by sending letter after letter to Ravenna, appealing to Honorius and Constantius to cease their relentless persecution of the Goths in Gaul. Athaulf took long walks alone in the rain. He'd often be gone for hours and Galla would sit silently in their tent, listening to the rain pelting the cowhide roof.

"Will this rain never cease?" Galla sighed one afternoon as she watched Athaulf don his heavy cape in preparation for one of his solitary walks. "I can't stand the endless din of rain out there," Galla said as she glanced up at the roof, which was now wet clear through.

"It's bound to let up soon, Galla," Athaulf consoled her as he pulled on his heavy boots. "Come with me today. You haven't been out of this tent since . . . It would do you good, even if it *is* pouring rain. At least the air is clean and fresh out there," Athaulf nodded to the door.

"No," sighed Galla, "I don't want to go out. I can't. Not yet."

"Well, I've got to get out of here, these walls are making me crazy," Athaulf ran his hand through his long hair, then placed his cape over his head. "Are you sure you won't come with me?"

Galla shook her head and turned her face away from Athaulf.

"All right, I'll be back later," Athaulf replied dejectedly.

Shortly after Athaulf left, Galla heard a voice outside her tent. "May I come in?" she heard Letta ask.

"Yes, come in, Letta," Galla replied, surprised that the woman would come to see her. Letta entered the tent and Galla indicated that she be seated.

"How are you, Your Highness?" Letta asked as she took her chair. "We haven't seen you for weeks and we are worried about you. Is there anything we can do?"

Galla looked at the woman seated across from her and wondered if she was truly as sincere as her clear blue eyes indicated.

"Thank you for your concern," Galla said stiffly. "No, there's nothing you can do . . . there's nothing anybody can do . . ." and Galla began to cry again.

"I'm sorry," Letta apologized. "I didn't mean to upset you. Perhaps I should go." She stood up and started for the door.

"No!" Galla sobbed. "Please don't go. I would like some company, really." Galla dried her eyes and tried to smile. "Besides, I never had a chance to thank you for what you did for us . . . for our son . . ." Galla's voice trailed off and the tears welled up in her eyes again.

Letta retook her seat and sat awkwardly, trying to think of a reply.

"Well," Galla said in a stronger tone, "tell me what's happening out there in the world. Has everyone washed away in all this rain?"

"No, but the rain has taken its toll. The grain in the storage bins has the rot and it looks as if our root crops are all destroyed." Letta paused and bowed her head. "I'm sorry, Your Highness, I didn't mean to bring more problems to you. Actually, I have had a bit of good news. Well, I think it's good news. I've had a message from Sarus' brother Sigeric. He's coming to Spain with his people. They have decided to move out of Gaul before the Romans move up into their area." Letta paused and tossed a questioning glance at Galla. Galla nodded for her to continue. "Well," Letta said slowly, "Sigeric is coming here. He says he wants to come for me."

Galla looked up with concern. "Come for you? Do you think he wants revenge for when you warned us about Sarus?"

"No, I don't think so. I don't believe there was ever any love between Sarus and Sigeric. As brothers they were always in fierce competition for power over their people. Sigeric finally took his followers north and left my husband and his followers in the south. No, I don't think he's unhappy at all about Sarus' death. He says he wants to reunite his people and to make peace with Athaulf and his people."

"Are you certain that his intentions are peaceful? It would be a very grave situation to allow these people into our midst if they are still allied with Rome," Galla warned.

"Yes, I agree, but I really do believe their intentions are good. I've even talked it over with Dubius. Do you remember Dubius?" Galla shook her head no. "Well," Letta continued, "he's the young boy that Athaulf spared after the battle with Sarus. Do you remember when Athaulf returned with my son Frel? Remember he also brought Sarus' attendant? His name is Dubius and he's still here. He works in the stable. I don't know why Athaulf saved Dubius--I asked him once and all Athaulf said was that he felt sorry for Dubius and that it wasn't his fault that his master had been so ambitious."

"Ah, yes," Galla nodded, "I know the young man you mean . . . I just didn't recall the name. Yes, go on."

"Well, Dubius thinks that Sarus really hated his brother Sigeric. He said he often heard them fighting. Dubius and I both think that Sigeric is coming in peace. And then there's . . ." Letta's voice trailed off.

"And then there's what?" Galla prompted.

"Well," Letta said nervously, "Sigeric has asked to marry me."

Galla looked up with surprise. "Marry you?"

"Yes," Letta replied, "it's the custom. Well, you know that by now, don't you? When a man dies, his brother marries the widow. It keeps the power and the wealth in the man's family . . . and the children. And I have little Frel, Sigeric's nephew and heir."

"Ah, I see," Galla said slowly, "but what about *you*? Do you want to marry this Sigeric?"

Letta looked down and shrugged her shoulders, "What are my options? No one in *this* camp will have me . . . I was Sarus' wife. I really have nowhere else to go except back to his people-- my son's people. I have to think of little Frel now, you know. And besides," she paused, "as near as I can figure, I'm twenty-six now. If I don't do something soon, no one anywhere will have me."

Galla sat studying the slim figure of the lovely blond woman before her. "Twenty-six," Galla thought to herself bitterly, "and how old is this Sigeric? Forty? Fifty? And *he's* not too old to take a new wife!" Then Galla thought of herself, "Twenty-six--I'm nearly that myself. I wonder if Athaulf is thinking of me as old. I *have* been rather dull company since . . ."

"I'm sorry, Your Highness," Letta interrupted Galla's thoughts, "I shouldn't be bothering you with my personal problems."

"No, Letta, it's fine. I'm glad you came to talk with me. I was just thinking about what you said about being twenty-six. You're still a remarkably lovely woman."

Letta blushed and lowered her eyes, "Thank you, Your Highness. Coming from one as beautiful as you, that is truly a compliment."

"Well, when can we expect Sigeric and his people to arrive?" Galla asked.

"Not until spring, perhaps even late Spring the way this weather is. They will come through the Pyrenees as soon as the passes are clear." Letta stood up to leave.

"Come see me again, Letta," Galla said with sincerity. "I have enjoyed our conversation. And bring little Frel. I'd like to see him. I think it would be good for me, for us, to have a baby around. Would you do that for us, Letta?"

"Oh yes, Your Highness," Letta replied excitedly.

"And Letta, I think we can dispense with that 'Your Highness' business. If you and I are going to be friends, you must call me Galla."

"Thank you, Galla, I'd like that. And I'd like to be friends, too." Letta walked towards the door just as Athaulf entered. Athaulf cast a wary glance at Letta, concerned that her presence might be upsetting Galla.

"Athaulf, darling," Galla said, "Letta has been visiting with me. We've had a nice talk."

Athaulf walked over to Galla and kissed her on the forehead. "You sound in much better spirits, Galla," he said as he sat down next to her.

"I am, Athaulf. Letta has helped me to realize that the world is going on with or without me," Galla said as she waved good-bye to Letta.

"And?" Athaulf asked hesitantly.

"And I've decided that I must go on, too."

Just as was expected, it was a very harsh and a very long winter. Snow covered the fields until Palm Sunday. It was May before the ground was soft enough to begin plowing for the belated spring planting. As the last seeds were tucked into the narrow furrows, Sigeric and his people arrived.

Galla and Athaulf stood watching, their hands shading their eyes from the bright June sun, as Sigeric and his refugee troops approached from the east.

"There's so many of them!" Galla said with alarm. "How will we ever feed them all?"

"We can't. I certainly hope they're carrying their own supplies. I expected a few hundred, but there must be over a thousand," Athaulf said in amazement.

Letta came out to where Galla and Athaulf were standing on a low ridge observing the arriving tribe. She was dressed in a light blue woolen gown and she wore spring flowers in her hair.

"You look lovely, Letta!" Galla exclaimed. "You don't look a day over twenty-two!" The two women laughed and Athaulf smiled to see how fond they had become of one another.

"Yes, Letta, your bridegroom will be swept off his feet," Athaulf added.

"The real question is, will Letta be swept off *her* feet?" Galla countered. "I have told Letta that if she finds that she doesn't like this man, she can stay with us as long as she pleases. I think she's worried that she's a burden to us . . . one more unmarried female."

"Nonsense, Letta," Athaulf said in a serious tone, "you will always be welcome with us--you *and* little Frel. I've grown quite fond of that boy of yours," Athaulf stopped himself abruptly, fearing that his comment might upset Galla.

"Yes, so have I," Galla added as she took Athaulf's hand in hers and gently reassured him that his comment about Frel had not hurt her. "Just remember Letta, you don't have to go with this man unless you want to."

"Yes, I'll remember. Thank you both so much. You've both been very kind."

The approaching band of Goths was now close enough to make out the figures. Leading the band was a short, heavyset man with a curly red beard.

"That must be Sigeric," Athaulf commented, "judging from his jewelry and silver horse trappings. It looks like your suitor has some wealth, Letta."

Letta strained to see the man on horseback. Nothing in her demeanor revealed her feelings upon seeing the squat, balding, overly dressed man.

Athaulf and his people prepared a welcome celebration for the new arrivals. As soon as the newcomers' tents were pitched, the festivities began. There were jugglers, poets and musicians from Barcelona, and as grand a feast as the hard times would allow. Sigeric had brought casks and casks of wine and ale from Gaul and he openly shared his bounty.

Sigeric sat at the head table alongside Galla and Athaulf. Letta took her place beside Sigeric and, without fanfare or speeches, it was assumed by all that a wedding was not far off. The party lasted until dawn. The sky was painted with shades of scarlet and orange as Galla and Athaulf entered their tent.

"Whew!" breathed Galla. "I haven't eaten or drunk so much in a long time!" She unlaced her bodice and threw herself down on the bed.

"Yes!" Athaulf agreed, "Neither have I!" He collapsed into a chair and pulled off his boots. "I think I'll sleep until sunrise tomorrow."

Galla rolled over on the bed and looked at Athaulf. "Well, what do you think of the bridegroom-to-be?"

"Who? Oh, Sigeric," Athaulf replied as he unlaced his collar and pulled his shirt over his head. He ran his fingers through his long hair and tossed his head slightly. "I can't say yet. He seems affable enough." Athaulf slipped out of his leather trousers and slid into bed next to Galla.

"Finish your sentence," Galla prodded.

"Well, it's just a feeling I have . . . like something's not quite right." Athaulf leaned over and caressed Galla's back. "It's probably just the wine." Athaulf put his arm around Galla and the two fell into a deep slumber.

The marriage between Letta and Sigeric took place in late July. Letta wore Galla's lovely saffron wedding gown. The ceremony itself was short and business-like, but the festivities that followed were raucous and uncontrolled. Galla had not seen anything like it since the night that Alaric disappeared all those years ago. She thought how much Sigeric reminded her of Athaulf's late brother Alaric--both Sigeric and Alaric were crude and bull headed. Galla thought that men like them deserved the title 'barbarian' that the Romans used to describe the Germanic tribes. She wondered if Letta felt as repulsed by Sigeric as Galla herself had once felt about Alaric. If Letta did feel disgust towards her new husband, she never revealed it. She stood with decorum throughout the ceremony and seemed to enjoy the frenzied celebration that followed.

Sigeric and his people stayed on into August. Athaulf became concerned. If the visitors remained through the winter, they might prove to be a burden too great for his people to bear. The crops looked promising but they would hardly support his own people, let alone Sigeric's people as well. Athaulf decided it was time to encourage Sigeric to take his people and to move on.

One evening at sunset, as the dinner fires were being lighted, Athaulf approached Sigeric who was seated by the fire quaffing a tall mug of ale.

"Eh there, Athaulf, come! Sit! Join me in a mug of your fine ale," Sigeric called out. Athaulf seated himself across from Sigeric and accepted the cool mug of ale that the stocky man handed him.

Athaulf sat sipping the ale for a while, listening to Sigeric slurping and belching. Finally Athaulf broached the subject.

"I've been thinking, Sigeric, about that nice plain of land over near Cadiz. You know of it--perhaps you've even been there. It's over near Gibraltar. I've heard the land is fertile and the trade to Africa is good." Athaulf paused and took a sip of ale.

"Yea, I know it," Sigeric said bluntly, his watery blue eyes scanned Athaulf's face.

"Well," Athaulf continued, "this land can't support us all, you know that. And you can't go back to Gaul--the Romans are still on the rampage there. So I thought you might go to Cadiz. I'll set you up with supplies and grain."

Sigeric's icy blue eyes continued to stare at Athaulf. Sigeric took a gulp of ale and frothy brown foam ran down his thick red beard. He wiped it off with the back of his rough hand. "So, Athaulf, you're doing my thinking for me now, eh?" Sigeric said with a toothy grin but his voice revealed his anger.

"No, Sigeric," Athaulf said politely but firmly, "I'm not doing your thinking for you, but I am thinking for my people. You've seen our crops--that's all we have to feed ourselves this winter."

"Crops!" Sigeric hissed and spit on the ground. "And you call yourself a Goth! No self-respecting Goth ever dug in the dirt like some mole! You won't find me or my people down on their knees in the dust," Sigeric added with a toss of his head, "not me or mine!"

"Well, do what you will, then," Athaulf sighed as he finished his ale and stood up to go. "We have been friends thus far--I don't want anything to cause problems between our peoples. I just want you to know that this land can't support us all. You've been here for three months. It's time for you to move on."

"All right Athaulf. Have it your way, then. You're the big fancy chief!" Sigeric slurred.

Athaulf paused and looked down on the drunken man. "I want to help you Sigeric. Let me know if you need anything for your journey." Athaulf turned and walked away.

When Athaulf returned to his tent, Galla could see he was in a state of great agitation. "What is it, Athaulf? What has happened?" Galla asked with concern.

"Oh, it's nothing, Galla," Athaulf sighed and ran his hand through his hair. "I'm tired, that's all. Having all these people milling about, all this noise day and night, it's making me tired. Sigeric's people never seem to settle down . . . they're so restless, they're making me restless, too." He threw himself down on a chair.

Galla walked over and began to rub Athaulf's broad shoulders. He took her hands in his and looked up at her. "Let's take a ride tomorrow, huh Galla? Just the two of us. We'll pack some baskets and ride down to the seashore. Think of it, Galla . . . a whole day just to ourselves. Will you Galla?"

Galla was pleased to see some of his old enthusiasm return and she laughed, "Of course, darling. That sounds wonderful. We could use a long ride and a day alone. I'll have Heda pack some things for lunch and we'll set off first thing in the morning."

"Let's leave before sunrise. I don't want anyone tagging along," Athaulf added. He put his arms around Galla's waist and drew her close to him, "I love you, Galla, more than you'll ever know."

The next morning Galla and Athaulf went to the stable before dawn. They saddled their horses and tied on the woven wicker baskets that Heda had carefully prepared. They mounted up and rode off before the first rays of sun peered over the horizon. No one saw them leave except the stable boy, Dubius.

Galla enjoyed the long ride to the sea. It was good to be on a horse again. Her long confinement and recovery had kept her from her rides and she was happy to be feeling completely well again. It was a beautiful ride down to the sea--a soft thin mist blew across the rolling meadows and settled on the sandy dunes. Galla and Athaulf laughed and talked as they rode along. Galla began to feel the life returning to her veins. The morning fog lifted and gave way to a sunny August day. Finally they felt the fresh sea breeze that heralded their arrival at the shore. They rode across the broad beach and into the shallow surf. The horses loved the feel of the foamy salt water on their legs and they happily galloped along the water's edge. When Galla and Athaulf reached a small sheltered cove with a sandy beach and a thick fringe of palm trees, they drew up the reigns of their horses and dismounted.

"Oh! It's absolutely lovely," Galla called out. "Why haven't we been here before?"

"We've been too busy working, that's why. I suggest we turn over a new leaf," Athaulf suggested as he spread out a blanket in the shade of the swaying palms.

"A new leaf?" Galla asked as she began unloading the wicker baskets.

"Yes. From now on we'll take more days off. Even chieftains need to rest."

"And chieftains' wives," Galla added, handing Athaulf a large bunch of ruby red grapes.

"Oh . . . and especially the chieftains' wives . . . but only the most beautiful ones . . ." Athaulf reached up and kissed Galla.

"Do I qualify?" she asked, putting on her most coquettish smile.

"Well, I don't know. Come over here and let me have a look at you." Galla walked over and stood in front of Athaulf. He put one finger on his cheek and studied her carefully. "Turn around," he ordered. Galla dutifully turned her back to him. "All right, turn back again." Galla giggled and turned back around to face Athaulf. "Yes, I guess you'll do!" he said as he pulled Galla down next to him on the blanket. "You're a bit on the thin side, though. Here--I think you'd better have another grape." Athaulf plucked a grape from the bunch and popped it into Galla's mouth.

She quickly swallowed it and said, "There! Do I look better now?"

"Oh yes! Much better! Now you're perfect!" Athaulf laughed.

"I have an idea!" Galla said and sat up on the blanket. "Let's go for a swim!"

"A swim?" Athaulf looked at Galla, "You'll get your clothes all wet."

"Who said anything about clothes?" Galla laughed.

"But Galla . . ." Athaulf stammered.

"There's no one here. Come on!" Galla leapt up, slipped out of her short riding tunic and ran across the beach into the sea.

Athaulf ran after her, leaving a trail of clothes behind him.

After their swim, the two stretched out on the beach and allowed the hot Spanish sun to warm their bodies. Athaulf sighed with contentment. "I feel so much better," he said. "I'm really happy. How about you, Galla, are you happy?"

"Yes, Athaulf," Galla replied as she looked up into the sky, "except for one thing . . ."

"What Galla? Anything . . . I'll give you anything you want."

"I'd like another baby," Galla said softly.

It was dusk before they began to pack up and it was completely dark as they rode back to camp. Galla hummed little melodies as they rode along and Athaulf made up silly words to go along with the tunes.

"It's been a perfect day, hasn't it, Athaulf?" Galla asked as they approached the camp.

"Yes, it has Galla," Athaulf sighed with contentment. "Let's plan to go again soon, shall we?"

When they arrived at the camp, the fires had burned low and the camp was still.

"Well, it looks as if they've retired early for a change. Perhaps we can get a good night's rest for once. I'm exhausted," Athaulf yawned. "Making babies is hard work!" he whispered to Galla with a wink. Galla looked down shyly and smiled.

"Here, Galla," Athaulf offered, "you dismount here and go into the tent. I'll take the horses to the stable. I'll be back in a few minutes."

Galla dismounted, grateful for Athaulf's considerate offer. It had been a very long day and she, too, was exhausted.

Galla lifted the flap of the tent and entered. "Galla, it's me!" a woman's voice startled Galla to alertness. "It's me, Letta." Galla's eyes adjusted to the deeper darkness inside the tent and she saw Letta standing close to her.

"Letta! What are you doing here at this hour? Why are you standing here in the darkness? Here, let me light a lamp."

"No! Don't light the lamp. Where's Athaulf?" Letta asked urgently.

"He's gone to stable our horses, why?" Galla asked, sensing something was very wrong.

"I don't know. I think Sigeric is up to something. He's been acting strangely all day. Maybe it's nothing, but I just wanted to tell you to be alert. Be careful, Galla, and tell Athaulf to keep an eye on Sigeric. I don't trust that man," Letta said hatefully.

"Where *is* Sigeric? How did you get away?" Galla asked with concern.

"Oh, he's drunk as usual, just like every night. He drinks until he falls into a stupor. Still, I'd better get back . . . just in case."

Letta started for the door of the tent but Galla stopped her. "Thank you, Letta," Galla said as she hugged the other woman. "You are a dear friend. You be careful, too."

Letta left the tent and Galla began to undress. Then she suddenly changed her mind and she pulled her tunic on again. She draped her shawl over her shoulders and headed for the stable. Just as she approached the stable door, it opened and the stable boy Dubius pushed past her and ran into the darkness. Galla felt an icy chill run down her spine. She ran into the stable where she found Athaulf laying on the floor, a sword lodged deep in his abdomen.

Galla screamed and rushed to her husband's side. He was unconscious and blood flowed from his wound in rhythmic bursts. Galla knelt down, pulled the sword from his body, and covered the gaping hole with her shawl.

"Help! Help!" she screamed as she struggled to stop the bleeding. Within seconds the barn was full of men and they carried the wounded chieftain to his tent. Galla stood motionless as she watched the men undress their leader and bind the open wound. "Send for the doctor in Barcelona!" Galla pleaded. "Someone, please, go fetch the doctor."

"From the looks of him, that won't be necessary," a rough voice growled. Galla looked up to see Sigeric standing in the tent door. "Guards, seize this woman!" Sigeric ordered. Two of Sigeric's guards grabbed Galla's arms and began to drag her from the tent.

"What are you doing?" she cried. "How dare you! On what grounds do you seize me?" Galla demanded.

"For the murder of the Gothic chieftain Athaulf!" Sigeric said coldly.

"Murder? Athaulf's not dead! He's not *going* to die! He's my *husband*! *Please*, you *must* help him!" Galla pleaded, tears running down her face.

"You're not the first wife to murder her husband. Guards! Take her away and lock her up."

Galla screamed and struggled in protest as Sigeric's men drug her to the very stable where Athaulf lay bleeding only minutes before. The burly men pushed Galla into a dirty stall and locked the door. Galla pounded on the rough wooden door until her hands ran with blood. She screamed and pleaded until her voice failed her. Finally, Galla realized that no human was coming to her aid. She knelt down and prayed.

Throughout the night Galla heard the sounds of men fighting and the screams of women being tortured. The mayhem lasted until dawn when two men threw open the stable door and drug Galla from the dirty stall.

"What's happening?" Galla pleaded as the men bound her arms tightly behind her back. "How is Athaulf? How is my husband?" The men pushed Galla out into the morning light. "Please, please, tell me how my husband is," Galla begged, "Where is he?"

"There!" one of the men pointed to a heap of bodies in the distance. "Right where he belongs, the filthy Roman-lover!"

A man in the distance yelled, "Get more wood over here. Get these bodies burned before they draw the vultures. Come on! More wood! Hurry it up!"

"No!" Galla screamed. "They're Christians! You cannot burn them! They're Christians!"

"Shut up," one of the men ordered and he slapped Galla across the face.

Galla began to pray,

> "The Lord is my Shepherd,
> I shall not be in want.
> He makes me lie down in
> green pastures,
> He leads me beside quiet waters
> He restores my soul"

"Go ahead and pray," one of the men scoffed, "a lot of good it will do them now," he laughed.

> "He guides me in paths of righteousness
> for His name's sake.
> Even though I walk through the valley
> of the shadow of death,
> I will fear no evil, for You are with me;

Your rod and Your staff, they comfort me.
You prepare a table before me in the presence
    of my enemies.
You anoint my head with oil; my cup overflows.
Surely goodness and love will follow me
    all the days of my life,
and I will dwell in the house of the Lord forever."

CHAPTER XI

Sigeric and his tribe moved west. Galla Placidia was forced to walk on foot in front of Sigeric's horse, her hands tied tightly behind her, as they traversed the Spanish countryside. Those of Athaulf's people who had been unfortunate enough to survive that night of bloody terror were forced to march alongside the bereaved Galla. The path that Sigeric and his band of ruthless warriors followed was along a line of small settlements that flanked the main road to Tarragona, a Roman settlement to the west of Barcelona. Sigeric's ragged assembly of Goths moved slowly, consuming or destroying everything in their path.

Galla saw few Goths whom she recognized as members of Athaulf's tribe. She feared the worst for the faithful Heda and her family. Only once did Galla catch a glimpse of Letta as the tall blond woman entered Sigeric's tent.

Long after darkness fell on the sixth night of the mournful march, Galla was awakened by a loud clamor of voices. Galla strained to see out the narrow spaces between the boards of the stall in which she had been locked. Torches flashed brightly and here and there figures ran about chaotically. After a few minutes, the camp was quiet again. Only one campfire still burned. The glow it cast lighted the faces of a circle of men who sat in solemn conversation.

At dawn, two guards entered the stall and dragged Galla to her feet. They led her across an empty courtyard and into a small house. In the atrium sat the men whom Galla had seen at the campfire during the night. At the head of the table was a man named Wallia, one of Sigeric's elder council members. The guards seated Galla in a chair opposite the long table at which the men were seated. She noticed that another chair in the room remained empty.

The men spoke among themselves in low voices as two serving women placed bread, cheese, and ale in front of them. Wallia called one of Galla's guards over to his table and whispered to him. The guard came over to Galla and untied her wrists from behind her. Galla looked at her bruised and bleeding arms. One of the serving women nudged Galla and handed her a mug of ale, which Galla accepted and drank greedily.

"All right, show her in," Wallia finally said in an audible voice. The door opened and Letta entered the room. Her dress was torn and she looked bruised and beaten, but she held her head high as she crossed the room and seated herself in the empty chair. Galla tried to catch Letta's attention, but the latter looked straight ahead towards Wallia and his men.

"We have two orders of business here today," Wallia began. "First, the murder of the chieftain Athaulf."

Galla gasped involuntarily and a cold tremor passed over her body.

"Second," Wallia continued, "the murder of the usurper Sigeric."

Galla gasped a second time and stared blankly at Letta who showed no reaction.

"You!" Wallia said pointing at Letta, "Tell us what you know about the murder of Athaulf."

Letta took a deep breath and spoke in an even, controlled voice, "I already told you what I know. I know that the stable boy Dubius murdered the chieftain Athaulf. I heard Dubius talking with Sigeric that very night. Dubius told Sigeric that he had done as Sigeric had ordered. Then Dubius asked for the money that Sigeric had promised him."

"And what else did you hear that night?" Wallia prompted.

"I . . . I heard Athaulf say that Dubius had ambushed him in the stable . . ." Letta paused and bit her lip as she drew another deep breath. Wallia nodded for her to go on. "Then Athaulf asked about his wife. He asked, if he died, that she be returned to her people." Letta's voice began to tremble. "He . . . he said he wanted peace . . . and . . . he begged Sigeric to spare his wife. His last words were that he loved her."

Galla sat rigidly, picturing Athaulf as he lie dying, his last words about her and about peace. Tears flowed down Galla's face as she stared blindly into space.

"And now," Wallia interrupted in a cold, loud voice, "item two . . . the murder of Sigeric." Once again Wallia turned his piercing eyes upon the blond woman.

Without a pause, Letta said coolly, "I killed him."

"Go on . . ." Wallia prodded.

"He killed Athaulf. And he killed the others of Athaulf's tribe who had been kind to me. And he even threatened to kill Sarus' son . . . *my* son." Letta paused and shrugged her shoulders. "I couldn't allow him to do that."

"So what did you do?" one of the other council members at the table asked quietly.

"I killed him. I waited for him to go to sleep and then I slit his throat."

A wave of nausea passed over Galla and she struggled to keep from fainting.

The men at the table spoke among themselves and finally Wallia said, "Galla Placidia, you are free to leave the room. We believe you are innocent of your husband's murder." He paused and looked down, "We offer you our condolences."

Galla struggled shakily to her feet. She was numb with shock. She walked blindly towards the door, then paused and looked at Letta who was still stiffly seated in her chair, her eyes straight ahead.

"Letta," Wallia announced, "you will remain under arrest until your punishment has been decided."

"Punishment?" Galla uttered hoarsely.

"Yes, Your Highness, this woman has murdered a Gothic chieftain. She will . . . she *must* be punished," Wallia said, irritated that Galla would intercede in the proceedings.

"But Sigeric murdered Athaulf! And he would have murdered Letta's son!" Galla argued.

"We will take that into consideration, Your Highness," Wallia replied. "You, of all among us, should know the laws that Athaulf introduced to our tribes . . . *your Roman* laws."

Galla lowered her eyes and said, "Yes, but Letta should have a trial by a jury of her peers. The punishment should not be meted out by a council."

"Guards!" Wallia commanded. "See that Her Highness is shown to a tent."

The two guards approached Galla and she knew to argue further with Wallia would be futile. Galla walked over to Letta and hugged her. "God bless you," Galla whispered and left the room.

By late afternoon, they were on the move again. Now Galla was permitted to ride in a wide cart with some of the other women. As the cart jerked and bumped along over the rocky hillsides, Galla wondered if Athaulf's dying wish, and now *her* wish too, would be granted . . . that she be returned to Rome. The years with the nomadic peoples had taken their toll and Galla felt drained and forlorn. She watched dumbly as the Spanish countryside passed under her.

When at last, after several more weeks of tiresome wandering, Wallia finally summoned Galla to his tent one evening, it was a thin and wretched creature who appeared before him.

"Your Highness," Wallia addressed the haggard form before him, "you do not look well. Have they been feeding you?"

"We feed her," one of Wallia's servant girls replied, "but she refuses almost everything . . . not good enough for her, I suppose."

Wallia threw an angry look at the servant girl, "Well then get her something that *is* good enough for her! We can't have her dying on us . . . not now when we're so close to Cadiz! Go on! Get her something decent to eat . . . and bring some of that wine we have."

Changing his tone, Wallia offered Galla a seat, "Please, Your Highness, be seated. I had no idea they were not caring for you properly. From now on you'll ride up at the front of the line with me--that way I can keep an eye on you to make certain you take care of yourself. I wouldn't want to be the one to tell the Emperor that his sister has starved herself to death." Galla did not reply.

"Well," Wallia continued as if nothing were wrong, "tomorrow we will reach Cadiz on the coast of the Atlantic. Have you ever seen the Atlantic, Your Highness?" Wallia asked as the servant girl poured a goblet of fine red wine for Galla. "It's a sight to behold, that ocean!" Wallia passed a plate of cheese to Galla, "Eat. What good will you be to anyone if you die? Don't you want to live to fulfill your late husband's dream?"

Galla looked up dully and searched Wallia's eyes. Underneath his red-veined skin and bristly whiskers, she perceived a look of kindness. She continued to stare at the heavy-set middle-aged man.

"You know as well as I that once you're gone there'll be all out war among all our peoples. You're the one thin thread that's holding this whole bloody world together," he said seriously as he pushed a plate of chicken in Galla's direction. "And if you get any thinner, you'll break. Now go ahead and eat something, you foolish woman."

Galla picked up a chunk of the dark yellow cheese and took a bite. She continued to study Wallia's face.

"Here," Wallia said as he unrolled a large vellum map, "look at this." Wallia looked up and saw a spark of interest in Galla's eyes. "It's a map of the Mediterranean. We're here," Wallia placed a thick finger on an inlet to the northwest of the strait at Gibraltar.

Galla looked at the map with indifference. "You're thinking of going across to Africa for grain?" Galla asked half-heartedly, sick at the memory of the earlier failed attempts.

"That was our first idea, yes. But we've had a message from your brother in Ravenna and we've decided not to go to Africa for grain." Galla looked up with curiosity. Wallia continued, "We've decided to go to Africa to settle."

"To settle? Who? Where?" Galla asked with concern.

"Yes, to settle," Wallia responded as he allowed the map to roll shut. "Your brother is a difficult and complicated man, Galla, as is his friend Constantius. We thought that now that you're a widow, your brother might cease his persecution of the Goths and renew his offers of grain for your return. But once again, Honorius has confounded us with his vacillations." Wallia picked up the scrolled map and tossed it on a table behind him. "We cannot wait any longer. Our people must have a place to settle--a place to be free of this Roman plague."

Galla took a long sip of the clear red wine. "The wine is good," she commented. "Thank you for ordering it for me."

Wallia looked at Galla and raised his eyebrows, "'The wine is good?' Is that *all* you have to say?"

"The cheese is good, too. That other food they tried to feed me wasn't fit for a pig."

"And what about our plans to go to Africa? What do you think about them? Are they good too?" Wallia asked in a bemused tone.

"Oh, yes, your plans are fine. *All* the plans to cross over to Africa have been fine, but each has ended in tragedy." Galla said as she picked up a chicken leg.

Wallia watched her as she carefully picked the flesh off the bones and chewed it delicately.

"So," Wallia said with irritation, "you don't think our plan will succeed?"

"It appears to me that *God* does not want your plan to succeed," Galla said as she finished the chicken leg.

"Bah!" growled Wallia, "You and your Roman God! You call yourselves civilized yet you believe in this resurrected Christ. A man! That's all that Jesus was . . . just an ordinary troublemaker. And you Romans make him a God. But then you Romans are *all* trouble-makers." Wallia leaned back in his chair and laughed. The grin faded from his face and he continued to stare at Galla. "I can see why they all fall under your spell, Galla Placidia--Athaulf, Constantius--all of 'em. You're a beautiful woman--and I can tell there's a brain behind those lovely amber eyes. It's *you* who should be the god . . . men would come from far a field to worship at your feet." Wallia leaned forward and stared into Galla's eyes. Galla instinctively leaned away from him.

"I'd like to ask you something," Galla said, breaking the tense silence in the room. "What did the council decide about Letta? Is she all right?"

Wallia leaned back again and dropped his eyes. "Yes. She's fine. The council decided to keep her in custody until we cross over to Africa. We don't want to take a chance on her running away and taking Frel with her."

"And how is little Frel?" Galla asked.

"He's fine . . . a bit too much like his father but we have time to change that. He's young yet."

Galla finished her wine and stood to leave. "When do you plan to cross to Africa?" she asked.

"Soon . . . before the winter winds set in. We'll leave as soon as all the tribes have arrived."

"And I suppose you plan to take me with you?" Galla said with bitter sarcasm.

"Well, we couldn't leave you here all alone, a poor defenseless woman? Who would care for you and protect you from life's harsh trials?" Wallia responded with a shrug of his shoulders and a grin.

The weeks passed and each new day brought hundreds of Goths to the camp at Cadiz. They arrived on foot, horseback, carts and boats. Soon an entire fleet was assembled in the harbor below the city. It was not a makeshift fleet like the one Alaric had assembled at the strait to Sicily, but this was a fine fleet of several hundred vessels, all well equipped and seaworthy.

On a clear November morning, the Goths set sail for Africa. The ships sailed from the harbor one by one, allowing sufficient room between them to tack and come about in order to catch the prevailing winds. Galla leaned over the railing of the vessel she shared with Wallia and watched the long line of sails disappear around the point of the harbor.

By late afternoon Galla's vessel had still not left the port. A stiff breeze started to blow, causing much trouble for the departing vessels in the bay. By dusk it was apparent that the ship Galla was aboard would not be able to leave that day, so the passengers went below to dine and to wait until daybreak to attempt to sail. During dinner the weather took a turn for the worse and a violent storm kept everyone awake through the night.

Morning came but still there was no relief from the storm. Wallia ordered all the passengers to disembark and they took shelter at an inn at the port of Cadiz. Three days later, just as the storm began to subside, news arrived from Gibraltar that all of the departed ships had been lost at sea, taking with them over twelve thousand Gothic men, women and children, Letta and little Frel among them.

Wallia and his tribes were at land's end. There was nowhere else to go but east again, back from where they came. Their numbers cut by half, their supplies nearing an end, the Goths began the long and tedious journey back to the Pyrenees. Their only hope was that some sort of reconciliation with Honorius might be effected. Each evening Galla helped Wallia to compose letters imploring the Emperor to cease his hostilities and to come to the aid of their beleaguered people. Each morning found the Goths on the road east again, more weary, more hungry, and more desperate. Any village that had been spared on the journey west, the eastward-bound Goths now fell upon like ravenous beasts.

The Goths were not the only Germanic group plundering the Spanish countryside. The Vandals had also ravaged their way down into the Iberian Peninsula. They offered to sell food to the starving Goths, but at prices twenty times its value. When the Goths were no longer able to produce the money that the Vandals demanded, the latter scorned their ancient rivals, happy to see the Goths nearing surrender and defeat.

As the first winter snows were falling, the Goths finally reached the foothills of the Pyrenees, only to find that snow was not the only thing blocking the mountain passes. There was a larger and a more formidable obstacle in their path--the Roman army. It was under the leadership of none other than Constantius himself.

Trapped between the Vandals and famine on one side, and the Pyrenees and the Roman legions on the other, the Goths finally offered up their last remaining item of value--the noble Galla Placidia. In return for Galla, the Goths were given 600,000 measures of grain and they were assigned to posts within the Roman legions. The Emperor Honorius had finally provided exactly what Alaric had originally requested over five years earlier . . . before Galla's sojourn with the Goths, before the devastation of Spain, Gaul and Italy, before the brutal sack of Rome in 410.

Galla's captivity ended on the last day of 415. She was released into the charge of an elite corps of Imperial Roman guards who escorted her and a large band of her Gothic followers over the icy Pyrenees Mountains. Constantius awaited her arrival at Arles, but Galla's party circumvented the Gallic town and continued east. By mid-summer, Galla and her contingent reached central Italy.

Galla left her followers at a small village north of Rome. She explained that there was something she wanted to do . . . something she *had* to do . . . before her entrance into Rome.

Taking only a mule and the clothes on her back, Galla headed south along the narrow coast road in the direction of her father's villa.

PART III

CHAPTER I
415 A.D.

Darkness was falling as Galla awakened from her reverie. She climbed slowly down from her seat upon the old fallen oak tree, and looked sadly around the valley in which she had spent her youth. Gone were the splashing fountains, the gaily-colored gardens . . . in their place were tangled vines and weeds. Galla sighed deeply, picked up the reins of the old mule, and walked falteringly up the hill towards her father's villa.

As she reached the crest of the hill, the fading sun caught the silver hair of an old woman standing near the stables. Galla paused briefly and squinted, trying to discern the features of the woman. A lump rose in Galla's throat--the hunched and aged woman in the courtyard was Eli. The years had taken an unkind toll upon the beloved nurse. Galla dropped the reins of the mule and ran down towards the courtyard.

The sound of Galla's approach startled the old woman and she dropped the bucket she was carrying. "Who's there?" Eli demanded as she peered out into the falling darkness.

"It's me, Eli . . . it's me," Galla called out.

"Your Highness? Is that you?" Eli asked with disbelief. "Is that really you?" Eli's voice began to tremble.

Galla ran to the old woman and put her arms around her. "Yes, Eli, it's really me. I'm home, Eli. I'm finally home!"

"Praise be to God, my Lady. Praise be to God!" Eli sobbed.

Galla and Eli walked arm and arm into the villa. The smell of freshly baked bread and the glow of a warm fire welcomed Galla into the familiar kitchen. Galla pulled herself weakly onto a high stool and she leaned on the old wooden table she knew so well. Her vision swam with tears as she ran her hand over the smooth surface of the old table.

Eli brought over an oil lamp and set it on the table in front of Galla. "My Lord in Heaven!" Eli whispered as she stared at

Galla in the lamplight. "What have they done to you? What have they done to you?"

Galla smiled sadly and ran her hands down the dirty wool sheath she wore. "I'm all right, Eli," Galla reassured the stunned old nurse, "there's nothing wrong with me that your cooking can't cure." Galla's flattering words failed to appease Eli's concern.

"Joseph!" Eli called out. "Joseph, come here!"

The sound of shuffling feet increased until Joseph turned the corner and entered the kitchen. When he beheld Galla he stopped dead in his tracks.

"No, you've not seen a ghost," Eli told him. "It's really her! Our Lady's come home again! Now, Joseph, go and prepare Her Highness' room. Then send to Rome for Julius. Oh, poor Julius," Eli fretted, "he's been next to mad with worry these last five years. He asked God not to take him until he had rested his eyes on you again." Eli stopped and stared at Galla. "Oh my Lady . . . it's you! It's really you!" Eli wiped the tears from her eyes. "Go on now Joseph! Get Her Highness' room ready and send one of the men to Rome to fetch Julius." Joseph turned and shuffled back down the hallway. Eli scurried around the kitchen, gathering every foodstuff in sight and placing it in front of Galla. "Eat!" Eli commanded, "Eat! Why you're as thin as a sparrow!"

Galla eagerly tore off a chunk of bread and dipped it into the thick hot soup in the bowl in front of her. The familiar aroma of Eli's cooking brought memories racing back to her. Galla ate until she could hold no more and then weariness took hold of her. "I think I'll go rest now," Galla said as she slid off the high stool and started for the kitchen door. "Oh Eli, will you see that the mule is fed and watered?"

Eli laughed softly, "Well, you might have changed on the outside, but you're still your old self on the inside, my Lady. You always did worry more about the animals than yourself. Now you go off and get some rest. Don't worry about that old mule, I'll see that he gets fed and watered."

Galla paused at the door to the kitchen. "Eli, what about Odysseus? Is he out in the stable, too?"

Eli shook her head sadly, "No, my Lady. The Goths took him." Eli began to weep again.

"It's all right, Eli," Galla comforted the old woman. "The Goths love horses. I'm sure he was well treated. I just thought I'd ask."

Galla left the bright warm kitchen and headed wearily for her room where she found Anta waiting for her. "Anta!" Galla said with pleasure. "How good to see you!"

"And you, too, my Lady. When Joseph told me that you had returned, I didn't dare believe it, but here you are!" Anta said as she helped Galla slip out of her filthy sheepskin dress and into a clean linen nightdress. Anta held up the smelly limp animal hide and looked at it with disgust. "Shall I burn this, Your Highness?" she asked.

Galla slid between the fresh cool sheets and she looked over at the dirty garment. "No, Anta, I want to keep it."

Anta looked at Galla with surprise, "Well, shall I clean it, Your Highness?"

"No," Galla replied slowly, "Just fold it and put it away like it is. I want to keep it just the way it is. Someday I may want it, someday I may want to remember . . ." Galla yawned, closed her eyes, and drifted off to sleep.

Warm sunlight and a soft breeze from an open window greeted Galla when she awoke the next morning. Anta and Eli sat dozing in chairs at the foot of Galla's bed. Galla looked around the room and blinked her eyes. It seemed so unreal. Had she been dreaming? Were the past five years all one terrible, long nightmare? Everything around her was unchanged . . . the furniture in her room was arranged exactly as she had remembered it . . . the books upon the shelves . . . the small writing desk by the window, it was all the same.

Then Galla looked at Anta and Eli . . . where once had been a young girl and a middle-aged nurse, now sat a mature woman and an elderly nurse. "No," Galla thought to herself, "I did not dream the past five years. They were, indeed, a nightmare, but the nightmare was real." Galla sat up in bed, eager to shake the memories from her drowsy mind. Her stirring wakened the servants.

"My Lady! You're awake!" Eli beamed. "I hope you rested well!" Anta scurried off to prepare a bath as Eli helped

Galla out of bed. "You have a warm bath, my Lady," Eli said to Galla, "and I'll go fetch your breakfast. Julius sent word from Rome that he'll be here at midday, so you have plenty of time to prepare yourself." Eli cast a sad look at Galla's hair.

Galla reached up and felt the tangled, dry mass upon her head. "Perhaps Anta can cut it," Galla suggested in a cheerful tone. "I believe I'm ready for a change anyway."

Eli went off to the kitchen and Galla enjoyed a long, hot bath in scented water. After her bath, Anta massaged Galla's body with perfumed oils. Galla devoured the fresh fruit and soft cheese that Eli brought her and the old maid returned to the kitchen for more. After breakfast, Anta managed to run a comb through Galla's damp tangled tresses. Galla sat in the warm sun in front of the open window as Anta alternately combed and snipped Galla's auburn hair. When Anta was done, Galla shook her head and felt her now shoulder-length hair. "It feels wonderful, Anta! So light and free! I feel like a new woman!" Anta smiled to see her mistress looking so pleased.

Galla then walked over to the cabinets that held her clothes and she marveled at how many lovely garments were there. She had forgotten her extensive wardrobe. In her years with the Goths, Galla had found that clothes were just more to pack and more to carry. Now she looked with amazement at the bounty of lovely silk gowns before her. Galla pulled out a delicate pale blue pleated sheath and she drew it on over her head. How light, and airy, and cloud-like it felt.

She selected a wide silver belt and wrapped it around her waist, but the belt only hung limply on her hips. "I guess I *am* thin as a sparrow, like you say Eli," Galla commented to her old nurse. Galla set down the heavy silver belt and instead drew a long white silk scarf around her waist, knotting it neatly and letting the ends drape down the side of her dress. "There! That's better," Galla said with satisfaction. She then stepped into a pair of fine white leather sandals. "These certainly aren't very practical," Galla laughed. "I bet I couldn't walk a mile without these failing me."

Galla picked up the polished bronze mirror and studied her reflection. "Well," Galla said as she set down the mirror, "I guess that's the best we can do for now." Galla reached for a bunch of grapes. "When Julius arrives, please tell him I'm waiting for him in the garden. I feel a need to be outdoors."

Galla was seated in the peristyle garden, watching the birds bathing in the shallow pool, when she heard Julius approach. "The Lord be praised!" the old man uttered as he stood in front of Galla. "The Lord be praised for your safe return." Julius sat down on the marble bench next to Galla and she could see tears welling up in his eyes. His silver hair had thinned considerably and his once straight posture now stooped slightly.

Galla put her arms around the elderly man's frail shoulders. "I'm home, Uncle Julius, I'm really home. I've missed you so much," Galla sobbed as she buried her head in the old man's toga.

The two sat holding one another for a long time. Finally, Julius pulled away and Galla looked up at him. "We didn't expect you to come *here*, Galla," Julius said. "We thought you'd go straight to Ravenna to meet with Honorius. He's expecting you there."

"Yes, I know," Galla replied with a sigh. "I wanted to come here first. I wanted to see you . . . and the farm. I wanted to come *home*."

"I'm glad you did." Julius cleared his throat and blinked back his tears. "Oh, Galla! You'll never know how worried I've been! I thought that God had forgotten us, and now you're here! Praise be to His Son!" Julius said as he lifted his hands towards Heaven.

"Yes," Galla said softly, "praise God and His beloved Son Jesus."

"Well, we have so much to talk about, I don't know where to start," Julius laughed. "What are your plans, Galla? Do you know what you're going to do?"

"First, I want to stay here and rest for awhile . . . just rest," Galla paused, "and *think*. Oh! And I want to send for my people who are waiting for me just north of here. They've been faithful to me. They helped bring me here. I want to give them some land and some grain to start planting."

"Honorius is a bit worried about those Gothic followers of yours, Galla," Julius interrupted. "He's afraid they're here to cause trouble and he's afraid that more will follow."

"They are simple peasants, Uncle Julius, not warriors. All they want is a bit of land on which to farm and to support their families. It's the least I can do for them, after all they've been through to see me safely home."

"Of course, Galla, *I* understand. I just want to let you know how Honorius feels, so you'll be prepared, that's all. The fields to the east and the north haven't been cultivated in years and the orchards have gone wild. It would be good to have the farm worked again. Good land shouldn't remain unattended."

Galla smiled gratefully. "When my people are settled, I guess I'll have to go to Ravenna to speak with Honorius face-to-face." Galla stood up and folded her hands. "Frankly, Julius, I don't know what I have to say to him after all these years--after all he's done--or *didn't* do!" Galla looked off into the distance, "I only know that I'm back now, back in Rome, and I'm going to take my rightful position as the daughter of Theodosius . . . Honorius or no Honorius," Galla said firmly.

Julius looked up at the woman before him . . . gone were the plump girlish curves and the sweet childish innocence. He saw before him a different Galla than the one who had lived there all those years before. Julius knew from his own experience what war and hardship could do to a person . . . what suffering and loss could do. Julius stood up and put his arm around Galla. He knew instinctively that he need not worry any more about his Little Acorn; she was now his Great Oak--ready to take her place in the Flavian dynasty.

"Julius," Galla said after a long silence, "how is Fortus? Is he well?"

Julius looked down into Galla's eyes, "Yes, Fortus is well. He came up with me from Rome this morning. He wanted to give you and me some time alone together. He's waiting for you in the library."

"Fortus! In the library! Now?" Galla exclaimed excitedly. She turned and started to run towards the house, but she stopped suddenly and turned back. "Julius," Galla said hesitantly, "is . . . is Fortus married?"

Julius looked puzzled and said slowly, "No . . ."

Galla turned again and ran into the villa.

"Galla! Wait!" Julius called after her, but she had already disappeared inside.

Galla raced down the long hallways, smoothing her hair and her gown as she went. She remembered the last time she saw Fortus, that fateful day so many years ago. He was standing in front of the window in the library . . . he wore his Roman soldier's uniform and he looked so tall and strong and handsome. How many times had Galla pictured Fortus standing before that window . . . the light playing over his soft brown curls and his muscular frame.

Galla paused briefly in the hallway in front of the library. She took a deep breath and silently opened the doors. There, in front of the tall window, stood Fortus, his back to Galla, exactly as she had seen him so often in her dreams. The light from the window silhouetted his hair and his broad shoulders. "Fortus!" Galla cried. Fortus turned and Galla flew into his arms, kissing him again and again. "Oh Fortus! Oh Fortus!" Galla sobbed as she clung to him, "I thought I'd never see you again! Oh Fortus!"

Fortus gently released himself from Galla's embrace and he held her out in front of him at arm's length. His sea-blue eyes were filled with tears. "Nor I you, Galla," he whispered hoarsely, "Nor I you." Fortus dropped his arms and lowered his eyes.

It was then that Galla realized Fortus was no longer wearing the short tunic and shining armor of a Roman soldier. He now wore a long simple black cassock and around his neck was a heavy chain from which hung a silver crucifix.

Galla stepped back with a gasp. "Fortus, no!" she cried. "No!"

Fortus looked at her with his light blue eyes still swimming with tears. "Galla," he stammered, "you were married . . . you had a child . . ." Fortus picked up Galla's hand and held it to his tear-stained cheek. "I saw no future for us . . . my only future lay with God."

Galla turned away and stumbled to a seat. She felt as if her one last, thin remaining hope of happiness had been wrenched away from her . . . her one last remaining hope of love. Fortus sat down alongside Galla and he held her in his arms. "Shh, Galla, don't cry," he consoled her. "We're both *alive* and we must give thanks to God for that." Fortus stroked Galla's hair as she continued to sob uncontrollably.

Julius entered the room and took a seat. He leaned his elbows on his knees and hung his head. "I'm so sorry, Galla," Julius apologized, "I thought you knew. I just didn't think. I'm so sorry."

Galla slowly regained her composure and dried her eyes. "It's I who should be sorry," Galla replied. "I'm sorry for acting so selfish, as if all the world would wait idly by for my return. Life goes on, no matter what the circumstances, doesn't it?" Galla managed a weak smile. "Are you happy, Fortus?"

"I am now. It took a long time, but God has His ways-- when one thing is taken from us, He finds a way to give us another. As you say, Galla, 'Life goes on,' perhaps not the way we had hoped, but perhaps in a way that's better. Only God knows what lies ahead for us."

"Yes, Fortus," Galla responded, "only God knows what lies ahead for us."

CHAPTER II

As soon as Galla's Gothic followers were settled on her land, Galla made the journey to Ravenna that she had dreaded for so long. In her company were Julius, who was eager to see Ravenna again, Pontus, who had remained in the service of the Roman army, and Claudia, who was now a widow with two small children. Galla was grateful for the company of her dear friends. Only Fortus remained behind, his duties at St. Peter's Basilica keeping him in Rome.

Ravenna had grown since Galla was last there. The presence of Honorius and his court had benefited the seaside city, both economically and politically. Galla marveled at the elegant new buildings as they rode east, past the main city, towards Honorius' palace. News of Galla's arrival reached the palace before her and she was welcomed with Imperial pomp and fanfare.

Honorius himself greeted Galla as she stepped from her litter. "Welcome, my sister," Honorius said with dignity as he offered Galla his arm and led her up the long marble staircase to the palace entrance. "We are glad to see that you have arrived safely. I trust you had a pleasant journey." Honorius continued chatting as if the separation between the siblings had been eight days rather than eight years.

Galla resisted the temptation to ask to which journey he was referring, Ravenna or Spain, and instead she merely commented, "Your palace is magnificent, Honorius. You must be quite comfortable here."

"Comfortable?" Honorius said in his pompous, slightly whining tone that Galla remembered so well. "Yes, I guess you could say that. I really don't have much time for comfort, I'm so busy tending to the affairs of the Empire."

Once again, Galla resisted the urge to respond unguardedly to her brother's thoughtless chatter. She knew these were the first of many such times that she would have to conceal her true feelings towards Honorius. So instead of telling her brother what she really thought, Galla merely complimented Honorius on the fine quality of the palace decorations.

Honorius allocated an entire wing of the vast palace to Galla and her entourage. Each item of frivolous expenditure that Galla observed increased her ire towards her brother. She couldn't help but imagine that while she and the Goths were starving in Spain, Honorius was spending vast sums on trinkets and baubles for his ostentatious palace. Galla declined the dinner invitation extended to her by Honorius, knowing that if she saw her brother that evening, she might not be able to contain her fury.

The next morning, rested and composed, Galla breakfasted with Honorius in the palace garden overlooking Ravenna's harbor in the distance. "After breakfast, I'll take you on a tour of the city," Honorius commented as he spooned honey on a wedge of bread. "I have a little present for you. I think you'll like it."

"I'd like to take a tour," Galla responded. "I haven't been in Ravenna in years and I'm interested to see how it's grown."

"Ravenna is the center of the world, Galla. Nothing happens outside Ravenna's walls, nothing worth noting anyway," Honorius said blandly as he finished his bread.

Galla looked down at her plate and wondered if Honorius was really as ignorant as his comments would indicate, or whether he was just self-absorbed and stupid. Either way, she promised herself, she'd remain cool and unaffected by his absurd comments. "Yes, it's a beautiful city. I had forgotten how lovely it is."

After breakfast, Galla and Honorius boarded his Imperial litter and they were carried through the streets of the bustling trade town. They made stops at several of the city's most elaborate buildings and Honorius bragged on and on about his lavish expenditures on improvements to the city.

Just about midday, after a leisurely drive along the road east to the seaside, the litter stopped in front of a charming old palace. Galla recognized it immediately. It was one of her father's palaces. Galla stepped down from the litter and admired the ancient edifice. "It looks just like I remembered it!" Galla commented as they mounted the steep stairs to the entrance.

"Yes," Honorius said proudly, "I've had it restored, everything is the finest, down to the last detail." A servant opened the tall bronze doors. Honorius led Galla inside and gave her a tour of the elegant old palace.

Beyond the main building was a vast peristyle garden with one long side open to the Adriatic Sea. Galla walked along the open colonnade and admired the view across the deep blue water. At the far end of the immense garden, a table was set and several servants stood waiting.

"Come, Galla," Honorius ordered, "I've arranged for lunch to be served here. Come, sit, have some of this fine Gallic wine." A servant poured wine into a jewel-studded golden goblet. Galla took the goblet and imagined how much grain could be traded for a precious object such as the goblet. "What's wrong, my dear?" Honorius asked as he placed a broiled quail on Galla's plate. "Is something wrong with the wine?"

"No," Galla said quietly, "it's excellent wine."

"Good! Good!" Honorius said gaily. "Remember I told you that I had a gift for you?" Galla nodded. "Well, here it is!" Honorius smiled as he looked around the garden. Galla looked around too, but she saw only the beautiful long reflecting pool and the manicured hedges and flower gardens. She looked quizzically at Honorius who laughed loudly. "*This*, my little sister, this palace! It's yours! Now that you are back among us, I know you will want to be near me. So I am giving you this palace," he said proudly.

Galla looked again at the fine old building and at the spectacular view beyond. "That's very kind of you, Honorius," Galla began slowly, "but I'm not sure if I wish to remain in Ravenna . . ."

"Certainly you do," Honorius interjected. "Ravenna is the center of the world, I tell you, and this palace is worth a fortune." A sharp whistle interrupted Honorius' sentence and they both looked up to see an unkempt middle-aged man approaching. "Welcome! Welcome!" Honorius greeted the visitor. "You're just in time to tell my sister what a valuable piece of property I'm giving her." The stocky man waddled over to the table, sat down with a thump, and wiped his balding head with a napkin. "Good to see you," Honorius said cheerfully as he patted the newcomer's back. "Have some of this fine Gallic wine."

The guest accepted a large goblet of wine and noisily consumed the contents. "Yes," the man said as he wiped the stubble on his chin with the back of his hand, "valuable. That it is," he agreed as he held up the goblet for a refill. "Good wine," he commented between gulps. "Is this some of that wine I brought back from Gaul?"

"Yes, it is," Honorius replied. "Galla was just complimenting the quality of the wine, weren't you Galla?"

Galla gave her brother a somewhat perplexed look. Who was this man with whom Honorius was conversing so freely and in front of whom he called Galla by her given name? "Excuse me, Your Highness," Galla addressed her brother. "I don't believe this gentleman and I have been properly introduced."

"What do you mean, Galla?" Honorius asked in a slightly defensive tone. "You've known this man since you were a child! *Everyone* knows *him*. Galla--this is Constantius!"

Galla felt a cool shiver run up her spine. She looked at the solid little man in the soiled tunic. "Constantius!" she thought to herself, "So this is the little upstart who has caused so much trouble!"

Constantius stood up and made a little bow. "I apologize, Your Highness, for my informality. It didn't occur to me that you wouldn't recognize me. I guess you *were* very young when we met at Serena's villa many years ago." Constantius picked up Galla's hand and kissed it clumsily, his ragged beard poking into her skin. "I'm sorry that you were unable to stop at Arles a few months back. I had rather a nice reception waiting for you there." Constantius looked directly into Galla's eyes and beneath his bemused smile she detected a look of anger.

"I was eager to be home again," Galla explained in a restrained tone. "I knew you would understand." Galla withdrew her hand from Constantius' sweaty palm. "It is an honor to meet you again, General. I've heard many things about you."

"All good, I'm certain!" Honorius added jovially. "Constantius is my right hand man. Oh, hell, he *is* my right hand! Don't know what I'd do without him. Tell me, Constantius, how are things going in Gaul? Any new reports?"

Constantius took another gulp of wine and wiped his mouth on the sleeve of his tunic. "Just this morning, a messenger from Toulouse, Goths and Vandals killing one another like flies! It's bloody wonderful!" Constantius laughed. Galla gasped and drew her hand to her mouth to silence herself. Constantius saw Galla's shocked reaction. "I'm sorry, Your Highness. You're having your lunch and here am I ruining it with talk of war."

"Yes," Honorius agreed, "we really must be more considerate, mustn't we Constantius? We so seldom have a member of the weaker sex among us, we forget how sensitive and fragile they are. Let's change the subject, shall we?"

"The subject is fine," Galla responded firmly. "I am just surprised to hear that there is still trouble in Gaul. I thought that everything was settled now . . . now that I'm back."

"Women!" Honorius scoffed. "They think the world revolves around them, don't they Constantius? For your information, my dear little sister, those barbarians have been fighting since before you were born, and they'll continue to fight long after you're dead. It's in their blood. They love it! Why do you think we call them barbarians?" Honorius chuckled and Constantius responded with a loud guffaw.

Galla clenched her teeth until the urge to argue with Honorius passed. She slowly folded her napkin and placed it gently on the table. "I don't believe I have thanked you for your magnificent gift, Honorius," Galla smiled sweetly. "I think I shall enjoy living in Ravenna. As you say, Ravenna is the center of the world. What better place, then, for me to live?"

Galla watched Honorius and Constantius as they cheered and toasted her decision to remain in Ravenna. She knew they were celebrating the success of their plan to keep her close by and under their control. Little did the two cats know that their little mouse had plans of her own.

Within the month, Galla and her retinue were established in her palace on the beautiful Adriatic Sea. Eli and Anta joined her household, as well as many of Galla's Gothic followers, including Candidianus, Athaulf's faithful friend. Honorius and Constantius objected to the presence of the Goths in Ravenna, but Galla steadfastly ignored their demands that she dismiss the Goths from her court. Pontus, who had accompanied Galla to Ravenna at Fortus' request, returned to his post in Rome. Julius and Claudia, however, remained with Galla in Ravenna.

Galla was glad to have so many familiar and friendly faces around her, and her palace became her only refuge in a town full of politics and intrigue. But politics and intrigue were exactly why Galla remained in Ravenna--it was there that Galla could keep an eye on Honorius and Constantius . . . and the Empire.

One morning, Galla joined Claudia and her children for a walk along the seashore. Claudia's two young children amused themselves by tossing stones into the sea and by looking for shells along the water's edge. The serene tranquility of the morning was broken when a messenger on horseback approached the little party. The messenger drew up his horse alongside the group, pulled out a large vellum scroll, and barked, "For Her Highness Galla Placidia from General Constantius." He handed the scroll to Galla and galloped off.

"Well, so much for a peaceful stroll along the seashore," Galla sighed. She took a seat upon a rock and unwound the heavy scroll. She sighed again. Claudia walked over and put her hand on Galla's shoulder. "We'd better go back to the palace," Galla told Claudia. "Constantius has asked for an audience with me. He's probably already there waiting."

Galla and Claudia folded up the little blankets, picked up the children's toys and started back to the palace. "What do you suppose he wants?" Claudia asked with concern.

"Oh, what he always wants . . . for me to send my Gothic friends away . . . for me to cease my communications with Wallia in Gaul . . . for me to forget the people with whom I spent five years of my life," Galla replied bitterly. She stopped walking and looked directly at Claudia. "Claudia, do you ever think about your husband?"

Claudia nodded sadly and glanced at her two small children toddling ahead of them. Yes, I do," she replied. "After he was killed fighting the Goths in Gaul . . ." Claudia hesitated. Galla smiled and indicated that Claudia should continue. "Well," Claudia began again, "when the news of his death reached me in

Rome, I didn't think I could live I was so heartbroken. But God is kind and he has seen me through. Each day is easier."

"I think of my husband, too," Galla said solemnly. "I know it's difficult for Romans to imagine, but Athaulf was a wonderful person . . . he had such dreams for his people. I don't want those dreams to die with him." Galla looped her arm over Claudia's and the two began walking again. After only a few steps, Galla stopped abruptly and announced, "That's why I'm going to marry Constantius."

Claudia drew back and stared at Galla in shock and disbelief. "Marry Constantius? But you can't stand Constantius! And after what you just said about your husband! What about your dignity? I don't understand."

Galla smiled sadly and stroked Claudia's lovely blond hair. "No, I don't expect you to understand, not yet anyway. And don't worry about my dignity. I learned long ago that our perception of 'dignity' changes with time and circumstance. Dignity is really of little importance to me now. What concerns me now is the future-- the future of Rome--and the future of the Church."

Galla took Claudia's arm and the two began to walk again. "Look at those two," Galla nodded at Claudia's two young children. "They don't know the difference between a Roman and a Goth. To them everyone's the same. Hatred for another people isn't something one is born with; it's something that is learned. Perhaps this next generation can be taught differently than our generation was. Perhaps your children, and someday my children, hopefully *all* children, can learn to accept others who are different. Perhaps our children can learn to be more truly Christian . . ."

Galla's thoughts were interrupted by a shout from the peristyle garden atop the palace retaining wall. "Hello there!" Constantius shouted down the terraced slope. Galla waved and, leaving Claudia and the children on the beach below, she mounted the steps to the palace above.

The interview with Constantius began much the same as the previous ones--questions about her Gothic followers, allusions to her uncertain allegiances. Today, however, Constantius' tone was softer, more civil, than usual. He sounded almost sincere when he said, "Galla, I think these people are poisoning your mind against me. You know how I feel about you. Honorius and I hope that one day . . ."

"Stop!" Galla ordered sternly. "I know what you are about to say and I won't let *you* say it. *I'll* be the one to say it--you and I should marry." Constantius slowly lowered himself down into a chair and he stared at Galla in total shock. Galla continued, "You will *not* ask *me* to marry *you* . . . I will ask *you* to marry *me*." Constantius opened his mouth to reply but Galla signaled for him to remain silent. "You may wish to hear the terms of my proposal," Galla warned, "before accepting."

Constantius leaned back in his chair and he folded his thick hands in his lap. "All right," he said in a reserved tone, "what is your offer?" His look was now serious and it reflected a note of respect that Galla had not observed before.

Galla drew up a chair across from Constantius. "First," she said as she took her seat, "let's dismiss protocol and sentiment and each speak candidly." Constantius nodded in agreement and Galla continued, "This will be a union of politics, not love, and as such, we must reach an agreement in regards to those politics. We are each strong and we each have our own agendas--yours are in the military, and on the battlefield, and, I might add, in the brothel." Constantius lifted his eyebrows, smiled slightly and shrugged his shoulders. "I, on the other hand," Galla continued, maintaining her most serious tone, "have set my priorities on two items--a peaceful settlement with the Goths and the advancement of the Christian faith."

"But Galla," Constantius interposed, "you know as well as I that Honorius . . ."

"Honorius is a powerless fool," Galla snapped. "*You* are the real power in Rome. Honorius can't spit without asking you. What I want is a deal--you need my lineage and I want your power. What do you say?"

"Well, it's hardly the romantic moment I had envisioned between us, but it will do. I agree. Just see to it that your priorities don't expand and begin to eclipse mine. Other than that, I say we have a deal." Constantius stood up, walked over to Galla's chair and leaned down over her. "When will the happy event take place?" he quipped.

"As soon as you have convinced Honorius to make you his Co-Consul."

"Co-Consul! Galla! Do you know what you're asking?"

"Yes, I believe I do. My ancestors on *both* sides of my family were Emperors, including the Emperor Constantine himself . . . my father Theodosius was Emperor as was my brother Arcadius . . . as is my brother Honorius in the West and my nephew Theodosius II in the East . . . *and as my son will be.*" Galla smiled shrewdly at Constantius. "You couldn't expect me to marry a mere *general*, now could you? Well, neither could Honorius." Galla stood up, led Constantius to the door, and ushered him into the hallway. "When Honorius appoints you as his Co-Consul, all Rome can celebrate our union," Galla murmured demurely as she closed the door behind him.

On the morning of January 1, 417, Honorius conferred the title of Co-Consul upon Constantius. That afternoon, Honorius joined his sister Galla Placidia and his Co-Consul Constantius in marriage. Constantius presented Galla with a huge gold ring engraved with the Imperial eagle. He placed the magnificent ring on the third finger of Galla's left hand. He never asked about the other two rings that Galla wore . . . one a crude silver ring carved in a Germanic interlace pattern . . . the other a small bronze oval bearing a tiny chi-rho cross.

CHAPTER III

Galla did not find her second marriage as objectionable as she had anticipated. Except for state and religious holidays, Constantius kept his distance from his new wife. He maintained his own palace in a different quarter of the town and his duties as Co-Consul of the Emperor often necessitated his absence from Ravenna altogether. During the brief and very public meetings that followed their marriage ceremony, Galla found her husband to be amenable to both her political and religious goals. It seemed to her that it was only in the presence of the Emperor that Constantius' placid personality would transmute into that of a misogynist and fawning supplicant.

Galla and Constantius attended Easter mass together that spring. It was a fine morning and the sea breeze was light and warm as they returned to Galla's palace. "Eli has set the table for lunch, Constantius. Won't you join us?"

Constantius looked at Galla and saw that her invitation was sincere. "Thank you, Galla. I would enjoy that." He alighted from the litter and helped Galla down. They entered the palace and found Claudia and her children waiting there to greet them.

"How was the service?" Claudia inquired sweetly as Galla and Constantius removed their cloaks.

"It was lovely, Claudia. I'm sorry you couldn't join us," Galla said as she took Claudia's arm and started to the dining hall. "How is your son feeling now? Is he better?"

"Yes," Claudia said as she watched her little boy heading into the hall. "I can't keep him in bed. Nor can I keep Julius in bed. He's insisting on joining us for lunch. I've told them both that these spring colds can lead to something worse, but they refuse to listen."

A large table was set in the dining hall and several chairs were placed around it. "I hope you don't mind, Constantius, if we dine at the table. I just can't get used to those dining couches again. I find it so much more comfortable and convenient to sit at a table, and it requires fewer servants to attend us."

"Not at all, Galla," Constantius replied, "that's very frugal of you. I admire that." He pulled out a chair and seated Galla. "Besides, I'm used to tables after all the time I've spent in the provinces," he said as he began to sit down.

Just then Julius entered and everyone started to rise again. "Oh, sit down, sit down," Julius scolded. "It is *I* who should stand for *you*." Julius glanced at Galla and Constantius at the head of the table and he nodded formally.

"It's good to see you up and looking so well, Uncle," Galla smiled.

"Yes, Julius, it is," Constantius concurred. "We've missed you at the Senate," Constantius added kindly. "I see you're still using that old wooden walking stick, Julius. What happened to that fine silver one I gave you for your birthday?" Constantius inquired.

"I guess I've just gotten used to this one. It supports me quite well," Julius replied. "I hope you'll indulge an old man." Julius lifted up the twisted oak walking stick and ran his hand over it. "This came from a very special tree, didn't it my Dear?" Julius winked at Galla.

"Yes, Uncle, a *very* special tree," Galla agreed with a smile.

After lunch, Julius returned to his room to rest and Claudia took her children to the nursery for their naps. Galla and Constantius went out into the garden to enjoy the lovely spring day.

As she plucked a rose from its branch, Galla commented casually, "Julius tells me that you've made great strides in the settlement of the Goths." Constantius stood silently looking out over the sea. Galla placed the stem of the rose into her belt, her face in deep concentration. "Why haven't *you* told me about the progress you've made? You never tell me anything about what you're doing. Do you think I'd be bored?" Galla asked with a slightly sarcastic tone. Constantius seated himself on a marble bench and continued to look out over the sea, but still he did not reply. "Or do you think I'm too ignorant or too stupid to understand?" Galla pushed.

Constantius looked up at Galla with his small gray eyes. "Neither, Galla," he replied somberly. "You're neither ignorant nor stupid. Yes, I've made some great strides in the settlement of the Goths. I've arranged for Wallia and his people to leave Spain and to return to Gaul. There's a great deal of good land along the Garonne River around Toulouse. The Goths can settle there."

Galla looked at Constantius with bewilderment. "Well why haven't you *told* me this? You know that's what I've wanted."

"Because . . . because I don't want you to have to feel grateful for what I've done." Constantius lowered his eyes and turned his face away from Galla. "You may find this difficult to understand Galla, but I do, truly, care for you."

Galla stood looking down on the man before her. A wave of pity washed over her. Here was a famous general, the Co-Consul of the Western Empire, and he was prostrating himself emotionally before her. "What a strange world it is," Galla thought to herself, "a world in which women seemingly have no power, and yet they hold the greatest power of all--the power over men's hearts."

Galla smiled softly and she sat down next to Constantius. He inched away from her and stared off across the sea, torn between his masculine pride and his affection for the beautiful woman next to him. "I know that wasn't part of our bargain," he spoke off into space, "but I had hoped . . ."

Galla picked up his hand and she held it in hers. It was a sturdy, manly hand, callused and scarred from many years of service--service to the Empire--service to Rome. Galla began to realize that the animosity she had felt towards him was really animosity towards her brother. Wasn't it Constantius who had continued the negotiations for her release? How could he have known how she felt about Athaulf? Constantius was just being a good Roman general in his offenses against the Goths and in his efforts to secure her safe return to Rome.

"I want to thank you for your help in settling the Goths," Galla said. "It shows you're a man of peace and I admire that. Isn't that what Virgil said? 'Generosity to the conquered'? You know something, Constantius? I think you and I are a lot more alike than either one of us realizes."

Constantius turned to look at Galla and she studied his face. He was neither handsome nor young, but his face had the look of a true Roman patrician. He reminded Galla of the Republican portrait sculptures she had so often seen, their faces reflecting the ancient Roman ideals of *virtus, simplicitas* and *gravitas*. Constantius had the same look of manliness, directness, and seriousness.

"I'm glad to hear you say that, Galla," Constantius replied. "I do so want to be friends."

Galla laughed and Constantius turned away from her again. "I'm not laughing at *you*, Constantius," Galla explained as she leaned forward to see his face. "I'm laughing at *us*! Look at us! Here we are, husband and wife, and we're discussing whether or not we can be friends. I don't know how we can manage to give the Empire an heir if we can't even manage to be friends." Constantius turned back towards Galla with a look of surprise and she continued to laugh. "I say we take one thing at a time," Galla proposed, "first an heir, and then perhaps friendship will come later." That night Constantius did not return to his palace.

Galla devoted the summer months to the restoration of several of the old churches in Ravenna. The most ancient churches were of wood and brick and were nearly a century old. The sea air, combined with Imperial neglect on the part of Honorius, had left the buildings in a sorry state. Galla enlisted the service of several of the Empire's finest architects but each time she found herself at odds with them regarding materials, construction, and particularly design. Finally, she dismissed them all and, with the help of manual workers, she herself oversaw the restoration and remodeling of the holy sites. Galla found the work immensely rewarding and fulfilling. She searched the libraries in Ravenna for books on architecture and construction. When she had read all the books she could find in Ravenna, she wrote to Fortus and asked him to send her all the architectural texts he could find in Rome.

One evening in early September, as Galla was working on some sketches for the renovation of the atrium of the church she was restoring, Eli entered and announced the arrival of Constantius. "Show him in, Eli," Galla requested. Then, turning to Claudia who was busy embroidering a tablecloth, Galla said politely, "Claudia, would you mind leaving? I'm sorry, but I'd like to speak with Constantius alone if you don't mind." Claudia picked up her sewing and was leaving the room just as Constantius entered.

"Good evening, Claudia," Constantius said jovially as she brushed past him. "Where's she going in such a hurry?" Constantius asked Galla as he crossed the room and took a seat beside the table where Galla was working.

Galla set down her quill and wiped her ink-stained fingers on a cloth. "I asked her to leave. I have something I'd like to discuss with you." Constantius sat quietly as Galla took a seat across from him. "The Empire is going to have an heir," she said matter-of-factly. Constantius looked blankly at Galla, obviously not understanding the meaning of her words. "You and I, Constantius, we're going to have a child."

Constantius rose to his feet and stammered, "That's . . . that's good. That's good, isn't it?" His face visibly reddened but he refrained from any display of emotion.

Galla laughed at the man's perplexity. "Yes, that's good," she assured him. How like Constantius, she thought, to be unable to express his true feelings. It was the same way when they made love--he was always on guard, always reserved. Galla felt it must be his lifetime in the military that precluded him from expressing himself. He had been trained for *pietas*--duty to the state over personal emotion. How different from the Goths, Galla thought to herself.

"Yes, it's good," Galla repeated, "*very* good." She stood up and put her arms around Constantius. "I'm very happy--for us and for Rome."

"If you're happy, Galla, then I'm happy," Constantius told her, pleased by her spontaneous show of affection.

Galla returned to her chair and sat down. "There's just one more thing. We have to tell Honorius."

"How do you think he'll react?"

Galla laughed, "You know him better than I! How do *you* think he'll react?"

"Well, he must have known this would happen. As long as he remains childless, the future of the Western throne lies with you," Constantius nodded towards Galla.

She patted her abdomen lightly. "Indeed it does!" she smiled.

Constantius was in Gaul when his daughter was born early in the year 418. Galla took the liberty of naming the child herself. She gave the infant the names Justa and Grata in honor of Galla's mother's two sisters, and then, knowing it would please her brother the Emperor, she added the name Honoria.

"Justa Grata Honoria," Constantius wrote from his army tent in the field, "that's quite a big name for what must be a rather small human being. Best regards to the new mother."

Constantius remained in Gaul for most of 418. He oversaw the settling of Wallia and his people in the area around Toulouse in Gaul. Galla was aware that Constantius' motives were not entirely altruistic. Constantius believed that if he could secure the loyalty of the Goths, then they would protect the frontier borders of the Empire from further Germanic incursions. By carefully placing the Goths in this particular area of Gaul, Constantius denied them access to the sea and therefore access to Africa. He had also strategically placed Wallia and his people between the other Germanic tribes to the north and the Romans to the south. Whatever the ulterior motives of Constantius were, however, Galla was pleased to see the Goths settled peacefully.

Just as Constantius was about to leave Gaul to return to Rome, Wallia died. Constantius stayed on until the Goths elected a new leader, a man named Theodoric. Convinced of Theodoric's suitability both as a leader of the Goths and as an ally of Rome, Constantius returned home to Ravenna at Christmastime, just in time to see Honoria take her first steps.

"She doesn't recognize you!" Galla explained when Honoria let out a plaintive wail as her father tried to pick her up. "Give her time, she'll get used to you."

"Well, here," Constantius said as he handed the tiny girl a large scroll. "I brought her this. Maybe this will make her like me." The infant struggled to take hold of the heavy vellum scroll.

"What *is* it?" Galla laughed.

"It's a map," Constantius replied with earnest excitement, "of the Roman Empire. I had it made especially for her. I thought she'd like to read it."

"She doesn't read quite yet, I'm afraid, Constantius," Galla offered, wondering just *how* little her husband knew about infants.

"Oh," he said thoughtfully, "when *do* they begin reading?"

"At about five or six," Galla replied, trying to conceal her amusement at Constantius' total ignorance about children.

"*Years?*" he said with disbelief. "Oh, well, I guess she won't be needing this for awhile then, will she?" Constantius picked up the map and laid it on the table, causing the little girl to burst into fits of sobbing. "What did I do wrong now?" Constantius asked, his frustration growing.

"Nothing, my dear, nothing," Galla laughed. "Claudia, will you take Honoria and put her to bed please? It's time for Constantius and me to leave for midnight mass." Galla handed the little girl to Claudia. "Are you sure you won't join us, Claudia? Eli and Anta can stay with the children."

"No, you two go on. I prefer to stay here and attend mass in the little chapel with Julius. I know Honorius is expecting you. You two go along now," Claudia repeated again as she bounced Honoria in her arms and the infant squealed with delight. "Come on, little Honoria," Claudia cooed, "come with Auntie Claudia and we'll go beddie-bye."

Constantius watched with exasperation as Claudia calmed his daughter and the two left the room. "I don't understand it, Galla. I can lead an entire Roman legion to splendid victories, but I can't get one little girl to stop crying."

Galla slipped her cape across her shoulders and over her head. "You will, Constantius, you will. Now, call the guards. We don't want to be late to mass."

When they arrived at the church, Galla took her place between Honorius and Constantius in the Imperial pew. As Galla watched the priests and altar boys taking their places, she recalled earlier, happier Christmas eves . . . with Fortus at St. Peter's Basilica in Rome . . . with Athaulf in the woods of southern Gaul. A slight pain tugged at her heart. She reminded herself that *here* was her rightful, her *proper* place . . . between the two Co-Consuls of Rome. "No," Galla thought to herself, "I'm not happy the same way I was then. This is a different type of happiness . . . it's the satisfaction one feels when one is doing the right thing, when one is fulfilling one's destiny."

Galla glanced at her brother Honorius, the Emperor in name, and then at her husband Constantius, the man who truly ran the Western Empire. "*This* is my destiny," Galla consoled herself, "to be the balance between these two men and to provide the Empire with heirs to ensure the future of Rome."

"Please Lord," Galla prayed, "give me a son . . . a son I can raise in Your Name--a son who will create a truly Christian Roman Empire. If You bless me with a son, I will dedicate great churches and monuments in Your honor, so that all the world can see the glory and the greatness of the one true God."

CHAPTER IV

On the morning of July 2, 419, Galla Placidia gave birth to a son, Flavius Placidius Valentinianus. He was named for his Imperial relations on both sides of his mother's family. Valentinian, as they called him, was an exceptionally small newborn, but he had a strong constitution and a voice to match.

"Not another screamer," Constantius jested as Galla placed the tiny infant in his arms. "One screamer in a family is enough," Constantius laughed as tiny Honoria asserted loudly that she wanted to hold the new baby. Constantius lowered himself carefully onto a chair and he sat staring at the newborn in his arms. Galla knew that Constantius was feeling the same profound sense of awe that she, too, first felt upon holding the future of the Roman Empire in her arms. Galla thought she could discern tears in the old veteran's eyes.

"Daddy me!" Honoria screamed, "Daddy me!" The little girl flailed her tiny fists against her father's thick thighs in her struggle to gain his attention. "Daddy me!"

"Stop that, Honoria," Constantius scolded. "I already told you that you're not old enough to hold the baby." Honoria lifted a tiny sandaled foot and kicked her father in the shin. "Ow!" he shouted. "Did you see what Honoria did Galla? She kicked me!"

"She's only a year-and-a-half old, Constantius. It couldn't have hurt that much. Let her hold the baby. Put Honoria on your lap and the two of you hold Valentinian together," Galla suggested.

"You're spoiling her, Galla," Constantius warned. "It's not good to let her always have her own way."

Galla watched the little girl as she climbed up onto her father's lap. "She's jealous of the attention we're giving Valentinian." Galla explained. "Try to give her equal time," Galla advised. "She'll have plenty of time in the future to be jealous of her brother. Let's see if we can keep them friends, at least while they're children." Galla stood up and called for Anta. "Please start my bath, Anta. It's time for me to get ready for the party." Galla turned to Constantius, "Aren't you going to change, dear?"

"No, I'm comfortable like this," Constantius responded, oblivious to Galla's hint.

Galla stood looking at the famous general who was intently balancing a baby on each knee. "Well, make sure Anta changes the children's clothes anyway. We don't want to present the heir to the throne in a shirt stained with grape juice."

"Like father, like son," Galla could hear Constantius repeating as she headed off to her quarters.

After her bath, Galla perused the garments in her closet, noting how small each one appeared since the birth of Valentinian. Anta helped Galla into dress after dress, each time holding the mirror for her mistress to view the effect. Finally Galla sighed deeply, "Well, I guess this one will have to do." She looked bleakly at the wine-colored gown she was wearing. "Tomorrow we will call the dressmaker. It's time that I admit I'm not a young girl anymore. I've had three children, and who knows? Perhaps I'll have still more. It's time for a new wardrobe, a proper Roman matron's wardrobe."

Galla's pregnancy had kept her out of the social scene in Ravenna and she noticed several new faces when she entered the huge dining hall. "Constantius," Galla commented as she reclined on a dining couch, "there are several new guests here. Who's that woman over there? The attractive one in the green dress?" she asked.

Constantius looked up from his plate of pickled sardines. "Which one? Oh, her? She's not attractive, too skinny." He made a sour face and shook his head.

Galla smiled at her husband's lie on her behalf. "Well, who is she anyway, that skinny *ugly* woman over there?"

"She's the wife of the general that Honorius is backing these days. His name is Castinus. He must be here somewhere." Constantius scanned the crowded room, "Yes, there he is--the big man with the dark beard. He's supposed to be a really good military man according to Honorius."

"What do *you* think, Constantius? Is he really good?" Galla inquired.

"Not from what *I've* seen. Oh, he can talk a good battle, but the proof of a good soldier is in the field. I'm not convinced yet." Constantius took a sip of wine and glanced around the room again. "Well, it looks as if all the guests are here. Honorius should be here soon. He always waits until all the guests are assembled so he can make a grand entrance."

Trumpets blew and Honorius and his entourage entered the hall. "Right on cue!" Constantius quipped as he helped himself to more wine. "I see he's got some of his new officers with him. That big light-haired fellow is here from Pavia, that shorter one next to him is from Dacia, and that young one there is from Marseilles." Constantius pointed last to a tall muscular man next to Honorius.

"Boniface!" Galla gasped.

"Yes, I believe that *is* his name. Do you know him Galla?" Constantius asked.

"He's the man who wounded Athaulf when we went to Marseilles to ask for ships. What is *he* doing here in Ravenna?"

"Honorius is planning a campaign to move the Vandals out of the Roman frontier region in Gaul and Spain. He thinks this Boniface might be the man for the job."

Galla slowly rose to her feet as Honorius and his group approached. "Welcome," she called out in her most cordial voice. "We are pleased that you could join us."

Honorius introduced his friends one by one. When he came to Boniface, Honorius gave a little smirk, "I believe you already know this gentleman, Your Highness. This is Boniface, Prefect of Marseilles. I think you've met before." Boniface lowered his eyes and bit the inside of his lip.

"Yes," Galla said in a calm, friendly tone, "we *have* met before. It's good to see you again Prefect Boniface." Galla held out her hand for Boniface to kiss. Boniface gingerly took her hand and brushed his lips quickly against it. He looked up uncertainly into her eyes. "I had hoped we would meet again someday," Galla continued. "Actually it was my husband, my *first* husband," Galla threw a quick look at Constantius, "my husband *Athaulf* who had truly hoped to see you again."

Boniface tensed visibly and he began to mumble, "Your Highness, please forgive me, you see I . . ."

"I see you were doing your duty to Rome. You did what any loyal Roman soldier would have done. That's what my husband . . . that's what Athaulf always wanted to tell you, that he admired you greatly. He said you were a fine soldier."

Boniface, bewildered, could only utter, "Thank you, Your Highness, thank you."

"Please dine with me, won't you?" Galla asked with sincerity. "I'm eager to hear the news from Gaul. Come, sit with me and we'll talk."

Galla, Boniface and Constantius talked for hours over course after course of food and drink. It was dawn when Galla and Constantius walked Boniface to the door. "Come see us again soon, won't you?" Galla asked. "I've enjoyed our evening."

"So have I," Constantius agreed heartily as he shook Boniface's hand.

"Yes, I would very much like to visit again. You have a truly remarkable wife, Constantius," Boniface commented as he mounted his horse.

"Yes," Constantius agreed as he took Galla's hand. "She grows more and more remarkable each day."

Boniface came often to the palace to visit. Both Galla and Constantius found him to be not only a fine soldier, but also a kind and reasonable man. They learned that they all shared the same views regarding a peaceful settlement with the Goths. By the following summer, the three had become devoted friends. Galla was pleased to have another Roman general take up her cause on behalf of the Goths. Constantius was happy to have a comrade within Honorius' military entourage. And little Honoria was delighted to have a pair of strong shoulders to sit upon to play "Giant."

"Again, Uncle Boniface!" Honoria demanded loudly when her "uncle" tried to set her down. "Again!"

"Now you leave Boniface alone, dear," Galla scolded. "Can't you see he's worn out? Go along with Anta now, your supper is ready." Galla pushed the little two-and-a-half-year-old towards Anta who held out her hand. The pair left the room and Galla let out a sigh. "Whew! It wears me out just *looking* at the two of you playing." Galla picked up her little son Valentinian and handed him to Eli who was waiting to take him to join Honoria for dinner in the nursery. Galla waved good-bye to her infant son and he let out a wail of objection at being removed from his mother's lap. The door closed and the room was silent. "Ah, peace and quiet, how rare it is these days," Galla laughed as she returned to her seat by the open window. "I wonder what's keeping Constantius. He said he'd be here to join us for dinner."

No sooner had Galla spoken than the doors to the dining hall opened and Constantius strode in. He was covered with dirt and mud.

"What on earth has happened to you?" Galla inquired as her husband leaned over and kissed her forehead.

"Chariot race," Constantius replied as he shook hands with the guest. "Good to see you Boniface!" Constantius said cheerily as he laid his metal helmet on the table. "Where were *you* today, Boniface?" Constantius inquired good-naturedly. "We missed you. It was a spectacular race." Constantius poured a goblet of wine and noisily gulped the contents. "You know that fellow Castinus, Honorius' general? Broke his leg . . . clean through," Constantius laughed.

"My dear," Galla chastised, "that's terrible. You shouldn't laugh at another man's misery."

"Oh! It's just Castinus. Bet it taught him a good lesson, too. He always does drive his horses too hard. Didn't make the last turn. Oh! You should have been there. Spectacular!" Constantius and Boniface both laughed and Galla couldn't help but smile at the two men's amusement at the plight of their not-so-dear cohort. "Of course," Constantius continued between bites of cheese, "that'll delay your campaign to Gaul, my friend."

Boniface's smile turned to a look of concern. "How long do you think his leg will take to heal?"

"Doc says maybe six months, broke it clean through. Spectacular!" Constantius broke out into laughter again.

"Six months!" Galla exclaimed. "That will put the departure date for the campaign to Gaul into the dead of winter. You don't want to cross those Alps in winter, believe me, *I* know!" Galla glanced at Boniface.

"Honorius will wait until spring," Constantius replied. "Truth be told, I don't think the Emperor is too eager to send troops to Gaul just now anyway. Might put a dent in his precious budget," Constantius added sarcastically.

"Why can't I go on ahead with my troops now?" Boniface asked. "Why do *I* have to wait until Castinus is healed? I've led my own contingent in Gaul. I don't need Castinus to hold my hand."

Constantius threw himself down on a dining couch and helped himself to a pork rib. "Honorius is afraid my wife has solicited your help in a generous settlement with the Goths. He's still convinced that the best way to protect our borders is to keep the Goths and the Vandals at one another's throats. If the Goths become a bunch of farmers, who will control the Vandals, and all the other Germanic tribes?" Galla and Boniface stared at Constantius. "Now, don't you two look at me that way. You know how *I* stand on the matter. I've been to Gaul, too, and I also know the Goths. I want to see them settled peacefully as much as you two do. Lord knows I've tried. I'm just telling you how Honorius feels about it."

The doors to the dining hall opened and Julius entered accompanied by Claudia.

"Julius!" Galla exclaimed. "How good to see you up! You must be feeling better." Galla started to rise but the old man signaled for everyone to remain seated.

"Welcome, Julius," Constantius said warmly. "You're just in time. I was just about to tell Galla some good news."

"Well, well," the old man repeated as he took his place on a dining couch and set down his oak cane. "I'm glad I came then. I'd enjoy some good news."

Constantius waited for the newcomers to be served. He then stood up ceremoniously and held up his goblet. "I'd like to make a toast," he announced, "to Valentinian, the *Most Noble Boy*."

Galla sprang to her feet and ran to where Constantius was standing. "Most Noble Boy?" she asked in disbelief. "Has Honorius promised the title?" Constantius nodded his head yes. "Do you know what this means?" Galla asked her dining companions. "It means that Honorius has acknowledged Valentinian as the successor to the throne--the Most Noble Boy in the Western Empire!" Galla explained, although her guests were all familiar with the most prestigious title that could be bestowed upon a Roman child. "I'm so pleased!" Galla exclaimed.

"Wait!" Constantius laughed, "there's *more*." Galla turned to Constantius with a look of surprise. "My Dear," he said seriously as he stood up straighter and took Galla's hand, "Honorius has decided to bequeath upon *me* the title of Augustus."

"*Augustus*!" Galla gasped. "That's the highest title in Rome, that makes you the *Co-Emperor*."

"Yes," Constantius chuckled. "Actually it worries me . . . all that pomp and formality . . . not my style really," Constantius shrugged. "And Galla," he said gently, taking both her hands in his, "Honorius has, at very long last, conferred upon you what you have always so rightfully deserved . . . the title of Augusta . . . the highest rank any woman has ever held in Rome."

Constantius' voice began to tremble as he uttered the last words. Galla stood staring at Constantius, stunned by this sudden and unexpected announcement. Constantius lifted Galla's hand in the air and he turned to face the dinner guests. "Ladies and gentlemen, I present to you Galla Placidia Augusta--first woman in Rome."

Claudia leapt to her feet and ran to hug Galla. Julius and Boniface followed closely behind. Even Eli could not preserve her usual decorum and she, too, gave Galla a tearful embrace.

Then, suddenly, something almost imperceptible happened. Galla thought of it often in the years to come but she was never able to explain it clearly. It was as if, at that exact moment, an invisible grate came down between her and her friends. It was as if that title, a thing that could neither be seen nor touched, dropped like an intangible barrier between her and her dear friends. It would, from that day forward, stand between her and those around her. Galla saw her friends pull away from her after their embraces and a new look was in their eyes. They were still smiling, sincerely pleased at Galla's good fortune, but from that moment on when they looked at Galla, they no longer saw Galla the woman, they saw Galla Placidia *Augusta*--the most powerful woman in Rome--and Rome was the most powerful empire in the world.

Galla had yet to realize the full impact of that barely discernible change within her friends, at this point she thought it was just in her imagination. "Augusta! I can't believe it!" Galla cried. "Oh, Constantius, are you sure? Why did Honorius decide to do this? I know my brother too well to think he would do this out of brotherly love. He must have a reason."

"Oh, yes," Constantius laughed as he sat back down on his couch, "Honorius never does anything without a reason. Of course he didn't *tell* me his reason, so I can only surmise." Constantius took a long sip of wine and dabbed his chin with his tunic. "Honorius is still childless and he doesn't seem to be making any wedding plans. Your late brother Arcadius' son, Theodosius II, who now rules the Eastern Empire, is reaching the age for marriage, he's nearly twenty now. If he were to marry and have an heir, *that* heir would stand in line to the throne, not only of the East, but of the West as well, if Theodosius played his game right. I think Honorius is assigning his own heirs now, just in case he doesn't have a child of his own, in order to prevent one of Theodosius II's heirs from usurping the Western throne."

Constantius picked up a stuffed partridge off the serving tray and he began to tear the tiny bird into bits. "I'm famished," he announced, "all this talk of politics works up an appetite." Galla cast a cautionary glance at her husband. "Now Galla," he protested, "what difference does it make what I eat now? I'm no longer a field general, I'm Augustus, and as far as I know there are no weight requirements to be Augustus," he laughed heartily and helped himself to another of the delectable birds.

Early in 421, Honorius publicly conferred the title of Most Noble Boy upon little Valentinian. Several weeks later, in a ceremony worthy of the auspicious occasion, Honorius proclaimed Constantius Augustus of Rome. Galla sat proudly as her husband ascended the throne as Constantius III, Co-Emperor of Rome. Shortly thereafter, Galla, too, received her official designation of Augusta, most revered woman in the Empire.

Sadly, Constantius was to enjoy his new position but briefly. On September 2, only seven months after being proclaimed Augustus, Co-Emperor of the West, Constantius succumbed to a bout of pleurisy. His death was sudden and totally unexpected. Galla Placidia, at age thirty-three, was left a widow for a second time, this time with two very small children and one very large title to defend.

CHAPTER V

The long-delayed campaign against the Vandals was finally scheduled to begin in early 422. Honorius raised his comrade Castinus to Master of the Soldiery in charge not only of the expedition to Gaul but of all the Roman troops in the West, the apex of a military career in Rome. Boniface was appointed to assist Castinus on the pending expedition to Gaul and Spain.

"I hate to leave you alone like this," Boniface told Galla as they shared lunch in her peristyle garden overlooking the sea. "Castinus is Master of the Soldiery, he doesn't need me to tag along with him on this campaign. We don't see eye to eye regarding the Germanic tribes anyway . . ."

"That's exactly why you *must* go," Galla interrupted, "so someone will be there to talk sense into Castinus." She refilled the cup Boniface was holding and smiled at him.

"I can't say two words to that man without causing an argument," Boniface sighed. "He thinks he's the only man on earth who knows anything about military strategy." He looked up at Galla and sighed again. "I'm sorry, Galla. I don't mean to ruin our last day together by talking about Castinus."

Boniface took a sip of wine and looked out over the sparkling blue sea. "Actually, there is something else I want to discuss with you before I leave tomorrow." He turned back and gazed at Galla with his large, dark brown eyes. "I know this isn't a good time, but since I leave in the morning, I don't see any other opportunity." He cleared his throat and carefully folded his napkin. "Galla, we've known one another for nearly two years now. For most of that time, you've been another man's wife. Now . . . well, now that you're free . . . I would like you to consider me as more than just a friend." Boniface stopped speaking and placed his hand over Galla's. "Do you think that is possible, Galla? Could you ever think of me as more than just a friend?"

Galla was not taken by surprise with Boniface's advance. She had known since they first met that he had found her attractive. What had surprised her was how he had controlled his feelings during their long friendship. Galla wrapped her hand around his and smiled sympathetically. "It's too early for me to consider another relationship right now, Boniface. It's only been six months since I lost Constantius. I must think of the children now and of myself. I simply do not have room in my heart right now for anything or anyone else." Boniface looked off across the sea again. "But when I *am* ready," she continued, "I will certainly think of you. I admire you, Boniface. You are a fine man and a good Roman." Boniface turned back, hope shining in his dark eyes. "And I will promise you one thing more," Galla proffered, "I will be praying for you while you are on campaign in Gaul and Spain."

The next morning Galla awoke to find a note from Honorius. He requested her presence at his palace. She arrived to find the villa in a state of confusion.

"What's happening?" Galla asked as she entered the library.

Honorius was seated behind a huge table piled high with maps and correspondence. "You don't know?" Honorius asked and then coughed deeply.

"No, how could I know anything? I only just now arrived. What is it? What's happening? Are you ill, Honorius?" Galla asked with concern at her brother's haggard appearance.

He coughed harder and took a sip from the glass goblet on the table. "No. I'm not ill. It's your friend Boniface, that's what's wrong. He's quarreled with Castinus again." Honorius stood up and walked around the table towards Galla. "What crazy ideas have you been putting in his head this time, little sister?" Honorius demanded in a strained voice.

"Ideas? Nothing! I don't know what you're talking about!"

"Boniface can't seem to get it through his thick head that this campaign is not a good will tour for the Goths. It is a *war*, Galla, a *war*. Boniface is treating it like a campaign to favor the Goths, rather than a campaign to annihilate the Vandals." He broke off into fits of coughing again.

"And what's wrong with that?" Galla asked defensively. "Isn't that what Constantius did? Settle the Goths peacefully? Isn't peace with the Germanic tribes preferable to annihilation?"

"Every man who gets around you takes your side regarding those damned Goths, Galla." Honorius drew out a large handkerchief and coughed violently.

"There are no 'sides,' Honorius. There is only right and wrong," Galla countered.

"Well, there are 'sides' now! Boniface and his followers are aligning on a pro-Germanic side while Castinus and his followers are aligning on an anti-Germanic side. I've got a Roman army marching off to Gaul and Spain and they're divided right down the middle on the very *purpose* of this blasted campaign!" Honorius shouted and pounded his fist on the table. "And it's because of you and your confounded female meddling! When will you learn to stay out of politics, Galla? Don't you have enough to keep you busy in the nursery? Can't you keep out of the men's world?" He was consumed by another fit of coughing.

Galla astutely read Honorius' mood. "Yes, Honorius," she replied softly, "I have plenty to do in the nursery. If I've caused any trouble, it was never my intention."

"Intention or not, you caused it, with all your Gothic followers right here in Ravenna! How do you think it looks, Galla, to have the Emperor's own sister promote the Germanic cause? Can't you see, Galla? The Germanic tribes are determined to destroy Rome! You're just as bad as Stilicho, you and your Goths!" Honorius bellowed.

Galla recalled Stilicho, her cousin Serena's Germanic husband. At the time, Stilicho's efforts to settle the northern tribes peacefully had seemed like treason. Suddenly Galla understood Stilicho and his motives. She saw that he was trying to avoid an all out confrontation with the Germanic tribes. Galla looked entreatingly at her brother, "Perhaps if we worked with the tribes, helped them, they wouldn't be so set on our destruction. We can't fight them all! There are too many of them. Our only hope to save the northern frontiers is to compromise with the Germanic peoples. We must accede to some of their demands. After all, they are only asking for their own survival!" Galla reasoned.

She looked at her brother and saw the angry fire in his eyes. She knew that to argue further would be futile and even counter-productive. Galla restrained herself from further argument, adding only, "I'm sorry, Honorius. I'll be more careful in the future. I am grateful to you, indebted to you. I don't want to cause you any further problems. This is a difficult time . . . we Flavians must stick together. I promise I won't cause any more trouble. Don't give another thought to me . . . you should be thinking of yourself, and your health. You don't look a bit good, Honorius. Is there anything I can do?"

"Yes," Honorius whispered hoarsely, "you can leave me alone and you can stay out of affairs that do not concern you."

"Yes, Honorius, I will do just that. Please do get some rest." With that Galla took her leave of the Emperor.

The quarrel between Castinus and Boniface only worsened as the campaign progressed. By the time they reached Spain, their differences were irreconcilable. Boniface decided to abandon the expedition and to cross over to Africa where he could counter the advance of the Vandals into Roman territory there. When Boniface and his pro-Germanic troops left Spain, the Goths took the opportunity to turn on Castinus and his anti-Germanic forces.

With a combination of diplomacy and feminine charm, and amidst the sudden turn of events, Galla convinced Honorius to appoint Boniface as Supreme Commander in Africa in return for his exceptionally valiant efforts against the Vandal advances in the Roman provinces there. Unfortunately, the appointment only served to broaden the gulf between the pro-Castinus and the pro-Boniface factions. Rioting broke out in Ravenna. Galla found herself once again summoned to the palace to answer to Honorius' accusations of pro-Germanic intrigue on her part.

"Don't bother to deny it!" Honorius shouted weakly, not bothering to rise from the bed on which he was lying. "Castinus has proof!"

"How can Castinus have proof of something I haven't done?" Galla argued. "I swear to you Honorius, I've been loyal to you and to Rome!"

"You haven't been loyal to Rome since you married that barbarian! No decent Roman woman would have done such a disgusting thing! Castinus is right! You *are* a traitor to Rome."

"Honorius! Please! You don't mean what you say. You're ill. You need to rest. If you felt better, you wouldn't say those awful things to me. I'm your sister. Why do you always listen to others and not to me, your own flesh and blood?" Galla pleaded. "Can't you see what Castinus is trying to do? He's trying to get me out of the way so *he* can be Emperor. He doesn't care about you-- he's just using you!" Galla thought about the upstart young general Castinus. It was not the first time that Galla had questioned the true nature of the relationship between Castinus and her brother. She wondered if Castinus was the real reason that Honorius had not married and produced an heir of his own. "Perhaps Castinus is more to Honorius than just a comrade," she thought to herself.

"How dare you insult my friend that way? You're just jealous, that's all! You've always been jealous of me, ever since we were children," Honorius fumed between seizures of coughing.

"Yes, Honorius, I *have* always been jealous of you . . . jealous that you were older than I . . . jealous that you were a male . . . jealous that you held the reins of government . . . jealous that you had all the power! But I'm *not* jealous of that feeble-minded Castinus! Can't you see him for what he truly is? He is stirring up trouble with the Germanic tribes just to bolster his own career. He's playing you for a fool! *He's* the traitor, not I!"

"Get out, Galla! Get out of this palace and get out of Ravenna! If you're still in the city by this time next week, I'll have you tried for treason!"

Galla stood dumbstruck. "Treason! You can't mean that, Honorius. It's your fever speaking, not you. I'm your sister. I'm a widow with two small children. I need your support and protection!" Galla stammered.

"You should have thought about that before betraying me! Now, will you leave or shall I call the guards and have them throw you out?"

"You needn't call the guards. I'll leave. May God forgive you, Honorius."

Galla and her household were packed and ready to leave Ravenna within the week. Each day she expected to receive word from the Emperor recanting his order for her to vacate the city, but no word came from the Imperial palace. Rumors reached Galla of anti-Germanic uprisings spreading throughout the countryside.

Galla's position in Ravenna grew more precarious each day. When the designated week was up, Galla and her entire entourage journeyed to her villa north of Rome. There, with generous monetary help from her friend Boniface in Africa, Galla was able to settle her remaining Gothic followers and to arrange her complex financial matters.

Word came from Ravenna that Honorius' health was quickly failing. Galla knew that if he were to die, nothing would stand between her and his fanatical anti-Germanic followers in Italy. It was imperative that Galla and her children flee the area. Julius was too old and ill to travel further, so Galla left him in Eli's dependable care at the country villa north of Rome. Since Claudia and her two children were in no direct danger from the recent turn of events, they too remained with Julius in the comfort and security of the villa. After bidding long and very sad farewells to everyone at the villa and then to her dearest friend Fortus in Rome, Galla, her two children, and her maidservant Anta boarded a sturdy trading vessel and set sail for their one hope of refuge--the court of Galla's nephew, Theodosius II, in Constantinople.

The journey by sea to the East was long and arduous. Galla had never enjoyed traveling by sea, and now, with two small children, the difficulty was compounded. The vessel was crowded and their tiny quarters were musty and cramped. Bad weather and choppy waters made the children violently ill. Even Galla and Anta suffered from bouts of seasickness as they struggled to care for the children and themselves.

Unfavorable winds and exceptionally rough seas retarded their progress and prolonged their agony. Soon the stores of fresh food and water were seriously depleted. At one point, a fierce storm so seriously threatened to destroy the heavy ship that all the passengers feared for their very lives. After several days of ardent prayers by all on board, the storm subsided and the remainder of the journey was calm. In her prayers, Galla had made a promise to St. John the Evangelist that if he delivered her and her children safely to their destination, she would erect a magnificent church in his honor in Ravenna. When they stepped off the ship in Constantinople, Galla vowed that she would one day return to Ravenna to keep her promise to St. John.

Galla and her little party were met at the ship by a conservatively small welcoming committee. Theodosius II reserved his welcome for a private audience with the newly arrived refugees. After all, Theodosius had his own political agenda to consider . . . to display too much public fanfare on the arrival of Galla Placidia might alienate Honorius and his court in the West.

Galla had not been in Constantinople since she was very young, but the foreign sounds and exotic smells of the Eastern capital were immediately familiar to her. She surveyed the bustling city with fascination and interest as the Imperial litter carried them from the harbor through the busy marketplaces to the magnificent palace of the Eastern Emperor.

"Mommy, I'm afraid!" little Honoria protested loudly when hungry beggars besieged their litter asking for coins. "Tell those nasty men to go away!"

"Shhh, Honoria, quiet. This city belongs to those men. It is we who are the intruders. You'll be safe," Galla assured her daughter. Galla noted with wonder how vastly differing were the two capitals of the Roman Empire. Both were cities teeming with hundreds of thousands of persons, both were major trade centers, and both were seats of an Imperial government, yet Rome seemed almost provincial compared to the Eastern ostentation of Constantinople. When they finally arrived at the palace, Galla was shown to a suite of elegant rooms and asked to attend a royal reception in her honor that evening.

After resting, Galla prepared herself and her children for the evening's festivities. She brought out the most beautiful and expensive garments and jewelry that she had brought with them. She knew that much of her advantage rested in the regal display of Imperial lineage and courtly pomp. She was Galla Placidia Augusta and her son Valentinian was Most Noble Boy . . . and she wouldn't allow anyone to forget it. She dressed herself and her children in the Imperial colors of gold and purple and they each wore gold crowns bearing the Imperial insignia.

What Theodosius had withheld from her welcome at the port, he now lavished upon Galla's reception at his court. Galla knew of the vast wealth of the Eastern capital, but nothing had prepared her for the luxury and the opulence in which she now found herself ensconced.

"Welcome, my dear Aunt," the young Emperor drawled as he leaned down from his golden throne and extended his manicured hand.

Galla curtsied very low and kissed the Emperor's jewel-studded ring. "Thank you, Your Highness, for receiving me." Galla smiled her most radiant smile and she could see that the young man was taken by her beauty, even if she were half again his age and the sister of his late father. "Your Highness," Galla continued, "allow me to introduce my children to you." Galla spoke softly as she directed her young son towards the Imperial dais. "This is my son, the Most Noble Boy, Valentinian. He is four years old. Say hello to His Majesty, Valentinian."

"Hello Your Majesty," the little boy said in a grave tone as he bowed deeply from the waist.

"And this is my daughter Honoria," Galla explained. "She will be six on her next birthday. Say hello to the Emperor, Honoria."

"He's not the Emperor," Honoria responded rudely. "Uncle Honorius is the Emperor!"

"We've been through this before, Honoria. Uncle Honorius is the Emperor of the Western Empire . . . Cousin Theodosius is the Emperor of the Eastern Empire," Galla elucidated once again to the child.

"Nonsense!" the little girl blurted out. "There can only be one Emperor!"

"Your Highness!" Galla gasped, "I'm so sorry! I apologize for Honoria's rudeness."

Theodosius smiled smugly, "Perhaps the child has the gift of prophesy . . . perhaps there *should* be only one Emperor!" The members of Theodosius' court laughed and then began to cheer him as the one, 'true' Emperor.

"She is young, Your Highness. I hope you will forgive her manners," Galla beseeched humbly.

"Of course, of course," Theodosius responded kindly. "And now, allow me to introduce *my* family. You remember my sister Pulcheria, don't you, Galla Placidia?" Theodosius gestured towards a skeletal figure with thin mousy-brown hair and dark circles around her bulbous eyes. Pulcheria made no effort to speak; she merely blinked as acknowledgment of the introduction. Galla marveled that this was the same young woman whom the Roman Senate feared held the true reins of government in the East.

"And I'd like you to meet my wife," the Emperor continued, closing his eyes as if consumed with boredom. "She has recently given birth and therefore cannot rise to welcome you. This is Aelia Eudocia. And with her is my beautiful new daughter Licinia Eudoxia." A pale blond woman held up a tiny bundle and Galla surmised that this was the wife and daughter of the Emperor, although he made no effort to point them out.

"A daughter!" Galla gushed, feigning happy surprise. "How wonderful!" Galla smiled broadly at the Emperor, but inside she felt as if one more thread in the thin rope of the Imperial succession had just snapped. She gripped little Valentinian's hand even tighter.

The welcoming festivities lasted until dawn. Galla was pleased to have received a lavish, albeit formal, reception into the Eastern Imperial household. She knew that her safety, and that of her children, rested in the hands of her twenty-year-old nephew Theodosius II and in his respect for and recognition of her Imperial standing and heritage.

Galla was also pleased several days later when the Emperor offered her the palace that she and her mother had occupied during their visits to Constantinople those many years before. The palace by right belonged to Galla's mother and now to Galla herself, but an Emperor could, and often did, usurp the rightful owner's claim on such property. But Theodosius had maintained the palace in good condition and he returned it to Galla's possession upon her arrival in Constantinople. Galla was happy to have the familiar palace as a refuge in the strange and exotic city. Soon she and her children were comfortably settled and she began to feel a modicum of security.

Galla had only been in Constantinople for a few months when shocking news arrived from Ravenna. Honorius, at age thirty-eight, had died of dropsy. By the time the news reached the

Eastern capital, Honorius' remains were already entombed in the family mausoleum at St. Peter's Basilica in Rome.

Theodosius II moved quickly to seize power in the West. He appointed Galla's archenemy Castinus as Consul of the West, a position of remarkable power and prestige. With this move, the Eastern Emperor hoped both to rule the West and to prevent Galla from any attempt at a claim for the Western throne for herself or her son. Theodosius was unaware, however, of two very important variables in his intricate formula for control of the West--first was Galla's devoted friend Boniface who, as Supreme Commander in Africa, controlled the essential grain supply from that continent; and second was that sometimes even the most carefully selected Consuls can turn on their benefactors and attempt to seize power for themselves. Over the course of the next year, Theodosius was to see both of those variables come into play. By the fall of 424, Theodosius was forced to recognize that he was not in a position to rule both the Eastern and the Western Empires.

Galla was surprised when an Imperial messenger arrived at her palace early one autumn day. She had seen very little of Theodosius and the members of his court during her sojourn in Constantinople. Theodosius, it appeared, preferred to keep his distance from his potential rival, and Pulcheria, she was told, was engaged in a nearly maniacal devotion to her religious duties. The arrival of a messenger from the Imperial palace, therefore, sent a wave of excitement through Galla's little household.

"Mommy! Mommy!" Honoria screeched. "A messenger! A messenger!"

"Yes, Honoria, I can see that," Galla hushed her young daughter. The man handed Galla an impressively large scroll and he saluted smartly. He made no effort to leave and Galla surmised that he had been ordered to wait for a reply. "Wait here," she commanded and she went into her study to read the Imperial dispatch. She returned a few minutes later with a small scroll, which she handed to the messenger. He saluted again and left.

"What is it, Mommy?" Honoria inquired.

"It's a message from Theodosius. He wants to speak with me," Galla explained.

"I want to go, too!" the little girl demanded.

"No, Honoria, Mommy must go alone this time, but you can help her find a nice dress to wear. Come on, let's see if we can make Mommy look nice for cousin Theodosius." Galla felt a sense of apprehension as she prepared herself to meet with the Emperor. She was well aware of the events of the recent months and of Theodosius' desperate attempts to secure power for himself in the West. She was also acutely aware that Theodosius considered both her and her son as threats to his Imperial claims in Rome. She nervously dressed and styled her hair, all the while imagining what terrible fate Theodosius might have in store for her and her son. When she was finally satisfied with her appearance, Galla kissed her children goodbye and she boarded the Imperial litter that was awaiting her.

Theodosius himself met Galla at the palace door and he led her into a small antechamber off the entrance atrium. "Be seated," the Emperor said courteously. Galla searched his eyes for a sign of his intentions and he astutely read her thoughts. "Don't be afraid, my dear Aunt," he said somewhat stiffly, "you are not in any danger. On the contrary, I think you will be well pleased with what I am about to offer."

Theodosius took a seat across from Galla and carefully smoothed the front of his purple toga. Galla waited patiently while the Emperor appeared to be searching for the right words. Finally he cleared his throat and addressed Galla, "It has always been my dream--the dream of *all* the Eastern Emperors--that the Roman Empire be united again. I had hoped that I could turn the untimely demise of my Uncle Honorius into an opportunity to fulfill that dream. Unfortunately, it now appears that dream will not be realized, at least not in the immediate future."

He paused and stared at his bejeweled red sandals. "The grain supply from Africa has been completely cut off by the Supreme Commander there, a man named Boniface. I believe you are familiar with this Boniface." He lifted his eyebrows and stared at Galla. She nodded slightly. "Yes, I thought so," he continued. "In addition to that, the general in whom I entrusted the *temporary* care of the West has also betrayed me. I believe you know that man too--his name is Castinus." Once again, Galla gave mute affirmation.

Theodosius took a deep breath and sighed, "It appears that I have only one course of action left. I wish I could say that I am doing this out of familial affection, but that is, in truth, not the case. What I do now, I do out of necessity. In return for this offer, I expect much from you, Galla Placidia." Galla felt her palms grow moist and she struggled to appear composed. Theodosius leaned forward in his chair, looked deep into Galla's eyes and said carefully, "If I cannot rule the West myself, then I believe it is in my best interests to have it ruled by one of my own family--a Flavian. I am prepared to name your son Valentinian as Caesar."

Galla gasped. "Caesar! Valentinian--Caesar!" she responded in disbelief.

"Yes, my Dear," the young Emperor said hesitantly. "You sound surprised. Isn't that what you always had in mind? That your son would rule the West?"

"Yes," Galla said slowly, "but I never really thought it possible . . . there were so many obstacles, so many variables."

"There still are," Theodosius interrupted. "Rule of the West does not come cheaply. Let me tell you its price. For years, the East and the West have struggled over the Prefecture of Illyricum." He paused briefly and cleared his throat. "In return for making your son Caesar, I want that stretch of land, *all* of it, from Crete and the Peloponnesus north to the Danube."

"Even if I agreed," Galla said with shock, "I couldn't just turn over a valuable Western province to you. There would be war!"

"I know," Theodosius responded calmly, "that is why you will wait to turn over Illyricum until later. And that brings me to my second demand." Theodosius rose slowly from his chair and faced Galla. "I am not going to give up my dream of a united Empire, Galla. If *we* cannot bring the Empire together again, perhaps our children can. I want you to agree to betroth your son Valentinian to my daughter Eudoxia. When the marriage takes place, *regardless* of whether or not the East and West are united, Illyricum will answer to Constantinople."

Galla sat thinking silently to herself for a long time. She knew that the Emperor's proposal was, in all probability, her one chance to see her child on the Imperial throne in the West. If things worked out the way Theodosius anticipated, Valentinian might one day rule not only the West, but the East as well. Whatever happened, the proposal would give Galla the reins of power in the West until her son reached his majority, and that was a dozen years in the future.

With her most regal bearing, Galla rose from her chair and faced Theodosius. "I agree," she said calmly. "You have my sincere blessing on the betrothal of our two children. And, upon their marriage, I promise that Illyricum will answer only to Constantinople."

On October 23, 424, Theodosius II appointed Galla Placidia's five-year-old son Valentinian as Caesar, second in the Empire only to Theodosius himself. In return for this great honor, Galla Placidia promised the valuable province of Illyricum, which included the territories of Greece and Macedon all the way north to the River Danube. The deal was sealed by the betrothal of Galla's young son Valentinian to his infant cousin Eudoxia, the sole heir of Theodosius II.

The next challenge for Galla and Theodosius was to wrest the Western Empire from the clutches of the treacherous Castinus. When all diplomatic efforts failed, a full-scale offensive military campaign was launched. Early in the year 425, with her two young children by her side, Galla Placidia Augusta accompanied the troops of the Eastern Empire on their march against the usurper Castinus and his forces to the West.

CHAPTER VI

Galla and her troops took the northern Italian town of Aquileia by surprise. She was joined in her offensive by a contingent of her faithful Goths, including her old friend Candidianus, and by the Alans, a particularly tenacious Germanic tribe. In order to counter these combined Roman and Germanic efforts, Castinus sent his assistant Aetius to secure the aid of the ferocious Huns. Had Aetius and the Huns arrived in time to defend Aquileia, the fate of Galla and her cause might have been much different. But Aetius did not arrive in time and Galla's victory won her young son Valentinian the title Imperator--victorious commander.

From her tent high upon a ridge, Galla looked down on the smoke rising from the devastated city below. "I want to thank you Candidianus for joining me here. Without your help a victory would have been impossible," Galla smiled broadly at the wizened old Gothic elder whom she had known for so long.

"A bit like the old days, eh Your Highness?" Candidianus grinned a nearly toothless smile.

"Yes, much like the old days," Galla agreed as she sat staring at the interlace pattern on the silver ring she wore. "You've been a loyal friend Candidianus. I will reward you well."

"Oh, I don't need a reward, Your Highness. It was reward enough for me to be back out on the battlefield again," the old man said as he helped himself to a second mug of cold ale. "And I'm proud to be of service to you, Your Highness. It's what our dearly departed Athaulf would have wanted, God bless his soul. Now perhaps you can fulfill the vision of the Christian state you two used to dream about."

"Yes," Galla said thoughtfully, "perhaps now I can." Galla glanced over at Valentinian and his sister Honoria who were fast asleep on the cot in the corner of the tent.

A messenger approached the door to the tent and he saluted stiffly. He handed Galla a large scroll, saluted a second time and left.

Galla opened the scroll and read it. "Bad news," she sighed. "It's from Ardaburius, the Alan chieftain whom Theodosius selected to lead the Eastern fleet from Constantinople to Italy. He says a storm overtook their ships and he barely escaped with his life. He's being held captive in Ravenna by Castinus and by that new usurper upstart John who now calls himself *Emperor of the West*. Ha!" Galla laughed sarcastically. "Emperor of the West, indeed! I imagine Castinus and John made Ardaburius send this note just so they could gloat. Little do they know, that at this very moment, our troops are heading south towards Ravenna!" Galla smiled and tossed down the scroll onto the table next to her.

"Poor lad, that Ardaburius. I pity him even if he is one of those heathen Alans," Candidianus commented. "I hate to see any man held prisoner by the likes of Castinus and John. No telling what they'll do to him."

Galla sighed, walked over to the door of the tent and surveyed the smoldering city below again. "No, there is no telling what those two maniacs might do. Come Candidianus," Galla said as she drew her cape over her shoulders. "Let's go over to the officers' quarters and tell them the news. We can all pray for poor Ardaburius." Galla walked out of the tent and Candidianus followed her into the falling darkness.

The next day Galla and her contingent headed south towards Ravenna in the wake of her advancing troops. Ravenna was a city ideally suited for defense. It was bordered by rivers and surrounded by swamps, making a direct attack by land impossible. The surest hope of a successful assault on Ravenna would have been from the sea, but Ardaburius' ships and the Eastern fleet had been lost during the storm. Galla knew that it would take a miracle to conquer Ravenna with only her foot soldiers. That night, in her tent outside the city of Ravenna, Galla lay awake for hours thinking about the attack. Finally, when it was clear that no earthly power could assure her a victory over the city, Galla appealed to a greater power in prayer. Comforted, she finally drifted off to sleep.

"What is it?" Galla asked as she wiped the sleep from her eyes and listened to the sounds outside her tent. "What's happening?" Galla drew on her robe and lifted the flap of her tent.

On the horizon she could see the silhouetted profile of the city of Ravenna against the opalescent morning sky. Columns of smoke rose from the town.

"Guard!" Galla called out to a man running past her. "What has happened?" she demanded.

The man ran over, saluted and smiled broadly, "It's the city Your Highness . . . we've taken the city of Ravenna!"

"Taken the city?" Galla asked in stunned bewilderment.

"Yes, Your Highness, last night. The Alan general Ardaburius somehow managed to send out a message ordering our troops to attack. He had already secretly arranged for a contingent of your followers from *within* the city to attack when your forces from *outside* the city attacked," the guard reported.

"But the swamps . . . how did our troops get through the swamps?"

"A shepherd came out of the city and showed our troops a solid dry path through the marshes. Everyone is saying that the guide wasn't really a shepherd . . . that he was really an *angel* sent by God to lead our troops to victory." The guard stood before Galla, his eyes shining with excitement. "Now, if you'll excuse me, Your Highness, I have been ordered to the city. Some of the troops have begun looting and we have to restore order."

"An angel . . . an angel showed us the path . . . an answer to my prayers," Galla whispered softly, her eyes transfixed on the city below. Then realizing the soldier was waiting to be dismissed, she replied, "Yes, yes, of course. You may go. Thank you for telling me this," Galla nodded and the soldier took his leave.

"Mommy . . . Mommy . . . what's all that noise?" little Valentinian asked as he came out of the tent rubbing his eyes with his tiny fists.

Galla picked up her little son and held him up to see the burning city in the distance. "It's your capital, Valentinian, look! Your troops have regained the Western capital."

"*My* capital Mommy?" Valentinian asked through a yawn. "What's a capital?" he asked sleepily.

Galla laughed and hugged her young son. "It's your home, Valentinian . . . it's your home."

By the evening of the next day, Galla and her family were installed once again in her palace on the Adriatic. Little Honoria squealed with delight upon seeing her old home. "Where's Eli?" the little girl asked when she entered the kitchen.

"We left her with Uncle Julius at Grandfather's farm, don't you remember darling?" Galla asked.

"Honoria wants Eli to make her some corn cakes," Honoria demanded, speaking of herself in the royal third person as she so often did.

"Well, I think you and I should be able to make some corn cakes ourselves," Galla offered, glad at the prospect of doing something mundane and ordinary for a change. Both mother and daughter set about stirring corn flour, eggs, milk and honey into a thick mixture. Then Honoria patted the dough into neat little cakes, which Galla placed in the huge oven. When the cakes were done, Galla seated her two children at the large wooden kitchen table and poured a tiny cup of watered wine for each to drink with their corn cakes. For herself, Galla poured a mug of cool dark ale.

"Honoria wants ale," the girl shouted.

"No, Honoria, you wouldn't like it," Galla explained.

"Yes, Mommy, yes! Honoria likes ale."

"All right," Galla sighed, "you can try some." She handed her cup to the little girl.

No sooner had the little girl taken a sip than she spit it out on the floor. "Oh, Mommy! That's bad. Honoria hates ale!"

Galla laughed and took the cup back from her daughter. Galla remembered the first time she had tried ale when Alaric was holding her captive. She, too, had found the thick liquid to be bitter and unpleasant. "It's an acquired taste, Honoria. You have to get used to it. You'll like it when you're older."

On the third day after the capture of the city of Ravenna, Castinus' supporter Aetius arrived outside the city with his contingent of Huns in hopes of retaking the capital. He found to his bitter disappointment that Galla's troops had soundly secured the city. Aetius disbanded his troops and ceased his efforts against Galla and her followers.

In order to appease the anti-Germanic factions, Galla ordered that no retaliation be made against Aetius and she allowed

Castinus to leave the city unharmed. John, on the other hand, was another matter. A man of petty ranking in the notary class, John had stepped forward following the death of Honorius and blatantly pronounced himself Emperor of the West. The law regarding the offenses of John was quite clear and the severest punishment was inflicted upon him. John was taken to Aquileia--there his hand was cut off and he was paraded around the hippodrome on a donkey. After suffering these and other gross indignities, the usurper John was publicly beheaded.

When matters were at length settled satisfactorily in Ravenna and the city was secure, Galla and her court headed south to Rome for the official crowning of her young son as Valentinian III, Emperor of the Western Empire. The Imperial procession that entered Rome that autumn day of 425 was as grand as any the city had seen in centuries. The parade was led through the streets by thousands of fully armed foot soldiers. The members of the senatorial class and then the patricians followed. Next came Valentinian, seated on a golden throne and carried on the grandest of the Imperial litters, followed by Honoria on a smaller but still magnificent conveyance. Last came the litter bearing the Augusta Galla Placidia. She wore the gold and purple robes of the Imperial family and a jewel-studded gold crown rested upon her auburn tresses. On either side of her were her two dearest friends--Julius, the respected Roman senator, and Fortus, now a bishop in the Church of Rome. Seated on the bench behind Galla were Candidianus, the Gothic elder, and Ardaburius, the Alan who had masterminded the attack on Ravenna.

The procession moved along the Flaminian Way through the gates of the same name and along the Via Lata to the Palace of the Caesars in the Forum. There, the six-year-old Caesar Valentinian was crowned Augustus, Emperor of the entire West.

Galla was proud to see her young son stand fearlessly before the cheering multitudes. She prayed that when her son became a man that he would be a fair and Christian leader for the Roman Empire and for all the peoples of the Empire regardless of their places of origin. She asked God to help her raise her son in His likeness.

Then Galla asked the Lord to guide her as well. Galla knew that until her son was old enough to take the reins of government himself, that she, Galla Placidia Augusta, would be the one true ruler of Rome.

CHAPTER VII

After a pleasant and restful visit at her father's villa north of Rome, Galla and her children returned to their palace in Ravenna. Galla's first order of business upon her return to the city was to begin the construction of a magnificent new church dedicated to St. John the Evangelist in fulfillment of her promise to the Saint for her safe arrival in Constantinople two years previous. This was just the first of many such sacred building projects that Galla undertook when she was settled again in Ravenna. Galla's primary interest from that point forward was the promotion and glorification of the Christian religion through the creation of splendid sacred buildings. She not only paid for the new edifices from her own funds, but she oversaw every aspect of their construction personally, from sketching the plans with her own hand to designing the interior decorations herself. Architecture and its application in the exaltation of Christianity became her first love and vocation.

Her second calling was government and law. Galla was not in a position politically to make sweeping changes or reforms in the crumbling Roman government, but she was able to enact measures to slow the decline and deterioration of the vast Roman bureaucracy. Galla enlisted the help and support of the Church, which she envisioned one day supplanting many of Rome's outdated and defective government structures. Her dream was to make a City of God out of the City of Man. For Galla, the Christian Church was the Phoenix that would rise-up out of Rome's ashes.

The years passed quickly as Galla engrossed herself in matters of church and state. Before she knew it, she was in receipt of a letter from Theodosius II in which he discussed plans for the wedding of his daughter Eudoxia to her son Valentinian.

"Could the years have gone by so fast?" Galla asked in amazement as she set down the royal decree from Constantinople. She looked out from the peristyle garden across the sparkling sea. "It seems like only yesterday that Theodosius and I betrothed the two of you," Galla said to Valentinian who was seated nearby playing a board game with his sister Honoria. Galla watched her two teenaged children in their heated competition. It was always this way, she thought to herself, each sibling trying to outdo the other. Even the most placid of activities always threatened to break out into violence when the two were pitted against one another.

"There! I win!" Honoria squealed and leapt to her feet, clapping her hands loudly. Her childish outburst belied the womanly figure of the nineteen-year-old girl.

"Oh, who cares?" Valentinian snorted as he threw down his dice. "It's only a game, Honoria."

"Yes! And I won it! That means I'm better than you are!" Honoria gloated.

Galla interrupted, "Have either one of you been listening to me? I'm trying to talk to you about your cousin Theodosius' proposal. Valentinian what do you think? Do you *want* to marry your cousin Eudoxia?"

"I suppose I have to . . . after all, you already promised, didn't you Mother?" Valentinian asked as he stood up, walked over to his mother, and put his arm around her.

"Yes, I promised, my dear, but I'd still like to know how you feel about it," Galla said as she looked up at her tall sandy-haired son who was now seventeen.

"It's not fair," Honoria interrupted. "I'm two years older than Valentinian and I'm not married yet. I'm the oldest, I should get married first."

"No one will have you," Valentinian quipped. "You're too ugly," he teased.

"Now stop it, you two. Your time will come Honoria, I promise. Marriage is a very important step, especially for a Flavian . . ."

"Oh Mother, stop!" demanded Honoria, shaking her dark curls. "I'm so sick of that word I could scream. What difference does it make *who* I am? I'm nearly twenty and I don't even have a suitor. It's not fair," she whined.

Galla ignored her daughter's tantrum and looked at her son. "What do you say, Valentinian? Do you want to marry Eudoxia?"

"Yes, Mother," the boy said gently as he kissed his mother's cheek, "if you want me to. After all, she *is* the daughter of the Emperor of the East and that *is* a good match for me, isn't it?" He smiled softly and picked up a strand of his mother's graying hair.

"Yes," Galla agreed, "an excellent match, my son . . . and very wise." Galla stood up and smoothed her rumpled gown. "Well, I had better tell the servants to begin preparations for your trip to Constantinople so you can meet your bride-to-be." Galla looked off into the distance across the deep blue sea. "And I'd better send word to the Prefect of Illyricum that he will soon answer to the Eastern Emperor."

Valentinian gave his mother a long, studied look and asked, "Isn't it enough that we're giving *me* in marriage, Mother? Why do we also have to give one of the most valuable Prefectures in the entire Empire?"

"Because I promised, Valentinian. I told Theodosius that he could have Illyricum when you married his daughter, provided he placed you on the throne of the West. He lived up to his bargain, now I must live up to mine." She smiled at her handsome son and ran her hand through his wavy hair. "Besides, the Huns have overrun much of that territory. We'll let Theodosius deal with them in the future. I'm too old to be fighting that fight."

"Oh, Mother, you're not old!" Valentinian put his arm around Galla again. "Look at you! The men still line up at banquets just to talk to you. You could have any one of a dozen suitors. Just yesterday I turned away Claudius Martius the famous senator. He's been asking for months to take you down to Naples for a visit to his country estate."

"Oh, and how would that look?" Galla laughed. "Galla Placidia Augusta accompanying an unmarried man on a weekend trip to the seaside?"

"Who cares what anyone thinks, Mother? You're your own woman! You should think of yourself for a change. I always hoped that you and Boniface would . . . Well, now that he's gone, you should think of yourself and your future." Valentinian urged.

"I *am* thinking of myself, and *I* prefer to keep my good name intact, thank you. Now," she paused and ran her hand over

Valentinian's smooth cheek, "we have a wedding to plan, *your* wedding."

In late summer, 437, Valentinian and his retinue set out for Constantinople. Galla, quite wisely, remained in Italy to protect her son's interests there. Although Valentinian was the undisputed Emperor of the West, several generals, including the powerful Aetius, were vying for greater and greater power. Galla Placidia could not afford to leave the West open to political intrigue during a prolonged absence from Italy, even if it were for the wedding of her only son.

On October 29, Valentinian and Eudoxia were joined in marriage in a wedding ceremony befitting the auspicious occasion. Coins were minted in celebration of the union between the East and West in wedlock. The newlyweds spent the winter in Thessalonica before making their triumphal entrance into Ravenna in the early spring. Galla welcomed the young couple when they arrived at the Imperial palace.

"How much you resemble your father, my dear Eudoxia," Galla commented as she led the young woman into the reception hall. "The last time I saw you, you were a tiny bundle on your mother's lap. And now look at you! You're all grown up--and quite lovely I might add."

"Thank you, Your Highness," Eudoxia said shyly. "I might say the same about you. My father was right when he said that you are the most beautiful woman in the Empire."

Galla laughed, "Your father hasn't seen me in thirteen years. I don't know if he'd have quite the same opinion today."

"I believe he would, Mother," Valentinian commented as he kissed his mother's cheek. "So, how have things been at court while I was away?" he asked as he threw himself down onto a couch.

"Much the same as when you left it, my dear. Your so-called advisor Aetius has spent the time consolidating the troops. If you ask me, it's time for *you* to take over as supreme military commander, Valentinian."

The young man laughed. "Oh, Mother, I'm no soldier, you know that. I have no desire to run the army." Valentinian leaned back and pulled off his boots. "See? I can't stand to wear these heavy old things. How could you expect me to march in them?" he grinned, showing a deep dimple in each fair cheek.

"But Valentinian," Galla argued, "the army is power. He who controls the legions controls the true power in Rome. If you let this Aetius continue with the army the way he has . . . and with his allies the Huns, I might add . . . there's no telling what he might try. Our dear friend Boniface gave his life fighting the Vandals in Africa in hopes of suppressing Aetius and his maniacal ambitions there, and you won't lift a finger to control that power monger!"

Valentinian groaned and smoothed back his light brown hair. He glanced at Eudoxia and noticed that she appeared somewhat confused. "Aetius is my advisor, Eudoxia. From what I've seen, he's very loyal. I have even appointed him Consul *twice* now and he hasn't abused that power. You'll meet him soon. Mother has never forgiven him since he sided with Castinus after Uncle Honorius' death. But that was years ago and he's been a loyal advisor ever since."

"He's a heretic!" Galla responded.

"He isn't a heretic, Mother. His *wife* is an Arian Christian-- that doesn't mean *he* is." Valentinian folded his arms and looked away from his mother with a deep sigh.

Eudoxia took advantage of the brief pause in the conversation to change the topic to a more pleasant subject. "Your Highness, speaking of Christianity, my father says you are interested in the preservation of Christian churches. I, too, am interested in glorifying our Lord. Perhaps you will show me some of your monuments." Soon the two women were engrossed in a deep discussion about Galla's latest architectural projects. Valentinian breathed a sigh of relief, glad that the topic of conversation had turned to a more pleasant subject.

In June, Galla received the devastating news that both Julius and Eli had succumbed to influenza in the recent epidemic that had ravaged Rome. Fortus himself came to Ravenna to deliver the shattering news to Galla.

"Perhaps I should return to Rome," Galla suggested as she shakily handed Fortus a cup of wine. She stared blankly out over the peristyle garden, tears streaming down her cheeks.

Fortus took a sip of wine and looked at Galla. "No, I don't think it would be wise. The epidemic is still raging . . . hundreds die each day. It's safer for you here in Ravenna."

"But what about the arrangements? I should be there to help."

"I took care of everything before I left, Galla," Fortus assured her softly. "Julius will be placed in the crypt at St. Peter's Basilica. And I found a nice plot for Eli in the yard of the church near your villa. She always loved that little church."

Galla wiped her eyes and looked over at Fortus. "Look at us Fortus--we're getting old. Soon we, too, will be placed in our tombs. Where did the time go, Fortus? It seems like yesterday that we were taunting Eucherius. Remember that silly race? They're all gone now . . . Eucherius, Stilicho, Serena . . . Arcadius and Honorius . . . and now Julius and Eli. Just the two of us left," Galla sighed.

"You still have Valentinian and Honoria, Galla. And, if the news I hear at Rome is true, by this time next year, you'll be a grandmother!" Fortus smiled his broad smile at Galla.

"Yes, the news is true. I am going to be a grandmother," she managed a weak smile. "The Flavian line will be continued. At least I can say I did that much--I saw to it that the family line went on."

"You've done a lot more than that, Galla. Everyone knows of your dedication to the Church. One can't travel anywhere in Italy without seeing a church you've either built or restored. Everyone also knows of the laws you have passed--important laws, like the one regarding the right to inheritances. The name Galla Placidia is spoken everywhere with respect and admiration. There isn't a man alive who doesn't know who the real power behind the throne is. You've made your mark on history Galla. You should be proud."

"Thank you for those kind words, Fortus. Yes, I guess I have made a mark. But sitting here with you . . . well, I think I still missed an awful lot, too." Galla looked up into Fortus' light blue eyes. "If only things had been different . . . I wonder what it would have been like--you and me."

Fortus looked down at the ground and Galla could see the muscles in his temples flexing. When he looked back up, tears shone in his azure eyes. "I think about it, too, Galla . . . God forgive me, but I do." Fortus blinked and looked quickly away.

"Come, Fortus," Galla said as she stood up, "there's something I want to show you." Galla called for her litter and soon she and Fortus were standing in front of a small, plain brick building.

"What do you think?" Galla said proudly as she surveyed the tiny edifice. "I designed it myself. Perhaps this will one day be my mausoleum. I've been working on it for some time now. It's nearly completed. Come on, I'll show you the inside." Galla led Fortus into the little cruciform-shaped building. Inside several torches burned and workmen were placing the finishing touches on a mosaic.

"I chose a Greek cross for the plan," Galla explained. "I think that's an appropriate shape for a mausoleum. That way the building will have four arms of equal length to house three tombs and the entranceway. I know, everyone wonders whom the other tombs are for. I don't know, perhaps Honoria would like to be placed here one day."

Galla ran her hand over the lowest course of the newly laid mosaics. "Beautiful, aren't they? The ceilings of the barrel vaults are done in stars to represent the heavens. Isn't that a lovely shade of blue? It's made from cobalt. The stars are of gold leaf pressed into the glass tesserae. And look at this," Galla took Fortus' hand and led him over to one of the short arms of the little cross-shaped building.

"This is my favorite mosaic--Christ as the Good Shepherd. See his sheep? Three on each side to represent the Trinity-- Father, Son and Holy Spirit." Galla led Fortus over to another mosaic. "And see this one? Christ is holding a book that says, 'Blessed are the merciful, for God will have mercy.'"

Galla continued to show Fortus around the little mausoleum, explaining each of the lovely mosaics one by one. "And this? What is this?" Fortus asked when his eye caught a long list of names.

"Oh, that's my dedication. See? It says, 'Galla Placidia has paid her vow in behalf of herself and of these . . .' and then I've listed all of my family, everyone from Constantine down to now."

Galla saw Fortus read the words "Theodosius, Most Noble Boy."

"That's for my first-born son. We named him Theodosius," Galla explained sadly. "I lost him when he was just an infant. He's still back there in Spain," Galla sighed. "Someday I'm going to bring him back to Italy. He's a Flavian, he should be here, don't you think?"

Fortus nodded and put his arm around Galla. "That was a terrible time for you, wasn't it Galla? You never speak of it."

"There's little use in speaking of the past. It just brings up painful memories. I didn't think I'd ever get over it, but I did. Life goes on, doesn't it Fortus?" Galla smiled weakly. "Well, let's get out of here and return to the palace. We've had enough talk of death today." Galla took Fortus' hand and the two went out into the warm sunlight.

"I think I'd like to walk," Galla suggested when they were outside. Fortus nodded his agreement. Galla and Fortus walked hand in hand slowly back to the palace.

CHAPTER VIII

Later that year, on her fiftieth birthday, Galla Placidia became a grandmother. Valentinian and Eudoxia named their daughter Eudocia after Eudoxia's mother. In gratitude to Saints Peter and Paul for the safe delivery of a healthy child, Eudoxia rebuilt the church dedicated to them on the Esquiline Hill in Rome. The building was called the Basilica Eudoxiana because she used her own funds for the reconstruction . . . it later came to be called San Pietro in Vincoli. This act of Christian piety greatly endeared Eudoxia to her mother-in-law Galla Placidia.

The birth of a child to Valentinian only fueled Honoria's animosity towards her brother.

"Oh, Mother," Honoria whined, "you don't understand. You never understand. You have no heart! You only think of Rome." Honoria threw herself down on a couch and pouted.

"Honoria, darling, I do understand," Galla consoled. "I know you want to marry, but now is not the best time. You are the sister of the Emperor, your husband must be carefully selected." A twinge of guilt tugged at Galla's heart as she spoke these words to her daughter. Galla remembered all too well what it was like to stand in the shadow of an Imperial brother and to be told whom she could and could not marry. Galla told herself that what she was advising Honoria was not just in the best interests of Rome, but in Honoria's best interests as well.

"I never get to leave the palace except to go to church!" Honoria fumed tossing her dark curls. "How can I meet any young men if I'm cooped up here like a nun?"

"Your husband can't be just any young man you meet on the street, Honoria. Your brother will select an appropriate husband when the time is right."

"To hell with my brother! And to hell with you, too!" Honoria hissed. "Look at you, Mother, sitting there drinking that vile ale! You ran off and married a *barbarian*! Who are you to tell me that I can't marry a man of my own choice?"

"That was different," Galla said slowly, drawing on all her will to contain her anger. "Besides, we're not talking about me, we're talking about you. For now your brother prefers that you dedicate yourself to your work in the Church. He'll arrange a suitable marriage when he's ready."

Honoria threw her cup of wine on the floor and stormed out of the room, pushing aside her brother who was just entering.

Valentinian asked sarcastically, "Well, what has my darling sister in such a fine mood today?"

"The same as usual," Galla sighed. "She wants to marry."

"Oh, that again," Valentinian scoffed as he poured a cup of wine from a golden pitcher.

"Well, Valentinian," Galla said slowly, "I can see her point. I, too, was once a young woman like Honoria."

"Oh no, Mother, you were never like Honoria," Valentinian interrupted.

"Well, I can see her point anyway," Galla responded. She could see that Valentinian was in no mood to discuss Honoria, so Galla changed the subject. "Well, what news have you from Africa?"

"It is a sad day for Rome, Mother," Valentinian sighed as he sat down next to Galla. "Geiseric and his Vandals have taken Carthage by surprise. We've lost the richest part of Africa. And, if that weren't enough, he's begun to persecute the Christians there."

Galla hung her head, "If only Boniface had lived . . . *he* would have kept Africa." Galla looked back up at her son. "Boniface was a true and loyal Roman, not like that Aetius of yours."

"Now, Mother," Valentinian warned, "let's not bring Aetius into this. I know how you feel about him, but the Roman soldiers love him. Only last week they erected a statue to him behind the Senate House in Rome."

"If he's such an excellent general, why didn't he go to Africa to defend Carthage from the Vandals?" Galla asked but Valentinian remained silent. "*I'll* tell you why," she continued, "because he doesn't want to get too far away from *you*, that's why. He thinks if he were to leave you alone for a moment that you might make a decision for yourself."

"I didn't come in here to argue about Aetius again, Mother. I came to tell you the news from Africa." Valentinian stood up and set down his wine goblet. "It looks like we're in for some rough times. It appears Geiseric and the Vandals aren't going to be satisfied controlling the richest grain province in the Empire. They are already assembling a fleet to cross over to Sicily. From there, well, it seems pretty obvious. I've ordered the port towns to secure their harbors and the army is already repairing the walls around Rome."

"Well, I hope your precious Aetius will earn your confidence now," Galla commented. "I've waited fifteen years to see him in action, perhaps now I'll have my chance. I sincerely hope he can live up to your expectations, Valentinian, for Rome's sake and for ours."

Galla stood up and put her arm around her son. "Uncle Julius once said that the Germanic tribes were just like rats, always gnawing away at our borders. Well, it looks like the rats have us surrounded now--Alans, Franks and Burgundians to the north, Gauls and Vandals to the west, Geiseric and his Vandals to the south, and Huns to the east. I'm afraid it will take a better man than Aetius to protect Rome now," Galla stated gravely.

The Vandals launched their offensive against Sicily early in the year 440. After a year of fighting, and with the much needed help of a fleet sent by Theodosius II, the Romans were able to repulse the Vandal onslaught and the invaders returned to Africa. The events of the Vandal siege on Sicily proved to Valentinian the suspicions his mother had harbored for all those years regarding Aetius. It now became clear to Valentinian that his trusted advisor was more interested in a military coup than a military career.

Putting Aetius back in his place became a necessary but Herculean task. Aetius commanded not only his own personal forces, but also the friendship and good will of the Huns, a formidable foe if unleashed against Rome. In order to counteract that threat, Galla and Valentinian decided to call a truce with their recently defeated enemies, the Vandals. That way, if Aetius decided to use the Huns to take power in Rome, Valentinian and Galla could call upon Geiseric and the Vandals to come to their aid.

Geiseric was only too happy to ally with the Emperor of the West. To prove his loyalty to the Emperor, Geiseric sent his son Huniric to Rome as a hostage. As always in dealing with the Germanic tribes, quid pro quo was the rule--Geiseric received the undisputed right to control the vast grain trade from Africa and, in return, Valentinian secured a trade agreement for that grain and a promise of no further Vandal attacks on Rome. As final security to assure performance on both halves of the agreement, Valentinian betrothed his infant daughter Eudocia to Geiseric's son Huniric. Tenuous though it was, this arrangement secured both a stalemate in the power struggle between Valentinian and Aetius, and a temporary peace within the Empire.

Peace within the Imperial household was quite another matter. The birth of a second daughter to Valentinian and Eudoxia once again opened old wounds with Honoria. She again demanded that she be allowed to marry. In order to appease her daughter, Galla decided to allow Honoria a modicum of independence. Galla provided her daughter with a household of her own in Rome. This new liberty seemed to placate Honoria, at least temporarily.

"What is it Anta?" Galla asked sleepily as her servant gently shook her awake early one morning. "What's happened?"

"It's the Emperor, Your Highness. He says he needs to see you immediately. He's waiting for you in the library."

Galla arrived at the library to find Valentinian pacing the floor.

"What is it, Valentinian? What brings you here at this hour of the morning?" Galla asked with concern.

"Your daughter, that's what!" he fumed.

"Honoria? What has she done now?" Galla asked as she sat down and wrapped her shawl more tightly around her.

"She has committed High Treason," Valentinian said between his clenched teeth. Galla didn't reply; she sat staring numbly at the floor. Valentinian continued, "Honoria has been having an affair with her household administrator Eugenius. He's been secretly visiting her bedchamber for months."

"Poor Honoria," Galla sighed, "she's so lonely. Of course, her actions show a gross lack of discretion but . . ."

"But nothing!" Valentinian snapped. "Her lack of *moral restraint* would be one thing, but I also have proof that Honoria and Eugenius have been plotting to overthrow *me*."

Galla rose slowly to her feet, her eyes wide with disbelief. "Honoria? Plotting to overthrow you? What proof do you have of that?" Galla demanded.

"Their confessions! *That's* what proof I have. And for that *lack of discretion,* I'll have their heads!"

"No!" Galla screamed. "Not Honoria! She's my daughter! It's not her fault. She's so young, so vulnerable. Please, Valentinian, she's your sister, your own flesh and blood. I beg you not to sentence her to death," Galla pleaded.

"The Claudian Law provides for death in cases of High Treason," Valentinian countered.

"It also provides for banishment," Galla interrupted. "Send her away if you will, but please don't execute my daughter. Her only sin is that of being human. She's a woman and she wants so desperately to be loved. Please, Valentinian, do not punish her simply because she's weak."

Valentinian looked at his mother, her face streaked with tears. "All right, Mother, I will have her spared, but I'm doing this for you, not for her. In my heart my sister is already dead."

The conspirator Eugenius was publicly executed based on two counts of Roman law--first, the act of having illegitimate sex with a member of the Imperial family, and second, the act of conspiring to overthrow the Emperor. Honoria was denounced publicly and then banished from Rome to Constantinople.

CHAPTER IX

The following spring, Galla kept her vow to have her firstborn son reburied alongside his Imperial relations. Enlisting the help of Fortus and the Church, the tiny body of Theodosius Germanicus was exhumed from his tomb in Barcelona and brought to the Flavian crypt at St. Peter's Basilica in Rome. With great pomp and fanfare, the infant was placed in a silver coffin, anointed with the title Most Noble Boy, and entombed with his hallowed ancestors.

"It was a lovely ceremony," Fortus commented as he helped Galla up onto her litter. The entire Senate was present; that's a very special honor." Fortus sat down next to Galla.

"Pope Leo gave an excellent mass, didn't he?" Galla asked with satisfaction. "Fortus, I heard that Pope Leo has nominated you for Bishop of Rome. That's wonderful. You must be very pleased."

"I will be if he allows me to remain here in Rome. I'm too old to go gallivanting off to the provinces."

"You're not old," Galla protested. "You're as handsome as you ever were--more handsome, I believe." Galla surveyed his strong features, which seemed even more distinctive with the addition of a few deep wrinkles.

Fortus smiled his broad smile and his light blue eyes revealed his pleasure at the compliment from the Augusta Galla Placidia.

"Did you hear those senators talking after the mass, Fortus?" Galla asked, her tone growing serious. "They were complaining about the peace we've had lately. Imagine-- complaining about peace! I'll never understand some men and why they always have to be embroiled in some war to be happy. That senator today claimed that the army was being weakened from disuse! He implied that *I* was responsible for undermining the Roman army with disuse!" Galla huffed.

"Don't listen to those warmongers, Galla. We in the Church know what you've done to strengthen the Empire. You've done a fine job redistributing the power from the ancient bureaucracy to the Church hierarchy. Those senators are just afraid that you'll find a way to relieve them of their privileged positions, that's all. A good war would take your mind off the peaceful transition from a government by man to a government by God."

"Yes, Fortus, you're right. I mustn't listen to them. I must listen to the Lord if this Empire is to survive."

After a lengthy journey, the litter finally arrived at the country villa north of Rome. The late afternoon sun stretched its rays across the rolling hills.

"It's good to be home again," Galla sighed as she slowly stepped off the litter.

"How long will you remain here at the farm, Galla?" Fortus inquired as he helped her into the palace.

"I don't know, Fortus. I'm working on a few projects in Rome right now. I'll stay here until they're completed."

When Galla and Fortus entered the library, they found a messenger from Constantinople awaiting them. "Your Majesty," the man saluted, "an urgent message from Emperor Theodosius II." He handed Galla a large vellum scroll and saluted.

"Thank you," Galla said politely as she took the letter from the exhausted courier. "Go to the kitchen for something to eat and tell them what you'll need for your return journey. Report to me before you leave in case I have a reply." The soldier saluted and exited the room.

"How curious," Galla commented as she took a seat behind the desk. She unrolled the scroll and began to read. Suddenly she let out a little scream. "Oh my God in Heaven! It's Honoria again! She doesn't use the brains the good Lord gave her."

Fortus walked over and put his hand on Galla's shoulder. She was trembling. "What is it, Galla? Has something happened to Honoria?" he asked.

"No, but something *will*, just as soon as Valentinian learns what she has done now." Galla set down the scroll and wiped her hand across her eyes. Fortus waited patiently until Galla was prepared to share the news.

"Theodosius writes," she began, her voice choked with emotion, "that Honoria has taken it upon herself to propose marriage to Attila, the King of the Huns! He's that maniac who's been causing so much trouble in the East. You know of him?" Fortus nodded. Galla drew a deep breath and continued, "Theodosius only recently tried to have that lunatic Attila assassinated, but the plot failed. And now my own dear daughter has offered herself in marriage to that savage!" Galla threw down the scroll and shook her head sadly.

"What does Theodosius propose to do about it?" Fortus asked with concern.

Galla smiled bitterly, "He suggests we *allow* Honoria to marry Attila. I guess he feels that the punishment would fit the crime."

"Do you think this Attila would agree to the match?" Fortus inquired.

"Honoria is the sister of the Emperor of the West and the cousin of the Emperor of the East. Of course he'd agree. He already has." Galla stood up, went over to the window and gazed out. "Honoria enlisted the aid of the eunuch that Valentinian hired to guard her. She sent the eunuch to Attila with her ring and her proposal. The Hun has not only accepted, but he's now *demanding* the union."

"What will you do, Galla? Will you allow this union?"

"No, Fortus, I will not. If we allow Honoria to marry Attila, we'll be playing right into Aetius' greedy hands. Aetius and the Huns have been in league with one another for years . . . a marriage with the Imperial family would give them the upper hand they've been waiting for." Galla turned back to look at Fortus. "No daughter of mine will hand Rome on a silver platter to Aetius and the Huns . . . not if *I* have anything to say about it."

Upon the orders of both Galla Placidia and Valentinian, Honoria was returned to Rome. As stipulated by Roman law, Honoria's eunuch was publicly tortured and decapitated. Then, as quickly as could be arranged, Honoria was married off to Herculanus Bassus, a minor court official with neither the desire nor the wits to plot against the throne. Unfortunately, Attila was not easily discouraged. For years after Honoria's marriage, the Hun chieftain pressed his claim to the Emperor's sister. He never succeeded.

After the tumultuous events of the preceding months, Galla decided to prolong her stay at her beloved villa in the countryside north of Rome. She worked on her architectural plans, read the Scriptures, and took long walks with her dear friend Fortus.

In early August, word arrived from Constantinople that Theodosius II had died from injuries he received in a riding accident. On August 25, the husband of Theodosius's sister Pulcheria, a soldier by the name of Marcian, was proclaimed Emperor of the East. Theodosius II's dream of a united East and West had died with him.

Autumn that year was mild. Except for a few brief public appearances, Galla spent the majority of her time in seclusion at her villa outside Rome. Galla's Gothic followers had turned the old neglected farm into a productive estate. The orchards were heavy with fruit like in the old days. Galla and Fortus arranged to have the extra fruit from the orchards distributed to the poor in Rome. The two old friends spent hours planning improvements to the various barns, stables, and outbuildings. Galla was pleased to have the farm restored to its former glory and to have her vast landholdings be of benefit to others.

After Galla had completed her public architectural projects in Rome, she devoted herself to some personal projects that she had thought about for a long time. She restored and rededicated the family chapel in the catacombs beneath her villa, in part to honor the stalwart early Christians who had faced such violent opposition to their new young religion, and in part to commemorate the ancient tunnels themselves and the very special place they held in Galla's heart.

One afternoon, after completing a design for a shrine to be placed at the catacomb entrance in Fortus' former room at the old bakery, Galla laid down her quill. "I think I'll take a walk," Galla said as she stood up and stretched. "Will you join me Fortus?"

Fortus shook his head, "I have to wait here for the monks to arrive. They're coming out to gather apples for the monastery," he explained. "I promised I would help them."

"Yes, of course. Well, I think I'll go ahead alone then. I haven't been up to the north valley in some time and I'd like to see the place again."

"If I finish early, I'll join you there," Fortus offered with a smile.

"Yes, do," Galla encouraged as she drew her cape up over her gray hair. "I'll wait for you there." Galla picked up the old oak walking stick that she carried as a memento of Julius and she left the room.

On her way out of the villa, Galla walked past the kitchen door. She caught the scent of freshly baked bread. Memories of Eli and Julius and their hours in the big warm kitchen came back so vividly that Galla thought she could almost see her dear friends seated at the old wooden table in the kitchen. And when Galla walked past the stables, she found herself looking for Odysseus, half-expecting him to be in the paddock waiting for her.

Galla took the well-worn path along the valley's rim and down into the glen below. She stepped carefully along the rocks of the nearly dry river bottom and instantly recollected the fateful chariot race with the young Eucherius. Galla remembered Stilicho and Serena and she imagined she could see them sitting in their elegant litter atop the far hill. When she reached the fallen oak tree, Galla sat down and leaned her back against the familiar old tree.

Images of places and echoes of voices reverberated through her mind. Galla looked down at the three rings she still wore--the massive gold Imperial Eagle, the simple silver interlace, and the tiny bronze chi-rho cross. The faces of the three men appeared before her . . . Constantius, Emperor of Rome; Athaulf, Chieftain of the Goths; and Fortus, Imperial soldier and now Bishop of Rome. Her mind drifted off into the past and Galla was led back through time. As the late afternoon sun made its way across the sky, Galla slept, her dreams filled with memories of days gone by.

It was dusk when Galla felt Fortus gently shake her awake. "Galla," he said softly, "it's late. It's time to go."

"Yes, yes," Galla mumbled as she awoke from her dreams. "I'm awake, I'm awake." Fortus helped the aging Augusta to her feet. She brushed the dried grass from her dress and pulled her heavy shawl up over her stooping shoulders.

"I was having such a pleasant dream, Fortus. I was dreaming that you and I were young again and we were racing our horses across this valley." Galla paused for a moment and her eyes scanned the wide glen. "It's been a good life, hasn't it Fortus? We've had our troubles, but all in all, it's been a good life."

Galla leaned on Fortus' arm and she started to take a step. "Wait," Galla said suddenly as something at the foot of the old tree caught her eye. "What's that?" she asked with curiosity. Galla lifted her old wooden walking stick and dug its tip deep into the pile of dried vines and leaves at the base of the tree. There, sprouting out of the gnarled stub of the old fallen oak tree, was a bright green stem of new life.

"Well!" Galla said with a smile. "The old oak isn't dead after all. Look . . . it's still alive! This old oak's roots must be very deep indeed to have survived all these years." Galla glowed with delight at the sight of the new growth springing from the old tree. "This is the future, Fortus," Galla said with satisfaction. "This new oak will be here for the children and their children's children." Galla proudly surveyed the tiny new sprout for a long time, her mind deep in reflection. Finally, she turned to Fortus and said, "Come, Fortus, it's late. It's time for us to go." Galla took Fortus by the arm and the two friends walked slowly out of the valley for the very last time.

*   *   *

Galla Placidia died on November 27, in the year of our Lord 450. She was buried in St. Peter's Basilica in Rome alongside the Great Fisherman St. Peter himself. Her son Valentinian III ruled the West until his assassination by a follower of Aetius in 455. As promised, Valentinian's daughter Eudocia was married to the Vandal Chieftain Huniric--their child, Galla Placidia's great-grandson, became Hilderic, King of the Vandals. In 476, Odoacer, a petty chieftain from the obscure Herulian tribe, became the first Germanic Emperor of Rome. Thus ended the Roman Empire in the West.